THE 13th DIRECTORATE

"The 13th Directorate, Mr. Cassidy, is the most lethal force the Western world faces today. It is an organization with the narrowest of briefs: one single operation that it has been planning, preparing, rehearsing, and fine-tuning for over a third of a century — the entire span of its existence."

Cassidy contemplated the tired, bloodshot but piercing eyes of the Russian.

"Tell me about it, Max," he said calmly.

"By the time I describe it all to you, Mr. Cassidy, and you believe it and convince your superiors and they draw up their ever-present list of options and run through the various Congressional oversight committees and the president's own arm, it may well be too late."

"Well, Max, we're starting with a bit of a problem here." Cassidy hesitated to underline the point. "You see, as I said, I'm afraid we have nothing in any of our records about this so-called 13th Directorate of yours."

"Perhaps," said the Russian somberly, "that is by design."

"Perhaps," Cassidy repeated.

The Russian sighed and closed his eyes. "Where would you like me to start?"

"Why not the beginning, Max? The inception."

Also by Barry Chubin

The Feet of a Snake

BARRY CHUBIN

THE **13**th DIRECTORATE

Mandarin

A Mandarin Paperback

THE 13th DIRECTORATE

First published in Great Britain 1990
by Mandarin Paperbacks
Michelin House, 81 Fulham Road, London SW3 6RB

Mandarin is an imprint of the Octopus Publishing Group

Copyright © 1989 by Barry Chubin

A CIP catalogue record for this book
is available from the British Library
ISBN 0 7493 0151 1

Printed and bound in Great Britain
by Cox & Wyman Ltd, Reading, Berkshire

*To my parents—for only now
do I appreciate how great is my debt.*

and

*H. Daneshvar—humble and considerate, generous
and unafraid, he is the one individual I know who has
remained unstintingly loyal to his beginnings, his
principles, and his late, benighted friend.*

AUTHOR'S NOTE

While most of the characters and all the events in this book are wholly imaginary, the arsenal of supersophisticated intelligence-gathering devices described here are terrifyingly real. Quite obviously these "National Technical Means," as the Soviets choose to call them, or "Technical Collection Systems," in the vernacular of Washington, are among the most closely guarded secrets of both superpowers. Hence only a trickle of accurate information ever surfaces; and then usually so distorted by disinformation that it is often next to impossible to comprehend the incredible capabilities involved—let alone keep abreast of the state of the art.

For my understanding I consulted—and consulted often—one source to whom I shall always be indebted. I shall call this source J.C. To J.C. I owe gratitude for opening my eyes, provoking my mind, providing focus and much guidance through the maze of technical assistance I was so generously afforded by others who also do not wish to be named.

Barry Chubin
London, 1988

In the wake of the disastrous 1980 hostage rescue attempt in Iran, the Pentagon established the closest thing the nation has ever had to a secret army. These clandestine operations and intelligence units are still around. . . . [This secret army's] small, specially trained units are designed to operate far more covertly than older elite paramilitary units, such as the Army's Rangers and the Navy's Seals. They have been given exotic code names, such as Yellow Fruit, Task Force 160 and Seaspray. New types of equipment have been developed for them, including small, high-tech helicopters and one-man satellite-communications radios and dishes. In addition, a far-ranging intelligence organization known as Intelligence Support Activity (ISA) gave the Army for the first time the ability to conduct full-fledged espionage using field agents. And all was done in such deep secrecy that to this day the very existence of some of the special units has never been officially admitted.

Time magazine
August 31, 1987

". . . They [the Soviet Union] are thinking of getting involved in an American election as they did in Germany."

President Ronald Reagan
January 2, 1984

| Prologue | # BEIRUT, LEBANON WEDNESDAY, JANUARY 23, 1963 |

Two lights swung onto the silent street, twin beams that pierced the dark storm pounding Rue Kantari.

Norman King slid down in the seat of his car. He squinted, gauging the path of the approaching headlights through the heavy rain running in jagged rivulets down his windshield. The headlights were set far apart. The vehicle was a big one; menacing. Probably an American V-8.

Slowly the two spotlights lumbered closer. Then the dark-green Ford flashed by, the spray from beneath its large, finned taillights splattering King's windshield. As he watched the vehicle disappear in his rearview mirror, he wearily raised his compact, muscular torso back to a sitting position and waited again, peering out into the black shadows of the windswept night.

For two bloody years now, he thought, that was all he had done—waited. Two god-awful, dreary years spent monitoring cars and cycles and pedestrians. The last eight months on this dismal street. Smoking himself to death watching for one small inconsistency. Waiting for one tiny error.

He crushed the half-smoked cigarette in the brimming ashtray on the dashboard and glanced at his colleague's car parked thirty yards away on the other side of this unexceptional residential street in West Beirut. He could make out the faint glow of John Swain's cigarette as he, too, inhaled a lungful.

King leaned forward over the steering wheel and looked up at the dark fifth-floor apartment housing his quarry. It was situated almost directly above him, its small semicircular terrace commanding a magnificent view of Beirut's rugged northern mountains and the dark blue of the Mediterranean Sea sweeping away toward Europe.

Suddenly the Arabian love dirge from the car radio seemed nauseating. He silenced it.

Two years, he thought dejectedly. Two whole years. And all for nothing. The man upstairs, as far as anyone knew, lived as quietly, as innocently as a village curate. Two men tailed him night and day; in six-hour shifts; twenty-four hours a day. His phones were tapped, his flat was bugged, his colleagues in the press were SIS plants assigned to monitor his every move.

And all for nothing.

Ten years now. No, twelve it was, King thought, adding the two years the man upstairs had just spent in Beirut as an SIS stringer working under the cover of a journalist for *The Observer and Economist*. For twelve years now they had suspected him. And still they had no proof. *"Guilt unproven but suspicions remaining,"* was the official verdict.

King weighed the situation for a moment longer. Was the effort beginning to pay dividends at long last? Certainly the man upstairs increasingly appeared to be losing control of himself. The new bout of "informal" interrogations under way with the new man sent out recently by London was straining him. He appeared tired, weak, a man shriveling under the constant pressure. His drinking habits were becoming even more prodigious lately, too. Starting earlier and earlier, practically every morning. And continuing steadily throughout the day—right up until the moment he passed out in a hazy alcoholic stupor late at night. Three weeks ago—on January 2nd, his birthday—he had keeled over in his bathroom after returning from an all-day New Year party and cracked his head open so deeply that it required six stitches at the Emergency Department of the American University Hospital.

How then could that alcoholic up there be one of the most brilliant double agents. . . ?

His thoughts were cut off by the appearance of another moving light—this time a dull single light in his rearview mirror. He watched the oval reflecting glass as the yellow glow drew closer in the pounding rain, stopping thirty, forty yards behind him.

Old "Hop-along" Habib, thought King, relaxing. The barman from the Normandy Hotel who lived in a small basement apartment at number eleven.

King glanced at his watch; it read 11:35 P.M. Knocking off early, he thought, watching the middle-aged man with the bulging belly waging his nightly battle with the stand of his white Lambretta and his frocky white *dishdasha*. Either that or it was a slow night. Who the hell would want to go out in this weather anyway?

Abruptly two brilliant beams swept the narrow road from the other end. King flicked his eyes in their direction. Again he squinted in concentration as he sank down in his seat. The car slowed and backed into the growing puddle that was a parking spot twenty yards in front of John Swain's Chevrolet. A sports car, King noted as it came to a stop by the curb.

Once again he raised himself to a comfortable sitting position as he recognized both the red Mercedes-Benz 190 and the emerging driver: Azarak, Raymond; local playboy. His *garçonnière* was on the third floor of building number twenty. King shook his head in envy as he lifted the binoculars lying on the bunk seat beside him.

Son of a bitch had a different girl every night. King focused the lens on Azarak opening the car door for his companion and watched as the carefree couple strolled arm in arm, totally oblivious to the pouring rain. Probably another stewardess, thought King, observing her long, straight blond hair, European features, and tall, slim frame. Her skin was tanned, her face young and pretty.

The couple stopped near Swain's car and kissed. It was a burning kiss—wild and passionate; their lips crushed against each other, their mouths opening wide ravenously, as the heavy rainfall lashed their unprotected faces. Slowly Raymond Azarak's free right hand undid the buttons of her tan raincoat, parted it wide and snaked inside. Gradually it slid down the girl's back. From the bare, suntanned skin of her shoulders, down the thin, sky-blue dress to the small of her back, squeezing her closer against his body.

King's pulse quickened as the girl complied willingly. She arched her body forward and subtly extended a long, slim leg between Azarak's thighs, pressing it firmly against his groin. He watched Azarak's arm moving slowly back around to the front again. Gently he started caressing the young girl's large, firm, braless breasts through the delicate, clinging wet silk of her dress.

"Shit," King blurted watching the slim, dapper Lebanese playboy brush away one of the girl's thin shoulder straps. Through the open raincoat he saw the man uncover a firm, round white mound untouched by the sun. Azarak's right hand cupped the moist, shining breast and fondled it. First all of it, or at least most of it, as much as he could handle. Then only the nipple. Slowly he bent down and kissed it, his tongue circling the small dark protrusion delicately—as if to stoke the fire building inside her.

"Fucker's going to take her right there," King whispered, a smile appearing on his face as he thought of Swain's ringside seat. The frenzied couple were no more than two yards away from his colleague and unaware of his presence. "In the pouring rain."

Abruptly he froze, his smile evaporating.

Something was wrong. Unnatural. The hand. Azarak's right hand. It had disappeared. It wasn't holding, supporting the large breast.

He snapped the binoculars to Swain, then back to the drenched lovers. The soaking right sleeve of Azarak's once immaculately tailored dark suit was bent inward, out of sight, buried inside . . .

A sixth sense suddenly knifed through him. To his left. Behind. Close. King snapped his head toward the side window, ducking, sliding, dropping himself to the floor of the car in a mad, desperate attempt to duck.

He was too late.

Too late to save his life. But not to late to see it all. In the one split second that remained he knew he had lost. Lost to the man upstairs. Lost to the KGB and "Hop-along" Habib and Raymond Azarak. He had lost the great game they had so doggedly been playing for two years. Lost because he had fallen for the oldest single con known in the game—the decoy.

The sexual decoy.

The bullet from "Hop-along" Habib Nasser's suppressed .22 caliber handgun penetrated King's skull squarely between his eyes. Thirty yards away the silenced bullet that ended John Swain's life entered his right temple. Neither of the British agents had had time to use the radios in their vehicles to sound a warning to SIS headquarters in Beirut.

Within seconds Rue Kantari was deserted again; normal in the midnight hour; no one the wiser. Raymond Azarak and his escort had hurried into the building at number twenty, Habib Nasser into his residence at eleven. Both men had been instructed to keep away from their windows.

A few moments later a dark-brown Mercedes-Benz 220 glided silently onto Rue Kantari and stopped, double-parking before the five-story building just in front of Norman King's car. The vehicle bore Syrian number plates with *Corps Diplomatique* markings.

Of the five men occupying the Mercedes, four disembarked, the driver remaining behind the wheel. One of the four men peeled off and disappeared into the soggy shadows just to one side of the entrance to the building. Inside, another stayed at the bottom of the elevator shaft. Two stepped into the tiny, coffin-sized lift and rode it silently to the fifth floor. There the last of the burly men took up position at the elevator doors, his eyes trained on the stairway that twisted around its shaft back down to the floors below. All of this was executed wordlessly—the practiced efficiency of a seasoned team. Only the tall, trim, swarthy man who had seemed strangely out of place among the younger ones with hard faces and muscular physiques continued onward. He approached the apartment to the right of the elevator, rang its bell, and waited patiently. He was about to press the simple white button again when the door opened. A short, stocky man with a disheveled mop of whitening brown hair appeared, dressed in a wrinkled pair of blue-striped pajamas.

The man's puffy, pit-marked face froze momentarily, his sleepy, bloodshot eyes flickering at the visitor.

"*Tovarich*," greeted the stranger.

Harold Adrian Russell "Kim" Philby looked down at his watch; it was 11:45 P.M. Then he smiled in his usual pleasant but reserved manner and extended his right hand.

"*Geidar Alievich.*"

The shrill ring of the telephone in the darkened room shattered Jane Irwin's sleep. She shook her husband.

"Darling . . . John . . . John?"

John Irwin's mammoth body leaped suddenly as if convulsed by an electric charge. "Who the hell—?" He reached for the green telephone on his bedside table. It was the secure line that was ringing. The luminous hands of the clock beside it stood at 12:07 A.M.

"Yes," he barked.

"Mr. Ambassador?"

John Irwin sighed deeply.

"Who else could it be, Crosby? It's my bedroom."

"You asked me yesterday to keep you plugged in on any unusual vibrations in the Philby case." The resident CIA deputy station chief paused, waiting for confirmation.

Ambassador Irwin jerked his body upward and felt for the bedside lamp. A faint yellow glow illuminated a small corner of the huge room. "That's correct."

"Well, sir," continued Stephen Crosby, "there's been a break of . . . ah . . . seven minutes now in communication with his surveillance team."

The Ambassador threw off his bed covers and abruptly swung his feet to the floor. "How many of them are there?"

"Two, sir. Per shift."

"Equipped?"

"Fully."

"Two radios out simultaneously?"

"According to the Brits both officers missed their hourly check at midnight, sir."

John Irwin's eyes flashed instinctively to the bedside clock again. "Well, for heaven's sake get over there, Crosby. See—"

"The Brits have just dispatched a backup unit, sir."

"Look, Crosby," fumed the Texan. "Those assholes can't arrange a two-car nigger funeral. Get over there yourself, Crosby. Get over there and bring the man in."

"But there's been no authorization from Langley, sir."

"What the hell does that have to do with anything under these circumstances, Crosby? You know we got the proof. You read the advisory. *Prima facie* evidence, for Christ's sake. That's why the joint Anglo-American team's arriving here in the morning in the first place." The Ambassador paused. "Now all we've got to do,

Crosby, is try to make sure the son of a bitch is still around when they get here."

The words had exploded in Kim Philby's mind.

But even now—as he was rapidly rummaging through his cupboards, drawers, and briefcases, stuffing essentials into a faded green canvas and pigskin suitcase—the impact of the sullen *apparatchik's* words had still not fully sunk in.

"We must take you home, Comrade Philby," the KGB man had said.

Home?

Moscow? Home? It had never occurred to him in that sense before. Oh, certainly he had always known that sooner or later it might well end like this. Somehow, though, it always seemed like something unimaginable—to be faced somewhere in the far-off future. Like infirmity. And death. It had always seemed so unreal, so distant, too dreadful to contemplate, really. *Moscow? Home?*

In four minutes flat, Geidar Reza Alievich Rezayov had briefed him on the need for his sudden departure: Anatoli Golytsin, a Major in the KGB's 1st Chief Directorate, the department charged with all Soviet clandestine activities abroad, had defected to the CIA in Helsinki some weeks ago. He had provided the Americans with information that corroborated the smoldering SIS suspicions about Philby. The case against the Englishman was no longer hanging in limbo between suspicion and guilt. Now it was airtight. And an Anglo-American team was on its way to Beirut at that very moment to take him in.

No, this was real. There were no choices.

But still? *Moscow? Home?* That weather. The humorless people. The dullness and misery of Moscow. *Home?*

Thoughts thundered through Philby's mind as he hurriedly selected an assortment of his favourite Hawes & Curtis shirts and polka-dot ties along with a couple of crumpled suits and sweaters. He knew these were not priority items—and Rezayov sitting there drumming his knees must think his actions odd—but he did want to take some mementos of his past and other life with him—however trivial and absurd they were. He grabbed the photograph of Eleanor and the children in its Victorian silver frame, which had belonged to his grandmother, then scooped up some pipes lying around on his desk. He unlocked one of its drawers and took out three neatly tied bundles of letters with English, French, and American stamps on them.

"Private correspondence," he muttered to the dour Azerbaijani who was watching him with mounting impatience. Philby chose a large brown envelope addressed to his American wife and read the brief, undated note he had prepared long ago, just in case this day arrived. It explained how he had to rush away for a short while—on a reporting assignment. She would find it when she returned from the party at Glen Balfour Paul's house. When he had finished, Philby replaced the letter in the envelope and stuffed it with two neatly stacked bundles of ten-pound notes. Each bundle contained 1,000 pounds.

"We must leave quickly," Rezayov replied. "We have a long drive ahead of us and a tight schedule to keep. To effect maximum security, the flight out has been arranged from a Syrian military airfield, close to the Lebanese border off the Beirut–Damascus road. If possible, though, we would like to arrange for you to be seen in the port area before we make the car journey north. The Soviet freighter *Dolmatova* should be weighing anchor shortly and it would be useful if you were thought to be on it." Rezayov looked at his Rolex watch. It read nine minutes after midnight.

Philby turned back to the suitcase. He looked at it thoughtfully for a moment. Then, seemingly satisfied, he pressed in the snap-up brass bolts on each side and picked up the valise.

"Comrade Philby," Geidar Rezayov whispered gravely as he reached out and touched the Englishman's sleeve. "From this moment on the 13th Directorate is no longer simply your brainchild. It is yours to command. Welcome aboard."

1 | MONDAY, DECEMBER 21

The shiny, stretched Zil limousines approached the triangular compound via different routes.

Along Marx Prospekt and Manege Street, up Revolution Square and the Kremlyovskaya Embankment, the imposing vehicles glided gracefully past the banks of powdery new snow that lined the enormous thoroughfares feeding onto Red Square. There the watery winter sunlight played off their waxed black finish as they swooped past Lenin Mausoleum and the Cathedral of St. Basil the Blessed and turned into Nikolsky Tower. Once past the heavily guarded checkpoint tucked beneath the turreted archway there, they entered the innermost sanctum of the Kremlin.

Inside the fortress compound, the vehicles veered left. One by one they stopped directly in front of the imperial portals of the Senate Building, situated midway down the avenue of snow-covered pines dotting Ivanovsky Square. As each car stopped, attending guards in gray uniforms rushed forward to open the rear door and then briskly slammed it shut once the passenger had alighted. The chauffeurs sped away toward the quadrangle that sat just ahead, in front of the high, gilded wrought-iron fence that cut off this, the real seat of Soviet Government, from the fabled conglomeration of magnificent onion-domed cathedrals and czarist palaces that adorn the southern two-thirds of the triangular enclave.

From each car a grave middle-aged man strode purposefully toward the steps leading to the dark-wood revolving door. Each was dressed in a sober single-breasted overcoat; each wore a somber hat: either a trilby or an astrakhan; and each had, wrapped around his neck, a woolen scarf.

Then abruptly the sudden rush of activity was over. All was quiet again. The inquisitive faces that had appeared in the windows of the ancient two-story Arsenal Building across the park returned to their daily chores. Below them, on the East Driveway of Ivanovsky Square, the captain of the guards extracted some papers from inside his long, cumbersome greatcoat and checked the list before consulting his men. They all cursed upon hearing that there was still one straggler left—for whom they had to wait. It was, after all, nearly twenty degrees below zero despite the sun. And they would have to endure the bitter southerly winds until he arrived and was tucked safely inside the building with the others.

Thankfully the wait was not long. Fifteen minutes or so later the nose of a dark blue Chaika automobile appeared in the guardhouse under the tower to the north. After the briefest pause, the car headed slowly down the curve leading to the Senate. The surprise of the guards at the distinctly modest make and model of the vehicle was heightened by the appearance of the passenger who disembarked.

He was an old man, slow and cautious in his movements, and shabbily dressed. On descending from the car he gave a throaty cough and looked up at the elaborate building as if taking in and delighting in its every detail. To ward off the bitter cold he clapped his gloved hands together a few times before smiling modestly at the guardsman holding the door of his car. Then slowly, with the help of a battered cane, he shuffled toward the stairs, his scuffed brown-suede shoes negotiating each level with the greatest of care.

"Who is *he*?" murmured one of the younger guards.

The captain looked at the bent elderly figure mounting the steps. He hadn't changed a bit. Not an iota in all these years. The *Anglichinin*—and they'd been calling him that ever since the captain could remember—had remained the same. The same disheveled professor's attire, the same mild mannerisms, the same deceptively

simply way. Strange though, thought the captain. His being here.
He hadn't been a visitor for a long time now. Years.

He looked at the young soldier harshly. "A legend," he snapped,
walking away.

At precisely that moment, high up on the slopes of the Alps, a
solitary figure descended toward the most distinguished, most extravagant ski resort in the world. He glided down, crisscrossing the
twisting 3,057-meter Piz Nair–Corviglia Pistes at a hurtling pace,
then more slowly, stopping occasionally in a glitter of spraying
snow to catch his breath and devour the breathtaking scenery.

He was an athletic figure, built solidly, like a middleweight
prizefighter but taller than most of that breed, perhaps. And his
grip on the steep *piste noire* slopes seemed almost in the same vein:
determined, pugnacious even, as if daring the mountain to fell him.

As he reached the flats surrounding the Corvigliahutte, the rest
lodge at Corviglia, the figure slowed and straightened to his full
height. He coasted in, pulling off his gloves, goggles, and stocking
cap. Then he ran a hand across his glistening reddened forehead
and thick crop of curly black hair as he threaded through the
droves of playful, rich teenagers buzzing with energy and excitement in the fresh mountain air. His clear green eyes seemed to
empathize with them even though he didn't smile.

At the *téléphérique* building he stopped, removed his skis, and
placed them in the rack there before strolling around the rest lodge
to the crowded open-air bar on the south side overlooking the
valley. He sat beneath a Martini parasol and ordered a Bloody
Mary.

It was a stunning sight: to the left and below were the villages of
Celerina and Pontresina and above them Mount Diavolezza and
the hulking 4,023-meter peak of Bernina. To the right, in the
combe, the village of Suvretta rose up to the Furtschellas and the
3,451-meter Piz Corvatch. In the center directly beneath him lay
the picturesque villages of Chantarella and St. Moritz, blurred a
little by the faintest of mists.

The skier stood and removed his parka. Then he took a sip of his
drink and recalled vividly—as he so often did—where and how it
had all started. Chicago. Cermak Road. And the stench of vomit
and sweat and urine. A different kind of winter to this one, too. A

different kind of snow and cold. That had been South Side snow, Cicero cold. The hawk, they called it on the street. And with good reason: it ripped through you like a giant claw. Nothing could save you from it. Nothing, that was, that you could afford.

"Ahhh . . . Mr. Delan. How very good to see you again."

The voice snapped the man out of his past. Even before he turned he recognized the distinctive elliptical tone of a middle-easterner attempting to affect an Oxbridge accent.

"I am happy to see you did not have any trouble finding this place."

He was a tall, fleshy man with thinning wavy hair and a sallow complexion.

"Hello, Keyvan," said the skier, smiling. "No, the instructions you left at the hotel were very precise."

"Good." Keyvan Naderi pulled out a chair and angled it carefully beneath the red-and-white parasol to avoid the bright, golden glare of the sun. "When did you arrive?"

"Yesterday. On the early afternoon train."

"From Zurich?" the Iranian asked as the two men sat.

"Yes."

"Ah, what a beautiful journey that is," Naderi said with very little conviction. "I must make a point of doing it again one of these days; one misses so much on these private planes."

He looked around as if to get his bearings, his watery eyes lingering momentarily here and there on this or that youth.

Delan studied the immaculate coiffure of his companion. Keyvan Naderi's face was not an unattractive one, even though nearly every feature about it was a little overgenerous and it was beginning to show the lines of his late forties. He was about six feet, but his weight was not distributed proportionately across his body, giving him the rotund frame of a well-fed penguin.

Naderi looked back; and down at the younger man's boots. "I see you didn't waste any time, though. You've been skiing."

Delan smiled, a boyish smile to disguise the distaste he felt for the man and the task he faced. Here was a creature who had turned the practice of playing both sides against the middle into an art form. Having to compete with his wiles made Delan uneasy. More so since his job was to foster as close a relationship as he could with the man.

"Well, I thought I'd make the most of the famous St. Moritz slopes now that I'm here."

"Is this your first time?"

"Yes, I'm afraid it is."

"Well, then," Naderi said, leaning forward to rest his elbows on the table, "I think it will be a visit you will always remember."

Delan felt a stab of excitement. Was this another hint? Was Naderi already going to reveal why he had summoned Delan here? Was he about to achieve the breakthrough he had worked so hard for over the last five months? Cultivating this cunning chameleon of a man, basking in his borrowed jet-set life-style. It seemed uncharacteristic of Naderi to rush into revelations. In all their earlier conversations, the Iranian had always sought to reinforce the image he liked to project: of a benign and amiable playboy forced to play the intermediary for patriotic reasons, a kindly man, helpful and generous to his friends—whichever side they were on—in the never-ending turmoil that had gripped his homeland. No matter that he would earn himself a fat share in the bargain. No matter that beneath the veneer of a simple innocent merchant he was trading in death.

As nonchalantly as he could, Delan angled his head and looked around himself.

"Tell you the truth, I don't think that's going to be very hard to do, Keyvan. I like this place already."

"You will like it even more, I assure you, after I give you the good news." The Iranian paused theatrically and smiled. "But first," he said, turning to flag a waiter, "we must have a little champagne to celebrate."

Delan nodded. It was a game they were playing now. But there was something missing from Naderi's style: polish. Or perhaps there was just a little too much of it.

Delan observed as Naderi intricately ordered a bottle of 1970 Dom Perignon. His ostentatious generosity—passing for what the Iranians called *luti bazi*—was always just that little bit forced, as if he was driven to establish his worth and sophistication.

Nevertheless it seemed to work. How else could the man's success be explained? In a profession that attracted the hardest, the meanest and most unprincipled of men, a vocation in which first and foremost one had to be clever enough not to be trapped in one's own intricate web of lies, this man had risen to the very top. It was important to remember that, Delan told himself. Always.

At last Naderi turned away from the waiter. He looked at Delan for one brief moment before smiling softly as he gently clasped his hands together. "Now let me tell you the good news."

Dutifully Delan shifted forward.

"In a word, I have managed to arrange the deal." Naderi paused. Delan held his gaze.

"Norman Oil Company has been found acceptable by my colleagues in Teheran. The National Iranian Oil Company is prepared to offer them a one-year, fifty-thousand-barrels-a-day contract beginning the first of March."

Delan sat immobile for a moment. *It was a breakthrough. A major breakthrough.* He had gained a foothold. He had entered the first half of the deadly equation. "Hey," he drawled, exaggerating his naive grin, "that's terrific, Keyvan. Absolutely terrific."

"Yes, I'm very happy about it myself. I can only hope there are no last-minute snags."

Delan frowned. "Could there be?"

"Not really." Naderi grimaced. "Unless they were to arise at your end. With your clients."

Delan stared silently at Naderi for a moment. No. He had absolutely no intention of reneging on their agreement. Nor did his colleagues. The bond they all wanted forged between the two of them was far stronger than any fifty-thousand-barrels-a-day deal. Still, making money together was the first—and perhaps most important—step with men like this.

"I really can't think what possibly could go wrong at our end. I mean, we—my firm and our clients—all came into this thing with our eyes wide open, and you were very up-front with us, Keyvan. So there can't possibly be any misunderstanding on that score. As for the mechanics—"

"Yes," Naderi interjected, casually pointing a crooked finger. "It is the mechanics that interest me at this juncture. Though quite ordinary, they are, you will agree, reasonably important."

Delan nodded uncertainly.

"Especially since this is the first time you and I are working together," the Iranian continued. "And even more so because I'm very interested in pursuing the Brazilian . . . ah . . . ah . . . nutmeg supplies you mentioned briefly at the George V in Paris at our last meeting."

"I'm completely at your disposal, Keyvan," Delan said, forcing himself to remain cool. The breakthrough was even bigger than he thought. So they were already prepared to broach the matter of arms from Brazil. It was a sudden flood tide of good fortune that was flowing his way. The fish was swallowing. Hook, line, and sinker.

For the next few minutes the two men discussed various details of the impending oil deal Naderi had arranged. It was not a complicated affair, not since the quantity, per-barrel price and duration of the "official" contract had all been agreed to previously. The only item left was the "unofficial side agreement" Naderi wanted personally. It was in the form of an "irrevocable, assignable, and divisible bank guarantee" provided by Delan's clients, Norman Oil Company of Oklahoma, and made out to an offshore, bearer-share company by the name of Xerxes S.A. The amount of this guarantee was to be the equivalent of thirty cents a barrel. A figure that added up to fifteen thousand dollars a day, or five and a half million dollars over the duration of the one-year contract. This was Naderi's share—the kickback he was demanding for himself and his colleagues in the mullocracy ruling Iran.

Strangely, though, the huge sum—a major portion of which without doubt went into Naderi's own pocket—did not even seem to faze the bastard, Delan thought as he read the proposed wording of the guarantee from the text he had extracted from his pocket. In fact, throughout their conversation Naderi seemed unusually distant, preoccupied, even. He listened and latched onto and debated the salient points, but time and again he found ways to divert the conversation toward the Brazilian arms supplies—and what precisely it was that Delan could provide.

On each occasion Delan felt his excitement mount. But he controlled himself. He had to be careful. He could show nothing but professional interest. This was a shrewd and experienced operator sitting in front of him. He knew very well that in the proliferating Middle East arms bazaar it was, more than anything else, a buyer's market. The purchaser determined the specifications of the arms needed. Was Naderi testing Delan? Or was it something more he was after?

And so each time Delan begged off evasively. Once he suggested he needed detailed information to ensure equipment compatibility. Several times, in different ways, he hinted that it would be easier to approach the subject after they had the oil deal tucked safely under their belts. His responses, he felt, only served to whet the Iranian's appetite—which was exactly what he intended.

"You are a good man, Nick," Naderi said in the end. "I'm satisfied with the wording of the guarantee. I will inform the oil company officials in Teheran that they can proceed as soon as you provide me with the final document. In the meantime, let me say this—"

The waiter arrived with the champagne and immediately Naderi switched moods. He became jovial and fussed elaborately with the ritual of tasting. "Is there not too much ice in the bucket?" he finally asked. Once the mystified young man had apologized and departed, Naderi's face snapped back to its previous mood. The sallow cheeks moved perceptibly as the muscles under his chubby face tautened.

"What was I saying? Oh, yes. This. My colleagues in Iran appreciate business partners who don't take too seriously their slogans about Satan and such things. I believe you understand that. I also believe many of your countrymen and commercial rivals could have made much more headway in my country if, like you, they did not take offense so easily. Abuse and rhetoric are part of the politics of the Middle East, Nick. You understand that, which is one of the reasons why you are such a pleasant man to work with," Naderi said slowly and earnestly. "I look forward to an expansion of ties with International Consultants Incorporated." He smiled, raising his glass. "To the future," he said, pausing. "And Brazil."

"*Salute,*" Delan offered, restraining the excitement he felt inside. And the revulsion.

"Tell me, Nick, are you by any chance free tomorrow night?" Naderi asked as he lowered his glass to the table.

"Yes, I am. Why?"

"I have arranged a little dinner with some friends; I wonder if you would like to join us."

Instinctively Delan recalled the beau-monde circles Naderi always had around him: fashionable industrialists, stateless nobility, hopeful starlets, and expensive whores. Might be a fulfilling evening.

"Sure, I'd love to."

"Comrade General Secretary, following the interim meeting of this extraordinary committee on November twenty-third we are assembled here today to discuss the specific steps necessary to dismantle the 13th Directorate and thereby immediately terminate the one operation that has always been its sole raison d'être."

Marshal Sergei L. Filatov, the Defense Minister of the Soviet Union, looked up from the papers he was shuffling and around the large, spare third-floor room that was the General Secretary's office. The conference table was flanked by eighteen chairs, ten of which were occupied; seven by members of this special ad hoc committee, three by members of the General Secretary's personal staff. Adorning the green-baize surface was an assortment of mineral waters, lemon soda, and small crystal tumblers filled with colored pencils. In addition there were the usual cut-glass plates of *pirozhki,* small pastries for nibbling.

The Marshal, a lean man with a full head of wiry salt-and-pepper hair and an intelligent if weather-beaten face that appeared ten years younger than his sixty-one years, shifted in his chair as his shrewd, hard eyes contemplated the General Secretary.

"Before setting out the plan which we have devised, however, some of us feel—and I have been asked to relay this concern—that it is our duty to inform you, Comrade General Secretary, that not all the views of other comrades conform with the decision that has been taken."

The large, intense, dark-brown eyes of the General Secretary silently bored across the table for a moment. Then they moved. Slowly, diligently, they contemplated the faces of the other men one by one. At length he raised his right hand to adjust his steel-rimmed glasses.

"How do they not conform?"

"It is held by some, Comrade General Secretary," Defense Minister Filatov responded, glancing up fractionally from the younger man's face to the cream silk wall covering bearing sepia-colored portraits of Lenin and Marx, "that opportunities to influence events on the other side are being unnecessarily sacrificed. It is further felt that while improvement of relations with the USA is, of course, a desirable goal at the prevailing dialectic of development"—he looked around the table and nodded at those sitting opposite him and to either side—"it is not yet possible to identify any specific advantages which may have accrued to us from this policy of appeasement and compromise we have more recently undertaken. Indeed, Comrade, there are many highly responsible and patriotic individuals in the security apparatus and the military services who show increasing concern at our inclination to take on faith so much of the rhetoric emanating from the other side.

"Of course," he added a mite haughtily, "it is the duty of *every* citizen in our country to show concern for the present economic inertia we face. More, even; to adhere unswervingly to the irreversible process of socio-economic transformation we have introduced. But, given the predatory appetites of the other side, many of our comrades believe it is no less our duty to ensure that the motherland's guard is permanently at full strength, too. Which brings us back to the dismantlement of the Komitet Gosudarstvennoy Bezopasnosti's 13th Directorate and the ramifications that this act might precipitate. You may wish to consider—"

"Comrade Marshal, you will permit me to interrupt," the General Secretary said in that soft, melodious, deep voice that had so captivated the foreign media. "The policies and activities of the leadership of our country are established by the Central Committee of the Communist Party of the Soviet Union and ratified by the Presidium of the Supreme Soviet. The authority vested in the General Secretary's office comes from the Central Committee directly and is endorsed by the Politburo."

The two men's eyes locked in a tense silence, two men representing huge, powerful, and conflicting factions, the ideological chasm between which was not closing. Here two worlds, two eras, sat locked in confrontation. One represented the new reformist wave that maintained that the Soviet Union's future interests lay in the strengthening of the home economic base and democratization.

The other embodied the more traditional Soviet view, one that saw a future dominated by a need to survive in an intrinsically hostile world—a survival that depended on unwavering ideological dedication at home and a capacity to demonstrate strength abroad.

The gap between the two perceptions was huge, their priorities irreconcilable. Worse, the divergence had dominated the nation for some years now. Indeed it had come to be the great delineator throughout the Soviet system. You were either for *perestroika*, "the era of change," or against it. Essentially it was that simple.

Across the long conference table in the General Secretary's room, the duel of eyes continued for a long moment before at last the much decorated, fully uniformed Defense Minister flinched just slightly under the building strain.

The other men in the room shifted in their seats, fidgeting with relief as the tension ebbed.

"The decision on the matter of the KGB's 13th Directorate was first communicated to the comrades presently gathered here last October," the General Secretary said in the same soft tone he had been using throughout. "The decision stands."

A hand holding a red pencil was raised above the table, puncturing the heavy air.

The General Secretary swiveled his balding head toward it. "Comrade Seleznadze," he said, looking at the pixielike, white-haired Foreign Minister from Soviet Georgia.

"Comrades," Nikolai Fedorovich Seleznadze started, "in the previous meeting of this special ad hoc committee I was performing state duties overseas. And since no written records are being kept on any of the meetings of this select committee's dealings in such a sensitive topic, I'm not familiar with the full details of all the points that were discussed—although, of course, I have familiarized myself generally with the extraordinary activities of the 13th Directorate. I should like to take this opportunity, then, to state that, from the perspective of the conduct of the foreign policy of our nation, to continue with those activities would jeopardize all the potentially sweeping and historic steps taken by us to achieve a degree of predictability and stability in our relations with the USA. It is worth noting that the other side has responded positively to many of our initiatives and that the relative normalization of relations has permitted us to turn our attentions to the domestic priorities of the Soviet Union."

"At the expense of the security of the motherland," barked Marshal Filatov. "Comrade Seleznadze's dealings with the other side cover only the more recent period. If, like some of us, the comrade had been monitoring the intentions of the metropolitan center of imperialism over a more extensive period of years, he would not be such a firm believer that what we are buying with this policy of compromise is a *peredyshka*, breathing space, but a—"

Abruptly a thunderous crash resounded across the room—freezing the words in the soldier's mouth. All eyes snapped toward the General Secretary. For one interminably long moment he glared at Filatov, the muscles around his eyes taut, his generous cheeks suffused with blood. Then, slowly, his angry silence seemed to pass as he opened the fist he had used as a giant gavel, raising it now to adjust his spectacles.

"For more than an entire generation we followed that line of thinking—military might. And what did we achieve, Marshal? We have become obsolete, a one-product state, a superpower in name only. No carrots, just sticks. And that alibi is no longer enough. Not when the momentum of the balance of forces is shifting so radically away from us. Look at the situation we have inherited, Marshal," the General Secretary said, his deep voice cutting across the room.

He lifted his hands and started emphatically ticking off on his fingers as he outlined "the international quagmire we find ourselves in.

"And we're facing all these enormous problems," he said once he had finished his long list, "at a time when we face a resurgent China. A China, I might add, ten, maybe twelve times the size of Japan and potentially that much larger in terms of economic productive capacity. China, comrades. That is where our future problems will come."

The General Secretary paused; and then continued with a brief but depressing account of the state of the nation's domestic economy, its lagging labor productivity, its technological backwardness, its cumbersome centrally controlled administrative system, its numerous and growing social problems.

He raised his eyes to the window before him and shook his head sadly as he repeated yet again how it was "the age-old economic bugaboo of guns and butter" that they were facing.

In front of him, through the puffy, white-silk curtains draping the four ten-feet-high windows, the city's streetlights suddenly came alive, glistening in the clock and the blood-red star atop Czar Tower, illuminating the fairy-tale onion domes and steeples of the Cathedral of St. Basil the Blessed in Red Square.

"No, my friend, our old ideology has become unsellable abroad and unserviceable at home. Sheer military might is simply not enough to win us the game. No. The age-old axiom still applies: foreign policy is an extension of domestic policy. And nations can only be assertive abroad when they are self-assured at home. Consequently, it is in our best short- and long-term interests to continue to attempt to reduce the tensions between the two superpowers. To concentrate on the positive elements between our two countries in order to reduce military spending on both sides still further—and thereby free up even more of our rubles for investment in the domestic civilian economy." He sighed heavily. "To do that, though, we must persuade them to trust us. And we, in turn, must learn to trust them more. This can only be done if we create more interlocking interests. And that is why the small but steady progress we have achieved in our relations with the USA must continue to be developed."

He paused and looked at Filatov grimly.

"That is also why the continued existence of the 13th Directorate serves no purpose. It is not only obsolete in its hostile, cold-war objectives. It has, too, a very real potential for getting out of control. And at this sensitive stage that would be disastrous."

The General Secretary's penetrating eyes continued to rest on the Defense Minister. "We have spoken of these matters before, so I will not take up any more of this committee's time on generalities. Now, Marshal Filatov, you were instructed to identify plans for the dismantlement of the 13th Directorate generally and in due course. And the halting of its operations specifically and at once. May we hear your recommendations, please?"

The Marshal spoke unenthusiastically. "Since the stratagem for the termination of the organization's single ongoing undertaking is nearly as complex and unconventional as its original goals, I took the liberty, Comrade General Secretary, of asking the man who has been involved in its day-to-day administration all these years to make himself available to answer that question. He is waiting next door."

The General Secretary frowned. The essence of collective leadership was collective responsibility—which, in turn, was the reason why layers existed: a bureaucracy to absorb the guilt. Besides, he thought warily, the resistance he and his team continued to face did not come so much from the old Party leaders anymore. They had nearly all been replaced by his own people. It came from the high- and mid-level career men in the security apparatus and the military. They were the ones who'd seen their roles and perks diminishing with the decreasing budgets. And it was the conservatives among them who were still putting up a rearguard action to his policies. So what was this machination of theirs all about? What the devil were they hoping to gain from short-circuiting the chain of command this time? Was it simply the usual reason? To avoid responsibility of any kind? Or was it something more Gordian?

He didn't know. He was sure there was a reason, though. The aged legend waiting next door was one of the abiding heroes of the hard-liners. A foreigner more mired in the insolvent ethics of the past than any Soviet citizen he knew of.

"I don't believe that's necessary," the General Secretary said. "This is, after all, a policy committee, not an executive one. As such we aren't likely to go beyond the general points of the plan, are we?"

"Ah, no . . . no," the Marshal responded uncertainly. Rejection of his proposal hadn't crossed his mind. He shuffled the papers in front of him in a single pile.

"We've considered all the options and have determined that we cannot pursue a conventional course in arresting the progress already made by the 13th Directorate in this operation. The plans are too far advanced and have acquired too much of their own momentum for a straightforward termination to be possible. The withdrawal of financial and other assistance would now be meaningless. In addition, for the very same reasons you wish to terminate the project, it is clearly not possible to liquidate the subject. The risk and potential repercussions of that approach, should something go wrong, would of course be disastrous."

The Marshal looked up from his papers. "In short, the only realistic option available to us is to take advantage of the subject's personal flaws and to arrange for them to be exposed in such a way as to achieve the desired effect."

"And how do you propose to do this?" the General Secretary asked.

Marshal Sergei L. Filatov raised his scuffed brown-leather

briefcase from beside his chair and extracted a thick folder from it. Carefully he replaced the briefcase on the floor beside his chair before fixing his half-moon spectacles on the bridge of his nose and leafing through the pages. At last he reached a large white envelope. He withdrew it from the stack of papers, every crinkle of the bending sheets resounding around the hushed room.

Slowly, with the greatest of care not to bend it, he extracted the thin, glossy, eight-by-ten black-and-white photograph—and placed it before the General Secretary.

2 | TUESDAY, DECEMBER 22

It was shortly after ten P.M. when Nick Delan knocked on the dark rustic, wooden door of the secluded building at the edge of the village of St. Moritz. The exotic silhouette of the towers and turrets against a moonlit sky created a strange setting, one unusually appropriate to the name of the establishment—The Dracula Club.

Only the faintest of amber lights broke the building's even blackness, adding to the mystery. The dim glow emanated from its low, wood-framed windows, decorated with ornate but sturdy wrought-iron bars. Not the slightest sound—from within or without—broke the stillness. Only the crop of Ferraris, Maseratis, Porsches and Rolls-Royces glistening in the moonlight gave any hint of the activities inside.

The door opened and immediately the tender voice of Julio Iglesias washed away the eerie silence. Delan turned his appreciative glance from the cars.

"Mr. Naderi," he muttered, engrossed by the delicately chiseled face and pallid gray-blue eyes of the maître d'hôtel. No more than twenty-five years old, she was slim and tall and polar-blond.

"Mr. Delan?" she asked, bending her head inquiringly as she threw off a warm smile.

"Yes," he nodded.

"Please come in. Mr. Naderi has been expecting you. He was worried you'd lost your way."

"Thank you." Delan stepped in and removed his overcoat. As he waited for her to log it with the *vestiaire*, he looked around to get his bearings. It was not an easy task. The light was sparse. In fact, it was nearly as black as it had been in the thick conifer forest outside.

"This way, please." She smiled again and brushed his arm, stroking it almost.

Her hair seemed luminous. He followed its bounce willingly, through a short hallway and past a rustic wooden arch, the sounds growing louder with each step. The music had changed now. It was a wild driving samba, laced with a heavy streak of Harlem talent. Viciously sensuous, a saxophone blared its tragic, earthy refrain from above the savage Latin–New York rhythm.

The small dance floor was a throb of movement, the bar behind abuzz with chatter, but the tables of the patrons were indistinguishable, hidden discreetly within private arched alcoves of black. Except for the bar and dance floor, which was a sea of ever-changing, multicolored psychedelic flashes synchronized to the rhythmic beat; the only lighting evident was pencil-thin white beams shining like lasers from the dark wooden A-frame ceiling upon carefully preselected targets. Here the exhausted eyes of a tormented old man dominated a dark, massive oil portrait. There the nipple of a sagging breast. An index finger of a pointed hand. The Devil's fangs. A flying bat. And the Holy Cross of Jesus.

Delan's guide ducked into an alcove and stopped at a long series of low, interlinking coffee tables that seemed to fade away into the darkness. She leaned forward and suddenly Keyvan Naderi rose from a stool.

"Ahhh . . . Nick," Naderi bellowed over the raucous din. "I was beginning to worry about you."

He was smiling his same old measured smile.

"I'm sorry I'm late, Keyvan," Delan said softly. "But I was on the line with the U.S., trying to get various documents in order before the Christmas holidays get under way."

Naderi looked at him. "Yes. The time difference can be a problem. But never mind all that now. You're here, that's all that matters."

Naderi's watery eyes sparkled as he turned away toward his guests. His left hand guided Delan forward. But the handsome group—men wearing casual chic and women bejeweled—seemed totally uninterested in a new face, engrossed as they were with one another.

"I'd introduce you, except one way or another they are all too far gone to care. Listen, somewhere in there," Naderi pointed haphazardly with his glass into the darkness, "there's a seat for you. Wait a minute."

He took a sip of his drink. "Clio?" he shouted into the darkness.

A few of the elegant entourage turned momentarily in their direction. A young boy whose punk-styled hair was undecided about its color, shaded from light blond at its tips to dark brown at its roots, lounged back slowly and invitingly. Left forefinger to left eyebrow, right wrist on his hip, he smiled seductively at Delan.

Delan forced a joyless nod before looking away.

For the most part the group appeared to be the usual mix that haunt these places, the new aristocrats: creatures who lived, and lived well, by their native wits—and exploitation. Monte Carlo residents, with Swiss companies, making their money across the world. Land speculation in Colombia, insider trading on Wall Street, or preferably London, where it was easier. A few percentage points for access to this or that contract in the Middle East; arms sales, no questions asked, to any buyer; or perhaps even ripping off their own husbands or wives. These were the middlemen, the dealers and fixers, in their own way paid-up members of what has come to be known as the International Business Community, weasels who burrow into the gaps between international laws, and more often than not make the lawmakers in several countries a little happier with their middle-class lot.

"Clio, can you hear me?" bellowed Naderi. "I'm sending in your escort. Look after him, will you?"

"How lovely. Of course, darling."

He turned back to Delan. "You'll be all right. Clio will look after you. My dear friend here . . . er . . . his name escapes me," he nodded to the table, "is just leaving. I'll see him off and join you."

Delan felt a slight shove into the darkness. He headed gingerly around the bodies sprawled on the couches and perched on stools toward the source of the husky voice he had heard a moment ago.

The guests were huddled around the low tables in threes and fours, pawing and nibbling and talking in a wide variety of languages. From the middle a slim, dark, bejeweled hand stuck straight up like a flag post. Four of its fingers plucked softly at the air.

Delan felt his way toward it.

"Hello." Her smiling, almond-shaped eyes looked up at him, two phosphorous reflectors in the dark. She extended a delicate, sun-tanned arm, arched at the wrist, and offered it to his lips. "I'm Clio."

Delan hesitated a fraction. Then he lowered her arm and shook it gently, all the while riveted by the ferocious beauty that was looking up at him.

"Hi," he practically shouted over the tumultuous din. "I'm—"

"I know," she interrupted, her thick lips parting sensuously in blood-red. "Kevi told me."

Delan smiled and nodded.

"What do you drink, Mr. Delan?"

"Martini, I think. A nice, dry vodka martini."

"Martini?" her husky voice repeated disapprovingly.

Delan nodded again; it was a move he had perfected into a hundred variations, each marginally different, each with its own distinct meaning. This one held surprise.

"Something wrong with that?"

She raised one of her thick, dark eyebrows.

"That depends on how you answer the next question."

Delan was intrigued; she had about her a lean, tensile quality, with all the beauty and presence of a Tartar princess.

He smiled. "Okay. I bite."

She looked into his eyes silently for a moment, a mass of dark-brown hair falling around her exquisitely sculpted high cheek-bones. "With onions? Or olives?"

Delan pondered playfully. "Olives. Now, what does that convey?"

She laughed and made a face. "I was afraid you'd say that."

"Afraid? Why?"

"Because I don't know you well enough yet to get that familiar," she said, turning to attract a waiter.

Delan was surprised. As she ordered he looked away, through the smoky black fog, and the gyrating bodies on the dance floor, to his surroundings. His eyes were adjusting to both the smoke and the dark. What an amazing place this was. He had never seen anything quite like it. Savage. Corrupt. Degenerate. Evil. He wasn't quite sure what he could call it. Whatever it was, it was arousing. And in the middle of it all was this girl called Clio.

The waiter departed and he dipped his head toward her again.

"You're not exactly a square shooter, are you?"

She turned and the whiff of a thousand perfumed petals filled his head as her long, billowing hair swept past only inches away.

"No, I'm not."

"And may I ask why?"

"Because it's childish. Square shooters only win in the movies, Mr. Delan."

Delan nodded, puckering his lips, absorbing the point. He let the pause ride for a moment.

"That seems fair enough. But do you think we could start at the beginning again—just for conversational purposes—because I'm afraid you have a distinct advantage over me: all I was told was Clio. There must be more."

"Bragana," she articulated proudly. "Clio Bragana."

Delan sank back more comfortably on the couch, closer to her. "Well, Miss Bragana, it's nice to meet you, even though you already seem to know me. What's your friend . . . er . . . Kevi been saying?"

She was silent for a moment, her lips pouting, her large, hooded eyes suggestive yet cold as she contemplated him.

"Nothing. Just your name, the fact that you're friends and that you're worth meeting or something. And harmless at the same time." She turned away.

Delan studied her sleek Latin profile for a moment. Then he brushed the corner of his right eye with his index finger and reached for the martini that had just arrived. She was a hard little girl, he thought. Tough and sure of herself. Obviously very, very experienced. Too experienced. Nevertheless, disarmingly beautiful.

Perhaps that was the link, he thought, his eyes scanning the room. In fact, one way or another, each and every person in sight had something on offer. Most were obviously exceedingly wealthy. The rest—male or female—were just as obviously decoration. Interim decoration. Beauty that was dazzling and changeable, buyable and sellable, the supply limited, the price high.

Abruptly he recalled an old proverb, one of the basic tenets of survival on the street: the buyer needs a hundred eyes—the seller but one. Which was young Miss Bragana? he wondered. A buyer? Or a seller?

And the jewelry, he noted as he looked around. Diamonds the size of sugar cubes, emeralds the size of grapes, rubies, pearls, gold by the kilo. A small wisp of a smile formed at the corner of his lips, his mind recalling another era, another jungle. Cicero and the abandoned, gutted ghettos of Lawndale. The smile broadened. Like taking candy from a baby, he thought. They'd have hit this place opening night.

He brought the long-stemmed Baccarat glass to his lips and sipped the martini. It was perfectly constructed: hardly a hint of vermouth. He sipped again and then replaced the glass on the table, plucking the miniature Japanese parasol cocktail stick that held two olives skewered to its end.

"Men should never eat olives," he heard Clio Bragana purr.

He stopped in midaction, his mouth half open, about to nibble one. He looked at the olive for a moment, then slowly turned toward her. "Why not?"

One of the thin straps of her white silk dress slid off her shoulders as her eyes looked straight into Delan's.

"Because olives taste like come."

Less than a mile southeast of the Kremlin, directly opposite the junction of the Yauza and Moscow rivers, a small peninsula extends into the meandering waterway, curving westward well past Borovitsky Square. The embankment at the nape of the isthmus, facing northeast across the river toward Izmailovski Park, is the Maxim Gorki Embankment. It is—along with the rest of the peninsula—among the most protected pieces of residential property in the sprawling eight-hundred-year-old city. For it is here that the most privileged reside, the elite of a police state: the senior officials of one or other of the many organs of the state security apparatus.

The elaborate eighteenth-century building, with its four columns, high portico and belvedere, marked number twenty-six and situated toward the center of Maxim Gorki Embankment, is arguably the most famous structure in the neighborhood from a historical perspective; notorious is probably a more accurate term. For it was from there that Rasputin helped to seal the fate of the Romanovs and imperial Russia. There, on the fourth floor, his Moscow residence. Having manipulated his patrons in St. Petersburg, it was to what is now number twenty-six Maxim Gorki Embankment that the monk would repair to savor the pleasures of the flesh. In 1984 the building was allocated as the residence of the Deputy Prime Minister of the USSR, a position now held by Geidar Reza Alievich Rezayov.

Now, deep into the night on this Tuesday, the twenty-second of December, a meeting was taking place there. Behind drawn curtains five men sat facing each other in comfortable purple-velvet armchairs placed around a priceless fading Tabriz rug. Between them squatted a heavy, carved wood-and-glass coffee table decorated with a large silver dish bearing fruit, plates of different *zakuski*, some small glasses, and a bottle of arrack from Azerbaijan.

"Comrades, please feel at ease. Our session tonight is above suspicion. As far as the General Secretary is concerned we are meeting with Comrade Philby here," Rezayov said, motioning to the frail, elderly man sitting to his right, "to consult about the dismantlement of his organization with a view to expediting the termination of its operations immediately. It is what I told the General Secretary myself today."

The tall, dapper Rezayov smiled politely at his guests. Only Kim Philby smiled back. The modest gesture, however, belied the discomfort the Englishman felt. He was never totally at ease in the company of these men. And even less so given the nature of this meeting. They were mostly unsubtle, impatient beings meddling in a highly delicate game.

"Nevertheless, Comrades," Rezayov continued, "it goes without saying that what we discuss must never be revealed to anyone outside this room. No notes will be taken nor will there be any recordings."

"It would be suicide," quipped Marshal Sergei Filatov, the slim, wiry-haired Defense Minister sitting to Philby's right.

"Yes," the man to Rezayov's left agreed, shifting nervously in his chair.

Philby turned to look at him. It was Gennadi Dmitrievitch Ivanov, Deputy Chairman of the KGB, a career security man who had established himself in the Special Operations section, Department V as in Victor, before moving up on the strength of his successes there to head the Planning and Analysis Directorate. He was a short, solid but not fat man with round ruddy cheeks and a shock of unmanageable straight white hair that he insisted on brushing to the right.

The elderly Englishman swiveled his head. The man sitting in the armchair directly across from him was bald with sleepy wet eyes and an immense girth. His fleshy face wobbled as he nodded solemnly, the lenses of his thick horn-rimmed glasses magnifying the drowsy dip of his eyelids to give him a deceptively dull and plodding appearance. But Anatoli Andeyev, the Director of the Institute of the United States and Canada, was anything but dull and plodding. He was, in fact, one of the shrewdest men Philby knew, besides being a scholar, an academician, a strategist, and one of the foremost chess players in the land. Perhaps the only man in the room capable of understanding the nuances involved, thought Philby. If he put his mind to it, that was. And when he didn't allow himself to be browbeaten into silence by the others.

"Well then," said Rezayov, "I think we can begin. We heard the directives of the General Secretary yesterday. I believe I reflect the views of all of us in saying we are in disagreement."

"Yes," snapped the Defense Minister. "But I must say I sometimes wish that other comrades would make their anxieties about these disastrous new policies a little more apparent. We are proceeding on a path that is perilous for the security of the Motherland. And almost daily some of the more senior elements of the military and security communities are becoming increasingly restless. They are even beginning to question *our* integrity and resolve to rein in our so-called progressive young friend."

Philby felt his uneasiness mount. Domestic politics was an area he had assiduously avoided almost from the first day he had arrived in the Soviet Union—what a lifetime ago now. It was a subject, he had learned very early on, about which his opinions were not welcomed.

"Your point is well taken, Comrade Marshal," Ivanov, the KGB Deputy, said, breaking into Philby's thoughts. "You have indeed borne the brunt of the burden of exposing the dangers. I think we are all aware of that."

"Absolutely," Rezayov added quickly. "You will forgive me, Comrade Marshal, for not interceding on your behalf in your discussions with the General Secretary yesterday. But, on the other hand, I'm sure you will agree with me when I say that what we agreed to at the outset is just as true today. Namely, that it is absolutely essential for me to continue to be identified as a keen supporter of the General Secretary's decisions. Unfortunately—but obviously—that includes his fervent desire to terminate the 13th Directorate's activities. After all, only by being part of the inner circle can I be constantly plugged in to all the various decisions being contemplated. And that, I submit, is how I can continue to serve our cause best: by acting as your eyes and ears."

"Yes, I suppose you are right." Marshal Filatov sighed reluctantly. "Now how do you propose we salvage elements of the 13th Directorate's operations without seeming to directly countermand the General Secretary's directives?"

"I believe Comrade Philby is in a better position to answer that than I," said Rezayov.

All the eyes in the room turned toward the slight, stooped figure with disheveled, thinning white hair. He seemed almost lost in the huge armchair in which he sat.

The Englishman stared back at the four men silently for a brief moment. Their faces were grim and determined. As certain of their path as any fundamentalist anywhere in the world might be about his faith or creed. There was no question of compromise.

Despite all their faults, this single-minded resolve was as it should be at least, thought the Englishman.

"What are your recommendations, Comrade Philby?" the usually reticent Andeyev prompted in his nasal tone.

"Pe—pe—perhaps it would be—be—better serve your purpose at this point if I were to outline the concept to you rather than going through the specific details of the plan."

The stutter was an impediment Philby had been afflicted with since childhood.

"Besides which many of the intricacies are still being worked out."

"Please, General." Again it was Andeyev who spoke, using Philby's official rank in the KGB as a handle this time.

"Le–le–let's see now," said the Englishman, mulling over his approach. "I honestly believe the best way I can explain it is by way of a rather appropriate old Azerbaijani anecdote about a mullah I picked up many years ago. From my philosophy tutor at Cambridge of all places, believe it or not."

The four men eyed Philby suspiciously. Here was a man whose very being automatically engendered wariness. He was a man of few words normally. So why was he now choosing a thousand where one would suffice?

"One day this mullah was passing through a narrow street in Baku when he caught sight of an incredibly beautiful and obviously wealthy woman," Philby began, rising from his chair with the help of his unsteady hands. He started shuffling around the room.

"Hypnotized and bewitched, the mullah began following the lady, trying in a variety of ways to catch her eye. But to no avail, I'm afraid. No matter what he did, she paid absolutely no attention to him. Not even acknowledging his existence.

"Stung by her beauty and wealth, the mullah went to her door-step each day at dawn. And then proceeded to follow her faithfully around the town as she carried out her daily chores. All the time, pining as only those who have known unrequited love can."

Philby turned and walked toward the drawn, dark-red velvet curtains fronting the three large French windows of Rezayov's drawing room.

"At last one day the lady noticed him and, taking pity, she had her maid call the priest inside the house. Thinking he was a man of meager means, she offered him food and clothing, but the tormented young mullah would accept neither.

"Instead he wept and wailed of his love for her; and how he would kill himself right there and then if the lady didn't consent to marry him."

Philby reached the end of the room. Carefully he parted the heavy curtain an inch or two and glanced outside. Across the wide waterway of Moscow River the sparkling city swept away from him on this crisp, clear winter night.

"The maid who had brought the food tried to reason with the

troubled mullah. She explained to him that the lady of the house was a respectably married woman with several children. She flattered the priest on his good looks and his bearing and his learning. All to no avail.

"So the maid tried a different approach. She told the priest how important the lady's husband was, how violent and jealous and mean. 'He will certainly cut your throat if he gets even a hint of this,' she warned.

"Abruptly the mullah sat up straight, his face contorted with horror. He grabbed at the maid's coarse skirt. Gone all of a sudden were the tears, forgotten was the passion and frenzy of undying love," said Philby, building the pace of his trembling voice and mimicking the mullah.

"'In that case,' said the mullah earnestly, 'I will fall in love with *you*. We will marry and live together forever.'"

Sitting in the middle of the room, the bald, overweight man in the loose dark-gray suit was the one who smiled tentatively at first. Then his fleshy lips parted, flashing a rare infectious laugh that bounced his body, the wide, biblike blue-striped tie rippling with the mounds of flesh protecting his stomach like a whale's blubber.

As the pregnant message sank deeper, the other three men followed suit, cackling buoyantly.

"Indeed, what do you do, Comrades, if you cannot win a race?" Rezayov asked.

"You cancel it," he explained, staring at each of his guests, pleased that the old man's story had had the same impact on them as it had had on him when he had first heard it that morning. "You cancel it, like the mullah. Or, better yet, you make your opponent do so."

The smiles on the faces of the three men Rezayov was looking at faded gradually, their narrowed eyes slowly betraying deep consideration.

"And you believe you can do that, General Philby?" Ivanov asked, his eyebrows twisting skeptically.

"Yes," Philby replied. "I believe we can both terminate and manipulate the termination of the original project in such a way as to achieve the desired objective. I also believe we can do it solely with the assets we have in place already."

"How?" General Filatov demanded.

"Essentially, it is a psychological operation I have in mind. Its goal is to disrupt Washington's thinking. Thereby destroying its morale and goading the White House into a huge miscalculation that will bring America to its knees."

"Do you have a car?" asked Clio Bragana as they stood waiting for their coats at the *vestiaire*.

"No," replied Nick Delan.

She turned toward the hat-check girl. *"Appelez-moi un cocher."*

"Il y en a déjà deux devant la porte, mademoiselle." The hat-check girl smiled and placed their coats on the counter.

"Sled?" he asked as Clio Bragana slipped into the heavy fur coat he held. "It's *freezing* out there."

Across her shoulder she cast him a small sultry smile, a world of promise sweeping across her almond eyes.

"You'll find the Swiss a very considerate race, Nick. As long as you can pay for it, that is. I'm sure they've thought of something."

The clacking hoofs of the furry miniature horse on the packed ice reverberated in the dark valley as the sled glided along the icy surface of the narrow lane. As they settled back on the ice-cold leather seat, Delan shaped the red, fox-skin eiderdown around their bodies and pulled it up toward his shoulders. The considerate Swiss had indeed made warding off the cold a pleasant experience.

"Where are you taking me?"

"The Chesa Veglia."

"What is that?"

"Somewhere you'll feel more comfortable. You can also try a Cafi-Fertig instead of those martinis of yours."

Delan looked at her, surprised. Nothing in her flickering moonlit profile indicated whether she was being serious or kidding.

"What makes you think I was uncomfortable in the first place?"

"Oh, come on, Nick," she shrugged. "Any number of things."

"Like?"

"Like?" she repeated sarcastically. "Like, when a man sits in a discotheque for three hours surrounded by beautiful, available women and doesn't dance, it's reasonable to assume he's not very big on dancing. Like, if in all that time he doesn't ease up or drop his guard even for one split second. And about half a dozen other reasons."

She was right. He had been uptight in there. "Has something to do with age," he kidded.

"And mentality."

"What does that mean?"

She looked at him. "Oh, I don't know. It seems to me you just didn't quite fit in with everyone else tonight."

"Why not?"

She shrugged and thought for a moment before she spoke. "I suspect it's because behind that friendly, polite, handsome face lies what the French would call *un homme sérieux*. Not at all the sort who feels comfortable frittering the hours away in the company of dilettantes and socialites."

This young woman's full of surprises, Delan thought. Now she turns out to be highly observant too. Perceptive. He studied her again: her windswept hair billowed about her exquisite features, her cold chin tucked into the collar of the heavy white-lynx coat she was wearing.

He reached over and pulled the eiderdown up to cover her shoulders. "You're right. But for the wrong reasons."

"So what are the reasons?"

Delan tried to sound aloof, determined to change the course of their conversation to a friendlier path. "Oh, I guess it's more a question of background. I'm not used to this sort of crowd. And I get nervous when the sophistication gets above a certain level." He looked back at her. "You see, in the neighborhood I grew up in the longest word we knew was fettucini."

The corners of her mouth turned upward slowly, two dimples forming on either side as she smiled.

"By the way, what the hell is a Cafi-Fertig, anyway?"

This time she burst into laughter. "You see, you're different already."

Two hundred yards behind the slow-moving *cocher* Keyvan Naderi stepped out of the Dracula Club. For a brief moment he stood at the top of the steps savoring the cold, clean, invigorating mountain air as his eyes followed the fading red rear lights of the sled. Then he descended the four wooden planks and walked slowly toward the parking lot in front of the club, tiptoeing warily over the icy surface of the makeshift path to compensate for the thin, slippery soles of the soft Italian patent-leather shoes he was wearing.

He headed toward a dark-colored Rolls-Royce and opened its door quickly. Once inside he started the engine and turned up the heater before reaching into the glove compartment and extracting a silver tube that held a Monte Cristo number two. He bit off the end of the torpedo-shaped Havana, struck a match and looked up just in time to see the two rear lights of the sled disappear behind the dark pines bordering the bend in the mountain road. He looked on for a moment, then checked the progress of the glow at the end of his cigar. Satisfied, he shook the wooden match gently until the flame died. He dropped it in the ashtray and lowered his hand to the small, light-gray cellular telephone just below, fitted beneath the walnut dashboard.

"Are you *sure* you want to walk?" asked an uncomprehending Clio Bragana, hugging herself for warmth even through the thick white-lynx coat she wore as she stood on the steps of the Suvretta-House Hotel. "It's cold and late and a long way."

Delan looked back at the dark, narrow road leading toward the village.

"Yes. Need to get some of this smoke out of my lungs."

"Okay," she drawled, as if to say she thought he was crazy.

He bent his head fractionally and kissed her forehead. "I'll call you tomorrow," he said softly.

"Do. I know a good doctor."

Delan smiled at her before he turned. Under his feet the packed snow crunched as he walked away at a determined pace, moving down the lane that was the winter address of the most fortunate of the fortunate. It was nearly two-thirty in the morning but his spirits were high and the walk would be therapeutic. It had been a most pleasant—if extraordinary—evening with Clio Bragana, one that called for contemplation.

He buttoned up his coat, pulled up the collar, and strode down via Marguns. Yes, she had an appealing freshness, an openness that suggested total honesty. And yet she was no innocent. There was nothing of the child about her. Quite the opposite. Presence. Experience. A strong personality. But had he been wrong in thinking he had detected a vulnerable streak, too? A painful sensitivity of some sort under that hard, self-assured surface? Was there a hint of something dark? Some dreadful disappointment masked by cynicism and affected hostility?

He quickened his pace. She had been right. The Chesa Veglia was an enchanting restaurant; and with far more to offer than just an exotic Irish coffee—which was what the Cafi-Fertig turned out to be. The local *Bündner* cooking, the Viennese cuisine and informal ambiance were both excellent and relaxing; they had talked and amused each other and when they had emerged from the restaurant their huddling together against the cold had in a very natural way turned into a warm hug.

Over dinner she had talked about her life in New York and made a savage mockery of the glamour world that employed her so handsomely.

"It's crazy. A whole flock of people fly down from New York to the Bahamas and spend a week making it look like the Côte d'Azur," she said. "All for a thirty- or sixty-second spot that's supposed to convince every woman in the States to tear out to the drugstore and buy a new French perfume. And all because some weird Polish art director who can barely speak English has convinced some Okie in the American conglomerate that is ultimately the client that the *smell*—can you believe it?—the *smell* filters through onto the film." She had smiled. "And they pay me two thousand dollars an hour to pout for a few seconds as I dab myself with what is supposed to lure American manhood back to its ladies' bedchambers. I spend ninety-eight percent of my time sitting around on my butt waiting for camera angles to be perfected. Or the lighting. Or the weather. Or script changes. Or whatever."

"Not a bad way to make a living. What came before the modeling?"

Her face had hardened momentarily and her answer had been slow. "Italy . . . Genoa, to be precise. But that was a long time ago."

Instinctively Delan had sensed tension. She seemed uncomfortable with the question. But it *was* their first evening together. And it *had* only just begun to go well. So there was no point in pursuing the subject and risking it all.

"What about you? What do you do?"

Delan studied the Christmas decorations lighting up the picture-postcard toy village of St. Moritz up ahead.

"I'm a consultant."

"Consultant!" she had repeated. "What kind of consultant?"

"Financial."

She looked at him, none the wiser. "Investments?"

"No. Opportunities. Projects. How to make money; and where."

She stared at him for one brief moment before returning to her moules farcies. "A wheeler-dealer?"

"If you want to be unkind."

"You enjoy it?"

"Well, let's put it this way. It beats working for someone else. The pay's better and the aggravations are less. Besides I doubt anyone would pay me *two* dollars an hour to sit around on my butt. Let alone—"

She had made a face as she cut him off. "Stop fishing for compliments. Where are your offices?"

"Washington and Los Angeles," Delan had replied, ignoring her mischievous smile. He remembered thinking then how comfortable they had become with each other. It seemed almost as if the ice had completely melted.

His mind lingered on that thought as he strode through the village. And slowly one thought led to another until an idea struck him. Could he swing it? How would it affect his life at this sensitive moment? And could he convince her, for that matter? Where could they go together for a couple of weeks? Alone—away from this plastic crowd she associated with. It probably wouldn't be too difficult for him to make the time. After all, Christmas was coming up and Naderi's documents were already in the pipeline. He had one thing working in his favor, too. The skiing this year was atrocious. There was simply not enough snow covering the ski runs.

Yes, he concluded. It was feasible. But he would have to wait for exactly the right moment to approach her.

His heart quickened at the prospect as he leaned into the antique, heavy, wooden revolving door of the Palace Hotel. It was a feeling he barely remembered.

Nine time zones away, high in the sky above the shimmering splendor of Century City on the west side of Los Angeles, there was pandemonium in the penthouse ballroom of the Century Plaza hotel.

The speaker smiled broadly and made a point to look into the eyes, however fleetingly, of every man and woman across whom his gaze swept. It was a youthful look in a maturing face, tanned and groomed to perfection. For thirty-one years that face had been his greatest bankable asset. For thirty-one years people from Manhattan to Melbourne, from Tokyo to Tierra del Fuego, had paid good money to see that face; to laugh with it and cry with it and suffer and love with it on their screens and in their lives. Now, as he approached his fiftieth year, the dark-brown hair was specked with white at the temples. The gray-blue eyes were perhaps more thoughtful. But the dimpled smile retained every ounce of the magic that had secured his career and stardom. He grinned a sheepish grin and again nodded his head humbly. And even the oldest women in the elderly crowd felt a slight lightness where their ribs met. Yes, this would be their man.

"Thank you, thank you," he mimed, soaking up the adulation. "You're very kind."

Each time he wanted to draw away from the lectern, the roar intensified—the audience demanding, insisting upon his continued presence.

Broadening the smile, he casually raised his right hand and pointed at one of the round tables just right of center stage, as if to single out a special friend. It was a gesture that Allan Sanford had perfected.

The thunderous applause became even louder. What made the flattery all the more astonishing was the extraordinary collection of the high and mighty who offered it so lavishly. The masters of industry were in that ballroom, political leaders from every wing of the party, two former presidents and five of the original astronauts, union leaders, twelve state governors occupying different tables, and scattered among them were nine chairmen of various House and Senate subcommittees, ex–secretaries of state, political strategists, former cabinet members, think-tank directors, columnists, all the elements of the American elite and their acolytes had seen the show and approved. The heads of the television networks were present to take stock and to plan. As were the chairmen and cochairmen and publishers of nearly every important newspaper or magazine in the country. Sprinkled among them were political analysts, university chancellors, professors, sporting personalities. And of course a host of film and television stars—in this their honeypot—dotted the assembly, adding their own special brand of glamour, and their mark of approval, to the occasion.

And each of them in that room had, independently, decided they had just witnessed something important; and each was thrilled to be there, in on the ground floor, at the very beginning of what could well be the dawning of another era.

The man behind the podium let the smile on his face ride. It was the beginning and the ending that were the essential moments of an appearance; the middle took care of itself. Knowing when to walk off—when the adulation was at its peak—was the key ingredient of any performance. He made a final sweep across the room with his eyes and arms, looked straight at the closed-circuit TV cameras which he knew beamed his face to the monitors on each table, mouthed a final "thank you" with a boyish grin and a wink at the lens before gliding elegantly from the stage.

The audience loved it. They loved his quiet confidence, his charm, his sophistication, his presence. But most of all they liked how he looked and behaved. He was what most people were not: suave and charismatic and articulate. Handsome and rich and self-made. He was modest and refined, almost in the European way. But not quite. Allan Sanford was all-American. The dream of every American mother; the hope of every father; the ambition of every son; the need of every daughter.

And of course they loved what he would do for them.

As he sat at the head table and reached for a glass of water, he caught the eye of a bald, bespectacled man with a stiff smile sitting five seats down.

"How'd I do?" his laughing eyes asked as he raised the glass of bubbling mineral water to his lips.

The bald man's response, equally silent and fleeting, was unambiguous: "You got it."

3 | WEDNESDAY, DECEMBER 23

Nick Delan—that was the very first thought of the new day. Even before she opened her eyes in her suite at the Suvretta-House Hotel, Clio Bragana thought of him; and willingly she let the moment take hold, surprised by the tenderness it evoked.

At last, reluctantly, she opened her eyes, afraid the joy would dissipate. But it didn't; the memory stayed, details flashing like shooting stars across the fuzzy skies of rousing consciousness. She gazed blindly at the hand-painted ceiling for a moment longer, savoring the pleasure, before lazily turning to the three tiny night lights on the side of the console labeled VALET, FEMME DE CHAMBRE, SERVICE D'ÉTAGE. She pressed the second two and lay back again.

What was it he had said in the sled? "You see, in the neighborhood I grew up in the longest word we knew was fettucini."

A small smile rose to her lips as she twisted leisurely and curled up again on the other side of the bed. But, like the apricot-sheathed down pillow she cuddled, the thought of him traveled with her. It was nowhere as funny as it was revealing, she thought. Self-effacement: the humility of the wise. Which was precisely why it was a warning to her. Prior notice not to get involved.

But it's been so long, she reflected. So long since she'd had any feelings about a man. The abhorrence of men that had been forced on her so many years ago had slowly faded until she felt nothing for them anymore. Neither good nor bad, just indifference. Oh, she had been attracted by one or two in a superficial way; intellectually or socially or in a crowd. But she had never allowed anyone close enough to develop a real friendship. She had no use for any sort of relationship with them: neither the need nor the inclination. Her life was complicated enough with the professional dealings she had to endure with them. Perhaps that was why she had acted so frivolously with Nick Delan at the beginning of the night. Perhaps flippancy was just the simple reflex mechanism that now seemed the natural response to the male species en masse. The guard that kept her sanity.

She thought back, back to a more simple time, when all her reactions were not defensive and fraught with fear, when life was innocent, simple, clean. And she remembered.

What was it now? Ten, eleven years ago. It seemed so very much longer. Another life almost. She recalled fondly the shy, introverted sixteen-year-old high school athlete and the innocent teenage love affair that was all she had ever experienced of normal love.

No, she thought dejectedly. Not since then had she felt anything for a man.

She sat up—trying to switch with movement the morbid channel her mind had selected so early in the day—and reached for the pink satin robe de chambre lying at the end of the bed. Standing, she covered her lissome nude body with the slinky gown and headed for the bathroom.

The gentle chimes of the doorbell interrupted her. She changed direction and walked across the small living room of her suite, through the tiny hallway to the door. It was the waiter and the maid.

She smiled at the waiter and ordered, in her flawless French, a light continental breakfast. Then she instructed the maid to draw the curtains, open the shutters, and run her a warm bath.

A few moments later, wallowing in the warm, jasmine-scented waters of the huge, old-fashioned white-metal bathtub, she again remembered Nick Delan. This time, however, it was accompanied by the tiniest thrust of excitement. A small, minute boost that tingled one second and was gone the next.

She pictured his tough yet boyishly mischievous face: the mop of curly jet-black hair, the cruel twist of those rich, wet lips, the greenness of his penetrating eyes, and suddenly the charge ran through her again. This time, though, the trembling stayed. It pressed against her lungs before spreading down slowly to knot in her midriff. Why the hell had she acted that way anyway at the start of the evening? Why had she toyed with him like a cheap tart? For the first time in a long, long while she had actually enjoyed herself. Maybe *that* was why, she thought. Because it was so unusual, so strange. A feeling that petrified her. One she had abolished from her life.

Again his memory superimposed itself in her mind. He was different from other men. A weird mix: seemingly considerate, humorous, polite, but— She stopped. But what? There was something else about him, too. A physical grace, a tough, animal-like assurance that conflicted sharply with his apparent sensitivity and gentleness. He probably knew how handsome he was, but he was totally unselfconscious about it, almost as if he didn't care. He was very successful in his career. That much she knew. But that too seemed unimportant to him. It was as if he was saying, "Take it away from me and I'll do it all over again. And if I don't, it doesn't make much difference anyway."

The excitement pulsed through her. Beneath the *mousse*-covered water she felt the burning sensation in her belly intensify as it worked its way down. Deep inside, like the pleasant pain of overworked muscles craving the relief of a massage.

She closed her eyes as she felt the heatwave spread up to her cheeks the way it always did, leaving them beet-red for hours after. She had never seen such animal magnetism in a man before. Nor, she remembered, had any of the other women in the Dracula Club and the Chesa Veglia last night. They stared at him like eager young teenagers out of control.

Gently her hand inched down her chest, down below the waterline that cut across her nipples, ruddy and swollen, toward the coarse triangular patch of hair that joined her legs. Her fingers glided—slowly, but with a will of their own—caressing the sensitive skin of her well-toned stomach as the heat and pressure beneath built to eruption.

She circled her fingers softly, tenderly, at the very top of the opening as gradually she let her body slide down in the enormous tub, raising her legs and opening them wider and wider until they came to rest on the rims on either side. She moved her wrist faster, the hand turning quicker, her fingers burrowing deeper and deeper until at last she could control herself no longer. She exploded in a fantasy of delight that she kept going, on and on and on until both her hands fell limply to her sides, exhausted.

She lay there, still, spent, for a long while. And realized the prisoner she had held captive all her adult life was becoming restless and defiant.

"Terrific. Absolutely terrific," beamed the tallest of the six men forming a halo around Allan Sanford.

Like seasoned blockers, the group flowed with him, a protective circle, as he sauntered toward the armchair closest to the main entranceway of the huge red-carpeted banquet room.

"The foreshadowing thing worked like a dream. I think the issue of your marital status went down about as well as it's ever likely to. It would be a big mistake for the President's people to raise the issue now. Especially given the strong showing you make in the latest polls among women—married and single. Let's remember to congratulate Andy for his research on the word bachelor. Old French for nobleman or knight, huh? He made it sound positively dishonorable for politicians to be married."

"It's not new," snapped Allan Sanford, slumping in the chair. He glanced at his watch. It was nearly 3:00 A.M. and the last of the guests had only just departed.

But the short, bearded, plump man, Stephen Raider, the pollster Sanford employed to gauge the pulse of his budding campaign, was not to be denied. He continued ecstatically, afflicted by the disease that is so prevalent among men whose profession it is to merchandise images and dreams—hyperbole. "Your assault on organized crime had them on their feet. I think we need to emphasize it even more in the weeks ahead. Make the Mafia one of the main building blocks of our entire campaign."

Sanford let out a heavy lungful of tension and glanced at the man wearily. He was exhausted, and the deflation that always followed such glittering but nerve-racking occasions was upon him.

"Let's skip the theatrics tonight, Steve," he said impatiently, turning his head to contemplate the rest of the group standing around him. They were his clan, the people who had been with him all along the way. The coterie that would some day occupy most of the West Wing and part of the East of the most prestigious piece of real estate in the world. They would dominate an era and create history. "What do the rest of you *really* think?" he asked of them all, quietly.

The others were no less elated; and they were more than familiar with this mood he was in. And so they smiled like sleeping alligators. "Great. Unbeatable. Terrific," was the unrestrained chorus. "Steve's not exaggerating," reassured one of the men. "For once he may even be understating it," he added, smiling at the bearded man. "The Mafia issue went over like a dream."

The destinies of all the men were long since linked to that of Allan Sanford. And every one of them felt the boost they had received in the last few hours.

"You were laser-sharp," said another—an older, experienced-looking man whose immaculate mop of hair was silver-white. "And your delivery was perfect."

Allan Sanford fought the sinking feeling of loneliness. His advisers were right. It had been a memorable evening, he told himself. Well worth five or even ten times its $65,000 price tag. He had shone. Even among an elite whose arteries had long ago hardened, who were as blasé to success as heavy rollers were to money, he had touched their nerves. He had impressed. The only question remaining was, when? When to officially declare his candidacy?

He raised himself slowly from the chair.

"I guess we have the day off tomorrow?" he asked one of the men, a bald, bespectacled, slender figure with the features of a squirrel. He was the unquestioned leader of the pack, the man who had personally selected each one of the team of specialists who formed what the press had affectionately come to label collectively as White House, Inc.. He was also the first person Allan Sanford had turned to after his speech; the man whose glance had given him a flash estimate of his performance.

"Yes, for the most part," replied Phillip Myers. "You have a couple of people scheduled for late afternoon and, of course, dinner with Richard Grossman and some of his CSA people."

Sanford nodded; he knew Grossman and his family well; he was the linchpin of the Hollywood moguls; an entrepreneur who had been part of the audience that evening; an old friend with un-equaled influence in the movie capital of the world.

"Fine. I guess we'll call it a night then." He smiled joylessly. "See you all tomorrow," he said, turning toward the door.

He walked a few paces, then stopped and looked back.

"Oh, Phil," he called out, instinctively lifting his right arm in a measured pose. "Why don't you walk down with me? A few things we need to coordinate."

Phillip Myers immediately approached him and the two men left the great hall together. Once outside, Sanford looked at his oldest and closest associate. They were a strange combination, he and Myers, Sanford had cause to observe once again as they moved down the hall. Poles apart in nearly every respect, they were still, nevertheless, a good team. They were very, very close in many ways. Closer than most husbands and wives, in a sense. And yet they were not friends. Not in the true sense of the word, despite a union that was complete, each utterly dependent on the other for their success. Indeed Phillip Myers had done more for Sanford's career than any other man. He had not only run their companies efficiently, he had engineered much of Sanford's climb from actor to superstar to tycoon. And thence from entrepreneur to one of the political pillars of the land.

But they were not friends. And not for any lack of effort on Sanford's part. The fact was Phillip Myers had no interests other than his work. He did not enjoy people. Nor did he need any emotional contact in his relationships. As far as Sanford knew that applied to the opposite sex as much as it did to male camaraderie. In short Phillip Myers was a workaholic—a cold, distant, severe man consumed with his profession. Nevertheless Sanford was fond of Myers. Not to mention extremely dependent on him.

"Well?" asked Sanford.

"Well what?" retorted Myers, adjusting to their usual private relationship of equals. In public it was different; Myers kept his distance and his place.

"Did you make the arrangements?"

"Oh, for Christ's sake, Al," retorted Myers angrily. "This is not the time. Or the place."

Sanford glanced at the shorter man as they walked down the hallway toward the elevators. As usual when upset, Myers' tight, narrow lips danced with nervous energy. First twisting one way, then another. Pursing. Biting. Moving.

Sanford looked forward again. "I don't need any aggravation tonight, Phil. Just answer the question. Yes or no?"

Myers stopped. "Aggravation?"

Two paces further Sanford turned. "That's right, Phil," he said. "Aggravation. Skip it tonight."

"What the hell is wrong with you, Al?" Myers walked closer and lowered his voice as he looked up at Sanford. "This place is packed with the media. Reporters are crawling the place like termites. Can't you control yourself for a few lousy nights? And before answering that, try remembering what happened to Gary Hart."

Sanford stared at him severely for a moment. Then he smiled and placed an arm around his slender friend's shoulder, gliding him to movement.

"You worry too easy, you know that, Phil?"

Myers was not amused; neither did he comprehend the humor. He grimaced and dropped his eyes as they entered the elevator.

"There's a whole Bible Belt out there," Myers said more loudly in the empty descending cubicle, thrusting his hand to the east, "that runs right smack-dab down the middle of this country, if you haven't noticed. One-fifth of the population, eighty-five percent of them white, who have what has euphemistically been termed puritanical ethics. The Christian Right they're called, and they happen to control thirty-five million votes that you risk losing every time you conduct one of these crazy escapades."

There was, Sanford thought as they alighted one floor below, no point in continuing the conversation. They had never seen eye-to-eye on this. And they never would. Phil Myers worried too much and nothing would ever change that. Slowly he eased a hand into his trouser pocket, dipped his head, and peered down at his colleague.

"Did you fix it, Phil?"

Myers glared back at him silently, the anger turning to frustration. Finally, he nodded reluctantly.

"The room is interconnected with the empty room next to my suite. It's been left unoccupied for 'security purposes,'" he said, spitting out the last two words venomously.

Halfway down the corridor the two men entered Sanford's suite.

There they used the connecting door to cross into Phil Myers' accommodations next door.

As usual it was Sanford who broke the silence. Myers was a brilliant man but moody, thought Sanford. He always enjoyed a good sulk. And he had a remarkable propensity for it, too. The only way to cut it short was to get him working.

"Phil," said Sanford, adopting the serious tone Myers preferred and letting it reflect on his chiseled features. "Do you have the California unemployment projections prepared?"

"No, not yet. Dan's still putting them together," replied Myers curtly as he removed his dinner jacket and tossed it onto the king-size bed.

"I'll need them tomorrow. Think they'll be ready?"

"They'll be ready."

"And the entertainment industry figures. I'll need those for Grossman."

Myers nodded, obviously placated a little. Sanford flashed him a friendly smile as he opened the connecting door and entered the empty bedroom that separated them from the accommodations beyond. At the far end Sanford opened another interconnecting door. Sitting in front of the television set, watching the blaring screen, sat a tawny blond call girl sipping a glass of champagne.

In his own room Phillip Myers sat on the side of the bed for a moment wrapped in thought. Then he picked up the small, compact Trimline telephone and punched out a series of numbers.

"Dan, it's me," he said, pulling out the top drawer of the bedside console. He extracted a small electronic remote-control device. "Just wanted to remind you we need those unemployment figures . . ."

In the two days left until Christmas, Clio Bragana and Nick Delan saw a good deal of each other. But rarely alone, rarely away from the crowd she frequented.

Part of the problem was that the warm weather had turned the already tenuous layer of snow covering the slopes into an icy mush, and so life suddenly became even more of a social whirl in St. Moritz.

"A ski resort without snow is like Szechuan cooking without

spices, darling," was how one heavily made-up matron put it at lunch one day. "So one simply has to change gear for a few days, provide one's own spices if you please, and hope the gods are kinder."

Changing gear in St. Moritz, Delan was soon to learn, meant more of the same—minus the skiing. A fiesta of lunches and dinners, tea and drinks, poker and backgammon sessions. Always, too, en masse, marauding gangs scavenging for amusement.

At first Delan tolerated the frenzied show, for all its ostentation and repetition. After all, it provided an opportunity to see Clio; and, perhaps, to manage to whisk her away for a few hours, to be alone together. But the occasions were sporadic and fleeting. Somehow she seemed to be constantly surrounded; and if not surrounded, otherwise committed, intently playing cards or throwing dice with passion. He had to content himself with the furtive looks she cast in his direction whenever she felt she could. And the warm feelings they stirred in him each time she did so. Just why two mature people were playing this teenage game of hide and seek was not entirely clear to Delan. It seemed as if he was conducting an illicit love affair with a married woman in the midst of her husband's best friends.

It was frustrating. Even more so because on another level Delan felt their relationship was developing. He could see the effort she made—albeit surreptitiously—to position herself as close as she could to him at lunches and dinners; and how in the Great Hall of the Palace Hotel, which was invariably where this circle met, she too would try to get him alone for a minute.

To Delan she became more and more of an enigma. In fact she seemed to have two distinct personae. The blasé socialite in public. And a tenacious but somehow vulnerable little thing in private. Just which was the dominant personality Delan couldn't decide. The problem was he was becoming increasingly curious to find out.

Christmas Eve found them yet again the guests of the ubiquitous Mr. Naderi. They were part of a very long and formal table set in the paneled restaurant at the Palace; but unfortunately they were separated by four bodies, and sat on opposite sides of the table. It was a difficult evening for Delan. In front of him sat a young Greek couple who quarreled openly. To his left a middle-aged Swiss woman, with a figure that was a testimony to the wonders of suction lipectomy, expounded on the life-style necessary to remain forever young. An hour of monologue exposition boiled down to two simple ingredients: fresh grapefruit juice and young men.

On Delan's right sat a very short Englishman. He was in his late fifties—but going on twenty-five if judged by his loud high-fashion attire and uniformly blond hair. Only the subject of his discourse gave away a clue to his maturity. He was consumed with the potential of his newly acquired bank in Zurich; and the prospects it had of making money for him quickly—and without risk—using other people's fiduciary money, of course.

Clio Bragana had noticed Delan's discomfort. Several times she had smiled sweetly at him, once even feigning powerlessness to help by shrugging her bare shoulder slightly.

He had smiled at her joylessly.

It was when the coffee was being served that he rose from the table, unable to tolerate the boredom any longer.

"Excuse me," he muttered to no one in particular as he stood and walked toward the restrooms. When he emerged Clio Bragana was standing there, waiting.

"You were leaving, weren't you?"

The question, coming that suddenly and out of left field, surprised Delan. He nodded slowly.

"Please don't."

Delan felt a tiny charge run through him. A charge tempered only by the pang of guilt the look on her face triggered off.

"We'll be going downstairs to the King's Club soon and I would like to dance with you."

Delan studied her silently for a moment longer. Her large, brown eyes looked up at him like those of a newly orphaned kitten. And they captured in that one brief moment all that was confusing about her personality.

"Why?" He could think of nothing else to say.

"I want to be with you."

Once they were installed in the discotheque downstairs, the evening took on a lighter touch. Clio Bragana sat with him and, in sharp contrast to the last few days, shut herself off from her friends completely. The two of them talked and laughed freely, each complementing the other even while they were at counterpoint much of the time. Their chatter ranged wide but not deep, always skimming the surface, somehow finding a humorous vein that seemed automatically to flow into another topic equally bizarre or farcical. And as the night bubbled along, Nick Delan found himself wondering why it was he was enjoying himself so much. What it was about her that made it so different.

It was only later, on the dance floor, that he finally conceded the point: he liked her. For the first time in a long while he actually enjoyed a woman—other than merely sexually. He pressed her just a little closer; and relaxed.

Gradually he let his right hand slip down the thin soft white material of her dress, down to the small of her back, pulling her still closer in the first whiff of intimacy. They danced like that for several moments, Delan delighting in the feel of her exquisite young body as they just barely swayed in rhythm to the delicate beat of a plaintive Lionel Richie. It was heaven. So he guided her right hand in closer to their bodies, tucking it in at the curve of his neck before sliding his left hand down her bare arm en route to the elbow—and thence to join his right arm behind her back. But it never made it that far.

Halfway down her forearm he froze. As casually as he could he moved his left hand back, tenderly entwining his fingers in hers for a moment. Then slowly he unlocked his fingers and gently stroked her hand, each caress moving lower and lower until at last his fingers rested on her wrist again.

For one split second he didn't believe it. He smelt her skin and the scent of the exotic perfume and cursed himself for being so paranoid. But his alarm refused to dissipate. For potentially it also answered a great many questions. Delan's right hand released her back and reached for her left hand dangling as it was loosely beside her body. Again as nonchalantly as he could he felt for it and their fingers knotted and then moved up toward their shoulders. Still they circled in a warm embrace on the crowded dance floor to the same gentle romantic rhythm.

He tucked the palm of her hand in between their bodies and gently splayed its fingers across his chest. Then slowly he moved his own hand downward. Across her long, slim fingers toward the forearm, his thumb circling around to the underside now, his fingers running gently down the soft skin covering her tiny knuckles. Gently it moved still lower. To the base of her right hand, on the inside of her wrist.

Behind her back his eyes closed. Across the silky surface her left hand held precisely the same roughness that he had felt on her right hand a moment ago. A coarseness that was almost perfectly hidden, tucked proficiently into one of the natural wrinkles of the joint.

Almost but not quite. There existed still the tiniest welt of scar tissue—and it extended across the entire surface of her wrist in an angry straight line that no amount of surgical wizardry could eliminate entirely.

4 | MONDAY, DECEMBER 28

In London, the watery winter sun suddenly broke through the dark clouds, momentarily eliminating the gray gloom that enveloped the city. The man stepped out of the Gore Hotel and looked up and down the tree-lined avenue. Then he glanced at his watch. It was 1:00 P.M. on the dot. A shiver of nervousness ran through him. It was a long trek that lay ahead. A hazardous journey that would have to be traversed alone—"naked," in the parlance of the trade, meaning no organizational backup to rely on. No partner. No team. No diplomatic cover or safe house to run to. No side even. Within the hour he would lose his past. With no guarantees of any sort of future.

He turned right, up Queen's Gate toward Hyde Park. The anxiety inside him mounted. He looked over his shoulder; then at his watch again. Barely a minute had passed. A short, vigorous walk, he thought. It would calm him. He could afford a few minutes. Who knew when he would next have such a simple, everyday opportunity again? Another shudder went through him. Or if indeed he ever would, for that matter.

He walked faster, slipping through the heavy Monday lunchtime traffic on Kensington Gore before entering the imposing black wrought-iron gateway to the park. Immediately inside, beneath the panoply of ancient trees, he turned right on South Carriage Driveway and lengthened his stride still further. Ahead loomed the Albert Memorial, across the street to his right the famous pinkish hulk of the Albert Hall.

He circled around the majestic Memorial, vaguely pondering its freshly refurbished ornate carvings and the angry billowing of the low, fast-moving clouds closing in. On the other side of the Memorial he mounted the steps to join the small, babbling crowd of Japanese tourists pointing their cameras at each other as they stood beside the statue of Prince Albert beneath the dome.

He drew a cigarette from the breast pocket of the rumpled dark-gray suit jacket he wore beneath his tan raincoat and struck a match, adroitly cupping its flame with his hands. The heavy intake of nicotine soothed his taut nerves. He puffed at the cigarette again, looking at the red double-decker buses towering over the stream of vehicles heading toward Knightsbridge.

It had to be done, he thought, toying nervously with the debonair Latin mustache he sported. There was no turning back anymore. There was nothing to gain from procrastinating. All that did was provide an opportunity for the doubts to start flowing again. The tingling sensation in his ribcage intensified. He could feel distinctively now his pounding heartbeat. He dragged on his cigarette again, deeper still. Reluctantly he started down the stairs, heading for the busy thoroughfare less than fifty yards away.

Badrutt's Palace Hotel in St. Moritz is a monument: a symbol of privilege and refinement. The century-old building, with its extravagant turrets and gables, is, however, something more than an antique-strewn landmark. For surrounding its opulence and magnificent service is a treasure trove of alluring tales. Stories that reflect the sort of flamboyant, reckless mischief that only the rich, the chic, the famous can get away with in the name of enjoyment. Yarns about kings and czars, princes and playboys, starlets and heiresses and their champagne baths, nude public chases, swings on chandeliers, and constantly interchanging partners and wives.

Many of these stories begin or end in the hotel's majestic old dining room, which is situated to the right of the Great Hall—the huge, wood-paneled lobby that is in a very real sense the heart of the hotel, indeed of the whole district of Engadine in which the village of St. Moritz is situated. And it was in there, at nearly three in the afternoon on this first Monday after Christmas, that Keyvan Naderi reached for the neatly folded bill in the small silver tray the waiter had just delivered.

"I'll speak to Teheran tonight," he said, squiggling a quick signature on the paper, "and advise them that the lawyers in Geneva informed me this morning that the informal arrangements are in order; and that they can go ahead with the contract. I presume your people are prepared to fly out to Iran as soon as the documents are ready?"

Delan nodded. "Wentworth Norman himself will lead the team. He's cleared his program to be ready to make the trip as soon as they're notified."

"Good," Naderi said. He paused, and for a long moment his watery eyes seemed to be measuring Delan.

The eyes of a crocodile, Delan thought, faking sleep: still, silent, poised to pounce. The Iranian was weighing the timing and the wisdom of prodding Delan on the Brazilian arms supply issue again. Delan could feel it. But abruptly the moment was gone. The wily operator had decided against it.

"Now, on to more immediate matters," Naderi began, resting back in his chair. "How did you enjoy the party last night?"

"Very much." Delan smiled, a little nervously. "She's an interesting and pretty lady."

For once Naderi's fleshy face seemed to take on an air of genuine sincerity and concern. "Yes," he breathed softly, "and an unfortunate one, too, I'm afraid."

"Why?"

"Has she told you anything about herself?"

"No." Delan shook his head. "She never talks about herself."

"Perhaps it is too early yet. Yes, of course it is," Naderi added quickly. "It's been, what? A week? Still, I must admit I'm rather surprised by the whole thing. I've never seen Clio do this before."

"Do what?" Delan asked, puzzled.

"Go out with a man. I mean regularly."

Delan stared at Naderi. "What does that mean? Why?"

For the first time in the five months Delan had known him, the usually self-assured Naderi seemed a little hesitant and uncertain. He fidgeted with the stem of his cut-crystal wine glass for a moment before taking a long sip.

"Well," he said at length, "I'm not certain I have the right to divulge any of this. It was, after all, told to me in deepest confidence; though I must say that was quite some time ago now. Nevertheless, I have a soft spot for both of you and it may help you both if I was to sound a warning, as it were."

"Well, I'd certainly appreciate it."

"Yes," said Naderi gravely, "but I must admit I'm rather more concerned about the effects of all of this on Clio."

"The effects of what?"

"This . . . this . . . budding intimate relationship," Naderi answered uncomfortably.

"Why?" Delan asked. "Not that there is one. In fact the last thing I would call it is intimate."

Naderi contemplated the point for a moment. "Perhaps all I should say is that she really has had a hard time of it all in her life." He leaned forward conspiratorially. "You know, the girl is very close to the precipice."

Delan glared at Naderi. "What exactly are you trying to say, Keyvan?"

Naderi stared back. "I understand you're going away together tomorrow."

"Yes."

"To the Plaza in Paris, I believe?"

Delan nodded unenthusiastically. He was not at all sure he liked Naderi poking his nose into his private life. Of all the people in the world, why the hell had Clio chosen this character as a father confessor?

"Well, that's a major step for her, Nick. Be gentle with her, for God's sake." Naderi looked away from Delan's frown and abruptly pushed back his chair. "Now perhaps we can join her. She should be in the Hall by now," he said, glancing at his diamond-crusted, gold Cartier watch as he stood. "Together with several other people I've asked to join us."

The two men silently crossed the long room with high gilded ceilings, each a little unsettled by their conversation. Nick Delan had any number of questions rolling around his head. But, while Keyvan Naderi seemed a little embarrassed by the last part of their lunch, from the curtness with which he had ended it, he showed no sign of wanting to make amends. He frowned studiously and walked quickly toward the stairs leading into the Great Hall. Just before they reached the stained-glass door at the entranceway, he turned toward Delan.

"You go on. I'll be with you in a few minutes," he said, pointing vaguely toward the restrooms.

He watched as Delan walked away. Only when he entered the Hall did Naderi turn and head toward the telephone booths situated in the short, gloomily lit corridor just to his left.

In London, the slender middle-aged man with mud-brown hair and a debonair mustache stepped out of a taxi beneath the huge spread-eagle emblem of the Embassy of the United States of America in Grosvenor Square. There was not a hint of urgency or agitation about him as he paid the driver and waited for change. On the contrary, he ascended the stairs and headed toward the main entrance of the building walking at a casual, contented pace. There he allowed three young women engrossed in conversation to precede him through the door and smiled politely at the third lady who thanked him.

Once inside he followed the women, left around the grayish marble-covered elevator banks and up the steps to a bulletproof counter of matching stone marked INFORMATION DESK. Again he waited patiently as the ladies were guided to the Commercial Library at the far end of the massive lobby.

"Can I help you, sir?" asked a muscular marine in full regalia, his cap carefully angled, shading the left side of his acned face.

The slender man nodded. "My name is Oleg Maksimovich Pavlenko. I am an officer of the KGB and I wish for political asylum."

The young marine looked blank. "Who is it you wish to see, sir?" he asked with the unwavering precision of a programmed robot.

Pavlenko closed his eyes. "I would think the man who I shall first see is Mr. Burns," he said softly, full of grace and patience. He opened his eyes and added a warm smile to his face. "Thomas Burns, the resident CIA station chief. After that, others—many, many others—will wish to see me."

Keyvan Naderi picked up the pay telephone in one of the two small wooden booths. He dropped ten one-franc coins into the appropriate slot, checking them as they registered in the small digital-display screen thoughtfully provided. Then he punched a series of numbers; and waited, shuffling from one foot to another impatiently. The staccato sound of long-distance connections abruptly turned to the bleeping rings of a busy signal.

"Zudbash, zudbash," Naderi urged in his native tongue as he slammed the receiver back into its cradle. He waited only the briefest moment before trying again, this time the palms of his hands suddenly sticky with moisture as he gathered the returned coins and fed them into the apparatus once more. Again it was busy and his frustration mounted. Suddenly he felt his bladder would burst if it wasn't relieved. But he dismissed the discomfort with barely a thought. This was far more critical. He was already at least a day late—an unacceptable delay, he'd already been informed.

Thankfully he heard the sound of intermittent rings just as he dried the moisture filming his left palm on his jacket and switched the receiver from his right hand. On the third ring a male voice answered. He recognized it.

"Plaza-Athénée, Paris, confirmed," Naderi said before cradling the receiver quickly.

5 | TUESDAY, DECEMBER 29

"Dago."

"With a name like Delan?" Clio Bragana asked incredulously. She lifted the champagne glass with two hands to allow for the sudden lurching of the old Rhetische Bahn train.

"One of life's revisions."

"How did it start out?"

"With an O."

"Delan-o?" she beamed, her eyes opening wide. The surprise turned to enthusiasm as she raised her drink a second time. "Well, *salute, paisan.*"

"*Cent ans,*" Delan mumbled, smiling back grudgingly. But as he reached for his martini he paused and the smile broadened. He raised the glass and took a long, stiff swig before nonchalantly plucking the toothpick from it.

She studied his outstretched hand only for a moment. Then a sultry smile spread across her face as she looked up to meet his challenge. Slowly, provocatively, she caressed the olive from the sliver of wood and placed it on her lips.

Delan felt a powerful charge of sexual wattage run through him. She was tough to fathom, this one, he thought as he watched her slowly, very slowly, make a meal of the olive.

Delan's left eyebrow lifted a mite. He had to force himself to concentrate. "Well, it seemed like one way to reject it all."

"What was it you were running from?"

"What they call South Side, I guess. But that was before I grew up. Before I realized it was all one great big South Side."

Clio Bragana looked around the immaculately preserved and polished paneling of the dining car. Making the trundling descent from St. Moritz down to Chur, the private Rhetische Bahn line was an appealing and nostalgic memento of the age of the train, the 1930s. The mahogany-covered walls, the starched white-linen tablecloth, the heavy silverware, the cigar fumes and the rushed but clearly professional waiters all combined to paint a picture of an older, more innocent Europe. Outside, the towering Alpine steeps of rock and the mountain villages and deep ravines were gradually giving way to cheerful, multicolored miniature farmhouses occasionally presided over by the brooding ruins of some distant ancient castle.

"This is South Side?"

"With a paint job." Delan nodded. "The ethics are no different. There are probably more killers, pushers, whores, and pimps per square meter on this ornate little toy than in the deepest ghetto. Only they're lacquered here. Successful. They camouflage themselves with silk and diamonds. But they're still thugs. Sharks living off minnows."

Clio Bragana looked at him intently for a long moment before she spoke again. The silence was filled by the charming clockwork clatter of wheels turning on strips of steel.

"So now that you know, why don't you change back? At least you'll have your real identity, your roots."

He paused momentarily, wondering why he was allowing the conversation to drift this way. Why he was answering. But he couldn't think of anything. Strangely, for once he didn't seem to mind it.

"Probably because of a woman I once knew."

"What woman?"

"My mother."

"Your mother?"

"Yes. She made one mistake. But it was enough. It cost her her life."

"Oh, I'm sorry," Clio whispered.

"Don't be. It was a long time ago."

"How did it happen?"

"She picked the wrong husband. A man who happened to be my father, but someone I'd rather not be associated with. Now, are you ready to order yet?"

There was a strained silence as she stared back at him, curiously. Then abruptly she looked down to her glass. "No, pour me some more champagne first."

Delan complied.

"One way or another everyone has a South Side," Clio said softly as she lifted her glass. "And I guess this is as good a time as any to tell you about mine. You see, I want to be very honest with you, too. I want you to know up front. Just so there's no misunderstanding."

Delan looked at her expectantly.

"It was in Genoa . . ." She hesitated and then a dejected smile spread across her face.

"Is that where you're from?" Delan asked, remembering the night they'd met.

"Was from. I ran away. As far as my legs would take me."

Delan shook his head at the waiter as he hovered to take their order for lunch.

"You see, Mr. Delan . . ."

She swallowed and turned to the flashing landscape as she fought to control herself. Finally she looked back, her eyes offering him the bravest gaze of defiance she could muster through welling tears.

"I was raped there," she forced herself to say. "At the age of fifteen I was raped and sodomized by four filthy, sweaty, drunken sailors."

She stared at him. "And somehow I look at men a little differently now," she whispered.

Delan felt a burst of heat surge through his body. Uncontrollably, as if with a will of their own, flashes of another time flickered in still frames before his eyes. Images of a two-room basement apartment. Warm. Well-lit. Filled with the sounds of a child's laughter.

His laughter. Of a mother's gentle hands fluttering across his body. Pecking, prodding, massaging. All the time her laughing eyes looking down to the sofa, delighting in the little boy's squeals.

Then the sudden knock. The door bursting open. Three men with hats. And fistfuls of steel. The terrifying pandemonium. The long screams of terror. Cut off only by two shattering explosions and the spray of warm blood across his face and pajamas. And then the final whimper—the haunting, everlasting whimper, of a mother's death.

He forced out the past and took hold of the present. Gently he reached out across the small table with both his hands and clasped her face, wiping away the meandering streams of tears with his thumbs. Then he raised her hand and kissed it softly.

"I don't blame you."

"Not even if I want a separate room?" she asked softly.

Nick Delan caressed her chin gently. Pain and regret, bitterness and shame mixed together to form the most heartrending look he had ever seen.

"Not even if you want separate hotels," he replied.

"The one thing I want everyone to remember throughout these debriefing sessions is that this man is not, I repeat not, just some sort of unknown walk-in defector with no bona fides. He's an agent we've had in place for three years now. A source who has more than established his credentials."

Thomas Burns, the brawny resident CIA station chief, looked up from his brown-leather armchair at the master counterintelligence operative and nodded his head. James Matthew Cassidy oozed leadership. With a Williams and Harvard background, the steely-eyed, tall and silver-haired Cassidy was a no-nonsense professional of vast experience and acclaim. More in keeping with the older generation of OSS veterans, his was an elegant country gentleman approach.

"Now," continued Cassidy, "that doesn't mean we foreclose in our own minds on any of the possibilities that exist. By which I mean the entire gamut of suspicions this sort of murky defection automatically conjures. What I *am* talking about is attitude. We have to establish a relationship of trust. And to do that we have to start on day one. That, and only that, provides the shortest and safest route to the most detailed picture possible."

The four others in the room, who listened intently, agreed.

"Sure as hell has to have a real good reason for such an abrupt and unexpected departure," Thomas Burns offered.

"Yes," James Cassidy said uncertainly. He slapped closed the file he was holding and moved out from behind the desk. He was as prepared as he was going to be: on the nine-o'clock shuttle flight from Washington to New York, the 1:45 P.M. British Airways Concorde, flight 194, to London—on a passport in the name of James Nolan, investment broker. Then the taxi to Claridge's, a quick shower and a shave before walking the two hundred yards to the Embassy (there was no sense in alerting the Soviets—or the Brits—to his presence in London), and three and a half hours of on-site briefings about the circumstances surrounding the defection to add to the "backgrounders" he had diligently studied last night and yesterday out at Langley—and he was prepared.

Twenty-five years of experience would handle the rest almost by rote. Almost but not quite. For every single defector he had ever encountered was different. They had different reasons: different worries, different guilts, a whole intricate web of unique concerns about their defections. It was, however, the other side of the coin that concerned him more at this point. The sheer scale of subtle ploys and deceptions the Soviets were increasingly employing. The time-release penetration agents and moles and bogus, dispatched defectors assigned to infiltrate the Western camp to disinform, destabilize, influence, confuse.

God knows how many have slipped through over the years, Cassidy thought as he paced toward the large window overlooking Grosvenor Square. And how much damage they have wrought.

The white-stone bust of Franklin Delano Roosevelt in the deserted park four floors below glowed in the yellow lights illuminating the streets' predawn stillness.

"The fact that the man refuses to go beyond name, rank, and serial number to anyone other than you could also have some meaning," Thomas Burns added. "Maybe he's carrying a heavy pay load?"

Cassidy turned from the triple-glazed opaque plexiglass window—designed to thwart any effort to pluck the words uttered within these four walls from the vibrations of the glass panes. This feature of the glass house—as the secure room is called in the trade—was just one of the variations from the standard embassy office facility. The others were the electromagnetic screening capability of the copper-lined walls, ceiling, and floor; and the telephone that was attached to an odd assortment of black electronic components resembling a coddled teenager's stereo stand.

"I hope you're right," Cassidy said. "It'll also be a whole lot easier all around if he's got an easily verifiable story. The problem is, you can never bet on these things. For a start, his unannounced arrival like this is totally out of character. On the other hand, I don't share your concern about his wanting to talk to me only. It could well be just a natural reflex action. After all, I've been his controller for years now, ever since he approached us, in fact. And defectors as a breed are a suspicious bunch. Every one I've ever known or read about suffers from guilt or loneliness or fear. Oftentimes all three."

"Postpartum syndrome," Burns murmured.

"Precisely. What's more, they know they'll be up against grueling interrogation and intense suspicion until their stories and motives are judged to be clean. After Yurchenko and his APEX ticket act even those we've known for years, like Pavlenko, realize they aren't immune from a frosty reception."

Following the CIA's humiliation in the on-again, off-again defection of Vitali S. Yurchenko in August 1985, and his subsequent redefection to the Soviet Union in a blaze of publicity in November of that same year, James Cassidy had been charged with a complete review of the U.S. counterespionage apparatus in general. His findings had resulted in a complete overhaul of the manual entitled *Procedures Applying to All Defectors*. The new PAD guidelines were to be rigorously enforced henceforth by all officials, in all cases—with no exceptions.

This was exactly what Cassidy would now do. He could not let his own personal feelings and the empathy he had built up over the last three years for Max Pavlenko enter into it. The fact that the Russian was a master espionage operative was beyond any doubt. He was, after all, the deputy director of KGB operations in North America; and as such the fifth most important man in the Soviet security apparatus.

"I guess that's it, then," Cassidy said, looking at Thomas Burns. "Let's get this show on the road, shall we?"

Cassidy moved to the midsize wooden desk and started stacking together the backgrounder files, pictures, computer printouts, and other folders that sat on its surface. It was the information the Records Integration Division of the CIA's Clandestine Service had provided; the dossier on one Oleg Maksimovich Pavlenko, KGB agent.

"All right, here's the way we'll handle it," Cassidy said as he donned his dark-blue blazer. "We'll start out with me taking him myself and see how that works out. Other than that there will be no divergence from the usual procedure."

He took out a small, brown plastic bottle from his briefcase, twisted its cap, and placed two sky-blue capsules in his mouth.

"Joe is familiar with that procedure," he said, pointing to the man who had traveled with him from Washington—a short, casually attired, bearded man with a mop of disheveled hair and lively, darting eyes. "For the rest of you, I'll give you a brief synopsis." He looked at the other three men one by one.

"I want the two specialized video cameras pointing at the target from the opposite corners of the observation window. We want his movements, facial expressions, and the retinal optical scanning, et cetera, to be conducted from two different angles at all times," he said, gesturing an example with his hands. "I want the shotgun mikes trained on his mouth, so we can pick up any changes in his breathing pattern, voice pitch, et cetera, along the way. Every sigh, every breath, every movement must be recorded visually and audiologically for later examination. Susan here," he pointed to the plump, Afro-haired black woman wearing a smart brown-suede dress who was his cryptographic stenographer, "will use the KW-7 to record what he says, and the recording will be code-faxed to the computers in Langley for instant comparative analysis with what we have on file there. That way I can get immediate feedback, cross-checks on his claims. One of you men will interrupt at irregular intervals; I need flap-potential readings on Soviet activity throughout the world starting at twelve noon London time yesterday. An hour or so, if I am not mistaken, before the target approached us."

"His approach was logged at one thirty-seven P.M.," interjected Burns.

"Fine. Just one other thing, Tom," Cassidy continued.

Sitting in his brown leather armchair, the CIA station chief gestured openness with his hands.

"I'd be grateful if you would ensure that everything stays normal around the embassy in the next couple of days. No extra guards or other security measures, especially on the outside. I want everything regular, like any other day."

"Sure."

"I guess that's it, then," Cassidy said, lifting his briefcase. "Oh, Joe, the usual refreshment cart, too: coffee, tea, whiskey, vodka, the whole works. All with the usual dose of Thorazine," he said, adding for the others, "Let's have him fall asleep before we do."

"Will you be drinking from the same lot?"

Cassidy smiled as he placed his briefcase back on the desk. He reached into his pocket and extracted the small bottle of blue pills which he had put there only a moment ago. Playfully he rattled it in front of Burns' face.

In Los Angeles it was nearly midnight; and a warm easterly breeze rolled in off the Pacific Ocean, carrying with it an aura of freshness, iodine gently wafting inland. In Westwood, a youthful enclave renowned primarily as the home of the University of California, Los Angeles, it sent the day's crop of litter scurrying along the sidewalks, into darkened doorways and quiet parking lots.

Up above, on the fourth floor of a low building just off Wilshire Boulevard, the man lolled back on his favorite settee—a deep, black Italian-leather couch that matched the rest of the modern furniture in his living room. He liked the color black. In every way. Especially the way it contrasted with white, in this case a backdrop of pure white—as in walls and carpeting.

He rested his tall, powerfully built brown frame on the couch and grinned slightly at the sight of the seventeen-year-old blond girl wobbling even as she sat on the floor in front of him. Texas beef, he smiled to himself. Fresh off the range.

It was just one of the many side perks of the job. Besides, that is, the visible income, the tax base, and the cover it provided for his real trade. The money itself was peanuts. Cigarette money compared to his real, tax-free source of revenue. He smiled again, watching the pretty girl's glazed, dilated eyes fixed on some distant point beyond the wall. She appeared cold, her slim body almost shivering as it turned in minuscule circles like a helpless mother twisting in grief beside her child's lifeless body. She was out of control, he judged. Numb. Ripe.

He felt the heat rising in his groin. Her oval face still held puppy fat, while her young body had yet to fully pad out.

Shit, he thought, feeling the glow inside him intensify. Man, about time. He had already invested more than a week on the broad.

He raised his long, shiny legs from the black-lacquer surface of the coffee table, and gradually uncurled his well-muscled body, straightening the flaps of his burgundy silk dressing gown and tightening its belt. Leaning forward on his seat, he tapped out a generous portion of white powder from the small vial he took out of his pocket. He cut the powder finer and finer on the small mirror lying on the table. Then he snorted the two lines he had finally formed, through a rolled-up C note, one line to a nostril.

"Ah," he sighed, exhaling the trapped air at last. For the first time he was suddenly into the soul music emanating from the stereo. K-ACE, he thought, thinking of the station. Only way to fly. He wet his right index finger, scooped up the dregs of the cocaine, and rubbed it around his gums. He was ready, the juices were flowing.

He looked at the dazed young girl still sitting just to his right on the carpet and grinned again at the tiny little prick-hole on the inside of her left elbow. Tomorrow, she's going to hate herself, he thought. She gonna sting. But like everything else in life, it was the first time that was a bitch. After that it was all downhill.

Using his long, sinewy arms against the plush chaise longue, the man pushed himself up to standing. He stuck out a large powerful ham of a hand, offering it to the young girl to assist her to her feet. But he was interrupted.

He turned and glared at the telephone. Only after a great deal of thought did he answer it. "Yeah."

"Baron, it's Johnny."

"What is it?"

"I got a problem down here."

"Solve it," the Baron said, moving to replace the receiver.

Sensing the Baron's impatience, John Proctor's voice came quickly. "It's serious."

Aaron "the Baron" Brown stopped himself from cutting off. "How would you handle it if I were dead, Johnny? Do whatever you would do then—now."

"I'd call the police."

Fifteen minutes later Aaron "the Baron" Brown deftly maneuvered his midnight-blue Jaguar to a stop in front of La Cheminée discotheque. The parking valet hopped forward to open its door. The Baron alighted without a word and strode into the club in that unhurried and casual manner that was his inimitable style.

"Where's all this happening?" the Baron interrupted midway through Proctor's explanation. He almost had to shout to make himself heard above the raucous din of a metallic guitarist trying to drown out thirty other musicians in full cry. The sounds poured through countless huge Gale speakers dotting the cavernous former warehouse. And they were complemented by the hoots and hollers of the customers ogling the six small, round platforms hanging from the ceiling. On them curvaceous young women wearing diaphanous one-piece swimming suits were thrashing their bodies and setting the theme.

"Table one seventeen," Proctor yelled back.

They threaded through the packed, gyrating crowds blanketing every inch of the floor, the Baron brushing aside bodies that stood in his way. He cared little for this place he owned and was forced to keep, with its stale odor of spilled beer and hard alcohol, the pungent reek of sweat, and a thousand fading cheap perfumes, all blending with burning tobacco, laced with hashish and grass. It reminded him of a time and place he wanted badly to forget.

"There," said Proctor. "That's the group."

The Baron stopped, his eyes slitting as they focused on the source of his troubles, sitting around the table reserved for him. There was nothing obstructing his view. He stood nearly one full head above practically everyone in sight. Everyone, that is, except a few of the group that had wrecked his evening, denied him his treat.

College kids, he observed. UCLA jocks.

"Who's the mouthpiece?" he asked.

"That mother there," Proctor replied, pointing to the tallest and biggest of the group. He was an immense young man with light-brown hair and an attractive smile. Perfect teeth above a classical, square-cut jawbone gave him a wholesome look. He wore a light-weight satin varsity-letter jacket and danced with abandon. Around him, his neighbors on the packed dance floor next to table one seventeen tried to give him as wide a berth as they could.

The Baron nodded. "Mark Richards. That's his name. All-American linebacker. UCLA."

As the Baron paused thoughtfully, studying the dancer, a shiver ran up Johnny Proctor's back. It was not an unusual sensation for Proctor. For although he had absolutely no reason, in fact he knew nothing about his boss, something about the Baron created an instinctive horror in Proctor. Perhaps it was just that he was so secretive about his life. In six years of working for him, Proctor could not remember one conversation they'd had about anything besides the business—let alone something personal or revealing. The Baron never got excited, never raised his voice. And yet for some odd reason Proctor always felt that he was in the presence of someone very evil. He studied the Baron and the veiled look on his face as he gazed on at the crowd. The blankness that seemed to emanate from those opaque pale-brown eyes flowed over to every feature, making his whole face appear totally expressionless, almost corpselike.

"Tell you what I want you to do," the Baron said softly at last. "I want you to go over to that man and apologize. Give him the table he wants so badly and tell him—"

"But you said never to give that table to no one without you knowing," retorted an uncomprehending and reluctant Proctor. "Shit, they beat up three of my men, Baron."

The Baron swiveled his thick, sinewy neck slowly and looked down at Proctor. "Right on," he said in a soft, flat tone. "And now I know, right?"

Instinctively Proctor looked away from the immotive eyes that he found so troubling.

"Give him the table he wants," the Baron repeated in the same quiet, deadly tone. "And tell him how it was all a big mistake and how sorry you are. Tell him the house will pick up the tab for him and all his crowd and— What have they been drinking?"

"Beer, mostly. A few whiskies."

"Fine. Open up as much champagne as they can drink. And tell Mr. Richards that's just the start. Tell him how bad I . . . the owner felt when you called and told me about the incident. Tell him I'm a big fan of his and how I'd like to make it up to him if he'd be kind enough to leave his telephone number and address with you. Tell him all of that. Just the way I'm telling you. And make sure he leaves here satisfied."

The Baron smiled coolly at Proctor as he turned to leave. Inside, however, he seethed. Usually the anger simmered beneath the surface. But sometimes the pressure built up to bursting point, demanding release. ·

Thankfully, with time and age, these moments had become more controllable. Most of the time he could switch the violence on and off practically at leisure. When he needed to summon the anger, all he had to do was what he was doing now: remember.

Remember 116th Street and Avalon Boulevard. The Japanese restaurant, the barber shop on the corner, the liquor store, all burned to ashes during one week. One week when the cry of pain from his neighborhood—Watts—reverberated around the country.

August eleven, nineteen sixty-five, the Baron recalled as he pushed his way through the crowds toward the front door. Six days that left thirty-four dead, over a thousand injured, four thousand under arrest, and forty million dollars of damage. And where was he when all that happened? Where was he when his own kid brother was being murdered?

In a jungle. Fighting a fucking war no one wanted won.

Something inside him had snapped. The ache he had always felt but kept hidden refused to lie dormant any longer. It acquired a tongue. A voice that told him to learn—and learn well—the skills the army was teaching for free: to hunt. And kill. And escape. The essential elements of survival in any jungle.

After that everything changed. Him and the war and Vietnam. Nam wasn't that bad. Just too many would-be fucking anchormen. Inciting. Whipping it up. What difference what jungle you died in, man? It was the dying that was tough. Not the fucking scenery.

Watts or the Ho Chi Minh trail never made no difference to no one, man. Not when he was done using his lungs.

And so he remembered. And remembered well. Everything—including all they had taught him in the marines and special forces, most especially Operation Phoenix, the famous psy-ops program that had taught him so many, many things. And so well.

Like patience. And planning. And surprise. And guile. But most of all, to always play for keeps—or never to play at all.

It was nearly two in the morning when the red Corvette pulled up in the parking lot behind the long, low-rise dormitory situated on the UCLA campus. From it emerged the tall, powerful frame of an obviously inebriated Mark Richards. With the greatest of difficulty he managed to slot the key in the car lock and then weaved noticeably as he crossed the apron of the car park toward the pavement leading around the building to the front door. The side of the structure was much darker than the front and the parking lot. It was crowded with bushes and eucalyptus trees, and unlit. Mark Richards staggered toward the foliage contentedly, thinking how great the evening had been and how he could have made Charlene if she hadn't thrown up all over him before passing out. Shit, he could barely walk himself. Wow, did we drink tonight. Dynamite.

He bounced off the wall as he turned the corner from the parking lot to the dark strip running alongside the building. Suddenly he stopped and laughed at himself. The "six-million-dollar legs," as the press called his, weren't working too well tonight. They couldn't even walk a straight line, let alone fly through the air to catch and dump a running back in full cry.

He straightened up and began walking again; or trying to. One more year, he thought. One more year and he'd be richer than his wildest dreams. He was definitely going to be the number-one draft choice, maybe even the Heisman trophy would be his. Either way, things looked great. And in this, his senior year, he was going to go all—

Abruptly he felt a strange sensation. And instantly all the alcohol in his body seemed to evaporate with the first intimation of rustling branches that he thought he heard just to his left. He turned sharply and instinctively tried to lean away from the shadow he saw coming toward him. But he was too late. A baseball bat was swinging through the air. Downward. In his direction. Almost in slow motion he followed the white blur as it arced lower and lower until it hit its target. Then all he felt was an almighty pain. A jagged, crunching, burning sensation that immediately saturated his body with cold sweat. The sound of breaking bones followed, it seemed, much, much later. After he had dispatched his arms toward the source of the excruciating pain around his left kneecap. It had swollen already. Felt like a mushed-up tomato, in fact, and blood was pouring out of the long gash on one side. He writhed in agony as he grew faint. Worse, the dark, indistinguishable shadow was swinging the baseball bat down again. In that one split second, for some inexplicable reason Mark Richards knew exactly where the bat was aimed. There was, however, nothing he could do about it. Except regret the highly lucrative career that never came.

He passed out—even before his right knee was shattered.

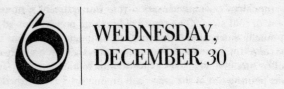# WEDNESDAY, DECEMBER 30

"Hey, mate, that's a fine-looking daughter you got there."

Nick Delan could not help but smile at the wimpy-looking young English soldier who had directed those words at him. He was one of a group who had obviously just arrived. They were walking in the opposite direction along the gleaming, sterile corridor at Zurich airport. The young corporal's mischievous, excited, alcoholic red eyes consumed the lithe figure of Clio Bragana dressed in a tight-fitting black-leather pantsuit, as she walked beside Delan toward their early-morning flight to Paris.

Abruptly, though, Delan felt Clio's hand drop from beneath his elbow. He looked at her just in time to see her turn and offer the parting soldier a maliciously inviting smile that stopped him in his tracks.

"I'm not his daughter," she said softly, her voice sincere to the extreme. "I'm his mistress. Now you can really eat your heart out."

It was difficult to say who was more flabbergasted, the soldier and his cronies—or Nick Delan. But Delan either hid it better or recovered first. Almost immediately he reached out, took hold of her arm, and guided her down the corridor, just as hoots of jeering broke out—jeering directed at the lanky corporal by his mates.

"What the hell was that in aid of?" Delan asked as they headed toward the boarding gate. But his voice held a tiny hint of pride mixed with all the surprise. She had been protecting him, he thought, feeling an unusual thrill.

"He was rude."

"I'm aware of that. But he was just a kid, a wise guy trying to impress his friends. Besides, basically it was more of a compliment."

"I didn't think so," Clio answered in a clipped tone.

"Listen, hold it a minute," Delan said, slowing her to a stop and turning her toward him. "You've been uptight all morning. What is it, Clio? What's bothering you?"

She frowned as she lowered her eyes. "I don't know, Nick," she said softly. "But I'm nervous. As nervous as a teenager about to have her first affair."

"But this isn't going to be an affair, Clio. We agreed on that last night at dinner here in Zurich. All we're going to do is try to have a little fun for a few days. Just the two of us. Alone. No friends and no aggravations. Now, this may come as a shock to you, but most thirty-five-year-old men can control themselves that long."

She looked up at him and smiled. "You're right."

Suddenly Nick Delan felt a great tenderness well inside him as the thrill he'd had only a moment ago slid from surprise to unadulterated pride. *She* had been trying to protect *him*.

James Cassidy stood and paced toward the smoked-glass surface of the far wall.

"Okay," he said more to himself than to Oleg Maksimovich Pavlenko, who remained seated in his unpadded wooden high-back chair. "Fine," he repeated more softly as if trying to correlate every detail he had heard throughout the long night.

The faces of both men were more haggard now, more disheveled, the stubble darker. Both had long since removed their coats. The collars of their shirts were open, their ties loose. All around them the sparsely furnished room was awash with the evidence of a long, arduous night's work.

Outside, a dreary new day had descended on the streets of London. But neither man was aware of the gloomy weather. Not a single window broke the powder-blue padding of the soundproof walls, and only a single door and the mirrored fourth wall served to complete its perimeters. The color blue to calm, soothe, and induce a sense of security. Or so the CIA's psychologists had stipulated—some years ago now.

Cassidy turned and ambled back silently. Everything the defector had said so far was valid. The reasoning behind his sudden flight was confirmed by the stream of information that had been coming through from a variety of sources for many months. The General Secretary's ongoing purge of the old guard to establish firm control had most recently focused its attention on the 600,000-strong KGB in general and the 1st Directorate in particular, of which Oleg Maksimovich Pavlenko was the key Deputy Director. The man in charge of all North American operations. His immediate boss—who coordinated all foreign operations—had been replaced only three weeks ago. He had been the fourth senior KGB official to be officially dismissed under the new leadership and it stood to reason that, even if Pavlenko's activities as a double agent hadn't been uncovered, then he'd inadvertently been caught in the bureaucratic purge.

Yes, Pavlenko's suspicions about his own shaky position made sense, too. A KGB Deputy Director's office and home telephones are not as a rule bugged—even in a society as distrustful as the Soviet world.

"Let's move on now, Max," Cassidy said finally. "Tell me about this 13th Directorate you mentioned earlier." What Cassidy could not even hint at was the interest it had sparked in him. If only because he had never heard of the organization before. Neither evidently had anyone in Washington. Demands had come through immediately, requests for "additional information."

Pavlenko sighed deeply, all the pent-up pressures of his tenuous position giving vent in that one breath. "At last," he said with relief.

"I beg your pardon."

"I said, at last. At last you are finished with your checklist and are ready to hear what I have to offer."

Cassidy smiled patiently at the Russian. "Come on, Max. You're a pro. You know the procedure."

"Yes." Pavlenko nodded. He pointed at the thick smoked mirror decorating the entire surface of the wall behind Cassidy. "I know, too, as you know I know, what is occurring behind there. And that you have by now been instructed by superiors in Washington to ask that question."

Behind the mirror Thomas Burns glanced at Joe Robinson. The chess game being played out before them was intensifying. Although he had been with the Agency since college, Burns had never before witnessed a defector interrogation. Nor did he have the slightest idea of the intricacies involved. The strict compartmentalization of the CIA allowed neither knowledge of, nor training in, areas of specialization. Interrogation was one such area. Safecracking, forging, surreptitious entry, sabotage, and assassination were others. They were the ultrasecret domain of TSD technicians—the Technical Services Department.

"You don't have too much faith in me, do you, Max? Do you really believe I need Washington to tell me I just heard something important? Something no one has, not to the best of my knowledge anyway, ever heard of before. Not in the Western world, at least."

Cassidy paced slowly toward the refreshment cart as he spoke.

"Let me make a suggestion to you, Max. A personal piece of advice based on the relationship the two of us have developed over the last three years—and the knowledge I have of how these things work on this side. If what you have to say is as troubling as you would have us believe, and if you have any interest in speeding up what is essentially a very long and arduous debriefing process, then just concentrate on your own role, instead of trying to guess what goes on behind mirrors, or in Washington, or what I am or am not instructed to do. It serves no purpose. Coffee?"

"Black, please." Pavlenko caught the sudden shift to a more businesslike tone in his interrogator's voice. But still that mirror worried him. He looked at the shiny dark glass. It was, he knew, standard interrogation procedure on both sides. Placed there as much to unsettle as to monitor. Still, it accomplished its purpose: he was totally unnerved by the thought of hidden eyes and lenses and microphones probing him, checking and rechecking every word he uttered.

Instinctively he found himself picturing the faces of the defectors who had preceded him—the Lyalins, Shevchenkos, Kuzichkins, Gordievskys—sitting before television monitors somewhere, studying and analyzing his every move. He wondered if their faces were the same faces—older but the same. Or if some surgeon's scalpel had altered them beyond recognition.

"Right on," smiled the bearded Joe Robinson to Thomas Burns behind the one-way smoked mirror of the wall. "We're getting to him."

"We are?" Burns murmured uncertainly.

Robinson's hands floated across the packed electronic control panel with the deftness of a concert pianist. They fluttered momentarily over the bass and treble knobs before moving on to adjust the angles of the six remote-control microphones trained on the target: four for sound, two for strain-symptom readings. Then, with other levers, he readjusted yet again the aim of the two complicated-looking video cameras whirring away on either side of his long electronic console and the beam of invisible, near infrared light that flooded Pavlenko's face, monitoring the movements of the cornea of his eyes.

He turned and nodded at Susan, the stenographer, who gently caressed the exotic-looking code-fax machine before her. It was the KW-7 cryptograph Cassidy had demanded, a machine that operated exactly like a fax only with one difference: it scrambled the letters and numbers typed onto it into an incoherent jumble of electronic pulses and fed them directly to the computers in Langley, Virginia. It was part of what is known as the privacy channel in the lingo of the trade.

"How you doing, Sue?" he asked.

She smiled, nodding silently, and he looked deeper into the room, to the team of white-coated technicians busily preparing the mystifying array of technological wizardry that is the leitmotiv of twentieth-century espionage. Every filing system that the United States Government possesses on "The Global Structure"—the mind-boggling multitude of information banks at its disposal monitoring and recording worldwide activities on a daily basis—was being patched in, readied, and held on red alert. These included the CIA's Records Integration Division and its Office of Central Reference, the National Security Agency's huge warehouses of minutiae obtained through its vast electronic surveillance network, and the data banks at the Defense Intelligence Agency, the Armed Forces, and the FBI.

The finest information storage and retrieval system available to mankind was in full swing. Cryptonyms were being flashed back and forth in digital codes between London and the United States, transferring their coded numbers and letters onto banks of television monitors. The United States was ODYOKE, the Department of State ODACID, the Department of Defense ODEARL, the FBI ODENVY, the CIA KUBARK, its Clandestine Services KUDOVE, the prefix AE for the Soviet Union, BE for Poland, DI for Czechoslovakia, SMOTH for M16 and UMBRA to indicate the top-secret nature of the information being transmitted.

"Thank you," the slender, pallid Russian said. He pulled his gaze away from the mirror and accepted the Styrofoam cup of coffee Cassidy was holding out. He shifted in his chair.

"The 13th Directorate, Mr. Cassidy, is the most lethal force the Western world faces today. It is an organization with the narrowest of briefs: one single operation that it has been planning, preparing, rehearsing, and fine-tuning for over a third of a century—the entire span of its existence."

Cassidy contemplated the tired, bloodshot but piercing eyes of the Russian.

"Tell me about it, Max," he said calmly.

"By the time I describe it all to you, Mr. Cassidy, and you believe it and convince your superiors and they draw up their ever-present list of options and run it through the various Congressional oversight committees and the President's own army, it may well be too late."

"Well, Max, we're starting with a bit of a problem here." Cassidy hesitated to underline the point. "You see, as I said, I'm afraid we have nothing in any of our records about this so-called 13th Directorate of yours."

"Perhaps," said the Russian somberly, "that is by design."

"Perhaps," Cassidy repeated.

The Russian sighed and closed his eyes. "Where would you like me to start?"

"Why not the beginning, Max? The inception."

Pavlenko stretched forward and picked up his coffee.

"The leadership of the Union of Soviet Socialist Republics has—and always has had—only one burning goal: to be the most powerful nation in the world. This driving urge was probably never more prevalent than it was in the late 1950s and early 1960s."

The Soviet defector leaned back in his chair.

"They were the most instructive years for the Soviet Union. Critical ones in the development of both foreign and domestic policies. On the one hand we accepted the superior military capability of the West and mounted a long-term attack on that lead. A policy that you will agree, Mr. Cassidy, has been remarkably successful."

The interrogator nodded silently. He lit his cigarette and rocked back on his chair, extending his feet to rest on the small wooden desk in the room.

"On the other hand, the Soviet leadership was well aware of the Western reluctance to use military advantage. Of course, as time went by, especially after Vietnam, it became increasingly apparent that this reluctance had degenerated to political impotence—witness Afghanistan, Iran, Nicaragua. Meanwhile the military edge you held was narrowing. Until, by the early eighties, it had disappeared altogether. And parity was something *you* sought."

Pavlenko lit a Winston and looked at it distastefully. He then returned his eyes to Cassidy's tired but impassive face. "All of which is not news," he said, letting out a stream of smoke.

"Right. Go on."

"What might be, though, is the Soviet perception of its relations with the U.S. given these developments."

Again the defector paused, to Cassidy's mounting irritation.

"The key, it was decided very early on, would lie eventually not in any battle of strength between our two countries. For no matter what transpired, the balance of power would remain more or less the same. We would both retain the capability to destroy each other easily and the winner would gain nothing but a hollow victory. So, we were engaged, then, not in a competition of relative strengths but one of relative weaknesses. Thus, it was in the weaknesses that the answer lay."

Cassidy smiled slightly, the corners of his sharp blue eyes crinkling.

"That's reassuring."

"Perhaps," Pavlenko responded.

The experienced old interrogator held his silent gaze.

"The weakness we assessed in your particular society," the defector continued, "was its openness, its complacency, its lack of discipline, morality, will. Its gullibility and innocence. What to you are institutional strengths, to us were opportunities for penetration. Opportunities to work within your system and influence events from inside, sub rosa. Using the very same propaganda machines you yourselves employ to sway, shape, and reshape public opinion."

None of this was earth-shattering, thought Cassidy. Nowhere near enough to justify the level of Soviet flap the Agency was monitoring.

"How did the Kremlin envisage exploiting these weaknesses?"

The Russian stood and walked away slowly.

"It wasn't the Kremlin, Mr. Cassidy," he said, his face adopting a pained expression. "Leaderships everywhere are not dissimilar. They are interested only in the maintenance of the status quo. For is it not the status quo that elevates them in the first place?"

Cassidy thought: This is new. Finally we seem to be getting somewhere.

He asked, "Who was it, then?"

Pavlenko turned to the smoked-glass mirror at the far end.

"A colleague of yours, actually," he said, sticking his hands in his trouser pockets. "And he managed to sell the idea to a broad range of people in Moscow."

Cassidy's back straightened. A mole? Was that what the Russian was leading to?

"Oh? Who?" he asked, his voice adopting an unprompted rasp.

"Harold Adrian Russell Kim Philby. Formerly of British Intelligence, now a general in the KGB."

James Cassidy felt the muscles in his jaw tighten. He tried desperately to stop himself from making a second telling move.

The Russian watched for a moment, waiting silently. Then he ambled back and sat on the chair facing his interrogator. "Did you know him?"

The American summoned all his discipline. "Kim Philby?" he asked. "Yes, I met him when I was a junior officer in Washington. One of the best in the trade. A truly admirable pro. Too bad he was on the wrong side."

Behind a now composed exterior, Cassidy's mind raced in another direction. The conversation was starting to head for uncharted waters. Among the Western intelligence agencies the

Philby enigma continued. No one knew what he was up to in Moscow. Or if indeed—at his age—he was up to anything.

Countless reports had come out about sinecure jobs in publishing companies and a post in Moscow's Institute of the United States and Canada, working with Anatoli Andeyev. There were even rumors that he worked in the public relations arm of the KGB, now that he was too old for active duty. Some had it that he had in fact long ago retired completely. But nothing conclusive.

One thing was for sure, thought Cassidy. The Soviets would never put Kim Philby out to pasture. No matter how old or impaired he was. His knowledge and instincts on the West were simply too valuable.

"How does he fit in now, Max?"

"He is what he has always been since he defected in 1963, Mr. Cassidy. The man in charge of the 13th Directorate," the Russian said calmly. "The author of the plan, in fact."

Cassidy cleared his throat. It was an old habit, one which appeared when he was nervous. But he couldn't recall a previous occasion when the tic had played up during an interrogation.

"And what are the objectives of Mr. Philby's organization?" Cassidy asked, careful not to show too much enthusiasm.

Pavlenko smiled meekly.

"Mr. Cassidy, it is very important that you understand," he paused, looking into his interrogator's eyes, "and believe this next point, for the basis of his entire operation, the core of his strategy was based on this one unique cultural asset: secrecy. Secrecy, and the weaknesses of an open society versus the strengths of a closed one. Without these ingredients this operation, this one initiative to which Mr. Philby has devoted himself for all these years, would not have been possible."

He stopped and brushed the air away with the back of his hand. "As you know, Mr. Cassidy, we Russians start with a distinct advantage over you in this regard. The clandestine mentality is an inbred Russian quality, a part of our very souls."

Cassidy was impatient to move Pavlenko away from philosophy. But he had to be careful not to put the Russian off his stride.

"All right," he drawled. "I'll go along with that."

"I hope so," said Pavlenko earnestly, "because this is undoubtedly the most covert—and sensitive—project the KGB has ever undertaken. So secret only a handful of people in the entire Soviet hierarchy were ever even aware of it in all these years."

"Not the Politburo, not the Central Committee nor its Administrative Organs Department knew about it. In all this time not even the Secretariat—the executive branch—was ever informed. Just a handful of carefully selected men; mostly the more youthful ones who were assessed to have the highest potential for upward mobility. The future elite who at that time constituted the core of the Soviet secret police." Pavlenko paused. "And today occupy some of the highest seats of Soviet power."

"Fine. But that doesn't answer my question, Max. What exactly is this ultimate objective of Philby and this 13th Directorate of his?"

The Russian looked at him severely. Then the right corner of his mouth curled in a menacing smile.

"To elect the next President of the United States, Mr. Cassidy. To own the White House."

James Cassidy felt the stab of a million frozen needles moving up his spine. *What the hell was this clown talking about?*

Abruptly the door of the interrogation room burst open and the head and shoulders of Thomas Burns appeared.

"Jim," he said with only the curtest nod of recognition at Pavlenko. "Can I see you a minute?"

A heavy cloud of fury passed through Cassidy's mind. What the hell did Burns think he was doing? Why was he interrupting? Now? At such a crucial stage? The interrogator pushed himself up, carefully holding in check the black anger he felt inside.

"Be right back," he told the Russian defector as he stepped into the hallway. He closed the door and turned sharply, his cheeks flushed, his hands placed threateningly on his hips.

"This had better be good, Mr. Burns, or I'll personally see to it that—"

"All hell's broken loose at SR," interjected the slightly shorter but more robust Burns, referring to the Soviet Area Desk of the CIA's Deputy Directorate, Planning.

Cassidy frowned and opened his tired, bloodshot eyes wider.

"There's been a huge increase suddenly in the flap reports coming in," Burns explained, raising the metal clipboard he carried. "You want to take a look?"

Cassidy waved the board away. "Give me a rundown."

"Starting a couple of hours ago there's been a spate of activity throughout the world. Deep-cover operatives are fleeing like rabbits. Golovkin, Titov, and Panzhevsky from Geneva; Mitkov, Laptev, Washington; Ivanov, Peking; Royko, here in London; and so on. Look at it," he said, a higher pitch to his tone as he turned the pages. "They're withdrawing their best men. The kicker is some of these characters we had no idea about. Thought they were diplomats, straight and clean."

James Cassidy massaged the tired flesh of his face silently for a moment, his eyes squinting into the distance. Then slowly he stuck his hands in his trouser pockets and gave Burns a solemn look.

"What do you say, Tom?" he asked reflectively.

Burns lifted his brow and puffed out a lungful of air.

"If he's a plant they're going to a hell of a lot of trouble to make it look real."

Cassidy dipped his head and contemplated the gray linoleum tiles beneath his shining brown wingtip shoes.

"Tom," he said at length, "I want the boys to run a Background Investigation for us." He lifted his head. "Send a CRITIC to CONSIDO. I want them to go back to the machines and get me everything we have on the KGB organizational setup. Everything," he repeated in a louder tone, stabbing the air with his right index finger.

CRITIC is the cryptonym for Critical Intelligence Message; CONSIDO stands for Consolidated Special Information Dissemination Office.

"I want what we know, what we suspect, even what we've dismissed over the years as uncorroborated crap. Have the Agency pull every Field Information Report we have on the KGB's structure, starting with their reorganization in 1961.

"I want the debriefing transcripts of defectors, NSA monitoring reports, and Division D decrypted summaries to be scrutinized again for any reference to . . . any hint of . . . this 13th Directorate that Max is talking about." He shook his head. "Has anyone come up with anything yet?"

"No," said the laconic resident station chief.

"Well, tell them to keep looking until they do. There's got to be something. The other thing we need to do right away is to find a deep hole for Max to crawl into. We don't want the Brits in here reminding us of bilateral relations and trying to take a piece of him."

"They shared Kuzitchkin and Gordievsky with us."

"Good for them. Doesn't mean we go the same route. The safest place to keep him would be right here. We can always deny his approach."

Cassidy thought for a moment. "Reassign the marine who logged his entry immediately. Send him home. And sanitize the visitors books so we have the necessary documentation ready. Yes. Let's keep Max in place until we can assess the fallout."

He glanced at the clipboard Burns was holding. The pile of communications traffic it held was an inch thick. The level of flap was incredible, Cassidy thought. Did it all have to do with this defection? Or was all this Soviet activity a feint? A vast, deliberate attempt to provide cover for a bogus defector? Had old Max been uncovered and turned? Or did Cassidy have a real live fish in his net?

One thousand five hundred miles away it was nearing noon, and the city of Moscow basked in a glorious morning of wintry sunshine. But the golden rays showering the old city failed to warm the atmosphere in the gloomy, high-ceilinged room on the second floor of the elaborate old building less than a mile from the Kremlin at number 2 Dzerzhinsky Square. Behind the tall windows in the headquarters of the KGB, the two men fixed each other with their stares.

"Is that necessary?" Kim Philby asked dismissively.

"What," inquired the other man, "is the objection?"

"It's clumsy and fatuous." Philby smiled superciliously. "Other than being a totally unnecessary risk, of course."

Geidar Reza Alievich Rezayov nodded thoughtfully. Over the years he had come to despise this antiquated old Englishman. Here was a man who, for all his correct political and historical analysis, for all the rejection of his class, was still somehow imbued with the social attributes of that class. He was arrogant, played shamelessly with his wit, and loved to affect cultivated airs. He was still a member of the English bourgeoisie.

Philby cleared his throat with a growl, spat into a soiled white handkerchief and continued to look at Rezayov through heavy-lidded eyes.

"I said, I think it's clumsy and unnecessary," he insisted with a hint of a smile and a cock of his head. "Which makes it highly risky."

His Russian was good, but the inflection in his quivering old voice was obviously a straight carryover from English.

Rezayov remained silent. He knew exactly what he wanted to say; and do. But he mulled it over. It was a habit his father had forced upon him at a young age: to think twice before speaking. And three times before committing. "Never get angry," his father had counseled with that shrewd Muslim peasant wisdom of his. "Get even."

Besides, thought Rezayov, he needed the *Anglichinin*. He always needed Philby—but now more than ever. However irksome and tiring the old man's eccentric ways were, he was without doubt still the most astute covert operations specialist in the business. Even more importantly, he was the perfect weathercock as far as Rezayov was concerned. Wouldn't he be the one who knew exactly how the operation was going at every phase? Wouldn't he be the first to know if all was not well?

"Comrade," the tall, trim, confident Azerbaijani smiled sadly, "I, as always, bow to your greater experience and expertise in such things. But unfortunately the Committee feels the risks are greater the other way. It is they who have decided that Pavlenko should . . . ah . . . remain in London, not I. And they insist on it, I'm afraid."

In London, the pelting rain had resigned temporarily in favor of a light fog. The defector and the interrogator met again, for lunch. The cold buffet of various salads and meats was served on a trolley table in the same sparsely furnished room in the United States Embassy on Grosvenor Square. But the "break of a couple of hours" that James Cassidy had introduced in between—after hearing the troubling update Thomas Burns had to offer—had seriously affected the rules of their game.

It was a tactical decision Cassidy had made earlier. As well as a practical one. Not only would an interruption at this sensitive stage serve to deflate the defector's ego and hopefully stop the momentum he had gained. It was also an opportune moment for Cassidy to catch up on the mounds of communications traffic coming in, to study the backgrounders and weigh the options Washington had forwarded for his consideration.

It proved a wise decision. For in the space of those two hours one thing became absolutely clear: that the huge octopus that was Soviet intelligence was stirring, moving into high gear. The incidents were innumerable, the humdrum routine of everyday monitoring suddenly shattered by a spate of unusual activity. And every indication—information from HUMINT, intelligence from human sources; ELINT, electronic intelligence; COMINT, communication intelligence; and SIGINT, signals intelligence coming in from intelligence as well as military and Department of State sources around the globe—suggested that the Soviets were "buzzing."

In England, exceptionally heavy communications had been detected emanating from the Soviet Embassy by GCHQ in Cheltenham. The same was true of their facilities in Washington, New York, and San Francisco as monitored by the National Security Agency. Soviet Ambassador Arkadi V. Khabalov, a senior GRU, or Soviet Military Intelligence, official now appointed to the Quai d'Orsay, had flown from Paris to Moscow for consultations. As had Vadim Popov, their Ambassador to Madrid. Separate reports indicated "the unusual sight of lights burning late into the night" in the Soviet embassies in several capitals of Europe; and Cuba and Canada as well. Increased activity had also been sighted in the headquarters buildings of the little brothers—the intelligence agencies of the Soviet satellite countries.

All of which "should be interpreted as a departure from the norm," Washington had advised Cassidy. And that "the sharp ongoing Soviet reaction tends to suggest a crisis, impending in nature."

In other words, the Soviet Union was in a hurry. Because they weren't fools. They knew the pickup in their activities would be detected. Consequently whatever it was they were after had to be big, something worth the suspicions their activities aroused, at the very least. Washington agreed: "Recommend intensification of debriefing mode concurrent with immediate plans to relocate AE NORTH PAW."

But why? What was the bug in the Soviets' tail? Was it really all because of the defection of this man about to sit across from him for lunch? Or was it something else? A huge, intricate ploy of some sort?

Either way it was a different game he was playing with Max now. A new element had been introduced. One that brought into play the most nerve-racking of an interrogator's constraints: the element of time.

It was one thing to pick the brains of a man at leisure—sometimes over years—in the comfort, security and controlled environment of one of the Agency's safe houses.

And quite another to pump him.

Not least because each individual was different. Some responded promptly and fully of their own accord. Others needed the help of medication, or the stimuli of psy-ops to whip up a little fear, or mental anguish, or perhaps even pain. Still others needed loving and attention and promises to assuage their guilts. All were frightened men, suspicious and wary. Few of them were fools.

But the sharp worldwide Soviet reaction had now severely restricted Cassidy's options. He had to grasp the full import of what Pavlenko was saying before the Soviets could regroup and engage in their own damage-control efforts. And yet he had to be careful. He could not push the man too hard, too quickly. For that was the surest way to unhinge any defector.

"Pumpernickel?" he asked as he held out a small wicker basket.

"Thank you." The defector took two slabs of the dark bread.

"Okay. Let's pick up where we left off, shall we, Max? The White House. How exactly does Mr. Philby plan on securing that property?"

The interrogator watched the smug smile that broke out on the defector's face.

"The same way you elect all your Presidents, Mr. Cassidy. Or, for that matter, sell your toothpastes."

James Cassidy stared at Pavlenko. No matter what happened, the American was forced to remind himself, no matter what he heard or felt, he could not show any sign of tension. Not again. He had to remain at ease, in control, unflappable. Abruptly, just as he was about to speak, Lenin's words echoed unsolicitedly in his mind. Words that were, now, the very first thing they taught at Langley in the Junior Officer Trainee Program:

"Communists must resort to all sorts of cunning, schemes, and stratagems; to employ illegal methods; to evade and conceal the truth . . . to incite one enemy against another . . . to use one country against another. . . . My words were calculated to evoke hatred, aversion, and contempt . . . not to convince but to break up the ranks of the opponent, not to correct an opponent's mistake but to destroy him, to wipe his organization off the face of the earth."

And Kim Philby, recalled Cassidy with grudging admiration, was a hell of a lot more dangerous than Vladimir Ilych Lenin in this arena. For one, he was better informed. For another, he was a former field operative. Not a philosopher. Still, to elect the President of the United States? Was it possible?

"Would you like to explain that to me, Max? I don't think I quite follow you."

"Well. Like you do everything in America, Mr. Cassidy. Through the banks and the boardrooms. Madison Avenue and Wall Street. And, of course, the media and Hollywood. Money. Money and, I believe, something you call hype."

A picture of Philby immediately superimposed itself in Cassidy's mind. The Englishman had spent three years, from 1949 to 1951, in Washington helping to set up the then fledgling CIA. He knew the U.S., its intelligence community and mentality as well as anyone in the world: he had the benefits of an insider's knowledge and an outsider's perspective. He had always been credited with being brilliant, analytical, and at the same time imaginative. If anyone on this sweet earth had the flair, the grasp for detail, the intuition and awareness to dream up, let alone pull off, a plan as brazen as what this defector seemed to be talking about, it was Philby.

Cassidy felt an eerie feeling run through him.

"That's oversimplifying it a little, Max. Besides which, you need an actual vehicle first, before you can—" Abruptly the interrogator stopped in midsentence. The gentle, knowing nod of the defector's head cut the words off in his throat as surely as would have a guillotine. For a long moment the two men stared at each other, a tense silence filling the air.

"Okay. Who is it?" the interrogator asked softly at length.

Pavlenko hesitated before answering.

"It will surprise you."

"Let me decide that."

"Very well," said the Russian slowly. "His name is Allan Sanford."

James Cassidy froze. The man *Time* magazine had called the most charismatic man in the world; *Newsweek* the most likely to succeed. *Playboy* had labeled him the sexiest man in America and *Harper's*, *Vogue*, and *Cosmopolitan* variations on the American Dream. What was this imbecile talking about?

Cassidy's stomach churned. That was what the Russian was trying to tell him. Allan Sanford *would* be the next President of the United States.

The only difference was, he was owned by the KGB.

It was precisely 7:30 A.M. when Phillip Myers slipped behind the wheel of an all-black Chevrolet Classic and circled out of the Century Plaza's driveway on to Avenue of the Stars. In the distance, the usual thick, gray-brown blanket of smog hung suspended above the metropolis, defying the Pacific breeze striving to nudge the poisonous fumes over the rugged, sun-drenched San Gabriel mountains on the eastern horizon.

It was unlikely, Myers thought as he guided the car across the wide thoroughfare into the far lane, that Allan Sanford would awake before Myers made it back. And even if he did, everything he needed was on his desk, ready for his attention. The Mounting Debt Problem report and The State of the Social Security Program were neatly prepared for the scheduled interviews in the manner he preferred—concisely, without an ounce of flesh.

"If you can't get it on a page," Sanford was fond of saying, "you don't understand the problem."

With that thespian mind of his, Sanford would within minutes memorize every word and digit on the two pages. And the two "friendly" journalists chosen for the separate interviews would, as always, be impressed. Whether he understood the historic trends, the present significance, the projected effects and how they related to real life and people and poverty and infirmity was quite another matter. What was important was that Sanford should appear to understand the detail.

Myers turned right on Santa Monica Boulevard, toward Beverly Hills. It was highly unlikely, in any case, that his own breakfast meeting would take that long. As a rule they only lasted an hour, an hour and a half.

He turned left on Rodeo Drive, heading for Sunset Boulevard and the Beverly Hills Hotel. There he stopped—among vehicles whose license plates crystallized self-imagery into a single word: STAR, ROCKY, OO7, BEAUTY, ANGEL, 1 X WIFE—and handed the keys to the parking valet.

Myers looked at his watch and hurried up the plush red carpet beneath the hotel's long awning. In the lobby, despite the shirt-sleeve temperatures outside, a roaring gas fire blazed in the stucco *cheminée*. He veered away from it, right toward the Polo Lounge, and the exit beside the bar-restaurant leading to the luxurious private bungalows hidden in the hotel's exotic rear gardens.

Approaching the famous watering hole, he reached into his side pocket and extracted a small square slip of paper. Across the top of the ordinary-looking message note the words CENTURY PLAZA HOTEL were printed. At the bottom of the slip the handwritten message read: "John Cambria's office called from the *Post*. Please call him back in the morning." It was dated yesterday; and the time six forty-five in the evening. He glanced at his watch. He still had five minutes before his breakfast meeting in the room up ahead.

Phillip Myers stepped into one of the telephone booths on his left.

High above and a few miles to the east, in a majestic five-bed-room Palladian mansion overlooking the Hollywood Hills, a woman in her late thirties was drinking coffee in her study when the shrill tone of the telephone interrupted her morning. Putting her cup down on the breakfast tray she noted it was her private number, and not one of the six interlinking lines connected to her thriving modeling agency on Sunset Strip. She brushed her shoul-der-length wavy red hair back from her ear and picked up the phone. "Hello?"

"Hi, Cath, it's Blackwell," a dour voice said softly.

"Colin!" Cathy Greene exclaimed with delight. "I have a sur-prise for you. But first, how did the dinner go?"

"Fine, I guess." The tone was louder but bored. "We'll probably need a reprise soon but whether the venue will be the same I'm not sure. Could be at Lido. We're moving down there in a couple of days."

"No problem, darling. Just let me know."

"I'll do that. Now, what's the surprise?"

"Are you ready for this?" Cathy Greene said smugly.

"Sure." There was the impatient sigh of someone pressed for time. "What is it?"

"She's arrived."

There was a long pause from the other end of the telephone. "I'll get back to you."

7 | THURSDAY, DECEMBER 31

"What will happen to me?"

"Nothing. You'll get some much needed rest."

The defector nodded. "Rest," he repeated desolately.

James Cassidy felt a twinge of pity for the man. His would be a lonely existence for the rest of his life, increasingly tortured by guilt and remorse for those he had left behind, his home, his family, his very roots. The conviction would grow—as it did in nearly all defectors—that deep down his new friends in Washington would never really trust or respect him. Yet he had shown courage, thought the interrogator. He deserved to be treated fairly.

"Yes. I would have thought you'd be happy to see the back of me. Even if it is only for a couple of days."

"When will you be leaving?"

"In a few hours. And you'll be coming over the day after tomorrow, in the early morning. As I explained, we've arranged a top security departure for you from one of our air bases up north over the weekend when things are very much quieter, as you know. You'll be accompanied, of course, by Tom Burns and some of his colleagues."

Oleg Maksimovich Pavlenko did not answer. Instead he stared at his interrogator, every exhausted wave of concentration searching for some sort of sign.

"You'll be far more comfortable in Washington," Cassidy added. "Things will slow down a little there, too."

The Russian looked away, and stood.

"Mr. Cassidy, we've been working together for some time now," he said slowly as he paced toward the mirrored wall. He turned and stared deep into Cassidy's eyes. "I think, too, that not only do we know each other reasonably well, but I have always sensed that there is a degree of respect between us. Am I correct?"

"Yes," Cassidy replied. It was true. The Russian had impressed him from the first day. He was extremely balanced, quite devoid of the psychological instabilities endemic among most defectors. He also had the encyclopedic brain, shrewd judgment, and sharp instincts of a first-class operative.

But he was also a disenchanted man—and, like all reformed addicts, disillusioned to the point of fury. The energy and conviction of his youth, the passionate involvement and unquestioning commitment to his ideology had all gradually crumbled to dust as he climbed up the ladder of the KGB.

Afghanistan had been his Rubicon. In his mind he defected then; but it had taken ten years before a propitious opportunity arose.

Cassidy smiled inwardly. The Russian would be surprised if he knew, the American thought. It was an open secret among the handful who knew about Pavlenko's existence: James Cassidy had been the sole reason why Pavlenko had never been pressured like most agents-in-place to "seek and obtain specific information about specified topics or subjects."

Cassidy had always defended his position on the grounds that the material Pavlenko was providing was not only valuable but substantive usually, and oftentimes absolutely new. Which was something with which no one could argue. But the real reason for Cassidy's unusual attitude had been different. On a personal level, which his Washington colleagues would never have understood, Cassidy was convinced that Pavlenko would refuse to provide anything that he felt might in any way be detrimental to his country. It was the system he abhorred, not his country. Underneath he was highly patriotic, a Russian through and through.

"Then, if I may, I would like to ask you two questions," Pavlenko continued. "And I would appreciate it if you would answer them truthfully."

Cassidy thought about the request. Unfortunately everything had to be held up to a suspicious optic in this trade.

"Depends on the questions, Max."

"They are both personal. Things that are worrying me."

"Such as?"

"The documents I left at the drops. Have they been collected yet?"

"Yes."

"Have they been of value?"

Cassidy pondered his reply. The answer was yes. An unqualified yes, he thought, recalling the last two lines of the advisory from Langley, printed in red across the softly gray-striped computer printout:

> PHYSICAL DOCUMENTATION UNDER OBSERVATION AND ANALYSIS. PRELIMINARY FINDINGS: RATING ONE: COMPLETELY RELIABLE CONFIRMED BY OTHER INDEPENDENT AND RELIABLE SOURCES.

Never, not in over thirty years in this profession, had Cassidy seen more impressive corroboration so quickly in a debriefing process.

"I haven't had any feedback yet, Max. You know these things take a little time."

Cassidy's instinct was to stay cautious. Nothing had been proved, not conclusively. And nothing would be, not until they could spend some time first uncovering the details: the names, dates, times, and other minutiae. Then cross-checking them all against "knowns" they had on file.

"And my family? My wife and two little daughters? Do you have any information about them?"

Yes, Cassidy knew. Four KGB officers had knocked on their apartment door late last night; and then, charging them with espionage under article 64 of the Criminal Code, carted them off to Moscow's Lefortovo Prison.

"No," he said as forcefully as he could. "I've issued specific instructions to . . . to all personnel to keep well away from your home. No point risking your family by chancing our people being spotted in the area."

This time, however, the lie was more difficult. He understood the depth of Pavlenko's pain and anguish for his family. It was a pain Cassidy knew and knew well from his own life, he thought, an image of his daughter Jenny flashing before his eyes. But now was not the time to break the news to Pavlenko. And Cassidy was not at all sure if he could ever bring himself to do so—even when the time came.

"Tonight is New Year's Eve," Pavlenko said softly.

"Yes, it is."

"Will you spend it with your wife? You will be there in time, no?"

"Yes, I'll be in Washington in time. I'm taking the Concorde. Whether I get to see her or not, however, is an open question."

The defector stared at Cassidy and for a long moment silence ruled.

"Do you have a picture of your wife?" Pavlenko asked at length.

James Cassidy nodded uncertainly, surprised. Then slowly he reached for his wallet and produced two snapshots.

"Is this your daughter, Mr. Cassidy?"

"Yes."

"She is beautiful. So like her beautiful mother. How old is she?"

"She was five when that picture was taken," said Cassidy, trying to sound matter-of-fact.

"And how old is she now?"

"She would have been seven next week."

The Russian stared at Cassidy in horror. Then he stepped forward hesitantly and hugged the American.

Everything about this New Year's Eve was new to Nick Delan.

Just as life during the last thirty-six hours in Paris with Clio had been an entirely new experience to him, so too was this night. For one thing it was the very first time in his life that he actually felt that the year being ushered in really might hold a promise of change—more in keeping with the fresh atmosphere of a budding spring than with the somehow forced and boisterous celebrations he had come to associate with past New Year's Eves. For another he found himself loosening up, gradually even relishing the pace and variety of the program Clio arranged for them.

Together, in just a day and a half, they had done everything. Like a Hollywood montage of a lovers' Paris, they had already marveled at the richness of Notre-Dame, dined on a *bâteau mouche* on the River Seine, explored the corners of Montmartre—and all during the first twelve hours, yesterday afternoon and evening. To top the night off Clio had taken him to Calvados—the establishment that, for as long as anyone could remember, was the last stop—where you simply had to be seen in the wee small hours of the morning.

Today they'd had a long, wet lunch—at the top of the Eiffel Tower. And then she had insisted on taking him to half a dozen haute-couture *maisons*, all on Avenue Montaigne, the elegant boulevard that links together like a string of pearls the houses of Ungaro, Dior, Chanel, Jean-Louis Scherrer, and Valentino, among numerous other boutiques and jewelers along its half-mile strip. Midway down the broad, tree-lined boulevard stands the luxurious Plaza-Athénée—the hotel she had chosen for them.

Despite the breakneck speed of the roller-coaster ride they were on, Nick Delan found himself savoring every moment. Paris with Clio Bragana was a city whose sounds were accordions, popping corks, and clinking glass—a far cry from the town he had previously known. She was charming and passionate and full of zeal; and gradually a most engaging relationship developed, one that reminded Delan of the male camaraderies for which most former athletes end up pining. She teased him about his conservatism, his age, his attraction to all the corny, touristic things—all the time clinging to him—and snuggling even closer if some passerby even so much as looked in her direction.

Each time Delan noted the bubbling pride he felt inside himself as she held on to and pampered him and openly let the whole world see her affection for him.

It was bliss. All he could see, all he could imagine, was her. So much so that he barely put up any resistance when she asked him if she could break the promise she had made to him over dinner in Zurich: the pledge that it would be just the two of them in Paris. Alone. Together. None of her plastic friends or haunts.

"Why, it's New Year's Eve, Nick," she beseeched like a little girl bursting with excitement. "And *everyone* goes to a party."

The "small affair," as Clio had called it, turned out to be at Régine's, thrown by the glamorous, red-headed owner of the discotheque herself. And it was wild. By eleven-thirty Nick Delan found himself wondering, a little light-headedly, whether every one of the chic crowd in the club had a guarantee in their pockets for 365 days of happiness—such was the reckless abandon with which they rushed in to greet the year ahead.

The self-indulgent spirit was catching. And Clio's presence beside him made the atmosphere even more pleasurable.

"Oh, Nick," she said suddenly, just barely one hour after the midnight celebrations. "I forgot to tell you. I accepted an assignment."

He looked at her for a moment. "Don't tell me. Let me guess. The one you were talking about on the phone the other day? The one in L.A.?"

"Yes," she said coyly, hugging a cushion in the corner of a large couch.

Delan leaned back, smiling happily; and kissed her on the cheek. "Great. When will you start shooting?"

"I have no idea yet. I'm still not sure it will materialize in the end. These things are always very tentative. Ninety percent of them usually don't work out."

"Well, I hope it does. I also hope it happens when I'm out there."

She nodded delicately, the smile evaporating as the lids of her large brown doe eyes became heavy. The gesture aroused Delan. Was this the first suggestion? The faintest show that the firmest no was perhaps sliding toward a maybe?

Delan felt a sense of frustration well inside him. How much longer could he go on like this? He thought about it. Should he test the waters? What the hell, he couldn't exactly expect her to make the pass—not even if she did change her mind. Go ahead, he decided. But don't rush it.

"You know what my grandmother used to say?" he asked above the tumultuous noise of the music.

"Oh-oh."

"What is it?"

"Oh, nothing. It's just that usually when someone quotes grandmothers or grandfathers they're taking the long route to what they have on their minds."

Touché, thought Delan. "Tell you the truth, this is no exception."

"Oh? What are you trying to hide? And why?"

"What am I trying to hide? And why?" Delan repeated. "Now that's a bitch." He thought a moment longer, using the blaring music as an excuse. "Can we go back to the long route?"

She laughed, rolling her head back. The heart-shaped diamond she wore above her slinky ivory satin dress twinkled as it rode up her bare chest. "Sure," she said lovingly.

But when she looked back at him again, Delan knew the moment had evaporated. Behind the air of casual laughter, her eyes carried the tiniest hint of caution again.

Who could blame her, he thought, backing off. It would take more than a few lunches and dinners, sight-seeing tours and pleasant small talk to erase the horror etched in her mind. No. One would have to go a long way to put her at ease, to win her confidence and trust. There was no point in pushing.

Suddenly he felt guilty. Now, in retrospect, it had been callous of him to have ever harbored that question the night they had met at the Dracula Club. It was so wrong. So utterly off target. She was neither. That was the answer, he thought, angry with himself. Not a buyer. Nor a seller. Just a very pretty bird—with broken wings.

The President of the United States looked thoughtfully toward Kenneth Ellender, his quiet, retiring National Security Adviser; then back again to the rumpled, elderly but feisty figure of the Director of Central Intelligence, Robert Wilson. The two senior officials sat next to each other, directly in front of his desk. Each was flanked by the one specialist they had selected to assist them in this, the latest of the string of briefings on the Pavlenko affair. Although it was the first time that specialists had been called into these meetings, neither of the two newcomers were strangers to the President. The CIA man, James Cassidy, sitting to his far right, he knew from his reputation as the nation's foremost counterintelligence operative. Deputy National Security Adviser Anthony Boyle sitting to his left he saw on a regular, if not daily, basis.

"Are you telling me," the President demanded finally, "that you believe the leading candidate for my job has had his career, financial affairs, and sex life controlled by Moscow for the last twenty years? And without our knowing it? Doesn't that stretch plausibility just a little *too* far, gentlemen?"

For one brief moment the four men sitting across the large ornate wooden desk in the Oval Office seemed reluctant to answer.

Then the youngest man in the room, Anthony Boyle, broke the silence. Except for the brief initial pleasantries, it was the first time the man charged with the political-military affairs portfolio on the National Security Council had spoken during the last hour, allowing the DCI and James Cassidy an unbroken run in the briefing, interspersed by only the occasional comment from his own reticent boss, Kenneth Ellender.

"The answer to your first question, sir, is a qualified yes. What we have no way of knowing for sure is whether or not and how deeply Allan Sanford himself is involved. As for stretching the imagination. No, sir. I don't believe it does. It's not at all inconsistent with the pattern of past Soviet conduct. More imaginative? Yes. A higher orbit? Perhaps. Nevertheless, it's a natural and logical extension of the game both sides play with each other all the time."

The President's gracefully aging face looked a little haggard suddenly.

"But this isn't just Machiavellian, Tony. It's insanity."

Boyle was unmoved.

"Why, Mr. President?" he asked. "If your avowed political intentions were—always had been and will be—the defeat of the other side, wouldn't you say that it would be a clean and attractive option to infiltrate your opponent's most sensitive organs? However outrageously?" He paused. "After all, we've got people in their Central Committee."

The President rubbed his double chin.

"What about our response? How would they have assessed that?" he demanded. "No one in his right mind would knowingly expose himself to the sort of retaliatory measure this kind of action is likely to provoke from this Administration."

"On the contrary, sir," Boyle retorted, "the Soviets have to be given credit for clear thinking. What we are witnessing here is a classic low-risk offensive. The risk to them is minimal—if not nonexistent."

"Why?" snapped the President.

"Essentially because we don't have a single viable response at our disposal, Mr. President. Not without overstepping our legal authority. Not without circumventing congressional restrictions and reporting requirements. Which they no doubt assess we cannot do politically. I don't believe it's unreasonable to assume that the lessons of recent history haven't completely been lost on them."

The President studied the tall, smooth, soft-spoken Boston Brahmin. He was an adviser the President held in the highest regard, an enormously competent human being, by nature conservative and cautious. His usually relaxed, open face, characterized by jowly cheeks, neatly parted auburn hair and gentle laughing eyes, now held a grave, intense expression. Anthony Boyle was the quintessential professional: a man whose field experience as a junior officer in Vietnam enriched his natural capacity for strategic thinking. It was the unusual combination of thinker, planner, and doer that made him so valuable to the Administration. He more than anybody else was responsible for the grip that the President was able to maintain on the details of the nation's foreign policy. What was even more refreshing about this young man was his utter abhorrence of a public persona, more in the vein of Brent Scowcroft and Walt Rostow than Henry Kissinger, Zbigniew Brzezinski or Alexander Haig. Such was Boyle's distaste for publicity, in fact, that he had turned down the post of National Security Adviser when the President had offered it to him. He had refused the job on "personal grounds," a reasoning that had baffled the President until Robert Wilson, his CIA chief and old friend, had explained Boyle's reticence. He simply wasn't keen on any visibility whatsoever. He had refused the National Security Adviser's post but had offered to stay on as his assistant on one condition: that the President's offer and his refusal remained between the two of them. He would not want to burden his eventual boss with the knowledge that he, Boyle, had been the President's first choice.

And it had. No one but the President and Boyle had ever known about the approach to Boyle. No one except for the CIA Director, Robert Wilson, who had originally suggested Boyle's name to the President.

"Why not?" the President asked Boyle.

"For a number of reasons, sir. All of which flow from two overall problems: credibility and timing."

"Go on."

"Perhaps we can sharpen the focus if we back up a minute. If we first construct in our own minds the precise scenario we're facing."

The President nodded.

"For over twenty years—slowly, carefully, methodically—the Soviets have built a national hero. Not just a glamorous star, or a popular politician or an envied entrepreneur—but all three: an honest-to-goodness American idol. And it is just conceivable that they've done it in such a way—what the intelligence people call false-flag recruitment—that the target himself is unaware of what's been happening."

"In which case," the President interjected, "isn't it possible to approach Sanford himself? Present him with the evidence and back it up by indicating our readiness to leak or otherwise make public the information?"

"That's clearly an option, Mr. President," Boyle replied. "But one that has two major flaws. Firstly, can we establish an absolutely watertight case implicating Allan Sanford and/or his organization? I mean, beyond a shadow of a doubt. After all, if he's clean, if he really doesn't know he's being set up, he's not going to be easily convinced that he's really not the prince he thought he was—but a simple pawn. After a lifetime of success in a number of highly competitive fields, including the entertainment industry and on both sides of the camera, he's not going to be too receptive to opponents telling him his success has actually all along been bought and paid for by the Soviets. No. To approach him directly we would need an absolutely watertight case, unimpeachable proof—which we don't have yet."

Boyle paused.

"And the second problem?" the President prompted.

"Well, in a sense the precise corollary of that," the younger man continued. "Can we be absolutely certain that Allan Sanford *is* a false-flag recruit as the defector has suggested? That he is a stooge as opposed to a willing accomplice? Because if our information happens to be wrong or incomplete in some way and he *is* involved personally, *any* approach we made could have potentially disastrous consequences. For a start the Soviets would be alerted immediately. Which means, in all likelihood, that they'd revert to a fallback position—an extremely well-camouflaged fallback no doubt—which we couldn't even begin to guess at."

The President studied Boyle's solemn demeanor for a moment. Then his eyes rose to the dark oil painting of Calvin Coolidge above the flickering fireplace embedded in the curved cream-colored wall directly in front of him. The clock on the mantelpiece read twenty minutes to eight in the evening.

"How quickly can we reasonably expect to know which track we're on?" he asked, addressing no one in particular. "When will we know whether Sanford's in on this or not?"

"Realistically we have only one source available to us at this point," replied Anthony Boyle. "The defector. Consequently Jim Cassidy is the man to answer that question, Mr. President."

The tall, slim, silver-haired counterintelligence officer shifted in his chair.

"Mr. President, that's a hard question to answer with any certainty," James Cassidy hedged. "From my experience there's only one way that information of this nature can be extracted *and* corroborated beyond question: with time. A long time—during which one can gradually establish rapport with a defector. That, and only that, provides the opportunity to check and recheck every minute detail of his revelations against knowns we have established. This process can be foreshortened a little, of course. But only at a certain risk."

"How?" the President of the United States demanded.

"Ah . . . chemicals, sir. Drugs."

The President's right hand began again to toy with his chin. "Please continue."

"If one is pressed for time, with no other options available—as is obviously the case here—one has to revert to foreshortening. Which is what we have elected to do. That's essentially why we're flying the defector over tomorrow. Nevertheless, Mr. President, I should warn you that drugs can only help so much. They cannot reliably extract what a man is trained to conceal."

"And in the meantime?"

"In the meantime, Mr. President," Cassidy replied, "one has to rely on the corroborating evidence one has. Which in this case appears to be very solid."

"How solid?" the President asked, turning to the stooped, disheveled figure of his oldest and closest friend, Robert Wilson. A veteran intelligence officer, Wilson had been a spymaster during the Second World War working in Switzerland with the wily old Allen Dulles. After the war he had returned to his law practice and built a fortune in venture capital projects. Armed with this wealth he had then wended his way into Democratic politics and soon found himself holding a string of important offices in Washington. In these posts he earned the reputation of an "outsider's insider"— a man who learned the rules quickly. And then how to get around them to achieve what he—or his patrons—were after. No one had been surprised when the President had appointed him to head the CIA. Not only were they old friends, but Robert Wilson had run his successful presidential campaign.

"More than adequately so, I would say," said the CIA chief. "But most of it is circumstantial, I'm afraid. Although, as you know, I'm a firm believer that that is usually the most incriminating sort of evidence. Either way, some points we've already corroborated with other sources. For instance, we've already put together a good deal of supporting documentation to back up the highly shady nature of the origins of the Sanford empire and the financing of his films; but much of the rest still needs to be collated. As Cassidy indicated, we'll be in a better position to work on additional evidence once we get Pavlenko over from London and isolated here. That will give us an opportunity to delve further and cross-check his verbal testimony and the documents he's provided with the supporting documents and NSA intercepts we have on file and other material to which we have or can get access."

"What sort of time frame are we talking about?"

The Director of Central Intelligence looked at Cassidy; then back to the President somberly. "It's not a speedy process. There's debriefing, collating, cross-referencing, corroborating, verifying— it takes some time. It may be weeks, months even, before we can put together an airtight case. If we ever can in such a way as to satisfy a court of law."

"What you're saying, then, is that there is no way of knowing quickly."

"That's right. There isn't. Not with any certainty. And perhaps not even within the required time frame either, I'm afraid. Vis-à-vis the upcoming elections, I mean."

The President held his intense gaze on his old friend for a moment. Then, gently, he swiveled his deep, dark-green-leather barrel chair away from the desk and stood slowly.

"You didn't finish with your scenario, Tony. What else is rooted in these two problems: credibility and timing?"

"Well, sir, exacerbating our problems above all else is the fact that Allan Sanford is ahead of you in every single national poll taken to date. That tends to severely restrict our retaliatory capability."

"In what way?" the President asked, treading slowly toward the fireplace.

"Credibility. And particularly now. Remember, Mr. President, the race has started—the November election campaign is under way and you're way behind at this point in time. As a result, the more traditional methods are out of the question: eliciting the help of the media with strategic leaks, a covert operation, even an attempt at a bipartisan approach—they're all too dangerous. They could easily be tainted, interpreted as a political ploy and backfire. For a start the media won't buy it. After all, Allan Sanford is their creation. They have vested interests in protecting him. They'd crucify you if you were to attempt a smear campaign."

The President frowned as he turned at the mantelpiece and paced back toward his desk. He looked again at Robert Wilson, as if pleading for some reassurance.

The Director of the Central Intelligence Agency shifted in his chair. The aged wrinkles on his florid, pugnacious face tried to twist kindly for a change. He understood the President's frustrations. He himself had experienced the very same sensations when the full weight of the implications of what Pavlenko had divulged had first begun to sink in.

Nevertheless the chief had to know, Wilson thought. His old friend had to be made to fully comprehend the exact nature of the limitations with which he was working. He had to see that there was no choice. Thank God for Anthony Boyle, he thought. The young man presented a case well: logically, intelligently, honestly, and he didn't pull his punches. No wonder he was a favorite of the President's.

"There would be a backlash the likes of which this Republic has never seen, Mr. President," Boyle continued. "You're talking about a very popular man here. Someone who is as close to a national hero as you can get. It would be like saying General Eisenhower was all along a German spy. Or Kennedy was a drag queen. Who is going to believe us?"

A tense silence suddenly filled the stately room. The President stopped at the three floor-to-ceiling curved windows behind his desk. He tucked his hands into his trouser pockets and stared out at the dark, snow-covered landscape outside. From above the bare cherry branches the tiny lights—five hundred and fifty-five feet high in the sky—on the tip of the Washington Monument twinkled through the falling snow and the thick, green-tinted bulletproof glass of the windows. Below, the tall globe lights of the path leading to the South Lawn and barren Rose Garden partially visible to his left shone brightly, hanging moons shimmering in the dark, stormy night.

"If that were to happen," he said softly at length, "come next year a KGB agent will be sitting behind this desk."

"The gutter."

Cathy Greene frowned at the striking French girl sitting across her desk.

"Come again, honey?"

"The gutter, Miss Greene."

"I'm afraid I still don't follow you."

The young blond girl sighed patiently.

"You're saying this man prefers his women with minds in the gutter."

"Yes," Cathy Greene murmured. She swallowed. The girl's instincts were incredible. She seemed to sense a man's sexual peccadillos like a shark smelling blood in the open sea. "Yes, I suppose so."

"They're the easiest kind." The French girl raised one of her hawk-winged eyebrows almost imperceptibly.

Never in her long career had Cathy Greene been so unnerved by one of her wards before.

"I know, Jacquie darling," said Cathy Greene, adopting a lofty approach for self-defense, "but it won't be easy. You're dealing with a demigod here. A man who has clawed his way up from poverty to international acclaim. I wouldn't be overconfident if I were you. He's a sharp cookie, and he's used to getting his own way and with the best broads around. He can be a real bastard."

For the first time in the past hour, Jacqueline Petit smiled radiantly; and suddenly her face became angelic: light-blue eyes, a slightly aquiline nose cresting above heart-shaped lips. A halo of hair seemed to complete the childlike vision, blurring her face slightly at the borders as a million hues of gold blended into the dewy skin covering her wide cheekbones.

She looked at Cathy with those misty blue eyes.

"Does he fuck?"

Cathy Greene was shocked. It was the contrast between the starkness of the words and the childlike innocence of her face that unnerved the older woman. She was positively feral, thought Cathy.

"Yes," she said, straightening the three matching silver picture frames on the left side of her desk. "Yes. Like a trooper."

"Then you have nothing to worry about. I'll get to him. All I need to help me is that parcel. And—"

"Oh, yes . . . of course."

This girl is flustering me, Cathy thought. I'd nearly forgotten. She unlocked one of the drawers of her desk and extracted a dark-brown leather book box. Indented on the cover and spine in golden lettering were the words *Jean de la Fontaine—Contes*. She slid it across the desk.

"Thank you." Jacqueline Petit left it there. "And a little information."

"What about?"

"Oh . . . what do you call them . . . his kinks."

"He's into threes," Cathy Greene replied slowly as she stood and moved away to the large picture windows behind her desk. She leaned against the wall and looked down at the late afternoon traffic. Seven floors below the offices of her modeling agency the never-ending procession of vehicles twisted on to the Strip at Sunset and Doheny.

"But he's careful. Out of two, one could be a potential witness. So he's very wary."

"Would you have someone perhaps that he likes, but clashes with?"

Cathy turned. "What do you mean?"

"Someone he likes physically but can't get along with. You know, their characters clash."

"Why?"

A chilling smile pulled the heart-shaped lips apart.

"It works."

"What does?"

Cathy Greene walked closer, fascinated but perplexed.

"Degradation, Miss Greene. Men love seeing one girl degrade another sexually. And who better than someone they clash with?"

Cathy Greene sat behind her desk. This girl was wicked. She had about her an aura of sadism Cathy had never witnessed before, not in all the years she had been in this business. The older woman flicked away some dust which may or may not have been on her sleeve.

"Maybe. When do you need her? Tonight?"

"Oh, no. First we need to tantalize him a little. Draw him out. Incite his fantasies." Jacquie smiled again. "Then we have to let him marinate."

For one split second Cathy pitied Allan Sanford.

She said, "How long do you think it will take you, doll?"

"To set up the scene?"

"Uh-huh."

Jacqueline Petit pouted. "Depends. Four, five days. A week at the most."

Cathy Greene watched Jacquie Petit run her fingers through her hair.

"What sort of girl do *you* prefer, Jacquie?"

"Me? I don't mind," shrugged the French girl. "As long as they are clean and attractive." Then she pouted again as a demure smile spread across her face. "I prefer older women usually."

Cathy Greene tried to ignore the tingle she felt across the surface of her skin. "I'm sure older women would love the opportunity, darling," she said slowly. "But this john likes young girls."

"What a shame," Jacquie purred. Her laughing blue eyes were quite bewitching.

"Would you like to see some pictures of the girls I have?"

"Sure. Why not? But what about this girl we just talked about? The one he clashes with."

"It's not any single specific girl really. It's a certain type."

"Oh. And what kind is that?"

"The innocent type, I guess." Cathy picked out a thick leather-bound photograph album from among the stack on a glass-and-chrome console behind her desk. She placed it in front of her and opened it. "The young, wholesome, naive type that gets nervous and talks a lot, instead of performing. That seems to upset him." She thought for an instant. "Maybe black girls, too," she added uncertainly.

Jacquie nodded, her eyes hard and thoughtful as if storing the information carefully.

"These are my best girls. A thousand dollars a night and up. Why don't you pick one out for yourself?"

Jacqueline Petit rose gracefully, her long, tapered legs kept together at the knee in a picture of correctness. As she glided around the desk the full curves of her firm buttocks and untethered breasts struggled against the light summer cotton of a simple khaki-colored Givenchy safari dress.

She bent beside Cathy Greene's chair, and petulantly propped up her chin with her elbow on the desk.

"Do you have any favorites?"

Cathy liked Jacquie's perfume. And the feel of the smooth, firm flesh of her young arm pressing against hers.

"No," she replied, nervously flicking her long, red hair over her shoulders. "Not really. I never mix business and pleasure."

Jacquie swirled toward her; and smiled slowly. Her face was now only inches away from Cathy's.

"Never?"

Cathy Greene looked into the younger girl's eyes, her heart pounding.

"Very rarely, doll," she said.

Slowly Jacquie looked away and turned the first page of the album. She studied the sharp features of a cool Nordic beauty in the glossy black-and-white photograph before turning another page.

"What's this one like?" Jacquie asked several pages later.

Cathy Greene contemplated the beguiling portrait of a beautiful mulatto girl.

"She's very nice. Half Tahitian. A little on the—"

"She looks gorgeous."

"She is, but—"

"I've never made it with a black girl."

The determined purr in Jacquie's voice stung Cathy. She hesitated. "But she's very inexperienced. Absolutely new to the—"

"Oh? How lovely. Not only is she delicious-looking, but I can break her in," Jacquie said softly. She paused exquisitely. "And Mr. Sanford can have his ultimate scene."

These men were right, the President of the United States mused. Given the established Soviet penchant for parallel planning, Bob Wilson was absolutely correct in wanting to assess Moscow's possible fallback positions. Particularly the option that entailed some sort of orderly, controlled retreat that could subtly lead to a different type of victory. What did Ellender call it? "Structured defeat"?

His advisers were right, too, about the importance and sensitivity of the eventual U.S. response. The Soviets would already be monitoring them closely, pulsing their assets for information on what exactly the defector had divulged so far. One hint and the KGB would move goalposts on them.

It was a delicate situation. Worse. This crisis could not have come at a more inopportune moment—not just domestically with the elections looming, but internationally with the fundamental change he had just introduced in Washington's arms negotiations policy. With it he had at last succeeded in overcoming the image of intransigence which was becoming a political liability. He'd also earned credit for placing the ball squarely in the Soviet court. It was of paramount importance to maintain this perception of a thaw. At the very least until after the elections.

"Is there any special significance in the timing?" the President asked, looking at his intelligence chief.

The elderly, stoop-shouldered Robert Wilson shook his head.

"It's real doubtful that the timing is in their hands," he replied.

"Essentially our information is that this is a twenty-, thirty-year-old project that has simply come to fruition."

"Tony?"

"The timing is hardly the central issue here," said Boyle with a hint of impatience. "The important point is the significant departure from established international norms of behavior that we're faced with."

The President leaned back in his chair. His right hand rose to massage the sagging flesh of his chin. Anthony Boyle remembered his golden rule: the President was not a cerebral man. It was the drama that moved him.

"During this last half-century, perhaps the most important tacit understanding established between the two superpowers is that we both need to maintain a certain level of predictability in our conduct.

"The Soviets have now broken this agreement. And that, above all, is why we must respond to this initiative promptly and in kind. We need to make it absolutely clear to them that we too have the capacity and the will to respond to this sort of destabilizing activity. And that it's in the interests of both sides to revert to a more traditional form of rivalry and competition as soon as possible."

"I'm aware of that, Tony," the President said testily. "But I'm still concerned about why. It seems totally inconsistent with Soviet rhetoric and actions over the past few years. Practically everything we've witnessed since the generational change in the Soviet Union has pointed to a radical and genuine departure from the old form of hostilities. So why the abrupt change? Why would they risk blowing everything on one mad machination?"

"From my vantage point," Kenny Ellender intoned, "that seems relatively clear, Mr. President. The gamble failed. The New Economic Policy, which promised deep transformations in the economic system, accelerated social development, and higher standards of living, has failed to produce. At least fast enough to appease the hard-line extremists. In short, the *nomenklatura* is unhappy. And this offensive is either a concession to them or an end run by them."

The President lifted his long legs to the heavy wooden desk and leaned back, slowly locking his hands behind his neck.

"Yes," he said. "But still, Allan Sanford a Soviet agent? Who the hell *is* going to believe that?" he whispered in an incredulous tone. "Why would a man like Sanford allow himself to be trapped this way?"

"I think *when* is the operative question," quipped Bob Wilson. "And the answer is: a long, long time ago. As much as thirty years, maybe. When Sanford didn't have a pot to piss in. That's probably when the Soviets first isolated him. They probably assessed Sanford as a great potential bet early on in his career and thereafter kept their eyes on him. Obviously, somewhere along the way they must have started backing him. And continued to do so ever since."

"Yes, Bob, but Sanford is an intelligent and shrewd operator. It seems absurd to assume this could be going on under his nose—and for so long—without his knowing. Is there any evidence, any indication at all, to suggest he's a willing traveler?"

The crusty former lawyer shook his head. "No. At least, nothing we have so far."

The President lowered his eyes slowly.

After a long moment it was Anthony Boyle who broke the silence.

"I'd like to raise a point of clarification, if I may, Mr. President."

"What's that, Tony?"

"We need to be very careful here, sir, not to confuse two issues. Their behavior may seem irrational from our vantage point. Madness even, as you suggest. But then again, 'There is a pleasure in madness that only madmen know.'"

"That's good, Tony," grinned the President. "One of your own?"

"No, sir, it's Dryden." Boyle smiled sheepishly before continuing. "And it's appropriate. Because this offensive is madness to the point of brilliance. A well thought-out, immaculately executed and timed initiative that effectively eliminates most, if not all, the legal options at your disposal."

The President's eyes narrowed perceptibly. He had worked too closely over the past three years with this astute young man not to detect the tone the Deputy National Security Adviser reserved only for his most crucial points.

"What are you talking about, Tony?"

"Well, sir, I think it's essential to keep in mind the fundamental handicap we're working with here. Every governmental organization at our disposal is basically a bipartisan concern. Roughly speaking they're split in equal parts between us and the Republicans. There's no way we can turn to them—not without seriously risking a leak. And that means all the various intelligence arms, Mr. President—military or civilian.

"If—however we choose to handle it—this leaked out, Watergate or the Iran-Contra affair would seem like kindergarten parties in comparison to the fallout we'd get."

"Jesus H. Christ," the President said softly. "Just what the hell does that leave us with?"

Anthony Boyle met his gaze unequivocally.

"One choice, Mr. President. And one choice only."

8 | SATURDAY, JANUARY 2

An ashen-faced Robert Wilson stood as the President walked into the small sitting room, tightening the cord on his dressing gown as he crossed the floor. The CIA director had woken the President fifteen minutes earlier, at just after three in the morning, with the request for an immediate meeting.

"Can't talk about it now. I'm in the car, on my way over," he'd said gravely.

On arrival he'd been ushered immediately into this peach-colored room in the private quarters of the First Family.

"I'm afraid we've got a serious problem, sir," Wilson said after the door was closed behind the President.

"What?"

"The defector is dead."

The President was stunned. "How?" he whispered eventually.

"Car bomb. On a highway north of London."

This time the pause was even longer.

"Why weren't they provided with an armored vehicle, for God's sake?" the President asked, disbelief mixing with anger.

"They were."

"So—"

"The bomb was placed on the inside of the vehicle," Wilson interjected.

The CIA chief paused to let the implications sink in. He looked down at the text of the telex he was holding. There was no point in going into the details now, he thought, his eyes resting on the last paragraph, the section quoting from the Metropolitan Police Special Branch preliminary report:

> EXTENSIVE DAMAGE CAUSED BY POWERFUL DEVICE IN SMALL EN-CLOSED ENVIRONMENT, SO PRECISE POINT OF DETONATION PROBABLY IMPOSSIBLE TO ASCERTAIN. NOT UNREASONABLE TO PRESUME—ANTICIPATING LABORATORY FLOW CHARTS OF BLAST—THAT LIKELY POINT OF DETONATION SOMEWHERE IN VICINITY OF DRIVER'S SEAT. BOMB DISPOSAL ESTIMATES THAT REDUCED THRUST TO POINT DIRECTLY TO REAR EXPLAINED BY PRESENCE OF SPECIFIC OBJECT—YET TO BE IDENTIFIED—THAT ACTED AS BARRIER AT POINT OF DETONATION.

The President of the United States sighed, "How many casualties were there?"

"Four, Mr. President. Three Agency men. And the defector, of course."

"How did the bomb get there?"

"I'm afraid it's all conjecture at the moment. We simply don't have enough information yet. We have to rely at this point on what's provided by Scotland Yard and MI5; and, for the moment, they seem to be playing it very close to the chest. Nevertheless there are only one or two possibilities."

"The British?" The President's voice was matter-of-fact now.

"No grounds for that kind of suspicion. Yet."

"What *are* the options, then?"

"Looks like an inside job. Can't be sure yet, of course. After all, it's only been a few hours. But that's how it looks to me."

"How is that possible? How could they have gotten access to our plans? Knowledge of this . . . this was to be kept strictly limited."

"That was with reference to the mode of response we were discussing. The actual administration of a defector runs through an entire slice of the bureaucracy. From point of entry: in this case the U.S. Embassy in London. And that means the State Department. To the Directorates of Plans, Intelligence, and Support at the CIA. The NSA, too, for the intercepts and communications traffic requested from them. All of which means they may have activated a 'sleeper.'"

The President sighed deeply again. A sleeper—the deadliest form of espionage agent. An ordinary, harmless man or woman, recruited, trained and then placed on site and often left for years to build a cover—before being activated at a critical moment.

"Two things are pretty certain now, though," Wilson continued. "One, that the Soviets went to great lengths to reach the defector; and at great risk. And two, that they're moving quickly. Both lend credence to the defector's claims and consequently to the veracity of the Allan Sanford story."

"Yes, Bob," the President agreed unenthusiastically. "Except it's going to be impossible to cross-examine him now. And that means we'll never know for certain."

"That, Mr. President," responded Wilson, "is probably the point."

MONDAY,
JANUARY 4

"Why don't you come with me?" Clio Bragana asked, attacking the tarte tropézienne. She lifted the stubby cake fork to her mouth. "It'll only take half an hour."

"I can't," Delan replied without looking up from the papers he was sifting through on the other side of the table. "I have to make a few calls to the U.S."

Between them the starched white-linen tablecloth was laden with assorted pastries and afternoon tea on her side. A single cup of black espresso coffee sat in front of him.

"Oh, come on," she implored. "How much difference can thirty minutes make?"

"Well, for one thing it'll take longer than that," Delan replied, picking up the papers as he stood. "It's over in Place Vendôme and this is the evening rush hour."

He walked away, across the sitting room in his suite at the Plaza-Athénée toward the traditional mahogany pedestal desk placed up against the far wall. Above it, hanging on the dark brown-cloth surface, two colorful impressionistic lithographs decorated that side of the room. They contrasted beautifully with the traditional furniture and thick, predominantly beige, Chinese rug covering the center of the parquet floor.

"For another, it'll be lunchtime back home by the time we

return," he added as he dropped the papers on the desk. He removed his dark-blue blazer and draped it around a chair.

"What is it, anyway?" Clio mumbled petulantly, her mouth full.

"A surprise."

"Yes, but what sort of surprise?"

Delan snapped open the briefcase lying on the desk and extracted several slim manila folders.

"The kind you only find out when you open it. Which means the sooner you move your butt, the sooner you'll know," he said, extracting the papers from one of the files.

He glanced at his watch. It was ten minutes past five. "Besides, if you don't hurry, you're going to miss your fitting across the street here. Don't you have to be there between six and—"

The sound of the telephone interrupted him.

"Can you get that?" he said, preoccupied with the documents he was sorting through.

"Hello," he heard her say as he selected a sheet; then, "I think you must have the wrong room."

Delan turned and started ambling toward the center of the room, his eyes busy reading the text.

"I'm afraid not," she said into the phone. "That's okay. No problem."

"Who was it?" Delan asked distantly.

"No idea. The man was looking for some guy called Bright-something-or-other."

"Who?" Delan asked.

"I didn't really get the name." Clio shrugged. "Douglas Brightonbark or Brightonback, something like that."

"Oh," said Delan after a short pause.

He looked up from the page and started walking slowly toward the marble-topped Empire console just left of the fireplace. The small cabinet had been adapted to hold a small refrigerator and a well-stocked bar. He poured himself a Scotch whiskey, adding a lot of ice and a little water. Then he took a long, hard sip.

"Give me your hand," he said as he approached her.

She did, looking at him curiously.

Gently he yanked her up.

"Out," he said with exaggerated strictness. "Go pick up your gift before the place closes and I get offended."

"Nick, please. Come with—"

But he rebuffed all her efforts at enticing him to accompany her. Firmly, but in a friendly manner, he shooed her out, picking up her fur coat, handbag, and shopping parcels and stuffing them in her arms as they went.

The instant he closed the door behind her, however, his face abruptly lost its mask of good humor. Suddenly it was severe, consternation flowing across its every feature as he snapped the heavy Fichet lock into place.

Immediately he moved to the telephone, picked up the receiver, and punched a series of digits, stopping after the first and third for the appropriate dial tones to fall into place.

He shuffled from foot to foot, twice sipping his drink while his eyes impatiently swept the room. The clicks stopped. The number rang twice.

"Good morning," said a stark, impersonal, American voice. "Transnational Enterprises. May I help you?"

"The name is Breitenbach. Douglas Breitenbach. S-C-I two-three."

At 414 via Lido Nord it was cocktail time; and it had been ever since brunch.

Between them Jacqueline Petit and Allan Sanford had enjoyed nearly three bottles of 1971 Dom Perignon; and in the marathon process languished the day away with some lazy, half-hearted sun-tanning and a lengthy ride along the shores of the Pacific in Sanford's sleek Tullio Abbate speedboat.

Even though it was midwinter in much of the world, thanks to the Santa Ana winds it was a little over seventy degrees in Southern California. Now, in the twilight hours, the sun's last rays fought to stave off the evening chill that accompanied the long shadows growing slowly across Lido Channel.

Sitting on the small, pot-bellied balcony off the main bedroom on the second floor, both refreshed by showers and changes of clothes, Allan Sanford topped up their flute glasses while Jacquie's misty eyes soaked up the spectacular sunset.

Allan Sanford replaced the dark-green bottle in the silver ice bucket and looked at her. It was getting colder. She was feeling the nip in the air. He felt a gentle ripple run down his stomach. Her nipples had hardened, their small, inviting contours pressing out against the white-silk blouse she was wearing, unhindered by any underwear. She was a remarkable young lady. Incredibly sensuous in bed, wild almost to the point of being corrupt.

It had been a long time, he thought looking at her heavy, marijuana-flushed eyes. A very long time since anyone had affected him, satisfied him like this. All he felt was desire—pure animal rage—for this girl. But why? What was it about this little number that got under his skin this way? And for so many days now? He contemplated her as she bent over the balcony, eying the immense, exaggerated curve at the small of her back and how it rounded out to her handsome, full derrière.

He'd sure needed it, he thought, looking away. This never-ending process of campaigning. Tension and fatigue and frustration. He was tired. To the marrow of his bones he was tired and he needed to rejuvenate himself, charge up the old batteries a little. It'd been fun, just stopping the world for a few days. Escaping with this broad into an irresponsible, painless ecstasy. He'd needed it, even if she was only a hooker.

He looked at her again as she turned and walked toward him. She wasn't just any kind of whore, he thought. She was what you'd call a natural. A real class act. And still only a rookie, too. On her first outing, in fact, according to Phillip Myers.

Jacquie Petit smiled as she sat next to him. Allan Sanford felt a flash of heat run through him. Deflowering innocence—that's what he enjoyed the most. I wonder if she has ever even experienced it, he thought. For real, I mean. It was impossible to tell for sure. She was so young, seemed so wholesome despite her new calling. Was it just a figment of his imagination, wishful thinking? Or had she really tossed off those lingering, come-hither looks at one or two of the more voluptuous young women they had seen on the beaches at Laguna?

"Tell me something," he said softly.

Jacquie turned slowly and looked at him across her shoulder.

"Sure," she purred.

"And I want you to be honest with me."

"Pourquoi pas?" She shrugged, smiling.

He fixed her with his most appealing stare—honed by a hundred different directors and a thousand scenes.

"Do you like girls?"

She blinked several times. And seemed to blush even though the color of her cheeks hardly changed.

"Physically? I mean . . . sexually?"

She looked away. Down and away to the long-stemmed glass in her hand.

"You want the truth?" she asked softly after a long silence.

"Uh-huh."

"I have never done it. *Jamais.*"

Sanford studied her again. Her young, inexperienced eyes were still downcast. Now the champagne glass she was toying with was spinning nervously in her lap.

"Yes, but does the idea appeal to you?" he asked. "Or, better yet, have you ever been turned on by a girl?"

Jacquie Petit shrugged demurely. At length she answered with great hesitation.

"I do not know. I suppose . . . I suppose I have fantasized about it. *Mais . . . c'est naturel, n'est-ce pas?* Everyone does, don't they? It's not abnormal to think about this, is it?"

"Would you like to try it?"

Abruptly color rose to her cheeks.

"I . . . I do not know. I suppose it . . . it . . . depends."

"On what?"

The glass was spinning faster now, the fresh champagne frothing.

"On the girl."

"Let's start with a brief recap of what it is we're looking at," rasped the Director of the Central Intelligence Agency, Robert Wilson.

The three men he addressed sat around him on the two opposing brown-leather settees in front of the log-burning fireplace in his office. The room itself was large—very large when compared to the Oval Office. It was also cold. As cold as the arctic winds blowing across the snow-covered Potomac Valley stretching away beneath this seventh-floor perch at CIA headquarters in Langley, Virginia. The coldness inside the room, however, was of a different kind. Cold as in sterile, sanitized, frigid.

Anthony Boyle glanced at his boss, sitting on the opposite couch.

Kenny Ellender sat listening intently to Wilson. Feeling impatient with these unnecessary preliminaries, Boyle let his gaze wander around the room.

It was designed in the carefully calculated style Robert Wilson affected: that of a man with many secrets to keep. There were no pictures or mementos in his office. Nothing on any of the coffee tables—no newspapers or magazines or flowers or any other decoration. The DCI's desk, like the long dark conference table at the other end of the room, was, as always, bare. No papers or files or reports sat waiting to be read. No in-box or out-box or pencils or pens. Not even his telephones were visible. Just the smooth, gilded red-leather surface of a wooden desk with an eye-catching geochron clock on the left corner, reflecting the time across the entire surface of the globe in colors and waves.

"We're working within two abiding parameters here," Wilson said. "First, given that all our formal intelligence arms are bipartisan in nature—and that includes the various proprietary agencies they run—we have no choice but to go to a deeper level, the deepest we have, in fact. The reason is simple. The days of nonpartisanship are past. In the old days it used to be that there were no political fingers in the pie. Now there are always two fingers in the pie. Which really means three. Because one or the other finger always drags in the press.

"Secondly," Wilson continued in an even graver tone, "we must all—each one of us—be very careful to keep the President distanced from whatever we do from this moment on."

He paused; and looked at each man somberly, the thick lenses of his dark horn-rimmed glasses making his irascible features even more pugnacious.

"I think we all know that what we're looking at here is a totally different set of circumstances and an altogether different issue than the Reagan-North/Iran-Contra affair or anything else this country has ever faced. But I believe, too, that all of us are aware that none of our liberal friends would see it as a defensive move, forced on us to protect national interests. They'd immediately pick up the legality issue as usual. And, given the precedents, we have little to rely on there. In the eyes of the law, what we are about to set in motion is illegal. Illegal in the extreme. As a result, it's imperative that the President is not, under any circumstances, tainted."

Again he paused. "The best way to ensure that, of course, is to make sure he does not know. And I'm not talking about plausible denial or spin control or ambiguous documentation, etc., here. I'm talking total ignorance about anything to do with the response we've chosen. Beyond a doubt, that is the best protection we can give him.

"If anything—anything at all—goes wrong, and it can be linked directly to the President, it would be a disaster. The biggest blunder any administration ever made. The American people may be willing to forgive and forget abuses of power or mismanagement and detached styles and overzealous subordinates abroad." Wilson paused and the moment lingered. "But they aren't going to stand for this. Not once the press gets through with it, anyway. There's no way the people will ever understand the deployment of secret—and, strictly speaking, illegally established—military-intelligence organizations here, domestically, and by a presidential directive. Christ, the Reagan people did everything, admitted to anything eventually, but they went to great lengths to limit the information coming out about these quasi-official secret soldier networks that Reagan hadn't even initiated himself. Carter did. It's a goddamn constitutional minefield we're facing."

"That and the fact that we have to accept one other thing," Ellender interjected. "Namely, that in today's United States it's virtually impossible to maintain a state secret for any length of time. Therefore the state cannot be involved in this venture. And if it's seen to be involved, then at least the symbol of the state has to be protected."

"Precisely," said Wilson. "Are we all still agreed on this point?"

A tense silence filled the room as Wilson turned his head slowly. His gaze rested on each of the three men in turn, observing their nods before moving on.

Which of these men, Anthony Boyle wondered, would actually have the gall to spurn the President? Which one of them would refuse to tell him if he demanded to know?

It was one thing to sit in a sumptuous office and boldly declare that the President would not—under any circumstance—be told. And quite another to turn down the most powerful officeholder in the world.

No, he, Anthony Boyle, felt no guilt at all for having promised the President to keep him informed—secretly—at all times.

"Good," Wilson said at last. "Now, Tony, as the Executive Officer overseeing this operation, perhaps you'd like to fill us in on where we stand. Start with the selection process if you will."

"Sure, Bob." Anthony Boyle turned slightly to look across the table at the tall, dark-suited, silver-haired man sitting on the opposite couch, next to his boss, Kenny Ellender. "James Cassidy and I have chosen the man we believe is the best potential candidate for—"

"Sorry, Tony," Ellender interrupted. "Can I ask you just briefly to touch on the criteria you used?"

"Yes, of course. Essentially it's the classic procedure. Jim and I wrote up an exacting job specification, a precise profile of the sort of man we need, including all the various physical and mental requirements: background, education, experience, street smarts, speciality, that kind of thing. Naturally, we broke each of these areas down into component parts and correlated them, detailing the required psychological makeup, the interplay between personal beliefs and the dynamics of the candidate's past actions, a meeting of personal and historic forces—"

As Anthony Boyle spoke, Kenny Ellender could not help but contemplate his deputy. This intense professional soldier upon whom the President had become so dependent. This responsible, committed, gifted and in many ways unconventional man who had led such a charmed life. Born to old Boston money, elite schools, Choate and Princeton, and the best that life had to offer, he had, nevertheless, chosen to dedicate his life to his country, in the old way—quietly. An approach that was now archaic, one that suggested a heavy streak of nonconformism in his character. Indeed, the better one knew Anthony Boyle, the more remarkable the dichotomy. For essentially, despite all that social polish and academic achievement, despite that engaging personality and impeccable grooming, Anthony Boyle had the instincts of a riverboat gambler: cunning, shrewd, devious, daring. The quintessential hands-on man of action in a city full of bureaucratic desk jockeys. Army intelligence in Vietnam, policy formation and coordination of strategic covert actions in Washington, these were not areas in which the reckless, the weak-kneed, the naive or plodding survived very long in the corridors of power.

Now Anthony Boyle had entered the dark netherworld of conspiracy on behalf of his President. He would have to be the shield, the cover, perhaps even the eventual target if anything went awry in this risky plan. Was he at all daunted by the prospect? Ellender couldn't tell. Nothing in his voice or comportment gave a clue.

"Then we added one last characteristic to the candidate's requirements," Anthony Boyle said, looking back to Ellender. "A blemish. Something that tainted the man in some way or other. The machines did the rest. They came up with this list of five names." He held up a sheet of paper. "We simply selected their number one choice."

"What was the last characteristic in aid of? Why does the candidate need a defect?" Ellender asked, his eyebrows furrowing like the curious but kindly academic he once had been.

"Well, we both felt it was wise to factor in a contingency at this early stage, Kenny," Anthony Boyle replied matter-of-factly. "Just in case something goes wrong and we need it. Experience suggests the simplest, most efficient and containable vehicle to have on hand under these circumstances is a scapegoat."

10 | TUESDAY, JANUARY 5

Orange phosphorus flames erupted in the deadly darkness, blazing seven stories above the dense jungle foliage.

Then came the first waves of searing heat and blinding light that made men a hundred yards away cringe in pain and terror. The Willie Peters billowed first to the left; then, with ear-splitting thunder, to the right. Then everywhere.

Suddenly pandemonium and chaos ruled. Tormented screams of agony pierced the ceaseless battery of gunfire. The stench of burning human flesh laced the choking clouds of nauseous cordite.

Then night again. Single-shot gunfire mixed with the occasional staccato burst. Then stillness and the same old lethal game of hide and seek. Played this particular time in the dense terrain of unknown jungles: An Loa Valley, Binh Dinh Province.

Again chaos. Night became day; day, night. Bombs, flares, tracers, helicopter gunships crop-spraying in strips. Then a deadly quiet. A longer blackness. Stillness. Fear. Sweat. And yet still more fear. Only the sky was theirs—a sky that showered megadeaths at random. Called in and directed by a twenty-one-year-old black man somewhere to Nick Delan's right. A microphone and airwaves their invisible umbilical cord to survival. Confusion their enemy. And their friend.

Eleven men in this jungle behind enemy lines were his—men who were silent—unable to attack unless attacked. The precise location and numbers of the enemy as always unknown. An enemy burrowed beneath in a maze of bunkers. Or nestled above, waiting patiently to pick them off one by one, camouflaged by the thick leaves of the trees. One sound, one dry twig was enough to give their position away. SOG—Studies and Observation Group— innocuously named technicians: specialists in operating behind enemy lines. Clandestine operators, covert soldiers, elite killers. Trained to parachute behind enemy lines to kill or destroy or rescue or steal. And somehow survive. To ward against leeches and body rot while fighting a phantom enemy, skilled only in silent kills.

This was the twenty-third mission for Delan, and no easier than the first. He had seen and heard it all. He knew the killing, maiming horror. And the role luck played in survival.

This particular sortie was a rescue operation. But what the hell difference did it make anymore? In this war reason had long ago departed, the right and wrong of any objective blending into an apocalyptic stew. Only survival mattered. And even that was becoming increasingly negotiable.

Abruptly a snap shattered the deadly quiet. It came from the dark ridge to the right. The Cong? Flanking? Circling to the rear? Or was it Hank? Had he broken from his right-tail position of the V-formation for some reason?

No night-vision goggles. No eyes.

Ahead—somewhere in that jungle—was a pilot. A downed A-1 Skyraider pilot and a crew of three intelligence specialists. Tired. Lonely. Hungry. Petrified. But most of all exposed. Across that tiny narrow stream ahead were Americans who had to be saved. Between, behind, and all around, the Cong. Patient, elusive, familiar. And determined. Were they circling? Closing in? Taking one man at a time, silently cutting a windpipe? Or tearing open a heart?

Another sound. Pebbles . . . rolling down . . . the embankment . . . down . . . into the stream.

Delan squinted and threw himself on his belly. Aware of trip wires that projected crude missiles, punji sticks dipped in festering human excretion; prepositioned booby traps that fell from the trees at the slightest provocation; poisoned darts that shot up from the ground at the brush of a denim.

He studied the ridge. Still. Quiet. The air coverage had passed. The darkness was total. He waited. Watched. Sweated. There was nothing. No sign of life. Only the smell of death and the final suffering groans of a dying man somewhere ahead.

Then suddenly a silhouette. A flash. From left to right. Coming toward

them. Sixty, seventy yards away. Beyond the flank. Then another, and another.
Goddamn it, who was it? The Cong? The pilot and his crew? Hank?

No night-vision goggles. No eyes.

Delan cursed and flicked the Ingram rifle from single-shot to automatic.
From one shot at choice to twelve hundred rounds a minute. Deadly rounds.
Pinpoint accuracy. Effective range two to three hundred yards. The finest
weapon of its kind in the world. Nonstandard issue. Stolen from a dead boonie
rat. Made in USA. But unavailable to U.S. forces.

He flicked the lever, but waited. Sweat poured from beneath the black grease
caking his face and body. The movements were getting closer. They could be no
more than yards away from Hank. If Hank was still there. Alive. Fort
Lauderdale Hank. With a wife and two beautiful black children. A boy, a
girl. Gorgeous brown eyes.

No night-vision goggles. No eyes.

Again movement. Closer still.

Delan could not wait any longer. He could not chance it. He raised the
Ingram. And squeezed, spraying from left to right, covering the dense foliage
of the small ridge. Emptying the cartridge into the darkness that held the
movements. Replacing it and firing again. Feeling the metal of his gun
heating . . .

And then the shriek, the scream that froze him. The split second the
nightmare always ended, the words tumbling between the twilight of abrupt
consciousness and the mists of sleep.

"Lenny, Lenny, I'm hit, Lenny. Oh, my God . . ."

Nick Delan opened his eyes and saw the dipped wing of the Air
France Boeing 747 as it circled, descending in the clear powder-
blue pre-noon sky toward Los Angeles Airport. He felt the warm
film of sweat drenching his brow and face and neck, dripping down
his shirt, soaking his chest and back. He cursed himself as he sat up
in his seat.

It was always the same; he should have known better. Whether it
was the airplane's vibrations or the high pitch of its engines, or the
claustrophobic environment, he didn't know. He didn't care. It
always happened. Without fail the nightmare was there. Sometimes—rarely—it occurred in bed. But on a plane it was unfailing.

He knew that, and yet he'd allowed himself to doze. And now the
young faces of the four dead Green Berets were staring at him. He
could again see their lifeless bodies being winched aboard the chop-

per. And the report he'd had to fill, signing his name and rank and serial number, attesting to the multiple murder he had committed. Four men, four widows, five fatherless children. For them there would be no yellow ribbons.

The only thing to save his mind was the two survivors they had airlifted out. Most especially one of them, a month or so later.

Nick Delan pressed the call button on his first-class seat and tried to shake the vision etched in his mind. He would never forget that man's name. It was that major who had brought him back from the brink.

He ordered coffee, black—and Kleenex. One to numb his innards; the other to wipe off the sweat.

The guilt would pass, he thought. It always did, thank God. Especially if he had more immediate concerns.

He gazed out at the endless housing tracts dotting the lush green hills that formed L.A.'s northern boundary. They swept down to the vast, sprawling metropolis, which spread away as far as the eye could see, to the sandy desert on the eastern horizon.

He thought of Keyvan Naderi. For the moment the situation would hold. The Iranian intermediary was satisfied with the arrangements—meaning, of course, he was assured of his multimillion-dollar cut. The deal was on a formal cycle now, with contracts to be signed in Teheran in eight days. So all of that was on course, but it wasn't enough. To make the necessary progress, Delan needed to get closer to the man. He had to increase the bonds of trust between them before he could get into Beirut in person. And only then could he burrow into that troubled city's heart. But to do all of that Delan needed to spend more time wooing Naderi. Finalizing the Brazilian arms deal would establish a more intimate link.

Shit, he cursed. He could not understand why he was being summoned to L.A. at such short notice, anyway. And at such a sensitive moment. It made absolutely no sense. He had to get back to Europe quickly. To be around Naderi, to be constantly under his eye.

He thought back to the privacy-channel summons he had received yesterday.

"The name is Breitenbach. Douglas Breitenbach. S-C-I two-three."

"One moment, please," the cold impersonal computer had croaked in response.

Delan remembered switching the receiver to his left hand nervously. What the hell did they want? he had thought. And so urgently? Douglas? He had never heard of the first name being used before. Certainly they hadn't with him. It was the classification for "Critical Communications Message Awaiting"; with a maximum delay of ninety minutes allowed for callback. It was also supposed to be merely a formality. A capability, in place, but counter to every one of the organization's canons.

What the hell could it be? Something to do with Naderi?

Nervously he had sipped his Scotch again, waiting. He knew it would take approximately fifteen seconds for the Westinghouse voice-entry system to feed the computer and the machine to run a voiceprint on him. He had been aware, too, that the codes of names and numbers he had used were only part certification. More essentially they were an excuse—a ploy to have him say enough for the computer's voice template to work with. The machine would then spectrographically produce the individually distinctive patterns of his voice—tone, pitch, vibration, syntax, breathing, phraseology. And run a comparison with the master recordings in its memory bank to determine positive or negative identification. The Secure Computerized Communications System was state-of-the-art. Fail-safe, they said, and its safeguards continued their vigilance throughout all conversations. They monitored and scrambled, pulsating misinformation to all but the two ends of the system's constantly sterilized lines. If anything came in between during the course of a conversation, the computer disconnected automatically.

"S-C-I two-three, you are cleared. Connecting you."

But he had learned very little from the ensuing conversation. In fact, it was even shorter than the wait for computer identification. All he was told was to return to Los Angeles for "urgent discussions" immediately.

Delan looked out of the small oval window beside his seat in the plane. The ceaseless procession of cars on the countless freeways and roads came up at him slowly as the jet engines made their final surge toward the runway.

Then there was Clio, he thought. Beautiful, bubbly, blissful but ultimately screwed-up, insecure Clio. So anxious to love, so capable of giving any man everything. And yet so deeply scarred by life's tough breaks. Petrified of any meaningful emotion or commitment, she seemed totally unequipped for any sort of mature relationship.

Still, Delan thought, feeling a strange ambivalence run through him. Even with all that, he was glad she was coming over. For some weird reason, despite all the complications that could arise from her presence here in Los Angeles, he was already missing her, already looking forward to seeing her again.

He thought back to when he'd broken the news to her about his imminent departure. It had been at dinner a scarce fifteen hours ago at Chez Eux, the marvelous little restaurant just off the Boulevard des Invalides that specializes in hors d'oeuvres of a thousand varieties. Instead of reacting badly, as he had expected, she had let out a screech of joy that had turned the heads of all the patrons within earshot. Immediately she had reached for the pendant dangling on the thin golden chain around her neck and kissed it.

"Nick, it works. I love it. It really works. It's lucky already."

Delan had been taken aback. He had looked at the pendant, his gift to her. It was a real four-leaf clover, pressed airtight between two round watch glasses by a thin band of gold.

"How so?"

"Because . . . wait a minute," she said rummaging through her bag. She extracted a small slip of paper and placed it in front of him. "Look. I'll probably be out there myself shortly. The modeling assignment's come through."

Delan glanced down and skimmed the short note; and indeed the telephone operator at the Plaza had scribbled down a message that seemed to confirm what she was saying.

"I'm *never* going to take this off," Clio said softly, looking at him lovingly. "Not even in the shower."

"I'm glad you like it."

"I love it. It's beautiful. Besides, I don't think I've ever seen a real four-leaf clover before in my life. Let alone owned one."

The 747 landed on the runway with a thud that snapped Delan out of his reverie. What an unholy mess, he thought. What he had planned on being a romantic interlude of a few days was turning into a cockamamy foul-up. He had absolutely no idea what it was that he was being called back for; or what lay in store in the days ahead. But there was one assumption that *could* be made. He wouldn't be able to spend the time with Clio that he'd wanted to, that he should. Worse yet, he couldn't even explain it to her. *Madonna*. Too many things were happening too quickly, and hers was not exactly a tranquil personality. She was far too complicated.

Outside, the famous arches of LAX airport came into view. First things first, though, he told himself. Right now he had more immediate problems to handle.

"Every indication is that Pavlenko did exactly what he was required to do, Comrade Marshal," said Geidar Rezayov. "In addition, the general reaction we're beginning to pick up is precisely as we predicted. The Americans have been pointed in a direction, and as usual they are tearing in like wild elephants."

Marshal Sergei Filatov nodded gravely.

"Which tends to endorse the wisdom of the distasteful but necessary course we were forced to adopt at your suggestion, Comrade Marshal," Rezayov added. "Despite General Philby's objections."

"Yes," concurred the man to Filatov's right.

The Defense Minister swiveled his head toward the portly, bald man uncomfortably sandwiched between the wooden arms of the simple pine armchair the Marshal had imported from Finland— along with the rest of the matching furniture in his spartan living room.

"I don't think anyone can dispute that the elimination of Pavlenko was a safer course to take," Anatoli Andeyev continued. "It rules out a major potential risk. And it does so without in any way affecting the overall plan."

Andeyev looked away from the Marshal, until his sleepy eyes rested on the emaciated-looking old man sitting across from him. You do agree, don't you, Comrade Philby, that your plans haven't been upset in any way?"

"They don't appear to have been. In fact, I'd be willing to go further than that. They may even have been advanced somewhat, given that the Americans seem a little discombobulated by the incident."

Filatov smiled. "Comrades, this is a moment we will recall with pride when we are old and retired. We can sit on the porches of our dachas and tell our grandchildren that once"—he paused, staring at Philby—"that once we heard an Englishman apologize."

Andeyev and Rezayov burst into laughter. Philby smiled.

When the mirth subsided, it was the Englishman who spoke. "Perhaps this is as good a time as any to raise another issue, if I may. I'd like to allocate a generous pension to Pavlenko's widow and children in due course. I presume there's no objection to that."

"No, no," Filatov replied brusquely, oblivious to the Englishman's tone. "Tell me, Comrade Philby, why were you so adamant in your opposition as well?"

Kim Philby contemplated the faces of all three men before he replied. "Two reasons, the combination of which I felt made it an unnecessary risk. To begin with, Pavlenko was a first-class operative, trained to withstand anything his interrogators could come up with and programmed to release only the information we wanted divulged."

Philby paused and sighed deeply. "I also felt that if something went wrong in our attempt to eliminate him two things were certain to occur. The first was that Pavlenko would have automatically assumed we were behind the attempt on his life. After all, that is the only sensible conclusion he could have drawn. And as a result, he would immediately have revealed everything he knew. The second thing was that those revelations would have been looked at by the Americans in a different light at that point in time. In short, we would have given them credibility with our own hands."

Philby looked around slowly. A vague hint of a smile seemed to be tugging at the wrinkled corners of his mouth and eyes. Suddenly a tense stillness filled the room.

"How much information did Pavlenko have, anyway?" demanded Filatov, breaking the silence.

"That's always a difficult question to answer," Philby replied. "I don't think there is ever any certainty about how much information a man who goes over to the other side—sanctioned or not—has managed to glean. The tightest security measures have been in place from the very inception of the 13th Directorate, and the strictest compartmentalization enforced. Nevertheless, in the final analysis, such things always boil down to individual extrapolatory faculties, and good men do not find it impossible to draw their own conclusions from the information available to them. And Pavlenko was a good man."

Marshal Filatov held his gaze on Philby for a long moment. "Is there any possibility at all that they had an opportunity to apply chemicals before they attempted to move him?"

"I don't believe so. But even if they had, I doubt it would have made much difference. As I said, he was trained."

Andeyev shook his head. The heavy horn-rimmed spectacles covering his deceptively drowsy eyes slipped down his nose a little. He pushed them back.

"It is interesting you raise that point, Comrade Marshal," he said, "because I put the very same question to our colleague, Ivanov, before he left for Prague this morning. He discounted the possibility, claiming the KGB, particularly since Yurchenko, is very familiar with the practices of the other side where the use of chemicals during interrogation is concerned. He said they steadfastly stick to two ironclad rules."

Andeyev shifted his bulky torso uncomfortably. "One is that the Americans do not resort to drugs until they have completed the debriefing process by conventional means. It seems they do not use chemicals to obtain information from willing defectors, but rather apply them to verify and broaden the information thus provided.

"The second rule is that they prefer to use serums only after they have the subject lodged permanently somewhere. In the United States, obviously. They rely only on their own clinical laboratory facilities and security conditions. They also prefer to conduct these experiments under what they call an open-ended time frame."

"Which puts them squarely in between a rock and a hard place," said Rezayov. "On the one hand, they have been handed potentially explosive information. On the other, they cannot corroborate it for certain because their primary source is dead. And that, Comrades, is exactly where we planned to put them at this particular stage. In a quandary."

"Yes," said Andeyev thoughtfully. He uncrossed and recrossed his short, stumpy legs, shifting his immense weight onto his left buttock.

"The essential thing now is to be fully mobilized for the next stage," Filatov said.

"Indeed, Comrade Marshal," Rezayov seconded.

Filatov looked at Philby. "Are we?"

"I believe so."

"Good."

"In the meantime, we must also protect against any undue commotion at this end," Rezayov interjected. "Absolutely no suspicions must be raised."

Anatoli Andeyev seemed suddenly to give up his battle with the chair. He stood, and the famous gray suit that was his hallmark unfurled. It was at least two sizes too large. Rumpled and stained, it enveloped rather than fitted him. He paced away toward the brown curtains draping the tall windows.

"What is the impression of your liberal friends so far?" Filatov asked.

Andeyev parted the curtains and looked out at the terrace.

"The General Secretary and his staff have made no connection between the defector and the 13th Directorate up to this point."

"Which is as it should be, of course," Andeyev heard Rezayov say.

In the distance, beyond the splendid, dark conifer forest that melted away, the city's night lights twinkled, five red ones just visible at the epicenter of them all.

Andeyev's eyes fixed on the stark mounds of the Kremlin's forbidding protective wall, then moved to Red Square, the heart of an Empire that now straddled eleven time zones and covered fifteen percent of the world's land mass, dwarfing by far any that preceded it, even those of ancient Persia or Rome. None of which had been achieved through excessive reformist zeal or democratization or *glasnost,* he thought resentfully.

He turned away, and paced back toward the sitting area in front of the fireplace.

"Yes, it is," Andeyev agreed. He looked at Philby for confirmation as he spoke now. "I believe the Hand of Imam Group, ostensibly directing their move against a regular American target, will claim responsibility at six P.M. Beirut time on Wednesday, January 6th. Tomorrow."

Filatov looked puzzled. "Why six in the evening, just for interest?" he asked. "And why only after four days?"

Andeyev stared at Philby.

"Finesse." Philby smiled politely. "Six o'clock to catch all the evening news programs in Europe before spreading to America. And four days to rejuvenate what will already be an old story in the American mind after the normal three-day cycle these events get carried on American networks."

Twelve miles north of Lido Island—beyond the lush rolling green hills and stained picket fences of Newport Beach and the glitter of Fashion Island, past the lavish condominium estates and immaculate golf courses girdling the San Diego Creek—lies a sinister three-square-mile strip of flatland barricaded behind a twelve-foot fence of barbed wire. Surrounding it on three sides are small, benign-looking high-technology companies and larger, inevitably green-mirrored-glass high-rise buildings housing the corporate headquarters of huge international concerns that have made the district of Irvine one of the most expensive industrial properties in the United States. Beyond, the manicured greenery blends gradually into the old barren desert beneath Loma Ridge.

In stark contrast to this miniature urban enclave, the flat tract of land behind the barbed wire lies almost bare. It contains only a central pod, surrounded by mostly arid wasteland. In that middle, however, two massive airplane hangars loom—each the size of two football fields, each covered by an eerie lime-green Perspex dome. Circling this entire gargantuan structure is an immense helicopter pad large enough to accommodate over five hundred assault helicopters at any given moment.

The clear land around the central pod, inside the fence of the U.S. Marine Corps Helicopter Facilities, is deceptive, however. For that flat, fallow strip of desert that is presented as a reserve center for all the world to see is, in fact, cropped with mines, sensors, and an underground bunker grid. It is constantly monitored by high-resolution cameras that can see through rain, fog, sleet, hail, and snow, day or night. In short, it is a high-security compound. One that specializes solely in covert combat operations of the most modern kind: low-intensity warfare.

On its southern perimeter, across from Von Karman Avenue, at 2345 Barranca Road, the sign beside the fluttering Stars and Stripes on the three-story red-brick colonial building reads: U.S. ARMY—U.S. NAVY ARMED RESERVES. And indeed that harmless, even gracious-looking building is as it appears to be: a recruiting center. But it is also more. To get to its basement one needs the very highest military clearance. And there are two separate checkpoints manned by veteran marines to ensure no one tries to circumvent these requirements. Beyond those checkpoints there are two electronic doors—one at each end of the half-mile-long electric walkway that runs the length of the gray stucco tunnel beneath the wasteland from this building to the central pod area. Again, both these portals need visual and electronic clearances.

With the assistance of Colonel Rutland and the papers he provided, Nick Delan had cleared these checkpoints quickly. At the last of these Rutland had dropped off, turning him over to a marine escort. The two heavily armed soldiers had accompanied Delan to an elevator and guided him up to a suite of offices at the top of the northern hangar.

Now he stood and waited patiently, looking out of the one-way floor-to-ceiling green photochromic windows that make up the entire western wall. Twenty floors below, the huge heliport lay still, the countless helicopters perched silently like a swarm of dormant grasshoppers—coiled, waiting to spring.

None of this made any sense, Delan thought. It was unprofessional. In this line of work even the best-laid plans went awry, so there was certainly no room for rushed jobs. He thought of Naderi and Beirut again and the fundamental importance of that project. He was pleased with the key breakthroughs he had achieved and cursed the man who had brought him here. Besides which, he was tired. He had not slept. He had spent over seventeen hours traveling one way or another—and still Colonel James C. Rutland had insisted on getting started immediately.

"We have a ninety-minute drive and only two hours before the meeting," the Colonel had said. "So you better get your ass in gear."

It hadn't been more than ten minutes after Delan had entered the duplex suite at L'Ermitage Hotel when the Colonel, dressed in civilian clothes, had knocked on his door. Delan had had neither the will nor the inclination to argue. All he had felt was strong doubt about the conduct of his colleagues. Their sudden reck-lessness worried him. But he was also curious. Why this sudden flap? Why this serious breakdown in procedures and security? Were they aborting his sensitive mission?

During the drive down from Beverly Hills, twice Delan had tried to probe the Colonel for information. The second time Rutland had made it crystal-clear it was a useless effort.

"Listen, Colonel," he had said in his southern drawl, addressing Delan by his military rank. "I sure wouldn't tell you if I knew. But I don't. All I know is that it comes from the top. And I don't even know how far up it is. What I do know is this: you're meeting with the Deputy National Security Adviser. Whether it goes any further I sure wouldn't know."

"Anthony Boyle?"

"He's flying out from Washington."

This was insane, Delan had thought. The Activity was a private network. Deep-cover. It was not supposed to have *any* official con-tact. Ever. That was the first of its so-called "ten commandments." Every one of which was basic to its survival.

As for the Deputy National Security Adviser, why the hell was he acting like this? What could possibly have happened? It sure wasn't in keeping with the character Delan remembered. His mind drifted back in time, back to their first encounter in Vietnam:

"Captain Delan?"

He turned in the mess-hall doorway.

"Major." He saluted informally at the figure mounting the wooden steps.

"You probably don't remember me," said the tall, robust, smartly tailored man with a friendly grin. "The last time we met, I was on a stretcher."

Delan had forced a smile. Unfortunately he did remember. It was some-thing he would carry with him for the rest of his life.

"You look far better standing up, Major."

"It must have something to do with being alive."

There had been a brief, strained silence before Delan decided the meeting must be over.

"Good to see you on your feet again, Major," he said, turning to go.

"Captain Delan?" The taller man reached out and caught his arm lightly.

"I'm up here at Quang Tri for the day. I thought I'd use the opportunity to thank you personally for saving my life."

"Glad we found you in time."

"I also wanted to tell you that I've recommended you be put up for the Congressional Medal of Honor."

Delan thought: *Four men, four widows, five fatherless children.* He said: *"Is that necessary?"*

"Captain, not only did you save two lives at grave risk to yourself, but some of the intelligence we managed to get back to MACV headquarters in Saigon was critical." The Major paused. *"I know about your buddies, Captain. But that intelligence has saved God knows how many hundreds of American lives."*

Delan nodded joylessly. He stole a glance at the man's name tag.

"Care for some lunch, Major Boyle? I sure could do with some good news and you have a cheery disposition."

In the years immediately following the war they'd kept in constant touch. Whenever Delan visited Washington, Anthony Boyle would always squeeze in a lunch or dinner, no matter how busy his schedule. Often, when the interlude between such visits stretched too long, Boyle would call Delan just to "touch base" and maintain contact. But slowly, and perhaps inevitably, given the different paths they traveled and the fundamentally opposite nature of their characters, the intervals began to stretch until Christmas cards sparked an occasional telephone call by one or the other of them. The last time they had actually met had been in Fayetteville, North Carolina—just over three years ago.

A small, dark speck in the balmy orange glow of the western sky snapped Delan's attention back to the present. How much had Anthony Boyle changed in the last three years? Power and success tend to alter a man, and not, as a rule, for the better. What was he like now? Or perhaps, better yet, what the hell was he after?

Steadily the fly-sized speck grew larger. To a bee, to a bird, to a dark-olive Sikorsky UH-60 Blackhawk helicopter. It descended slowly, drifting menacingly above the bumper-to-bumper rush-hour traffic on Route 55, the Costa Mesa Freeway.

Nick Delan looked at his watch. It was 4:58 P.M. At least Tony Boyle was still punctual.

The large transport helicopter breezed lower, a cloud of dust spewing in its trail as it glided over the barbed-wire fence and across the desert sand toward the heliport. Its alarming, rhythmic roar grew ever louder as it floated sideways, dropping slowly until it touched down.

Nick Delan smiled nostalgically as a tall, powerfully built man appeared in the doorway and adroitly negotiated the assault stairs. He restrained himself from the instinctive reaction of the average person—ducking beneath the rotor blades churning three feet overhead. Instead he held his hat firm with his left hand, a briefcase in his right, as he walked briskly away from the swelling tornado, looking neither left nor right.

Behind him another man followed. A tall, slim man with silver hair who also carried a case in his right hand. His was much larger, though. It was square and new and black.

Delan squinted. The document bag seemed to be affixed to something.

A chain.

A chain that was attached to the man's hand.

The large Queen Anne house buried off Butterfly Lane in Elstree, just north of London, stood dark and lifeless. The gentle glimmer of the quarter moon in the cloudless sky shimmered through the tall, thick trees that surrounded it, highlighting the immaculate slate tiles of its roof and its white-painted trimmings.

Below, a curved gravel driveway extended into the depths of the woods on either side of the house. A gray moat separated the mansion from manicured front lawns that sloped away toward a small natural pond, the stables, and the rectory in the fields beyond. All sparkled with dew beneath the bright moonlight. And all stood serene, tranquil, a great country manor reposed.

A quarter of a mile away, the powerful headlights of a dark-green Rover 800 swung right on Aldenham Road and glided gently to a stop at the gates of the estate. To one side of the black wrought-iron bars blocking the car's path the simple wooden sign, half hidden in the bushes, read: PINE MANOR.

As the electric gates began to part slowly, the friendly, moon-faced guard in a dark-blue private uniform waved in the car from behind the thick window of a small, half-hidden guardhouse.

Speeding again toward the manor house, the Rover shattered the nocturnal silence as its wide, heavy-duty tires crunched against the gravel. Immediately, dark-uniformed figures appeared, silent, furtive silhouettes looming in the shadows on the borders of the rectory and the woods. Several of them held back large black dogs straining at the end of a leash.

In the background now there was a chorus of quacking and flapping wings from the flock of geese on the pond at the end of the front lawn. Geese, with their acute hearing and nervous disposition, are regarded as among the most sophisticated, dependable, and economic of all sentinels. Especially by those with a need for discretion in their security.

When the driver of the car slid his vehicle to a stop at the steps of the manor house, two passengers disembarked just as the carriage lights on either side of the front door came alive. The third passenger, an older man, emerged more slowly. As the driver held the door ajar, the other two men stood waiting. When the last man had joined them, they followed him at the surprisingly fast clip he set, his determined gait digging into the tiny stones, crunching them beneath his feet.

Unlike the others, the tall, elderly man wore no coat. Despite the sharp chill in the night air, he sported only a thick, brownish Harris tweed jacket, with dark-leather elbow patches, and cavalry twills above his polished dark-brown ankle boots. His shock of silver hair was cropped closely at the sides; his refined if weatherbeaten face sported a smile of permanent courtesy. The smile combined with his archaic round wire spectacles to reflect a particularly polite, resigned, timid look. The regard of an experienced and worldly man, with an infinite capacity for patience.

As the three men approached the bottom of the sandstone steps, the door of the mansion opened. And out stepped a British Army sergeant-major in full dress blues.

The tall, elderly Englishman modestly acknowledged the stiff, unmoving figure and raised his right hand a mite in answer to the man's military salute. He strode past, entering the majestic oak-paneled lobby whose high ceiling extended up past the first-floor railings. As he entered, a young man dressed in a white tunic and flanked by two assistants stood ready to greet him.

"Colonel Stuart-Menteath," said the younger man, shaking his hand rather hurriedly. "I'm Dr. Dai Davis. Sorry to drag you out here at this ungodly hour, but it's rather urgent, I'm afraid."

"Don't mention it, my dear man."

"Just the same," the doctor said, clasping his hands together. "Rotten hour. Just hope neither of your colleagues is very squeamish. What you are about to see is not a very pretty sight."

We want you to take him out . . .

The words reverberated in Nick Delan's mind. They etched into every cell before moving down to knot in his stomach and pound in his heart.

He squinted at the man sitting beside him at the vast conference table.

"Allan Sanford?" he asked in a raspy whisper of disbelief.

The Deputy National Security Adviser stared at him impassively for a moment; then he nodded almost apologetically.

"Yes."

Take him out . . .

Innocuous war-game talk. Pentagon language. It was called murder in polite circles: assassination. This was madness. Boyle was nuts.

Adrenaline surged through Delan's body, carrying with it suspicion and fear, vigilance and mistrust. But it also held a tiny hint of excitement—that invigorating, almost sensual chill of danger that he had always found so enticing.

But life had rules, he thought. It was all ratios and percentages and angles. Winning demanded judgment, discipline, timing. Not feelings or emotions.

Boyle was painting a lethal scenario. It was a minefield. If the second rule of combat was to know your opponent, then the first was to identify your friends.

"Why me?"

"You're AISA," replied Boyle, leaning forward to rest his elbows on the shiny table top.

"So are seventy other people, give or take a few."

The tall, distinguished Presidential Adviser looked at Delan gravely. "Because you're the best."

"Oh, come on, Tony." Delan grimaced. "You can do better than that. This isn't a beauty contest. There are a dozen or more outfits at your command better geared to this type of action than us. Christ, we're classified under Clandestine Military Intelligence, slash, Surgical Combat Specialists. Not assassins."

"That's true, Nick. But the Soviets have isolated an enormous weakness in our retaliatory capability with this scheme. They have hit a nerve that effectively leaves us with very few choices."

"Why?"

"Two reasons," Boyle replied honestly as he stood and started walking slowly around the Situation Room. "One as sound as the other. First, every other available instrument at our disposal has an unacceptably high leak potential. The more conventional the approach—if there were such a thing as a conventional assassination—the larger and more comprehensive the organization would have to be. That means people, layers, bureaucracy. We just can't risk it.

"Second," Boyle continued, his hands buried deep in his trouser pockets, "is capability. Capability as in flexibility and versatility. AISA is the sole organization with acceptable levels of secrecy, autonomy, and expertise. It's also the only truly deep-cover strike force the United States Government has at its disposal. The other agencies—military or intelligence—are on the books, for a start. They're also too structured, too formal, hampered either by interservice coordination problems or divided commands or both. And/or they're too severely restricted by mandatory Congressional disclosure requirements to be effective instruments for an operation as delicate as this. They'd be incapable of handling something on this order of magnitude with the required nimbleness."

Boyle turned at the far end of the antiseptic conference room. Behind him, the usual string of official portraits adorned the wall.

"That's why we turned to AISA," he concluded. "And to you, Nick. According to the machines, you're the best man we've got."

Delan toyed with the corner of his right eye. Boyle was lying. Or being flattering. Which was always one and the same thing. The Army had far more experienced secret soldiers, special-operation-forces men, at its disposal. For a start there were all the former Delta Force men, the Army's 1st Special Forces Operational Detachment, conceived as the nation's primary antiterrorist strike force that had been the harbinger of AISA.

Every instinct in Delan's body—reflexes honed in all the various theaters he had survived in his life: from the ghettos of Chicago to the jungles of Indochina and El Salvador, from the theoretical and educational competitiveness of Northwestern University to the rough-and-tumble world of college football—all decreed caution.

And yet still the exquisite chill remained—the thrill that the cutting edge of danger always aroused in him.

He sighed heavily. "I'm already on an assignment, as I'm sure you know. What you may not be aware of, or perhaps don't fully appreciate, is that I've just made a breakthrough. And after a hell of a long time at that." Delan paused. "Unless I'm very much mistaken, the infiltration of the Islamic Jihad movement is still a primary goal of ours, isn't it?"

"Not as primary as having a President that is ours," Boyle snapped back. "Contact your man. Get him off your back. Tell him . . . tell him . . . hell, tell him anything but buy yourself a couple of weeks."

"With all due respect, Tony," said Delan, forcing a sudden rasp to his voice, "I still think you've come to the wrong address. Neither I, nor anyone else I know in AISA, is psychologically equipped for this assignment. Basically we're military men; soldiers motivated in another direction."

He paused, throwing off a hard look. "What you need is a nut. With a strong self-destructive streak. Maybe you should try the CIA; they're more experienced in that line of work."

On the opposite side of the brightly lit conference table, Anthony Boyle stopped in midstride. He turned slowly and looked at Delan, his haggard eyes strained and weary.

"We don't have that kind of time."

Delan frowned in puzzlement.

"It would take too long," Boyle explained. "The brainwashing process takes anywhere from six to twelve months or more."

The perplexed look on Delan's face deepened.

"I'm no expert on this. But as I understand it there are essentially only four known impetuses that can be effectively exploited in the brainwashing process," Boyle explained. "Other than fear and the more exotic and less reliable things like hypnosis and drugs. MICE, they call it. Money. Ideology. Compromise. Ego. Even if the Agency had a potential candidate with the right psychopathic makeup ready on hand, and even if that candidate had the precise required mental makeup and/or motivation levels in one or more of these areas, it would take six months to a year or more before we could be certain that he or she was fully primed."

Nick Delan pursed his lips as he shook his head forlornly. "How long do you have, Tony?"

"Let's see now," said Boyle looking at his watch. "It's the fifth of January. Eleven days."

Delan's eyes snapped toward the presidential adviser.

"That's the drop-dead time," Boyle explained, using military jargon. "We believe that Allan Sanford will officially declare his candidacy in exactly twelve days."

"What difference does that make?"

"For one thing, increased security. Once a major candidate declares, he automatically qualifies for Secret Service protection."

Delan nodded slowly, an understanding grimace spreading across his face.

"I guess that makes sense. But the rest of it sure as hell doesn't. This sort of thing requires time; it needs meticulous planning."

"Yes," the Deputy National Security Adviser replied slowly. "But first we need a volunteer. The rest is somewhat easier to arrange."

"Don't bet on that," Delan said harshly. "Planning covert operations has never exactly been our forte."

"Maybe not," Boyle snapped. "But we had better get this one right."

Delan looked at the man whose life he'd once saved and suddenly felt a great deal of sympathy. The old Anthony Boyle he'd known and befriended in their military days had been a very strong personality, cool and immensely confident under pressure. The figure standing before him now was an older man, burdened with responsibility, exhausted, frustrated, unsure. And with good reason, perhaps. If the Soviet defector was not a bogus plant of some kind; if this man Pavlenko had not been injected into the mainstream of American intelligence to confuse or entrap in some carefully calculated Machiavellian scheme—then Anthony Boyle had much to worry about. The perceived threat was real. Very real. And the anxiety he reflected was entirely justified. What's more, if the scenario Boyle had painted was real, then the Deputy National Security Adviser had a point. The Activity *was* the only viable alternative. The most reliable and covert arm at the government's disposal.

Delan stood and walked slowly toward Boyle. Still, he thought, it was a treacherous course that this man was proposing.

He stopped beside his friend at the huge windows framing the Californian dusk.

"What would it take to sway you?" Boyle asked quietly.

Delan cast his eyes downward. Twenty floors below, the swarm of helicopters languished on the massive asphalt, their shadows elongating eerily as twilight descended.

"Proof, Tony," he said softly at length. "Unmitigated proof."

Anthony Boyle turned slowly until he faced Delan. For a long moment his tired brown eyes stared at Delan, silently, intently. Then he nodded cautiously as he backed away and turned, his pace picking up with each step he took in the opposite direction. At the far end of the room he opened the dark-wood door.

"Would you come in now, please," he said, looking to his left.

Delan felt his heart skip a beat the instant he recognized the figure entering the room. It was the man he had seen earlier, the silver-haired figure who had followed Boyle out of the jet helicopter a little while ago. Now, as then, he held a large square black document bag in his right hand. And it was chained to his wrist, just as it had been before.

"Nick. I want you to meet James Cassidy."

"Medically speaking, there's no reason why he should still be alive," said Dr. Dai Davis cheerfully as he accompanied Stuart-Menteath along the oak-paneled corridor on the first floor.

"How much longer do you think he has?"

"Not long, now. A few more hours at the most. We've exhausted the possibilities, I'm afraid. It's a miracle he's survived this far."

"Oh. Has he mentioned my name again?"

"Yes. Every time he becomes compos mentis that's about all he gurgles before slipping off again."

"Well, we'll just have to see what he wants," Stuart-Menteath said calmly. "Probably has something or other he wants to get off his chest."

"Wouldn't doubt it if that is all that's keeping him alive. There's a sort of desperation when he hisses your name." Dr. Davis grimaced. "Of course, it could be the pain."

"Banged up, is he?"

"There's hardly a thing left. Only a torso and head; and not much of those, actually."

"Have you been able to determine yet what the other thing he keeps repeating is?"

"Not for certain. The technical fellows were up to record his mumblings to play around with the speed or something. They'll get in touch with us as soon as they can. Ah, here we are," the doctor said, indicating a room. Two military policemen in full dress came to attention on either side of the double doors.

"Oh, just one thing before we go in," Stuart-Menteath said, raising his right arm to touch the younger man's elbow, stopping him. He made no effort to speak softly, out of earshot from the guards. "I should like to be in there alone while we speak, if you wouldn't mind, doctor."

"Certainly, Colonel," Dr. Davis replied, not quite able to disguise his disappointment.

"Most kind of you."

The two men entered the room. To his left a bank of monitoring machines sat against one wall. The rest of the large room, however, looked more like a well-tended and frequently used guest room in a dowdy country house. Two well-worn high-back wooden armchairs flanked a mahogany chest of drawers which faced a large Edwardian wardrobe sitting across the floor. The curtains were chintz, of autumnal hues backed by a heavy lining.

Three green-masked nurses monitored the screens and dials on the machines. Crisply dressed in starched gray uniforms and white-linen caps trimmed in rose, they were Queen Alexandra Nurses, or QAs as they're called in the Army, where their training included the somewhat more demanding needs of the military. One of them, a plump, middle-aged woman with a most severe demeanor, flourished a clipboard with gusto as she swooped around the space.

In the very center of the room was situated a large chrome hospital bed. Covered in by a clear plastic dome, it had several oxygen cylinders at its foot and any number of tubes of different sizes running in. One intravenous infusion on a drip stand fed the body plasma to replace the constant loss of blood being sucked away by a thicker one beneath. Another pumped in a saline solution to rehydrate the invalid. Mixed in with it was a small quantity of Narcan, a respiratory stimulant, and albumin, a protein solution used for shock, severe bleeding, and burns. The tentacles of a urinary catheter and a cardiac monitor were also apparent.

John Stuart-Menteath peered at the hyperbaric chamber as he approached the bed slowly. In its center a short stump of a body lay—motionless. No hands, no arms, no legs, it was a gruesome sight. What little was left of the mutilated figure appeared contorted, too, deformed even further by yards of two-and-a-half-inch clear-plastic bandage that was stained dark red and appeared squishy in many parts.

Stuart-Menteath beckoned Dr. Davis closer.

"Do you think I might take a look at him?" he whispered in the doctor's ear once he stood beside Stuart-Menteath.

"It wouldn't be of much use, I'm afraid. He has third-degree burns on his entire body. Which means he's shriveled and charred where he isn't blistered or bloated."

"Even the eyes?"

"Particularly the eyes."

Stuart-Menteath nodded, his bushy white eyebrows twisting gravely. He walked forward slowly, his face no longer impassive. At the tent he gazed at the bandages as if his eyes held the power to bore through the crinkled plastic, to focus through the distortion they created. He stood for a long moment, still, quiet, full of concentration. Then slowly he unzipped the hyperbaric tent and bent down and in, close to where the head rested. Behind him Dr. Davis motioned the nurses out of the room before following them.

"My name," Stuart-Menteath whispered, softly but with some authority, "is John Stuart-Menteath. I understand you wish to speak to me."

The wrinkled clear-plastic bandages across the patient's upper torso strained slightly as his chest expanded.

11 | WEDNESDAY, JANUARY 6

From his perch above Newport Beach Nick Delan trained the lightweight but powerful trimode general-purpose binoculars across Lido Channel. Allan Sanford turned off his bedroom lights.

Unfortunately, the proof had been conclusive. It convicted the poor innocent man he was now watching. And it did so without a shadow of a doubt.

Even a cursory glance through James Cassidy's documents, computer printouts, and facsimile sheets was alarming. Let alone all the additional data that flashed onto the screen patched in to CIA headquarters in Virginia. With every question from Delan, Cassidy's nimble fingers, playing on the computer keyboard, elicited a response from Langley. Each was more damning than the last.

Still Nick Delan had been unwilling to commit himself without further study, without more proof. Despite the fact that in the end Boyle had given Delan only twenty-four hours to make up his mind, yesterday he'd spent fifteen of those hours diligently going through all the material Cassidy provided. Then he turned his attention to the mound of supporting documents he'd requested, analyzing and scouring for one hint of a flaw in the evidence.

But to no avail. Ultimately there was only one conclusion that could be reached: no matter how unprecedented the operation was, no matter how unorthodox, illegal, and potentially explosive, it was the only realistic option available. And it necessarily followed that he was one of only a handful of operators capable of carrying out such a mission. All of which meant Delan didn't really have a choice. Neither did Washington. Anthony Boyle was being on the level. Washington really needed Nick Delan.

Even worse, the more Delan studied the documents, the more this conclusion was confirmed. The case against the man he was now watching solidified with each page: from NSA intercepts of recent conversations between Allan Sanford's top adviser and a shadowy Swiss lawyer named Claude Bernard, to thirty years of financial transactions that on close scrutiny made no pragmatic business sense. In addition, there were documents hinting at a sordid tale of anonymous political contributions, payoffs, and intrigue. Most of this had an international connection, one that brought into play a dizzying array of murky offshore companies, bearer shares, and cash transactions.

The final damning touch was the Pavlenko transcript—a document whose authenticity was beyond doubt, coming from a deputy director of the KGB.

Delan's eyes followed Sanford—the binoculars still operating on normal vision—down the well-lit stairs and into the ground-floor living room. He heard the jingle of ice and the gurgle of bourbon intrude on George Benson's rich voice in the background.

The one-inch-long, pencil-thin, high-sensitivity directional microphone, capable of pinpointing a specific sound while filtering out background noises, extended from the side of the binoculars. The sounds it plucked were being received on the SSB band of a normal Sony ICF-2001D FM/AM PLL synthesized radio. On a sound-magnification scale of one to ten the arrow on the microphone attached to the binoculars—that in the vernacular of the trade are called the penetrator—stood at two, meaning its capabilities were hardly even being tested.

Delan twisted the lens of the penetrator fractionally, and watched and heard Allan Sanford add some more ice to the glass and then walk out onto the small veranda fronting his house. Now he stood contentedly, looking directly up at Delan's fourth-floor suite—or at least at the twinkling night-lights of the Balboa Bay Club where Delan was staying. The sprawling building lay a little over one hundred yards away directly across the smooth, shiny surface of Lido Channel.

Delan flicked the switch on the penetrator to thermal vision.

The concept of thermal, or heat-seeking, vision is rooted in the principle that all matter (above zero degrees) emits thermal energy. A fair portion of this heat is absorbed and scattered by atmospheric conditions. But certain wavelength bands are more receptive since the atmospheric distortion, or attenuation, along those paths is relatively low. These atmospheric windows reflect the peak temperatures of objects: from the 450° C heat output of a running engine—to the 20° C warmth exuded by a clothed human body. The different degrees of heat emitted are reflected through thermal vision devices exactly as the colors of the spectrum are seen in the concentric bands of a rainbow: the heat is measured by the intensity of the colors running from the colder beams of violet and indigo, through to blue, green, yellow, orange, and finally red.

Thus a human body under normal conditions generally appears as logic would dictate: from the violet and blue hues of the outer skin and much of the limbs to the yellow and orange glows inside the torso. Burning red appears only at the most vital parts: the kidneys, intestines, heart, brain, liver, and sexual organs.

Through the walls of Allan Sanford's house three other figures came at Delan. In a constantly moving kaleidoscope of colored squares—depicting the heat emitted by various objects—the outlines of two women appeared behind the wall of another bedroom on the second floor. They were dressing.

"That's a gorgeous dress," said a girl's voice on Delan's receiver. She had a French accent and long hair that bounced in a neon powder-blue through the goggles. Delan could not distinguish her features. But he could make out both the young ladies' shapes. They were statuesque.

"Thank you," replied an American accent. Her hair was cut short, almost like a man's, and it came through the binoculars in a baby-blue color that made it even more exotic.

"What is it?"

"Alaïa."

"Azzedine Alaïa? The best. Let me see it. Turn around."

The short-haired girl swiveled on the ball of her left foot—a swirl of changing colors through the binoculars. Her dress was so diaphanous that it barely diluted the multicolored thermal lights outlining her body. The different colors of heat, flowing from her organs and the surface of her skin, glowed straight through it—unaffected.

"Fabulous," said the French girl. "But it would look even better without underwear, darling. It ruins the lines."

The blue- and mauve-colored lights of her arm reached out and caressed her friend's purple buttocks. "Look."

Nick Delan pursed his lips and smiled; but he turned the penetrator away: he had other things on his mind.

Delan flicked the switch on the penetrator again, not to normal vision but to night vision this time. But he was careful to turn to the image-intensification mode, which employs available light, magnifying the particles of light that nearly always exist even in the darkest environment by twenty-five thousand times. He purposely avoided the infrared capability the binoculars held. Since infrared is a low-frequency, invisible beam of light, it is detectable by other infrared devices if not by the human eye. And that was an unnecessary and unacceptable risk given the riskfree capabilities he had.

He moved the lenses back to the figure on the veranda.

Allan Sanford had disappeared. Delan scanned the bridle path that twisted around the island, between the narrow strip of sandy beach and the luxurious residences. To the left, he followed the dimly lit path for a hundred yards. But even in the near daylight of the glasses there was no one. Instead a sign attached to a fence caught his eye. It read: DO NOT BEWARE OF DOG. BEWARE OF OWNER OF DOG.

Cute son of a bitch, thought Delan, as he swiveled back to monitor the right side of the building. Abruptly he stopped: Allan Sanford appeared from behind some bushes in front of his house. He was toying with the petals of some flowers.

Delan studied the familiar handsome features of the former actor—tinged, as is the way of night vision, in a murky lime-green. Was it really possible this man was being duped? Was it conceivable that for thirty years this exceptionally gifted manipulator of public emotions had himself been manipulated?

Why not? Show business and professional sports—to name the most glaring fields—were replete with stories of idols, people who had made fortunes, ending up on skid row. Usually compliments of unscrupulous business associates. Besides, how many people ever questioned success? Especially their own success. It was only failures who were prone to self-scrutiny. As his empire grew, Sanford came to rely more and more on one man—a lawyer by the name of Phillip Myers. And that, in essence, according to the documents Anthony Boyle had collected, was the root cause of Allan Sanford's problems.

The overexpansion and resultant liquidity problems that plagued Sanford's empire during the reign of the previous chief executive of Sanford Enterprises could not be halted in time. Investments flopped, a huge hotel project in Hawaii proved catastrophic, Sanford's record company—a gold mine only two years earlier—suddenly lurched heavily into the red. Even where others were succeeding effortlessly, Allan Sanford's projects failed.

In addition, all this occurred at a time when the unimaginable happened: the public was no longer flocking to see the latest Allan Sanford movies. His career—as he underwent the always tenuous transition from young hero types to more mature character roles—was on a sharp decline. In two years, from 1961 to 1963, four Allan Sanford films were disasters at the box office. And suddenly Allan Sanford was in serious financial trouble. An empire that had assets of over thirty-five million dollars in 1958 was on the skids. Even worse, outside funding for new films proved harder and harder to raise and so abruptly windfall revenues stopped flowing in. Only the pittance from residuals remained to support a high-rolling lifestyle and a retinue of hangers-on.

Nick Delan raised his glasses, flicking them to normal vision: the young girls were nearly ready, putting on the final touches before a full-length mirror. He could see them clearly now through the bedroom's picture window. He zoomed the lenses forward by pressing the side button, focusing on the shapely, short-haired girl's face. She was a mulatto girl with sensuous high cheekbones and moist, pouting, generous lips shaped like a flattened heart. Her eyelashes were long and heavy, giving her young face a mystic look. Delan lowered the binoculars to her breasts. Then to her thighs. Neither held the slightest trace of underwear now.

He smiled as he lingered on the scene and turned the binoculars away reluctantly, switching to thermal vision again. The kaleidoscope of colored squares swept through ever-changing shapes and hues. Delan turned the instrument off, slipped the leather sling off his neck, and walked to the bar in his comfortable modern suite. As he mixed a Scotch and water on the rocks, his thoughts turned to Phillip Myers.

It was at that crucial juncture in Allan Sanford's life that the man who was rapidly becoming his right hand, Phillip Myers, had worked his first miracle. He'd found an anonymous group in Switzerland looking for short-term tax losses. The group was not only willing to invest in Sanford, they were willing to do so on a multimillion-dollar package of films. In return they sought not altogether intolerable conditions: a first option of up to thirty-three percent on any Allan Sanford undertaking in the future (for which they would make commensurate or proportional payments toward capitalization requirements on a project-by-project basis); given the traditional conflicting needs of artistic and commercial considerations, that Phillip Myers be entrusted with arbitration rights on behalf of both parties should the need arise; that hereinafter the accounting company Sanford Enterprises would retain be a small, conservative, well-respected firm with its headquarters in Palo Alto but with branches and affiliations all over the world, including a large office in Zurich.

It was at about this time, too, according to the FBI documents Boyle had provided, that J. Edgar Hoover's eager antennae began picking up hot gossip about Allan Sanford's extracurricular activities. And the man who catered to these prolific sexual needs: the versatile, ubiquitous Mr. Myers was, it seemed, a man for all seasons.

But just how versatile and ubiquitous was not absolutely evident. Not back then, anyway.

Nor was it fully evident in 1977 when a scandal was fortuitously avoided. In fact few people even believed the testimony of the former Mann's Chinese Theater usherette, a voluptuous twenty-two-year-old Iowa lass, who made wild accusations about being "outraged at discovering a film, surreptitiously taken," of her exploits in bed with Allan Sanford.

Alas, the girl was found to be a heroin addict. Who not only had a history of such hallucinations, but overdosed in a dingy West Hollywood motel just two weeks after her ravings.

Delan picked up the penetrator. Was it possible? he asked himself again as he walked toward the windows. Was this man really as innocent as he appeared to be? Just another princely figure totally blinded by ambition and greed? He would not be the first such animal who aspired to the White House—and made it.

Delan raised the binoculars and peered through them across the waterway. The girls were about ready: one still stood at the mirror rubbing the rouge a little lighter on her cheeks, while the other stood beside the open door, waiting. They were both obviously stunning. And very young indeed.

One thought stirred another, and suddenly a picture of Clio Bragana entered his head. He missed her.

The girls were heading down the stairs. With the penetrator, Delan followed them, his mind five thousand six hundred miles away, running a montage of Paris in slow motion—with Clio's smiling face superimposed over the passing scenes.

The low whistle coming over the speaker snapped him out of his reverie. He concentrated on the happy smile crossing Allan Sanford's face at the sight of the two girls.

"Wow, you look terrific," Sanford said with all the sincerity of an Academy Award winner. "Both of you."

The girls smiled.

Despite all his reservations, Delan felt a strange empathy for the man he was watching. For, he thought, it was essentially on that Monday, the twentieth of January nineteen sixty-four, when a desperate Allan Sanford had so unwittingly signed that agreement with a Swiss consortium—a day that Allan Sanford had rejoiced at as a turning point in his life—that he had signed his own death warrant. The rest—all of it—was just icing on the cake. For the men who came for drinks that night had planned all along to stay the night.

Delan lowered the binoculars, perturbed.

It was only today, though, that the executioner for that death warrant had been appointed.

Twenty-five miles east of the Moscow ring-road, deep in the dense pine forests off Gofkovskoye Shosse, stands a vast thirty-square-mile compound known simply as *D'e'vachka Adee'n.*

The black Zil limousine sped along the narrow black-top lane toward the picture-postcard mirage in the heart of this snowbound wooded tract. Inside, a single passenger occupied the lush burgundy suede rear seat.

Two billboards loomed ahead, one on each side of the road. The vehicle slowly decreased its speed. The elderly passenger ignored the red type on a white background. The stark Cyrillic letters were indelibly branded in his mind: HALT! NO TRESPASSING! FORBIDDEN ZONE!

The vehicle rolled to a complete stop at the orange-striped steel barrier that spanned the lane. Two KGB officers, in uniforms and greatcoats bearing the distinctive green piping of the elite Border Guards, approached the vehicle. Several others observed, partially hidden behind the snow-covered bunkers on either side of the road.

Not a word was said. The driver showed his pass, and the sturdy barrier was raised. The long black limousine started up again, lumbering down the narrow forest lane. It proceeded slowly, however, adhering strictly to the prominent signs that read: WARNING! DO NOT EXCEED 30 KPH! VISUAL AND RADAR CONTROL IN EFFECT!

As always, General Kim Philby felt a tinge of excitement at the thought of what lay ahead. *D'e'vachka Adee'n* was, after all, his brainchild. What had started off as a small spark in his brain so many years ago would in all likelihood be his only legacy. Suddenly he recalled something he'd once read. "The only thing you can take with you is what you leave behind in this world."

This was what he was leaving behind—*D'e'vachka Adee'n*. And it was a worthy bequest. One that said far more about him—far more truth—than anything he had ever read about himself. The drivel was never-ending, as well. Even now a spate of new rumors were circulating once again in the West—sparked by the premiere of yet another new play in London's West End pretending to analyze the motives of a band of young men nearly half a century ago.

The publicity, no doubt, would sell some tickets. But how the Brits loved to delude themselves. "Poor Philby wouldn't half-love to return." "Poor Philby, who's he got to talk to?" "Poor Philby's short on Glenlivet." "Poor Philby still gets his books from Hatchards." If it weren't so arrogant it would be funny. Did they really think he found their company and their decrepit society so scintillating? Most of the blighters he knew couldn't afford their Travellers and Reform Club dues anymore unless they went off and became some decorative puppet in the city.

The truth, he supposed, was difficult to accept. He'd done that which had to be done. That which he had felt. And he'd never regretted it, not for a single day. But it made much better copy to go on about his Oedipus complex, his stammer, his drinking, the neglected childhood and hatred of his father. Poor old pa, getting it in the neck for what Kim had done. Mind you, pa was a bit odd. Even now, he couldn't forgive the old man for foisting onto the family some half-Arab siblings.

Still, for the Brits it represented complete ignorance of his worldview to assume that he could not make a rational decision without some dark force from his family background guiding him over a supposed precipice. They simply did not comprehend the workings of history.

The sting of bitterness perked him up. Besides, it was incredible how much damage one could create in Whitehall with just a little mischief. A few strategic words to a Sunday paper and all the old wounds were open again. The same old tortuous discussions and guilts and incriminations began anew. Imagine, he thought, the havoc this little foray would cause. Suddenly he felt a renewed sense of determination take hold. *D'e'vachka*, where his authority was unquestioned. As the nerve center of this now doubly complicated mission, it offered him security. Complete security and absolute control.

A high chainlink fence flashed by suddenly, breaking his thoughts. It was topped by razor-sharp accordion wire and swept by remote-control cameras. They whirred in three-hundred-and-sixty-degree circles, turning at exactly six degrees per second in a confusion of directions. Below the wide-angle lenses, spaced at fifty-yard intervals for as far as the eye could see, signs hung from the wire mesh. The sharp red letters read: HIGH-VOLTAGE ELECTRIC FENCE! TURN BACK! FORBIDDEN ZONE!

The Zil stopped at the elaborate security post that was the road's end. Kim Philby did not wait for his gaunt young driver, who scurried to open the rear door. Gingerly he alighted, adjusted his furry astrakhan hat, and breathed in the crisp wintry air. The scent of the pine trees always elated him on trips out here, no matter how frequently he came. Before heading toward the guardhouse to the left, he buried his hands deep in his fur-lined duffle coat.

He looked around as he walked, the arctic cold forcing tears to his eyes. It was amazing what one could accomplish with a little imagination and initiative.

Philby opened the door marked SCIENTIFIC RESEARCH CENTER/SECURITY CLEARANCE. He ignored the stiffness that seemed to descend suddenly on the burly uniformed men in the antiseptic guard room.

"Zdrah'stvooit'e tavah'reeshch," he murmured in answer to their salutes.

A short, stocky captain, all eyebrows and lips, stepped forward quickly.

"Do'broye oo'tro, General Philby," he said obsequiously. *"Pazhah'lsta. Pazhah'lsta,"* he repeated, sweeping his hand toward the heavy security door on the other side of the room.

Philby smiled affably as he headed toward it. A soft buzzer sounded briefly, unlocking the metal door. The old man waited as the captain pulled back the heavy steel door. Then he stepped out and entered the time machine he had created.

"Where to, buddy?" the American cabbie in the front taxi asked through the open window of his idling yellow Pontiac.

The two girls kissed.

Softly at first, as if their lips were dainty, like the fragile veins of autumn leaves. It was a touch full of tenderness; and perhaps uncertainty. Then slowly it turned wicked; the uncertainty gave way to sin. Their mouths crushed against each other, their tongues entwining in a combat long and cruel.

Nick Delan zoomed the lenses on the binoculars fractionally. He peered out across the dark, moonlit bay, through two walls and into the guest cloakroom in Sanford's house a hundred yards away. The penetrator's thermal lights outlining their mounting body heat flickered, each color rising a notch. Their lips became hotter, turning from yellow to amber; the searing blood pumping through their orange hearts darkened to red. The surge of changing colors descended, too, pooling in their loins in an amalgam of reds and golds. Then the lighting started cooling off again, gradually running back down through all the colors of the spectrum to the cooler blues and violets of the limbs.

Gently, amorously, the French girl caressed the mulatto's face. She stroked her sharp, high cheekbones and then slowly moved her hand down until her fingers outlined April's thick, hot, parted lips. They collected moisture from her open mouth and cooled the golden color on her lips. Silently, sensuously, her index finger taunted the girl with silent promises of forbidden dreams.

"Let's have another line," she purred.

The twinkling thermal colors of the mulatto's slim but curvaceous torso stepped back from their embrace. She nodded the orange lights of her head bashfully, even as her purple outline tottered a little on her unsteady feet.

Jacquie Petit turned and extracted the cocaine paraphernalia from her bag. The colors of her fuller body, too, were hotter than they had been—but nowhere near as hot as the heat engulfing April's frame.

"It's great shit, isn't it, April?" she asked in her attractive French accent, her voice coming through clearly on the small receiver in Delan's room. She placed the dark-blue outlines of what looked like a small, square mirror, a short straw, and a file on the cooler, deep-purple marble counter surrounding the two washbasins.

"I've never had anything so good. But why does it look like that?" April asked, regaining her composure.

Jacquie held up a Ping-Pong ball–sized lump of mauve.

"Direct from Leticia, *chérie*. It's one hundred percent pure."

"Wow, that must have cost a fortune, Jacquie. Where do you get it?"

"A friend."

Jacquie turned and the neon blue contours of her arms started filing the lump of cocaine.

That girl is carnal, Nick Delan observed. A predator, dominating and devouring. Relentless, too. Much to the delight of Allan Sanford, who, throughout the evening, had been more than content playing a passive spectator's role. All night the French girl had plied April. Until finally the younger black girl had become anesthetized. Gradually but systematically she had done it; and with a great deal of savoir faire to boot. It had started with grass. But four times during the evening Jacquie had enticed April to the wash-room, away from the steady flow of champagne Sanford provided, to vary the diet of marijuana and alcohol with a little cocaine. Pure, one hundred percent coke, too—as it turned out now.

"Here," Delan heard Jacquie say. She pushed the dark-blue outlines of the mirror across the purple counter and held out a straw. "Go ahead."

The tall, sinewy April took two wobbly paces forward and bent her frame. With a great deal of difficulty she held her trembling hand steady long enough to aim the straw at the powder. Then she inhaled. Deeply and with appetite. Twice, once in each nostril.

"Aaah," she sighed with delight as she threw back her head and let out the trapped air.

Through the penetrator Delan immediately saw the stimulant spread its fire. The kaleidoscope of lights depicting body heat reflected the change instantly. Like a stone dropped on still waters, the ripples spread: up from her nostrils and into her brain. Then quickly back down again, diffracting through the neural system, meandering down the length of her body. Along the way the rush of excitement ignited the glands, boosting their secretion into streams of gold.

The sensuality of the X-ray vision and coloring was startling. Nick Delan could feel the arousal. And it was spurred by the excitement and sheer wickedness of the moment: the systematic, relentless seduction of one girl by another through a breakdown of will. Sparked by the ultimate high that a benign-looking white powder known as the *Dama Blanca* induced.

Poor Allan Sanford, Delan thought. If only he knew. Then again he probably does. Either way he was a lucky man. And in more ways than one. He was also in for one hell of a night.

Jacquie Petit was busy preparing another line for herself. Delan turned his glasses to Allan Sanford. He was lounging comfortably on one of the deep, white Italian couches in his living room, preoccupied now with the television he had only just switched on.

While Allan Sanford had participated in one of the smoking sessions, to Nick Delan it seemed he preferred good old *Cuba libres*. Throughout the evening he had devoured the rum and Coca-Cola continuously; but not once during the evening had he showed any indelicate side effects. He had behaved like a contented man: correct, polite, controlled, charming. Only occasionally did he look at the two playful young girls assessingly, seeming to be gauging the most opportune moment to join in.

He was encouraged at every turn by Miss Jacquie Petit. Whenever she could, it seemed from Delan's vantage point, she would aim her body language—at times her very body—at Sanford. She would brush by him, making sure one part of her tall shapely figure caressed his. Or she would bend; just enough to allow him a tantalizing peek of her generous, untethered breasts.

Delan turned the binoculars back to the two girls. Abruptly he felt a surge of excitement run through him. The mulatto girl, outlined in neon blue, was sitting on the dark counter between the two washbasins. Her legs were splayed apart, her dress riding high on her thighs. Beneath the diaphanous material, Jacquie's arm extended, her hand moving gently, her fingers caressing the bright-red triangular swath in between. Softly, tenderly they circled, feather touches that were promising her bliss.

The American girl had long ago lost her inhibitions.

"Aaah," she breathed passionately. Heavier and heavier, louder, more often and with mounting insistence she repeated her rhythmic sighs of ecstasy.

"Breathe in," ordered Jacquie Petit suddenly. "Deeply."

With her free left hand she raised a tiny purple object. Abruptly the sound of thin glass popping erupted on Delan's receiver.

April did as she was told. Over and over and over, each time more fervently, she inhaled. She grabbed Jacquie's hand and brought it closer, breathing the wafting vapors from her fingertips, savoring the rush of glandular juices igniting this fever she had never known before.

Through the binoculars Nick Delan saw the vapors spread quickly, cutting a bright path of gold through her nasal passage, spreading down to her chest and heart. The fiery stream of color descended further, too. Coursing like a stream of molten lava, it burned down through her veins, down toward the depths of her innards, pooling in the very pit of her belly.

Cardiovascular response, Delan observed. Amyl nitrite.

But the fingers of Jacquie's right hand cut him short. They dug deeper into the black girl's womb, more fervently, until very gradually April slumped backward helplessly. She slouched her shoulders against the large mirror backdrop and thrust her hips forward, pivoting them round and round and increasing the fury with each frantic churn. Her mouth was opening now, wider and wider, her face the very image of a pained, savage yearning. Simultaneously the red-and-yellow strobe lights in her head began thundering too, as her body jerked around epileptically, sliding lower and lower on the purple marble counter with each frenzied spasm. Further and further it slithered down slowly, until at last she rested her right shoulder and stretched out on the dark surface, the agony growing beyond endurance now, contorting every feature of her perspiring young face, her lips a twisted pout of pain. A pain that bordered on ecstasy.

"Holy shit," Delan whispered. This was wild.

Abruptly Jacquie stopped; and slowly—very, very slowly—moved her hands away, her palms caressing April's skin as they inched outward. Now they tenderly stroked up past the bare, silky inner thighs of April's long legs, up across her red-colored groin and her hard, flat orange belly to her delicate model's breasts.

There they stopped. And then started again, circling April's amber nipples, protruding now against the thin silk dress.

"Let's go upstairs," Jacquie wheezed.

April groaned, a world of unbridled animal rage giving vent in that one short frustrated cry. Then she smiled weakly and closed her splayed legs and sat up on the counter.

"What about him?" her childlike voice slurred.

"Don't worry about that," Jacquie responded reassuringly. "I'll take care of it. You just go upstairs and get undressed."

Nick Delan bit his lower lip. This is going to be a long night.

He watched the two girls separate at the foot of the stairs. April struggled up them, unsteadily, clutching the white banister for assistance and balance. While, in sharp contrast, Jacquie Petit bounced into the living room, not only very pleased with herself but sober too, absolutely in control.

Nick Delan switched quickly to normal vision as he followed her in. Allan Sanford sat framed in the small glass panes of a French window and normal vision in the light of the living room was not only clearer, but three-dimensional.

Jacquie plopped herself down beside Allan Sanford; and then offered him a sly wink.

"It's all set. Tonight you're in for the ultimate American dream."

"Auditorium, please," Kim Philby directed in English as he stepped into the yellow taxi. Behind, ten other yellow cabs stood in line, the vehicles a credible cross section of all the American makes and models.

The hefty cabbie wearing an oversize red-and-black plaid lumber jacket wrote the destination on his clipboard. He dropped the gearshift to D, and the powerful V-8 engine surged forward noisily.

"Stevenson Hall comin' up," he replied.

Briefly Philby studied the back of the burly, light-skinned man with the short blond crew cut before looking away.

The route entailed a deeper foray into the ever-thickening forest. The lane narrowed too, until the snow-laden branches of the immense evergreens on either side brushed occasionally against the yellow taxi. Then, abruptly, the darkness of the tall, heavy foliage ended. Sun splashed upon a vast natural clearing, its soft rays glistening off the fresh white snow.

In the distance a village drew steadily closer. A town as serene as any midsize New England village, clumped in a valley beneath gentle rolling hills and dotted with red-brick buildings—Georgian and colonial in style. Several steeples poked up at the sky and a dozen larger, more modern structures of concrete and glass could be seen, built around a large reflecting pool at the bottom of a gorge.

The car stopped at the imposing black gates that divided the red brick wall encircling the hamlet. Beside the ornate wrought-iron portals a simple white colonial sign read: LINCOLN UNIVERSITY/MAIN ENTRANCE.

Immediately, two tall, muscular, fair-skinned men stepped out of the guardhouse.

"Hi, how ya doin'?" one of them greeted. Beneath the Ray-Ban glasses he wore, he munched rhythmically on a wad of pink chewing gum.

"Pretty good," responded the cabbie.

"May I see your pass, please?"

Silently, Kim Philby handed the security guard his card.

"If you gentlemen would like to wait here for just a moment, we'll be right back."

Philby nodded patiently. He made a habit on each trip to catch a faulty detail here, a compromise there. As he watched the towering man turn in his Brinks Security uniform and pace toward the small colonial-style gatehouse, he made a mental note to have the man's smoking habit corrected. The pack of Astra cigarettes tucked in the open pocket of his windbreaker looked out of place in New England.

Philby looked up at the road widening to a freeway behind the closed gates; and the easily recognizable green highway signs that read: VINCE LOMBARDI FIELDHOUSE, WALTER CRONKITE SCHOOL OF JOURNALISM, ALBERT EINSTEIN SCHOOL OF SCIENCE.

The guards reappeared almost immediately, handed Philby's card back, and waved the driver on. A few minutes later the cab stopped in front of a large, circular, bunkerlike building made of a reddish-brown stone.

Kim Philby stepped out and handed the driver a twenty-dollar bill. As he waited for change he turned and looked down the knoll sloping away behind him. At the end of the gentle incline of snow-covered lawns, the reflecting pool stood frozen and deserted. Behind it, above the bare poplar trees that provided shade for the children during the hot summer months when the campus became an open sports camp, the fluorescent lights of the large, modern Science Department buildings were burning even in the sunlight. To the right of their glass façades, numerous identical four-story red-brick dormitories rose up the tree-lined hill in the distance to the Liberal Arts college and the ever-popular cafeteria. Not a brick was out of place. It was a perfect composite of any small American university.

"Here we go," said the driver.

Philby collected the change and tipped him modestly before heading up some steps and following the path leading to the large glass entranceway. Yes, he thought, looking around himself with an intense sense of satisfaction. Any small American university at all. Or perhaps Canadian university would be more precise. A Canadian university in the winter when life is all indoors and underground. When no one is seen wandering around the campus grounds, when everyone, students and faculty, stays indoors and commutes via subterranean passages and closed-off malls.

The perfectionist in Philby had always regretted this deviation from the American norm. But there had been no other way of circumventing the American photo-satellite capabilities, those prying eyes in the skies that zoomed down to capture and record everything in sight. Which did not include all those green highway signs and brown-and-white building ones. Or the yellow paint on the taxis. All of those had been done up in a special reflector paint that etched the lenses of those vaunted satellites, making the letters indecipherable and the colors all uniformly brown.

Other than those two concessions, Lincoln University was perfection itself. Drake University, Iowa. Or Oberlin or Swarthmore or Wellesley or Brown. Pure Americana writ large.

The Yanks called Bykovo, the old spy school on the other side of Moscow where they taught "illegals" American culture—baseball and hot dogs and apple pie—Little Chicago, Philby thought. *I wonder what they'd call this place—if they knew?*

It was an offensive masterpiece; a testimony to the ancient Egyptian art of *Kamsihk:* sexual domination through self-discipline.

Three times she had taken the American girl to the brink of bliss in the last half hour. But on each occasion she had turned her away hungry. Before her burning desire could explode to joy. Before her body could satisfy its craving.

Even more, on each occasion the French girl had timed the disappointment immaculately: one split second later than the time before, just that much closer to ecstasy. Each time, too, she had done it with just a little more disdain. Each time she had increased her contempt—until finally a viciousness emerged. A harshness that had driven the younger girl to the brink of desperation.

It had been a delicate transformation, though; one marked by subtlety and a great deal of experience. Only very gradually had Jacquie Petit tilted the tables, manipulating April Morgan until their roles were the exact opposite of what they had been originally. Until the once passive April wanted to please. More—much more—than she wanted to be pleased.

Now Jacquie's head lay on the pillows, her shapely nude body stretching down the huge bed, her long, glistening legs splayed. Between them rested April, her head burrowing in.

Jacquie's hands guided her. Tenderly she encouraged her, caressing her, rewarding her by responding enthusiastically. But at the same time constantly demanding more; and making the younger April ~rk for her. High and low and all around the sensitive bank of nerves there; and then very, very deep. Then lower still—to the most forbidden, the most degrading part of all—and in between.

All the while she let Allan Sanford watch and wonder; only occasionally did she pull him toward her from his ringside seat, lying as he was on the bed beside her, for a passionate kiss.

Even from a hundred yards away, across the dark-blue moonlit waterway leading to the Balboa Bay Club, the scene was all-engrossing. Through the penetrator binoculars the colors ceased to have meaning. The thermal lights indicating their body heat had long ago blended into one huge flickering fire: every hue of yellow and gold, all the shades of red, had fused together in shimmering balls of flames. And it was not the wild scene alone that was so all-absorbing to Delan. Not the lights; or the exotic colors; or, indeed, the eroticism of it all.

It was the French girl.

She was wicked.

Delan rubbed his tired eyes momentarily before quickly returning to the scene. The French girl's arms were gently but firmly prying April's head away now. Away, coaxing her head upward slowly until the younger girl lay on top of her, their lips meeting. It was a passionate embrace, long, lustful. And as it held, Jacquie's hand descended, down toward April's legs. Between them it lingered.

Gradually, delicately, her fingers started caressing. Then slowly they picked up steam. Touching, turning, twisting, taunting; and then nipping in.

But again—at that one precise moment when April's fervent panting was about to segue into an ecstatic wail—Jacquie's hand froze. She stopped, reached for April's head and turned it away from herself. Forcefully she guided it down to the right, toward Allan Sanford's midriff.

April Morgan was all but out of control now. She slid off Jacquie's body and into the empty space on the bed in between and tore in, devouring the aging skin around Allan Sanford's stomach with her lush, ravenous lips. Around the hair her famished tongue traced an outline down toward his thighs. Through the binoculars, the moist saliva left a cooler neon trace on the golden surface of Sanford's skin. But it was momentary. Like the instantaneous bright swath of white that trails a shooting star, it almost immediately melted away, evaporating on the hot skin.

Suddenly a hand intervened again. This time almost savagely. It grabbed April's short hair and yanked it up until her mouth opened just in time to take Allan Sanford in.

Nick Delan saw Jacquie Petit smile as she urged April's head down; gently, slowly, rhythmically and yet deeper and deeper with each beat. Simultaneously her other hand slithered around April's back—down toward her limbs. It twisted around her buttocks and began massaging again, a penetrating touch that almost immediately had April bucking her head and body like a bronco being broken in.

Through the extraordinary colorful lights of thermal vision, Nick Delan could see the excitement slowly etching into Allan Sanford's brain too. Like the mercury of some exotic thermometer on LSD the colors changed, heating up from the yellow range through orange to gold. Sharp, jagged little rivulets of red—burst veins in an eye—slowly descended into his brain, growing gradually to wide rivers of blood as they spread out. Increasingly his breathing became more desperate as his head rolled faster and faster, side to side. He groaned with pleasure. A moan that was about to erupt with bliss.

But like a maestro conductor with an unerring ear, yet again Jacquie intervened. She tore April's head away from Allan Sanford's manhood and turned it until the American girl had made a complete about-face from her right side to her left. She embraced April's sweat-laden body and kissed her voluptuously. Then, as their kiss lasted, slowly Jacquie's left hand started creeping downward again.

Nick Delan watched as the blue outline of Jacquie's arm twisted down behind April's back. It grabbed Allan Sanford's manhood and urged it closer, guiding it forward until slowly it approached April's buttocks, lying as she was now on her left side. There Jacquie held it for a moment—tempting, taunting—before ushering it past.

Allan Sanford slowly arched himself forward toward April's back—but he was met halfway with a snapping thrust. Through the binoculars Delan saw the stream of burning red lava flowing inside April's belly engulf Sanford instantly. And immediately the heat spread its color into his groin, etching upward into his stomach, and down toward his knees. Almost reflexively Sanford reached under the black girl and pulled her backward until her firm buttocks pressed into his soft belly. Rhythmically, in the most flowing sequence of all the natural motions, he repeated his actions. With each reprise Delan saw Sanford feel the fire more potently; and each time he sought the pain more ferociously, more often, more rapidly.

Nick Delan needlessly adjusted the focus. Then he fidgeted with the sound level, turning the volume of the shotgun microphone up a little. Allan Sanford's breathing was becoming heavier and heavier again; more and more desperate, too. Through the binoculars the multicolored sparks depicting his body shimmered with ever-increasing heat. The red-hot meandering stream was panning out too, out across the entire surface of his body, flowing from his groin and belly.

Gently, the neon blue outline of a hand inched toward the source of the heat. It twisted between April's long, sinewy legs and gently stopped the torrid scene.

Nick Delan saw Jacquie grab Sanford's manhood with great authority; and extract it. She moved it up, one small inch.

"She's a virgin here," Delan heard her tell Sanford, purring viciously. "And she wants to lose it."

Allan Sanford entered—and exploded instantly.

Across the cool, serene, dark-blue waters of Lido Channel, it took fully ten seconds before Nick Delan lowered the binoculars. And only then very slowly, puffing out a heavy lungful of air as he rubbed the back of his neck, flabbergasted.

"I have been instructed to be as brief as I can on the background—the origins, organization, development, targets, and techniques—of the 13th Directorate in order to concentrate on the two variations under consideration for immediate activation."

Arkadi Anatolevich Zubko coughed a little self-consciously. He lifted his hand and cleared his throat, looking down sheepishly from behind the podium on the pot-bellied stage. Four men sat bunched together in the second and third rows of the small amphitheater.

"Nevertheless, to fully understand our options and the present status in terms of both assets and their strategic positioning on the playing board, it is necessary to touch on the goals of the operation as originally envisaged.

"During the mid-1950s it became increasingly clear that an entirely new system of politics was evolving in the United States of America. One that created a totally new political system and politician. This spelled the end of wards and precincts and of the bosses who delivered package votes at national conventions."

As Zubko warmed to his task, Kim Philby saw self-confidence gradually descending on the young man he'd recently appointed as his Deputy. With each sentence the tall, thin analyst with thick brown hair, a long, drawn-out face, and intelligent if close-set eyes, consulted his notes less and less. Increasingly he looked directly into the eyes of the men in the dark-green-leather seats and stridently outlined for them the rapid technological evolution that had revolutionized American politics over the past thirty years.

"In a nutshell," Zubko said after talking for almost ten minutes, "what was projected back then is exactly what we see today: a political system in which the voters are entirely dependent on a reality that is created and unfurled for them by a small handful of individuals: the television producers. So total was the spell of television, so clear the emerging pattern of future American political life, that our side detected a window of opportunity."

Of course, what they were hearing was not new to any of the Comrades. And yet as Zubko delved into the background and achievements of the 13th Directorate—its grasp and use of media-dominated American politics, its selection and molding of a media star into a political force, the intricate management of his financial and professional fortunes until the persona of the player and the politician fused into one—a swelling excitement filled the group. Like children familiar with all the details of a story who on every new telling look forward to the next well-worn climax, the elderly gentlemen were positively enthralled by Zubko's story.

All of them, that is, except Kim Philby. To him this was more like a lament for what might have been. All the planning, all the effort would at best now yield little of long-term consequence, and at worst yield nothing at all. His colleagues, so obviously taken with the whole scheme, had to be given credit for daring to defy the directives of the General Secretary to immediately abort the entire scheme. They had to be complimented for trying to salvage some sort of gain for the Soviet Union. But they could not be expected to relate as personally as he did to the program that might have been—a program that might well have meant the permanent crippling of capitalist America.

Zubko's soft, flat voice interrupted the old man's thoughts. "So you can see we are extremely well-positioned within the Sanford camp. Now let me move on to the two variations we are now considering. The sexual entrapment program . . ."

A nice touch, that, thought Philby. This was the part of the fairy tale the children always liked the best. He picked up one of the thin scuffed gray files sitting on the small table that folded out of the seat in front, a dossier no one else in the room had or would ever see in its entirety.

Née: KROTOVA, Raya.

Date: 14 June 1964.

Place: Ventspils, Latvian SSR.

Enrolled: School of Higher Learning, 104 Gofkovskoye Shosse, Moscow.

Date: April 1977.

Scholastic Observations: Outstanding pupil, practical and theoretical levels. Graduated June 1981. Activated early, field-work application parallel to formal education.

Operational Experience 1:

—1979 (Aged 15) Sexual Entrapment Program M/SEP/21-10-1CD.

Target: French Ambassador, Charles Pierre Guidot.

Status: Successful.

Operational Duration: Seven months.

—1980 (Aged 16) . . . Hymenoplasty.

Operational Experience 2:

—1981 (Aged 17) Sexual Entrapment Program M/SEP/8-01-2CJ.

Target: Newsweek Magazine Bureau Chief, Moscow, Juliet Mary Warner.

Status: Successful.
Operational Duration: Three months.
—1982 (Aged 18) . . . Hymenoplasty.

Kim Philby skipped the rest of the thick file that summarized another half a dozen or so successful sexual entrapment operations played out in Europe and the States. Instead he flicked the pages until he reached the last section of the report, specifically the first six lines.

Infiltrated and Legended: Paris, December 1985 (Aged 21).
Allocated Income Level: Monthly net yield U.S: $5,000.
Assigned Source: Swiss trust fund (Banque Worms) provided by deceased parents (under established legended background).
Psychological Classification: Sadistic orientation.
Sexual Classification: Classic bisexual tendencies.
Comments: Continues to show unusual aptitude and enthusiasm.

Philby closed the file. How far they had come over the years, he thought, picturing the immense facilities of Lincoln University outside this small amphitheater in Adlai Stevenson Hall. From two-room broken-down apartments—to this. From press-ganging ugly lumps of lard to. . . . The photograph of the girl in the file flashed before his eyes. For a moment he considered her, what a truly beautiful woman she was, how valuable an operative she had already been in her young life, how efficiently penetrating the very concept itself was. He found himself wondering how that little girl must have looked when she was first enrolled at Gofkovskoye Shosse at the tender age of twelve and a half. How she had felt.

Philby thought: Like any of the thousands of Soviet track stars, swimmers, weight lifters, ballerinas, or other "swallows" dragged away to cold, hard institutions do at that young age, I suppose. The public schools in England were much the same. At least, Westminster School certainly had been in his day.

What had it been about this girl—about any of the girls for that matter—at that young age that had stood out, though? What wrinkle had been detected? He did not know. Certainly it had to be far harder to pick out a potentially good swallow at twelve or thirteen than it was a future Olympic athlete. So many of the necessary qualities were intangible. Especially at that tender age. How could one project sexual aptitudes, sexual appetites and preferences, physical appearance at maturity with any degree of accuracy? There were no performance sheets to analyze; no muscle tone, mobility, reflex speeds to compare; no track records, no yardsticks at all.

Or were there?

Because the doctors did. In ever-growing numbers. And with increasing accuracy. As that beauty in the picture lying there on the table attested.

Was it the training? The four years of intensive courses in male psychology and sexual technique?

"That is where the first alternative—which is a simple task really at this stage—would end," Philby heard Zubko saying. "With the vivid public disclosure of Allan Sanford's personal life. Photographs and films collected over the years would be discreetly leaked. Unquestionably this would stop his career in its tracks. This, we feel, is decidedly the best way to terminate as quickly as possible, and with the least amount of risk, the original goal of the 13th Directorate."

Sitting near Philby, Marshal Filatov shifted in his comfortable padded-leather seat. He glanced at the Englishman.

"Now, the second alternative is one that is already built into the system as a fallback option. It was conceived as a secondary goal to that of electing Allan Sanford to the White House. The advantage of this option is that we achieve many of the same goals initially sought by the 13th Directorate. And we do so by utilizing only the very same equipment and assets we have and have had in place for a long time now."

It stood a splendid chance of working, Philby mused, suddenly feeling an excitement he hadn't felt in years. And when it did, it would create a furor in America, a crisis of such proportions that policy-making would be derailed and their national self-confidence undermined for a generation. All the ingredients were there. All that remained was to come up with one last twist, one final blow, to keep Washington in its present state of shock for just a few days longer. One new element to push them over the top.

Zubko's voice encroached again. "Now let me run through some of the assets we have in place or on standby at this moment."

He turned a dial on the podium and the lights dimmed.

Abruptly two pictures flashed on the screen behind the tall lecturer.

"No doubt," Zubko said, "all eyes are on the picture to the left."

Philby remained silent as his three Russian colleagues chuckled, gawking at the same picture he'd seen only moments ago in the file. It was a photograph of the same girl Marshal Filatov had shown the General Secretary a few days ago.

"Her name is R. Krotova. She is presently working under the alias Jacqueline Petit. The one to the right is L. Markurian, alias Catherine Greene. Both are members of the illegals department. And both have been successfully inserted and are in place. The younger one only recently; Cathy Greene for many years."

The picture changed.

"This is N. Elshtayn . . ."

The sudden silence that descended on the room impressed Zubko. It was a hush, he noted as he paused, that was tinged with a certain respect.

". . . and it seems, for obvious reasons, you all recognize the face."

12 | THURSDAY, JANUARY 7

In California, the golden morning had gone by slowly for Nick Delan; and it had opened up a can of worms.

Yet again he pointed the penetrator across Lido Channel at Allan Sanford's house and eyeballed the surrounding area for weaknesses: shadows that could hide a figure; the corridors between some of the houses, the general makeup of the targeted area. It was those shadows, those spaces and indentations, the side routes and bushes and trees that could possibly save his neck. All of which required complete familiarity with the area—and that meant a physical probe.

Earlier that morning the penetrator had picked up a conversation between Allan Sanford and someone on the telephone. Sanford had said he wasn't planning to leave his house for the next five or six days. He had a grueling, nine-state midwestern campaign tour scheduled and he was resting up for it in preparation. The conversation confirmed what Anthony Boyle had told Delan at the briefing. There was sure to be tighter security provided on the campaign trail. Especially if Sanford declared his candidacy, as Boyle suspected. That would mean Secret Service protection, for one. And even if he didn't, there would be hordes of reporters, cameras, supporters, staff; and constant movement. Sanford would not stop in one place long enough for any sort of calculated strike. Nor would he be alone for a moment.

No, the house across the bay was the only option, Nick Delan concluded as he lowered the binoculars. There was practically no security. For all intents and purposes, he had a one-week stationary target. All that remained was to find a hiding place. One that provided a swift, efficient approach—and a decent enough escape. But that he would have to find at night. In the exact operating conditions. The reconnaissance had to be accomplished as soon as possible, too. Tonight, in fact.

Therein lay the can of worms. How the hell was he going to slip away from the delicate young Miss Bragana on her very first evening in town?

He didn't know. He would, however, have to rigidly compartmentalize his life in the next few days. Somehow he would have to explain to her that something urgent and unforeseen had cropped up. That he was going to be extremely busy for a few days. He also had to do it without alienating her. For that was another factor in the can of worms. His was now a very lonely task and a part of him welcomed the warmth, distraction, and companionship she would provide. He might not be able to open up to her, tell her anything about himself or his life, but her warm presence would provide a wonderful escape from the dark reality he faced. Besides, there was just a chance that he'd need her, that she'd conceivably be useful if something went wrong. If it did, he couldn't count on having a single other friend in this world. The United States Government had a notoriously short memory where its friends were concerned—a "hardening of arteries," it was called. And Anthony Boyle was the quintessential symbol of that approach: a practical, pragmatic, expedient weatherman attuned to the slightest change of the breeze.

Abruptly Delan recalled an old axiom from the ghettos of Chicago. One of the laws of survival he'd first learned in that aching wasteland of derelict factories, vandalized playgrounds, and instant slum blocks.

> If you have a friend,
> Loyal and true,
> Fuck him royally,
> Before he gets you.

It was good advice, he told himself. Something to remember when it came to Anthony Boyle.

* * *

"Yes, of course, Miss Bragana. Your suite is ready."

Clio Bragana smiled at the short, moon-faced assistant manager with thinning blond hair as he looked back up from the computer screen hidden behind the elegant counter. He collected the key and politely indicated the way. The atmosphere of the lobby was distinctly old-world. In fact, the L'Ermitage Hotel looked charming, more in the tradition of small European luxury hotels. It seemed modern and efficient but discreetly so, hiding the cold pragmatism beneath warm parquet flooring, rare European oil paintings, and tasteful leather furniture. It was quiet, too; calming. Not like the usual maelstrom in the lobbies of even the most prestigious of American hotels, large or small.

"Mr. Delan requested the suite next to his if possible and we managed to arrange it." The assistant manager affected the usual supplicant's pitch that receptionists at elegant establishments manage so adroitly. As the doors of the elevator opened and the two of them entered, Clio looked at the mirror just in time to catch the man's hooded eyes glance up the long side slit in her canary-yellow cotton dress.

A few yards down the corridor on the fifth floor the employee darted ahead of her.

"Here we are: Suite five-oh-two." He opened the door.

Clio Bragana stepped into a large, sumptuous ocean of white. Embellished with a host of different bright colors, it created a spectacle that immediately brought to mind the fan across a peacock's crown. The reception area spread out before her with a sunken living room and a roaring fireplace, private balconies beyond. To one side stood a dining table, glazed with a sharp black shine. Four matching chairs surrounded it, their upholstery covered with the same bright, multicolored chintz pattern that draped the windows.

"Let me show you the upstairs."

Clio looked at the glass-and-chrome stairs of the duplex curving up toward a glass-fronted landing overlooking the living room. "No, that's all right. I presume it's the bedroom."

"Yes, ma'am. And an en suite bathroom, of course."

She unbuckled the H-snap on her crocodile handbag and handed him a twenty-dollar bill.

"Thank you, ma'am. Do let me know if there is anything you need," he said, backing toward the door.

"I will."

The man turned and walked away. Then suddenly he looked back again.

"Oh, I almost forgot, Miss Bragana. I asked Mr. Delan if he wanted the interlocking doors between your suites opened and he said to ask you."

Clio felt a slight tingle of embarrassment. You slimy bastard, she thought. First the money, then the tough question, huh? She smiled at the assistant manager, cramming into that one brief glance a world of sensuality: the ultimate weapon of feminine beauty.

"Why on earth not?" she asked.

"I'll have someone right up," he replied, looking away sheepishly.

After he had left, Clio wandered around the suite, casually inspecting and marveling at all the convenient gadgetry American hotels manage to include. She had only just reached the sophisticated stereo set, though, when the gentle two-tone chime sounded. The security man did his job quickly. With his master key he unlocked the two doors connecting the suites. One was on the upper level of the duplex, at one end of the tiny mezzanine. The other was a door that led off from the right of the reception room, to the side of the sunken living-room area.

Once he had left, Clio controlled her inquisitiveness and stepped out onto the balcony. Above the host of tall palm trees, the skyline of Beverly Hills was trapped against a gorgeous light-blue sky. But slowly her curiosity increased. Would there be any clues about him in his room? Surely something of his personality, his life, his job was contained there? How strange, she thought, feeling guilty. They had practically lived together for nearly a week, going in and out of each other's suites in Paris, but still neither of them had ever entered the other's bedroom, witnessed the other's private world. She wondered again what she would find. What she would learn if she entered.

Hesitantly she turned back into the room from the balcony and moved toward Nick's suite. It was darker than hers, more traditional. She walked a little closer to the open door. A large glass coffee table rimmed in gold metal came into view, surrounded by dark-blue couches. In its center stood a huge crystal vase, brimming with bright flowers. It smelled divine. Tiny petals of a million different shades of lilacs mixed with roses, tulips, gardenias, and jasmine blossoms cascaded down to a bright yellow ribbon tied neatly around the base of the bouquet.

Clio Bragana looked around her own suite. Complimentary strawberries and cream were on display; as was a basket of fresh fruit. But there was not one single flower. She looked back again at the large arrangement in Nick's suite. Particularly the envelope that lay half-open beside the yellow ribbon.

Slowly she approached, stepping through the doorway. She looked around again before walking closer still, up to the low coffee table. There she cast one final cautious look around the room before dipping and picking up the envelope. One word was written in block capitals on the white surface: CLIO.

She ripped into the envelope and looked inside, relieved and happy, but very surprised. She turned the card over to the inscribed side.

"Thanks for the confidence. Nick."

The dinner at La Scala had gone a long way toward soothing Nick Delan, softening and pushing into the background the anxiety, doubts, and ambivalence that had been building inside him all day. Anxiety about the task he had been assigned: to kill a man—and not just any man—an innocent one. And doubts about the direction the Activity was taking, too. Questions about the propriety of this deviation from a basic tenet of the American system: the military should never be used for domestic law enforcement or domestic politics.

It was disquieting.

So, too, was the arrival of Clio, about which he felt a strange ambivalence. He was happy to see her again, excited even. But he still hadn't decided how he was going to handle her. He needed to think of a way to convince her that something important had come up, something beyond his control. But it had to be a story that would also win her over. And he needed to do it before the evening was through. Because he simply *had* to cross that channel that night. To identify acceptable infiltration and exfiltration routes, and eyeball the target area for viable staging posts.

Clio had been asleep when he walked into her suite. So he had called La Scala and booked a table for nine-thirty. Over dinner her delightful company, along with a bottle and a half of full-bodied '73 Grand-Puy-Lacoste to wash down the excellent homemade fresh pasta and veal piccata, had helped to unwind him a little.

It was almost midnight when they stepped back out onto Little Santa Monica Boulevard. The night was warm, tinged with the fragrances of a spring that seems to rule eternal in this blessed part of the world. A warmth that has about it a cocktail of sensual fragrances, not least of which is the aura of glamour. The mystique—that lure, that enticement of materialism, of hedonism, of instant success.

Clio Bragana took his arm and pulled him closer as she moved toward the opulent, well-lit shop windows on Rodeo Drive.

Delan smiled at her, but it was a perfunctory gesture. His mind had moved back to the problems he faced and how he was going to handle them. This, he was thinking, was as appropriate a time as any to tell her. The evening had gone well. It was coming to an end. The later he left it, the more difficult it would become.

"There's something I want to tell you, Clio," he said, squeezing her arm warmly as he tugged her away from her window-shopping. "And I want you to take it the right way."

She seemed a little surprised by his sudden stiffness. "Oh-oh. Let's see now. You're really married? And you have three—"

"Come on, Clio, be serious a minute."

"I tried being serious, Nick. All I could get was secretarial work."

"Look, this is difficult enough without your clowning."

"Okay," she said slowly; but suddenly the good feelings between them seemed to have ebbed.

"And for a start, stop seeing shadows," Delan said harshly. "Look, if every time I want to say something serious I have to go through a checklist of possible interpretations, it's not going to make conversation very easy."

Clio looked up at him. "I'm sorry," she said softly. "It's just something that's always there. Right on top of everything else." She paused and looked down.

Delan reached out with his left hand and circled her back. "Well," he said, bending his head closer to hers. "Tell it to go screw itself where I'm concerned. I promised you once, in Paris, that I'd never lie to you. And I meant it."

Her brow wrinkled momentarily before a small smile spread across her face. "You're right."

"I have a problem, something I have to do. There's not a whole hell of a lot I can tell you about it. And there are reasons for that, Clio, believe me. But there are things in my life right now that require a great deal of attention." Delan felt the muscles of her arm, wrapped as it was in his, tauten. "Now it's not going to take very long—a week, ten days. And I know it's come at a bad time for us, but it's something I have no control over. So I want you to trust me. Just this once, I want you to trust me. Who knows, it could just become a habit."

A wave of mistrust swept across her face. "What kind of things?"

"I can't talk about any of this, Clio. I wish I could but I can't. Not now anyway." He hesitated before he added, "Maybe someday. In the meantime, I want you to take it on faith." He leaned down and unlocked the passenger door of his rented black Ford Thunderbird.

The thin silk of Clio's delicate turquoise dress drifted up onto her supple thighs as she swiveled her long legs into the cabin.

Delan closed the door. And felt the razor-sharp point of a knife in his back.

"Move, fucker. Just move," a high-pitched voice hissed in his ear.

Delan felt the sudden sharp jab of a blade dig through his dark-blue jacket and pierce his skin. His heart froze. He breathed deeply and looked down. Clio hadn't noticed anything yet. With his body blocking her window she couldn't see to her right. He had to get this over with quickly. It was too close to the trauma she had suffered the first time around.

"What do you want?" he asked. "There doesn't have to be any trouble."

"Trouble?" the man repeated, mixing utter contempt with surprise. "I ain't looking for no trouble. I just want you to move, man," the grating falsetto whispered with exaggerated slowness. "I want to rip you apart."

The kid was nuts; or spaced out; or both, Delan thought. He had to turn around. He had to establish who it was, if he had friends and what it was he was after. It sounded like one man. About twenty years old. Caucasian. But Delan had to be certain.

"Why? Why don't you just take the money and go?"

The voice cackled. Then another raucous laugh followed.

Two, Delan thought.

"You motherfucker—"

Abruptly Delan felt a crushing pain on his left shoulder blade. A blow that sent a sharp jab halfway through to his lung. For a split second it felt like the stab of a knife.

Abruptly the voice dropped its anger. Now it gave vent in the same taunting whisper again. "Man, the money is already mine. Question is, what else you got in the car to offer?"

Delan fought to breathe. It wasn't a knife. Whatever it was hadn't cut him. There was blood, but only a trickle. He had to turn, he had to see.

"Look, I don't want to fight. Just take the money and leave."

"Whooee!" cried a third voice in the background. "Man, we're going to tattoo a number here tonight." It sounded like a Texan.

Madonna, three, Delan thought.

"Turn around," whispered the first voice, jabbing Delan in the back with the point of his knife. "I want to see the fear in that pretty face."

Delan turned. There were four of them. One knife, one gun were pointing at him. But the other two were also obviously armed; their black leather jackets bulged. They were not the problem, though. Nor was the knife. The hulking Texan with the gun was the problem. He was too far away. He had to be coaxed closer. Surreptitiously Delan moved his left foot forward and placed eighty percent of his weight on his back foot. The back stance. Designed for frontal attack.

"What's going on, Nick?" Clio Bragana asked anxiously from behind. The soft whir of an electric window accompanied her voice.

"Nothing," he snapped. "Just stay there."

"You don't give no orders here, man," spat the southern boy, darting forward to join the delinquent with the knife. He looked like a weight lifter and held the gun in his right hand. With his left he grabbed Delan by the ear and twisted it painfully until Delan's head rested on his shoulder. "If the lady wants a hunk of good ole southern snake inside her all you're gonna do is oblige. Maybe she ain't never had no real prick before. Now, you gonna open that door and invite her."

"Right on," cried the first boy, threatening to pound Delan again with the vicious-looking blackjack that was the handle of his knife.

"Nick . . . *Nick* . . ." There was panic in Clio's voice. "What do these men want? Nick?"

It has to be now, thought Delan. These kids are half-crazy on something. If she gets out of that car . . .

The four punks, all attired in spikes and spangles of various sorts, had drawn closer to him now. Reachable. He bent the middle finger of his open right hand slightly, lining up the tip with the index and fourth finger to form a deadly spearhand.

"I don't want any trouble. I don't want to fight," he said.

The muscular Southerner twisted his ear again, more violently. "Fight? Sh-e-e-et. Ain't gonna be no fight, man. Not if you open that fucking door."

Delan jerked upward—one hundred and ninety pounds traveling at more than fifty miles an hour and propelled at less than one square inch of nerves. He buried the rigid spear of his hand deep into the epicenter of the hollow under the boy's armpit. A howl of pain erupted as the Southerner's body instantly went limp. Paralyzed, the bulging muscles of his right hand dropped the gun while his left hastily released Delan's ear. Desperately, he clawed at the excruciating pain. Instinctively Delan curled his fingers as he withdrew his hand, tearing the vulnerable nerves and muscles apart. The man's yell became a whimper.

Simultaneously Delan's body was spinning, the left leg sweeping around in an aerial arc to the temple of the boy with the knife. There was a crunch of breaking bones as a high-pitched shriek pierced the night. Delan had missed his target. The heel of his shoe had smashed instead into the left side of the man's nose, shattering it. A spray of warm blood shot up into the air, showering Delan.

He turned. Two weapons lay on the ground. But two more were on their way out of black-leather jackets.

For one split second Delan's body was still. Then his left leg snapped out, catching one of the two remaining thugs on his elbow just as he withdrew his hand from his jacket. The short, brawny figure with a spiked Mohawk haircut screamed as he fell. But already Delan was moving again, his right foot lashing out with the speed of a striking cobra. The fourth youth—medium build with frazzled pink hair—dropped a half-drawn snub-nosed revolver and grabbed his groin, sinking to the ground.

"Nick . . . Nick . . ." he heard Clio call out in a terrified whisper.

The hulking Southerner was moving again, his hand reaching for the gun on the asphalt. With a reverse stamping kick Delan crushed the boy's fingers with the back edge of his heel.

"Nick," Clio Bragana cried above the cacophony of confusion.

Delan swiveled again, to the first punk, the one with the high-pitched voice, the leader. But his eyes caught a movement in mid-turn. It was the fourth boy. He was trying to totter to his feet. Delan dispatched the toe of his left foot to the boy's groin again and a stream of vomit spewed out onto the tarmac.

Clio Bragana screamed, a terrified sound that reverberated through the empty parking lot.

Delan ignored it: there was still the leader. Delan looked down at him squirming on the ground. How many times? he thought, hatred raging inside him. How many women had he frightened or raped or beaten up? How many kids . . .

"Please . . . Nick . . ." Clio Bragana wailed through her sobbing. "Please . . . please." She was fumbling to open the car door.

Delan aimed his kick for devastation. He brought it down on the boy's ankle, shattering it.

Swiftly he looked around himself again, his cold, glazed eyes sweeping the space for any last signs of danger.

"Jesus Christ," he heard her whisper behind him.

He turned.

"Oh, my God," she said, her bulging eyes surveying the destruction.

Delan exhaled. He relaxed his body slowly.

The groans and wheezing agony of the four toughs fawning on the ground had faded the color from her cheeks. Her legs seemed rubbery and weak.

Delan reached out and took her arm. "Don't look."

"Holy Mother of God," she mumbled. Her eyes were locked on the pool of blood she'd stepped in.

"Come on, get back in the car."

She looked up at him, eyes agape, horror etching every feature.

"You didn't have to do it," she whispered pathetically. "You didn't have to hurt them like that."

"I did what had to be done, Clio. Now get in the car, please."

She turned away, looking back at the groaning figures. She was pale. Her body trembled.

"Get in the car, Clio," Delan ordered, pointing to the open door. There was no point in trying to talk to her: she was in a state of shock and they had to leave quickly to avoid spending the night answering questions. He walked to the driver's side.

Gingerly she backed toward the car and got in.

Delan reached across her to close the door before backing the car out of its parking space. As he turned right on Rodeo and headed north toward Santa Monica Boulevard, they heard the approaching wail of police sirens.

"Why?" she whispered incredulously.

He turned toward her. Tears meandered down her cheeks.

"Very simply, because there was no other way. It was either us or them."

She answered slowly. "But why the mayhem? Why the willful mutilation?" she sobbed, losing the battle for control.

"I grew up with people like that, Clio," he said softly, anxious that she should understand him. "I know them. I know their mentality. And violence is the only way. They're crazies—spaced out on a bowl of shit. You give them half a chance and they'll tear you to pieces."

Very slowly she lifted her head and looked at him. "So what the hell is the difference between you and them?"

Jesus Christ, Delan thought.

"Nothing," he said sadly, too preoccupied to notice the pair of headlights following two hundred yards behind. "Not a thing."

It was nearly one-thirty in the morning and Nick Delan was still only just preparing to leave for Newport Beach. As he changed into a pair of jeans and a lightweight, navy suede windbreaker, his mood was glum. The evening had ended as an unmitigated disaster. One that had also affected the timing of his reconnaissance mission. And he simply had to glean some of the information he needed to plan his assault tonight.

He picked out a pair of dark socks from the closet and sat on the bed. Clio Bragana had not said another word, not even a perfunctory goodnight. She'd walked frostily with him up from the garage, and once inside his suite had gone straight through the connecting doors and apparently to bed. Her response had agitated him. Had he exaggerated? Had he been an animal? Had his South Side instincts for self-preservation been absolute?

Madonna. What the hell had he gotten himself into? And what was he going to do with Clio now? There were a hundred more important things he should be concentrating on. Why had he allowed himself to . . .

"Nick?"

Delan snapped his head toward the whisper from the semi-darkness. Clio stood in the doorway, resplendent in a salmon-colored satin *chemise de nuit*. It was bare at the shoulders and stopped just short of her knees. Half in and half out of the dimly lit room, she was hesitant: the firm breasts of her young body pressed against the door, her eyes cast down demurely.

"I couldn't sleep," she whispered.

"Neither could I," he retorted.

"Are you going out?"

"Yes."

"Where?"

"Business."

"What sort of business starts at two in the morning?"

"My kind."

Delan started putting on a pair of dark-blue tennis shoes. At length it was Clio who broke the long silence.

"I wanted to apologize," she said softly. "I didn't mean what I said. Earlier, in the car, I mean."

"Don't worry about it."

"I . . . I don't know what came over me," she murmured, her fingers toying nervously with the fine lace bow dangling on the nightgown between her breasts.

Delan stood up. She looked as if she'd spent the last half hour crying. She obviously wanted to talk. Meanwhile, he had to cross that channel while it was still dark and he still had over an hour's drive before him. He approached and reached out for her, and she moved eagerly toward him, leaning her head onto his shoulder.

"I guess . . . I guess I just went berserk. Instead of thanking—"

"Forget it," Delan murmured, cutting her off. Tenderly he hugged her closer—like a father bolstering a repentant child. "It really doesn't matter."

She pressed back, fitting her head between his shirt and the soft curve of his neck. Silently she clung to him for a few moments, her lips occasionally pecking his skin. Then she spoke again, very, very softly. "Nick?"

"Yes."

"I want you to make love to me."

Delan's heart leapt. For one split second he felt tempted—there was always tomorrow night to cross the channel, the hell with Boyle and the presidency, Sanford and the KGB. But that was all it was—a fleeting fantasy. He knew himself too well to savor dreams.

"Tonight's not the right night, Clio," he whispered, a wisp of a sad smile curling his lips.

She looked up at him with those large brown eyes. "Why?"

"It's for all the wrong reasons, Clio. And come morning you'd regret it."

"How extraordinary," Sir Basil Ramsbotham exclaimed. "And you say the Americans persist in this story of theirs?"

Colonel John Stuart-Menteath nodded earnestly. "Yes, I'm afraid they do. Claim there was no question of not respecting the reciprocity arrangements. Say they were planning to share the chap with us. Only a question of when. Their Ambassador reiterated several times that it was solely a precautionary move to have the fellow ensconced in the safer quarters of their base at Alconbury before we were to be called in."

"So presumably they're still unaware of the man's fate?" asked Sir Peter Grey.

"Yes," replied Stuart-Menteath, his face taking on a pained expression. "Thought that was a little premature at this stage. Don't you agree?" He pressed the old-fashioned, round wire-rimmed glasses at the bridge of his nose.

"I see what you mean, John," Sir Peter concurred. The Deputy Director of MI5 was a man he not only held in high regard, but one upon whom, to a very large degree, he depended. "Quite right, too. But what of the bodies? Won't they be making a claim on those sooner or later?"

"I presume so," Stuart-Menteath replied. "Through the usual channels, I suppose." He paused. "And we shall provide them with their own, of course."

"What about the fourth?" Sir Basil inquired in his low-pitched reedy voice that always seemed to carry its own echo.

John Stuart-Menteath turned to face the Cabinet Secretary. He wasn't taken in by the polished naiveté on Sir Basil's rumpled scholarly features. Hardly anyone, he thought, could be gullible enough to believe a man could reach the status of Cabinet Secretary unseasoned or easily confused.

He looked away, to the dark oil painting of Sir Robert Walpole hanging over the marble mantelpiece. It was embedded in the center of the north wall of the briefing room, deep in the basement of the Cabinet Office below Whitehall.

"They have no legal claim to the remains of a deceased third-country alien," Stuart-Menteath replied matter-of-factly.

The answer seemed to satisfy the Cabinet Secretary, who sank back in his chair pensively.

"Any idea why he asked to see you *personally*?" Sir Peter asked.

In contrast to Sir Basil's slight, almost inconsequential air and the dark-blue pin-striped suit he affected, the head of MI5 was a natty sort. A little younger, too. His tall, erect body was attired in a beautifully cut gray-flannel suit that instantly marked him as a retired cavalry officer. His jaunty pink-and-orange kerchief showed his tolerance for the conventionally unconventional. What was left of his overlong fair hair was brushed across his head and held firm by a touch of hair cream.

"I think so," Stuart-Menteath replied. "After he identified himself it was rather obvious, actually. You see, I had some dealings with young Pavlenko during his Aden days. Which is what concerns me just a little."

Sir Peter stared at his deputy in anticipation. "I have the impression I missed something, John," he said at length.

"Well, I'm not really certain—"

The sound of the telephone interrupted Stuart-Menteath. He stopped as Sir Basil picked up the old-fashioned jet-black receiver.

"Ramsbotham," the Cabinet Secretary identified himself. "Yes, certainly," he added. "Please inform her that we are on our way."

He replaced the receiver and gave his colleagues a tired look.

"Gentlemen, the Prime Minister is ready to see us now."

It was a few minutes past three in the morning by the time Nick Delan swung his car off Pacific Coast Highway into the Balboa Bay Club. He slowed immediately: a flimsy but obtrusive red-and-white luminous arm across the entranceway blocked his path. The alert night watchman leaned out of his cubicle before the black vehicle came to a complete stop beside him. The Ford Thunderbird, though luxurious, was not an exceptional model on the streets of Newport Beach. Which was exactly why Delan had rented the vehicle in the first place. It was unobtrusive in this neighborhood whose wealthy residents had a penchant for foreign cars, especially Mercedes-Benzes and Porsches, and various antique vehicles.

"Hi, how can I help you?" the burly guard inquired with a casualness that belied his vigilance. His right arm hovered above the holster at his side. "Cocked and locked," as they said in the Army, Delan observed to himself.

"Suite forty-four eighty. Cavalante, Joe Cavalante."

The rough, moon-faced man checked a list on the small counter before him. Then with a certain aplomb he pressed the button that raised the barrier.

"Have a good night, now," he smiled, his leathery face crinkling in a friendly manner.

"Thanks," Delan replied, looking squarely into the guard's eyes so the man could see his face clearly. "But I could use a little fresh air first." He tapped his lungs. "Get a little of this smoke out."

"I hear ya," the guard drawled. "I hear ya."

"Maybe down by the beach. Get a little of that iodine."

"Hey, can't beat it," the guard agreed. "Where the elite meet to breathe," he added, reciting a popular local jingle.

"Take care," Delan said before gliding off. As he followed the twisting driveway left, toward the virtually empty parking lot in front of the health spa, he removed the heavy brown-framed spectacles with the plain glass he'd been wearing and placed them on the passenger seat. Then he extracted the small wads of gauze he had stuffed around his teeth to puff out his cheeks and lips during the drive down. In fair weather, he had been taught, prepare for foul. And a confused, conflicting trail was no trail at all—should something go wrong.

Once he stopped, he opened the door slowly, emerging at a leisurely pace. In his hand he held a canvas bag the size of a large camera. He stretched the muscles in his back and then locked the car before ambling toward the beach with seeming casualness.

A few yards down the path he turned right and mounted the steps of the wharf. He strolled at the same contented pace—anyone who happened to be watching would see a bachelor savoring the dregs of a perfect evening. Up close, however, his face was a picture of cold concentration as he scanned the area ahead: the luxurious yachts moored to the wharf on his left, the narrow strip of white sand bordering the island across the waterway. It was quiet; not a sound broke the rhythmic roll of the tiny waves lapping on the white moonlit sand.

The houses on the opposite beachfront were dark. Only the occasional dim night-light and the tiny colored bulbs of Christmas trees and other decorations in downstairs living rooms broke the even blackness.

The windows of Allan Sanford's brown-brick colonial-style house were pitch-dark on the second floor. Downstairs the pot-bellied bay windows and French doors of the living room were dimly lit. Through them a golden saucer light on a stand could be seen, sending a soft spray of illumination up to the snow-white ceiling.

Delan descended the stained dark-brown wooden steps at the end of the wharf, stopping on the bottom step and casually surveying the scene. He saw and heard nothing but the wind rustling through the clump of trees to his right and the gentle roll of the waves to his left. He stepped down the last step and looked again—up and down the strip of sand stretching toward the South Shores Sailing Club and the bridge on Newport Boulevard connecting the mainland to Balboa Peninsula in the distance. In between an armada of boats—of every conceivable shape and size, from tiny one-man sailboats and dinghies to the very largest private yachts—bobbed on the gently rolling waters.

He sat and waited; watching, listening. Still nothing. He massaged the back of his neck and rose to go back up the stairs. But suddenly he dipped his head and nipped under them instead, adroitly stepping beneath the wharf, out of view.

Again he stopped and waited, carefully monitoring the area. His senses were sharp despite the hour and lack of sleep. The zimeldine tablet he had taken back at the hotel had totally reversed the effects of the wine. He undressed, stripping down to his bathing suit. The chill of the night air was invigorating.

He dropped to one knee and extracted the Baird night-vision goggles from their olive-green canvas bag. The binoculars were waterproof, coated with a thin film of colorless rubber that could withstand pressure up to a depth of one hundred feet. He used them to scour the target area and peripheries with both modes: available lighting and infrared vision. Neither produced anything of note, so he looped its strap around his neck.

He was ready. On the actual night of the hit he'd be carrying a lot more equipment, equipment that was far too dangerous to be carting around on a simple reconnaissance sortie in harmless terrain. So, for the purposes of tonight, he was ready.

Abruptly the beat of his heart picked up. Gradually the adrenaline pumped through his system, producing that icy thrill he always found so enticing. In an instant a lifetime flashed through his mind. A lifetime peppered with the same sensation. He remembered the daily quarter his grandmother used to give him as lunch money back at Lawndale Junior High School. And the dime he had to fight not to pay in "tolls" to the "wardens" of the street gangs. He recalled the cheers of thousands of Northwestern fans going wild at the quarterback draw play for a forty-five yard gain. He remembered it all. Vietnam, Laos, Cambodia, Teheran, El Salvador. And now Los Angeles.

As always at such moments an old habit forced itself on him. He stood absolutely still for a second, dipped his head, and closed his eyes. Then, after a moment's stillness, he crossed himself slowly before opening his eyes.

He looked around carefully before stepping out of his hiding place onto the sand. But as he slid into the water his mind reverted to where it had left off. Danger. The heat of the game. That was the only sensation that thrilled him anymore. His sole antidote to age.

Slowly he traversed the channel, dog-paddling mostly so he could monitor the way, memorize as much as he could of the area. The channel was deserted at this late hour, not a boat was moving. As he drew closer to the opposite side, he passed small motorboats moored to private buoys. Then wooden wharfs extended on either side of him, harboring luxury yachts. He could make out a few of their names as he drew closer: *Cheryl, Toyan Around, Enchilada.*

Soon he felt land under his feet and stopped for a moment. He scrutinized the narrow path going both ways, then glanced back to the opposite shore where his clothes lay, just to get his bearings.

He turned again, his heart beating faster, and walked up the sandy beach. To his right lay half a dozen or more houses with patios opening onto the beachfront. Then a small park with a playground. To his left the path was longer. In the distance it disappeared, curving out of sight with the beachfront. Up closer the bend led to several private wharves. It was this direction he chose to take.

The beach approach was essential. It would be far too restricting to rely on the single two-lane bridge that was the only land link to the island. Especially since intelligence had it that a police car was almost always on the Lido Island side of the bridge, absent for only as long as it took to drive around the narrow mile-long island. Besides, now that he was closer, he could see plenty of potential hiding places around Allan Sanford's house. Quite a variety of emergency escape routes too: alleys running inland between the houses to Lido Nord, the island's main artery. From there a veritable maze of little side roads branched out.

For the next three-quarters of an hour he reconnoitered, specifically designing IADs—Immediate Action Drills—emphasizing readiness for any eventuality. Twice during his search he had to hide and wait for a night watchman with a dog to pass by, before heading on to inspect the right side of Allan Sanford's house. Each time the dog barked, the patrolman gave only a cursory glance before moving on.

The more Delan studied the area, the more confident he felt. All told he had chosen three potential hiding places, two possible angles of fire, and, other than the sea, six, maybe seven, possible evade and escape routes.

He had also detected only two conceivable complications. From Sanford's house to the nearest alley on either side was forty-five, fifty yards. To the right it was via Genoa. To the left via Palermo. The other corridors were even further away. If anyone approached the house simultaneously from both sides, Delan was trapped. Except, of course, for the water.

The second difficulty was that both his potential angles of fire were from very close range: the bay windows on the right side of

Sanford's living room, or the French doors on its left. Either way it meant getting close enough to see Allan Sanford's face as he fired.

And that was not an appealing proposition. It was going to be hard enough killing an innocent man without seeing the horror in his eyes at that last split second.

Hiding behind the ivy on the railing of the wharf at the end of the tiny park, he peered across the channel at the looming hulk of the Balboa Bay Club and checked his return route one last time.

Slowly he scanned to his right, along Bayshore Drive to Linda, Harbor, Collins, and finally Balboa Island. Reaching the last of the islands, he turned back and looked to the left. In the distance the lights of Hoag Memorial Hospital sparkled on the knoll above the tall, modern Japanese bank buildings around the intersection of Pacific Coast Highway and Newport Boulevard. Behind the Balboa Bay Club, the ridge at Crestview was dark and lifeless.

Delan lifted the Baird goggles and viewed the hills through available lighting. He saw nothing of consequence. The painted wooden houses on Kings Road and Cliff Drive were dark and silent. Yet again he swept the binoculars in both directions: to the islands, then back to the hospital off to the distant left before he was satisfied.

No, he thought as he tried to locate his own room in the club across the way through the goggles, it was going to be a simple mission. Surprising that a man like Sanford had no protection, though.

Idly he flicked the switch on the side of the goggles forward to infrared—and instantly he froze.

For one brief but interminable moment he could not move. It seemed as if he was nailed there, paralyzed by a loss of all feeling in his limbs. Then just as suddenly the moment vanished as a stronger instinct shunted the fear aside. Furiously he tore at the small switch, turning it back again in a desperate attempt to stifle the invisible rays it beamed. Simultaneously he threw himself to the ground, twisting and rolling over and over to gain as much distance as he could from where he had been standing.

"AISA?" the Prime Minister exclaimed doubtfully. "And what is that?"

"I believe, Prime Minister," replied Sir Peter Grey, "that they could best be described as their SAS. With a number of refinements."

"Yes?"

Sir Peter turned to his deputy sitting beside him.

"AISA, or the Activity, or the Enterprise, as it is more commonly referred to," Colonel John Stuart-Menteath explained, "is the acronym for Army Intelligence Support Activity. It is the spearhead of the American Special Operations Forces in what, in the lexicon of American intelligence analysts, has come to be called low-intensity warfare. Essentially the organization is merely an extension of the traditional concept of special forces. But that one small step makes them *secret* soldiers. A private network of elite former covert-action intelligence agents and counterinsurgency, antiterrorist, and military harassment specialists banded together under the deepest cover."

The lady sitting behind the Chippendale desk immediately latched on to the key word.

"You said 'former' operatives, Colonel." She inclined her stiffly coiffured hair toward Stuart-Menteath. "What did you mean?"

"I mean, Prime Minister, that it is an organization made up entirely of operatives who have formally severed all previous links to the military and intelligence communities in which they served and now function as a deep-cover elite available as and when they are needed. They are a parallel structure under the direct command of and responsible only to the executive branch of the United States Government."

For once the unflappable lady seemed a little surprised. "Isn't that illegal, Colonel?"

"Yes, it is. The organization has never received a presidential finding, the legal certification required by Congress from the President for major intelligence activities. Nor has it ever officially been tasked. On the other hand, it's hidden so well and its personnel are so committed that, despite all the congressional inquiries resulting from the Irangate fiasco, despite all the media attention and financial inducements from the media and offers of use immunity from the various investigative bodies, not a single fact about AISA or its activities was uncovered. Neither that it exists nor that it doesn't, let alone what it does, its responsibilities, or chain of command."

The Prime Minister's eyes glistened and her nostrils flared slightly.

"I'm not sure I'm familiar with the word 'tasked,' Colonel."

"I'm led to believe they mean: to assign or to direct, ma'am. As in to a specific task."

The Prime Minister's brow wrinkled. "What is this organization's background?"

An expression of pain passed fleetingly across Stuart-Menteath's weather-beaten face. "It's rather a jumbled story, really. The by-product of all these violent psychological moods to which our cousins appear prone, particularly in their perceptions about national security, executive-legislative authority, covert actions, and so on. It was a convergence of events that led to the birth of AISA. The first factor was the radical change in the rules of the covert-action game, terrorism and hostage-taking and so forth, in the last twenty years. The second was President Carter's decimation of the American covert-action capabilities, what they now like to call 'the tool of middle resort.'"

Stuart-Menteath went on to explain how the concept of AISA, as a "deep-cover surgical strike force," evolved under a frustrated President Carter after the disastrous attempt to rescue the fifty-two hostages held by the Iranians in 1979. He explained how the Activity had become a pet project of Ronald Reagan's, "who took to them like desert flowers to rain"; how it grew in size and scope during his two terms; how the organization's brief had gradually evolved from a military intelligence-gathering organization to what were called "overt covert active measures."

"And what does that mean?" the Prime Minister asked.

"They define it as 'a clandestine low-intensity prevention, pre-emption, and retaliation capability,'" Stuart-Menteath replied with a touch of sarcasm. But when he proceeded to list some of the operations AISA had secretly undertaken during its existence, the Prime Minister was genuinely taken aback. She stared at him silently for a long moment before speaking.

"These are important interventions you're talking about, Colonel. How on earth can a paramilitary organization undertaking operations of such magnitude, be kept so secret so long? Antiterrorism in Italy; counterinsurgency in the Philippines, Central America, and Africa; infiltration of fanatical religious groups in the Middle East; and so on. How on earth have they managed to keep it secret? For a start, surely they are based somewhere. They must have headquarters, barracks, housing, equipment, and—"

"No, Prime Minister. They do not."

He went on to describe how the nation's top military operatives—Delta Force men, Green Berets, Rangers, and agents from
the various intelligence organizations—resigned their commissions
and entered the private sector. "From there," he explained, "behind a wide assortment of fronts—commercial cutouts, as they call
them—they operate as a sort of private network or clandestine
army. Highly motivated mercenaries willing to do their government's bidding off the books, so to speak."

"I suppose we had plenty of this sort when there was an Empire
to run," muttered Sir Peter. "Dedicated adventurers doing odd
things in the various corners of the world."

"Possibly, sir. The fronts they use range from security and defense consultancy work to a variety of small, privately owned busi-
nesses and private investigation concerns, all subsidized by the
Defense Department or the CIA in the form of consultancy, service,
freight, or procurement contracts.

"All of which means there is no paper trail, Prime Minister.
Nothing to lead anyone to them at all. Which is precisely why they
escaped unscathed during the Iran-Contra scandal."

The Prime Minister's stern eyes were thoughtful and intense.
"So it's in their hands now, is it?" she asked at length.

"That is what we are led to believe, ma'am," Sir Peter Grey
answered. "We are, of course, querying our people in Washington
and elsewhere for additional information." He grimaced as he
turned toward Stuart-Menteath. "Even have a name, don't we?"

"Yes," replied Stuart-Menteath. "Fellow called Delan. Nicholas
Delan. How they intend to proceed, though, is still a bit of a mystery."

The Prime Minister leaned forward to rest her elbows on her
desk. Outside, a watery midday sun broke through the low gray
clouds, abruptly lighting up her gloomy office.

"Be that as it may," she said a little curtly, turning toward Sir
Basil Ramsbotham, her Cabinet Secretary. "As far as we are concerned, I don't—in all honesty—doubt for a moment the course we
should take."

"No, Prime Minister?" Sir Basil inquired, aware of her affinity
for prompting.

"Certainly not." She paused, then added in a deeper tone,
"There is every chance the Americans are being quite honest with

us. That they would have contacted us when they had this Russian fellow safely settled.

"And even if that were not the case," she emphasized, "this is hardly the time for one-upmanship. There seems to me to be a far more important issue here: the question of what exactly this defector meant, and what can be done about it. Consequently, I would urge you all to establish contact immediately. Put your heads together with your counterparts in Washington and proceed accordingly. After all, this man's words on their own are useless, aren't they? Unless they're fitted into everything else that's known. And they have most of the equation, don't they? They at least know what the defector divulged and thus are in a far better position to know what this trick the defector mentioned could be."

The Prime Minister looked away, gazing blankly for a moment at the Johann Zoffany painting to the left of her desk. "What were the defector's exact words again?"

"My name is Oleg Maksimovich Pavlenko," Stuart-Menteath intoned slowly. *"I am an officer of the KGB. My assignment was to defect and plant a story. It's a trick. A deception. A double-edged sword. You must get word to the Americans immediately. They must act with utmost caution and cunning. It is a trick to . . .*

"The rest wasn't very clear, I'm afraid," Stuart-Menteath added. "Nevertheless, I did get the impression that somewhere in the middle of all his murmurings I heard the word 'mole' mentioned. Can't be certain, though. Damned frustrating when you think about it. A few more breaths and everything would have been quite clear. The technical people couldn't help very much, either. It was simply too garbled to isolate on their recordings."

"How unfortunate," said the Prime Minister. "Still, perhaps the Americans can fill in the blanks. Certainly they're in a better position to make a judgment about any mole, aren't they?"

"Perhaps, Prime Minister," Sir Peter observed. "But they seem to be taking an . . . ah . . . an unusual approach."

"Oh? Why?"

"Odd sort of man they've turned to."

The Prime Minister leaned forward on her desk. "And what sort is that?"

"I think Stuart-Menteath should answer that," Sir Peter replied, looking toward his deputy. "After all, this fellow Delan *was* a former colleague of his."

"Well, he's a success story of sorts," Stuart-Menteath said. "But a sad one in the end, I suppose. Humble beginnings. Good scholastic and athletic achievements. Promising career in an American sort of way. Professional American football; then using his intelligence and looks to become a celebrity, I suppose. Television, advertising, that sort of thing.

"Vietnam changed him, though. His record there was one of unstinted bravery for which he was highly decorated. But something apparently happened there to scar him, too. Became a bit withdrawn. After Vietnam he chose to stay on, moving into antiterrorist activity. That's when I met him. Up in Hereford, Bradbury Lines, 22 Special Air Service Regiment, when he was sent over by the Delta Force for training. Must admit, though, he was always a bit of a puzzle to me."

The Prime Minister waited for an explanation.

"Why?" she asked when it did not come.

"I'm not really sure. It just didn't make much sense to me—his staying in the Army. What with all that potential and all that talent. Put it down to loneliness after reading his file. Came from a very hard background. Didn't seem to have anything to go back to. No home. No wife or children or, for that matter, any other family." He paused.

"Yes, well, he seems to be more than qualified for the job," the Prime Minister replied. "So what is it that concerns you all? What is it that strikes you as unusual about this approach?"

"His specialty, I suppose, Prime Minister," Stuart-Menteath replied.

"And what may that be?"

"He's an assassin."

13 | FRIDAY, JANUARY 8

Who?

The question thundered in Nick Delan's mind as he drove north toward Los Angeles in the early morning light. To his right, off the San Diego Freeway, the vast, idle South Coast Plaza shopping mall drifted by unnoticed, his mind consumed with that portentous scene etched on its eye.

What did it mean? Every possible answer only raised more doubts, more apprehension, more suspicion.

Maybe he was wrong. Had he moved too quickly? Was what he'd seen some sort of mirage? A reflection, perhaps, of other lights.

His brain stood still for a moment—blank, bare. Then the photograph appeared again. A frozen still shot of the precise scene. And there in the middle, bright and clearly visible through the infrared scope, were five of them: piercing spotlights targeting, flooding one small square.

No. It was real. They had been there. There, waiting, ready. Someone had been watching him every step of the way.

But who?

And why?

Was it Boyle? Had he put his sidewalk artists on to him? Had him tailed and monitored all the way? And if so, why? To gauge Delan's progress? But those projectors were huge nodes. They were far too powerful for mere close-range surveillance. So what were they doing? Why were they there?

If not Boyle, who? Was it a political game? Had there been a leak? But how could there've been? This was top secret, classified UMBRA—the highest rating of all. Besides, there simply hadn't been enough time to run through the usual rumor mills by which all Washington's secrets are inevitably exposed.

Who else was there, then? Who else stood to gain?

For the next hour, as he drove past the same monotonous vistas of parking lots and burger stores and pizza parlors, up through the various towns that make up the long chain that leads to L.A., Nick Delan was racked by doubt. All the time four words ran through his head like a jingle he couldn't shake loose. Four Latin words remembered from his college days: *Inter Arma Leges Silent.*

Amid the clash of arms the laws indeed grow silent. All laws—including those that govern loyalty and ethics. Friendships, even.

By the time he reached the tall palms in front of L'Ermitage Hotel on Burton Way he'd made his decision. It was not one he felt particularly comfortable with. For no matter what the explanations, certain doubts and fears were bound to remain. Nor did he congratulate himself on his creativity. Only the reality of the plan appealed to him. And the truth was he needed to be practical, to admit he was in above his head.

Once in his suite, he immediately headed for the interconnecting door between his living room and Clio's. He listened for a moment for anything that might suggest she was awake at this early hour. There was not a sound.

He entered his bedroom, locked the door, picked up the telephone, and dialed a number. He waited for the inevitable click that would come after the second ring. The stark, impersonal voice asked: "Good morning. Transnational Enterprises. May I help you?"

"The name is Breitenbach. My number is S-C-I two-three. I need Esquire."

"One moment, please," the computer croaked.

Delan looked at his watch. In Washington it was nearly 9 A.M.

"White House," a perky female voice replied after nearly one full minute, during which the line was secured.

"Deputy National Security Adviser's office, please."

"One moment."

"Deputy National Security Adviser's office," a more elderly, less ebullient lady replied.

"I'd like to speak to Anthony Boyle."

"I'm afraid he's occupied just at the moment. Who shall I say is calling?"

"Breitenbach. Douglas Breitenbach. And it's urgent."

"I'm sorry, sir," the lady said severely. "But he can't be disturbed."

Delan sighed and rubbed the tired, aching muscles beneath the stubble coating his face. "I have a feeling, lady, that he's going to be a whole lot more disturbed if you don't go in and tell him I'm on the line. And that it's urgent."

"One moment, please."

Within seconds Anthony Boyle was on the line. "Nick, what is it?"

"You got yourself a problem, Tony."

"All right, Nick, what is it? On the telephone you sounded like you saw the Devil."

Delan sat back on the edge of the black-leather collapsible chair in the center of the vehicle's spacious cabin and looked severely over his right shoulder at James Cassidy and Anthony Boyle on the bench seat behind. He scanned the two men's faces for the smallest hint of deception.

"Let me ask you a question first," Delan said softly, reaching for the leather strap hanging on the side of the cabin. The silver limousine was surging forward, twisting around the steep curve of the exit ramp that led out of the colossal parking lot beneath Century Square.

"All right," replied Boyle cautiously.

Suddenly Delan did not want to hear the answer. For there were no answers. Or at least none that could be trusted. It was a game with no rules that they were playing. In an arena full of mirrors. Strategically placed to confuse.

"Did you order a surveillance grid on me?"

Boyle shook his head and frowned. "No. Why?"

Delan stared at Boyle silently. Outside, the sienna rays of the setting Californian sun bounced off the black one-way windows of the limousine as it turned left on Constellation Boulevard.

"Are you sure, Tony?"

"Yes." Boyle shifted his large frame, his eyes narrowing slightly.

"Well, you better get back to your drawing board, then, and come up with another idea after you consult with your Russian defector friend."

Anthony Boyle glanced at James Cassidy before looking back. "What do you mean? Why?"

"Because we're being watched, Tony. And God only knows what else."

"You want to explain yourself?" Boyle asked slowly.

"I mean, it's a setup of some kind. A simple, old-fashioned, cheap, divorce-case-type setup. Only with the latest in cameras and artificial lighting devices being used."

The Deputy National Security Adviser's back straightened as his eyes darted toward James Cassidy again. This time the two men exchanged longer glances and for one brief moment the only sound to fill the tension inside the car was the soft, shrill screech of compressed rubber as the limousine swung onto Avenue of the Stars, not more than two hundred yards from the famous Century Plaza Hotel.

"What the hell are you talking about?" Anthony Boyle asked at length, looking back to Delan.

"When I went in to eyeball the area last night, I switched the night-vision goggles from available light to infrared at the last minute. It was an unnecessary move but a lucky one, as it turned out. At first all I could picture was a laser-aiming device beaming back at me somewhere in the general area of my eyes. But not for long. Within seconds it dawned on me that the light was bigger. Much, much bigger than the pencil-thin beam of a laser sight. So I took a calculated risk. I took split-second viewings from a number of different positions. Activating my infrared capability only for very short bursts. Just long enough to see. Too short to be detected. Or at least to be a sitting target."

Delan's eyes flickered toward the dark one-way glass to his left. Outside, the railway tracks running alongside Santa Monica Boulevard flashed by the window frame.

"And?" Boyle prompted anxiously.

"And there was more than one light," Delan answered in a tired voice. "There were four or five. At least that I could make out in those conditions."

"What kind of lights?"

"Nodes. Infrared kind. Huge mothers, too, and deployed in an arc up on the hills above Pacific Coast Highway. But all targeted on Sanford's house. Flooding the place."

Delan paused to let the tense silence linger. He wanted the two men to fully absorb the impact of his words. He needed, too, to gauge their responses. To assess whether they were leveling with him. On Club View Drive, ahead and to their right, Delan vaguely saw the lush green fairways of Los Angeles Country Club fade into the giant trees bordering the most exclusive strip of Wilshire Boulevard: the high-rise buildings dotting the gentle incline around Beverly Glen.

"Somebody was out there waiting for me, Tony," Delan added at length. "And it could be worse."

"In what way?" Cassidy asked.

"Because they were the lights I could see, Jim. Operating on infrared. God only knows what else was out there. Whoever it is could well have a backup surveillance system employed, working off VLS."

"Off what?" asked Boyle.

"VLS. Visual Lighting System. It's a photo-surveillance capability that works off available light. The process magnifies the smallest amount of available light to levels with which to work efficiently."

"Undetectable," Cassidy clarified, looking thoughtfully at Boyle.

"And if we don't know exactly how many VLS operators there are, and we don't have a precise fix on their location," Delan explained, "there's no way we can get around them to go in and find out what the hell is going on with these infrared monitoring posts. Not without totally exposing ourselves to any and all of the potential VLS operators out there."

"There are a couple of other problems that come to mind," James Cassidy added slowly. "I guess we also have to assume that, even if we did go in after the detectable infrared monitoring posts, all we would find would be a bunch of simple, innocently contracted professional technicians hired by some unknown face or front. Tools who in all likelihood don't have a clue about the *real* reason they're out there. Some cleverly disguised stakeout for some television special; or another investigative piece on Sanford's sex life, for all they know."

Boyle shook his head. "Yes, they're too visible. We have to assume there's a layer in place between them and whoever ordered them there."

"Besides which," said Cassidy, "we've got to retain some element of surprise by not letting on we know they're there. Otherwise we'll never find out who they are or what they're really after." He paused, adding in a softer tone, "Until it's too late, that is."

The Deputy National Security Adviser nodded as he turned toward Delan.

"What do you think, Nick?" he asked at length.

"It's immaterial who's *actually* up there," Delan replied. "What we need to know is why they're there. And what it is they're after. Even worse, is it something specific they're looking for? Some sort of reaction they're trying to instigate?" Delan sighed. "I don't know. But whatever it is, it looks awfully elaborately planned to me."

Anthony Boyle shifted uncomfortably in his seat. Then he picked up the receiver fitted in the console on the black-leather armrest beside him.

"You can head back now," he said, speaking to the burly young blond driver on the other side of the bulletproof glass partition.

Immediately the car veered left, threading back down through the lushly manicured narrow lanes in the rolling hills of Bel Air Estates toward Sunset Boulevard.

Anthony Boyle replaced the receiver and looked at Delan.

"I don't know what we can come up with, Nick, but you'll have to leave this with us for a little while. You're right, maybe the answer lies with Pavlenko. Let me get back to you."

It was only a tiny movement. Perhaps so minute it never took place. Maybe Delan sensed it rather than saw it. But something happened, something was there. Immediately some sixth sense triggered a flood of suspicion in him. It had come from James Cassidy. Was it a movement, the flicker of an eyelid, a tiny nervous twitch at the corner of a lip?

Delan nodded earnestly to hide the disquiet he felt. Boyle was lying to him. Or hiding something. Or both. That much was clear. He had known Anthony Boyle too long. Casually he looked away from the Deputy National Security Adviser, and searched James Cassidy's face for a clue.

Twice so far Delan thought he had caught uncertain expressions on the CIA man's face during this conversation, instinctive reactions both times to something Boyle had said. It was impossible to say just why, but even now Delan thought Cassidy seemed a little uncomfortable.

"Let's just take stock a minute," said the CIA man, looking away from Delan. "The knowns we have going for us for sure are these. One, that there *is* an ongoing operation in progress. Two, that it is in every likelihood of Soviet origin. Three, that while we are uncertain as to its ultimate goals, there is no doubt in our minds that it's a highflyer.

"Now one or two more general facts can be added to this list of knowns: tradecraft—it's not at all inconsistent with the Soviet style. Soviet intelligence operations have always been characterized by their long-term view of events, their intricate planning, their devious, careful, thought-out style. All of which goes to say that most Soviet intelligence schemes are extremely complicated, sometimes multitargeted, with one goal being chosen at the very last minute. Which in this case means they may well still be on dual tracks, keeping their options open, measuring our responses before deciding on their final run."

Cassidy paused.

"And all we have to do," Delan interjected sarcastically, "is figure out what that is, right?"

"Maybe," Anthony Boyle murmured softly. His eyes were slits of concentration now. "But then again, maybe not."

"What the hell does that mean?" snapped Delan.

"I don't know," Anthony Boyle mumbled in the same soft whisper. "I don't know," he repeated as if in a deep trance. "Not yet, at least."

The limousine swerved to descend into the tunnel beneath Century City. Its screeching tires abruptly snapped Anthony Boyle out of his thoughts. Very slowly, he turned away from the dark window until his gaze rested on Delan. Now his eyes were cold and determined. As hard and cruel as the eyes of a hunter looking down the cold metallic blue of a rifle, lining up the hairs of its telescopic sights.

"Well, you better come up with something, Tony," Delan said slowly, trying to fathom the meaning of Boyle's gaze. "Something very, very good; and real precise. Because there's a trap of some sort here somewhere. That much I can smell." Delan allowed all the anger he felt to overflow into his voice. "More. Unless you can come up with some additional information from your defector friend, I want you both to know that I—and I'm the man who has to go in there to kill Sanford—think we need to do a little rethinking. Abort, even, and go a different route."

Boyle nodded, softly but gravely, his glazed eyes staring at Delan.

"And I want *you* to know we'll take into account your position in any decision that is made," said Cassidy trying to sound reassuring as he broke the ensuing silence. "We'll get to the bottom of all this and get back to you. In the meantime, let me give you a piece of advice," he added, as the limousine came to a stop in the underground parking lot. "You have some long hours ahead of you, Nick, and when I was in the field I always found a good piece of ass helps pass the time more quickly." He smiled paternally. "Get laid, Nick. Have a little fun. We'll get back to you."

"Yes," Anthony Boyle halfheartedly agreed. He seemed a million miles away, his eyes glazed in thought. "I think . . . I think you just may have hit on something, Nick. Inadvertently or not." Again he seemed to snap out of his reverie. "We'll get back to you," he said, nodding his head by way of good-bye.

Nick Delan eyed the two men grimly, one at a time. Then silently he alighted.

As he moved to close the door he heard Cassidy speak again, obviously to Boyle, "Speak unto us smooth things, prophesy—"

But the heavy limousine door Delan had already launched closed with a thud, cutting off the CIA man.

Strange, thought Delan, but those words sound familiar. Had he not heard them before?

14 | SATURDAY, JANUARY 9

On Connecticut Avenue at De Sales Street NW, in Washington D.C., it was nearly twenty past three on Saturday afternoon by the time the slim figure with the French passport had completed the registration formalities of the Mayflower Hotel.

"Now let me show you up to your room," smiled the young receptionist with the page-boy haircut, fresh skin, and dimpled cheeks.

"You are very kind," replied the shy Frenchman in a heavy accent. "But I wonder, have you received a packet for me? I was to be awaiting something left for my attention."

The receptionist broadened her high school smile as she looked at the mustachioed foreigner whose fashionable black, mat Carrera eyeglasses clashed with his otherwise nondescript appearance.

"Sure. Let me just check to see if we're holding anything for you."

She returned almost immediately, carrying a heavily taped shoe-box-size parcel wrapped in brown paper.

"Here we are," she said, holding the package out as she came around from behind the heavy wooden counter. "Sorry about that."

The Frenchman smiled self-effacingly. "Thank you. You are very kind."

"Okay. Would you care to follow me, please."

The gaze of the Frenchman, walking a few paces behind the young woman, moved slowly up the seam of her cappuccino-colored stockings to her dark-brown skirt as her shapely legs took her through the extravagant Beaux Arts lobby.

When they reached his room on the seventh floor, the Frenchman placed both the package and the small canvas overnight case he carried on the bed before tipping the young receptionist and seeing her to the door.

Gently he closed the door after her. And instantly his demeanor changed. Now he stood fully two inches taller as he straightened his back to its accustomed posture and stretched the aching muscles created by the slouch he had been affecting ever since he had first entered the lobby downstairs. He rolled his neck around to loosen up the tautness that stretched all the way down his spine and walked toward the bathroom. Looking in the mirror, he first took off the trendy plain-glass spectacles that he wore solely to attract attention to his extra-light-blue eyes. Then he ripped off his heavy black mustache. Both he stuffed in one of the pockets of his raincoat, which he took off and turned inside out, the expensive brown-suede surface of the reversible lining now apparent.

The man smiled at the mirror as he reached up to his face with his gloved hands again. Already he looked five years younger. Expertly he popped the blue contact lenses out of his eyes. Beneath, the dark-brown pupils stared back with intense satisfaction at the sudden and profound change; more comfortable too in the now strikingly Mediterranean face.

He placed the contact lenses in their box in his raincoat pocket and then stripped down completely. Completely, that was, but for the black gloves which he left on. Meticulously he placed every article he removed from his body on the bed beside the black canvas bag before entering the bathroom again. There he showered, thoroughly shampooing the oily *crème défrisante* out of his hair with the special Bioscalin shampoo he had brought with him.

After he had stepped out of the shower, he dried himself quickly before turning to his thick crown of shiny black hair. That he rubbed vigorously, twice switching to a dry towel from the pile that stood beside the large, angled mirrors in which he was monitoring the progress. Meticulously he toweled out the moisture—until the natural curls of his thick black hair formed a youthful, trendily fluffy shape.

Only when the physical transformation had been completed, checked in the mirrors of the bathroom for perfection, did the man remove the only item he was still wearing: the thin black kid gloves, which were soaking wet. But he merely took them off and exchanged them for an identical pair, dropping the wet ones on the pile of clothes on the bed.

From his overnight case he extracted a sober dark-blue blazer, gray-flannel trousers, light-blue shirt, and a red-and-blue-striped tie. Then he turned the bag inside out, transforming it from a black canvas bag into a soft-leather beige holdall. He changed the straps to match before dressing himself in the fresh set of clothes and packing those he had been wearing. With great precision he placed the items in the bag as if adhering strictly to a memorized checklist: starting with the wet gloves that were on top of the pile, down to the heavy brown shoes at the bottom.

When the chore was completed he stopped and looked around again. Satisfied, he approached the shoebox-size package wrapped in brown paper. He swiftly slit the Scotch tape with a small red penknife, then took out the contents. After checking the thirteen-round load in its magazine, he slid the holstered Browning BDA Auto Pistol onto his belt and twisted it around until it nestled in the curve of his back. The small, slim cardboard envelope that bore the words U.S. ARMY and various letters and numbers in heavy red and black print and that he knew weighed less than five ounces he placed in his right-hand blazer pocket. Another, even smaller package, perhaps the size of a book of matches, and a gadget resembling a pocket calculator went in the left. The last item, a simple circular key ring with three keys on it, he placed in his trouser pocket.

The Frenchman patted everything into place before stuffing the shoebox, with every last shred of the wrapping paper and protective Styrofoam chips inside, into his bag, which he now zipped up.

When he emerged in the corridor a few moments later, he looked like any other affluent young American middle manager, except for the kid gloves he continued to wear. He looked up and down the corridor casually—before throwing the room key back inside and slamming the door shut. Then in a distinctive loping gait he headed down the hall. At the elevators he lingered a moment, looking both ways. When he was satisfied no one was approaching he slid through the swing doors to one side and went down one flight of stairs. As he approached the door marked 636 he took out the key ring, inserted a key, and entered the suite.

Without any ado he went straight to the bedside table, picked up the telephone and, with the same Swiss Army knife he'd used earlier, undid the screws in its base. Within three minutes he had completed his task. It took him another two to screw the base back onto the telephone, pick up his bag, and step out in the hallway again. Downstairs, he alighted from the elevator and headed toward the De Sales Street exit of the hotel—far away from the reception desk in the main entrance.

"It's fabulous—my favorite meal," said Clio Bragana as she bit into the overstuffed chili dog.

Delan smiled at her and held out a paper napkin. "You said the same thing about steak tartare in Paris."

"I was lying," she mumbled through her full mouth. She wiped away the sauces dribbling from her lips. "Don't you want to change your mind?"

"No, I'll stick with the coffee," Delan replied, dodging a young man wearing yellow earphones barreling down the broad sidewalk on roller skates. Like the miracle of Moses crossing the Red Sea, the tide of people making up the crowd in front of and behind Delan cleared a path for the young man just in time. Gloriously unaware, the teenager went through jiving to a rhythm that only he could hear.

Up ahead Venice Beach was bustling on this Saturday afternoon. Droves of boisterous, tanned Californians were performing—primarily for each other—feats of incredible agility and daring. Roller skates, skateboards, and bicycles looped the loop and jumped over countless barrels and did a hundred other impressive stunts. Still others pumped iron in large chicken-coop-like enclosures. Muscles bulging, veins protruding, bodies glistening with a little perspiration and a lot of oil, they saved their best for the biggest audiences. Scattered in the midst of this theater were the aging hippies, preening punks, winos, and junkies. All of which added up to a carnival of attractions that was a rarity in Los

Angeles: people, crowds, in the streets, walking about. And all in a city where streets were made not for people, but for cars.

The spectacle was being played out against the perfect backdrop of a beautiful springlike day, white beaches, rolling ocean waves and a constantly changing variety of music. Rhythms blaring from everywhere—moving up and then away in an instant—emanating from portable radios and cassette players transported not only by the kids on wheels, but many of the onlookers as well.

Clio Bragana threw the hot dog wrapper in a bin and reached for Delan's coffee. She sipped it and handed it back before tucking her arm under his.

"If you'd rather go back to the hotel, it's okay with me," she said softly.

Delan looked at her. "What . . ." He stopped and grimaced as the late Bob Marley's voice blared from a pair of Pioneer speakers whizzing past his ears. "We only just got here. Why would I want to go back?"

"I don't know." She shrugged.

"What made you ask, then?"

She looked at a chimpanzee sitting on his owner's shoulders. He stood among a group of scraggly people congregating in front of the doors of a dilapidated drug rehabilitation center.

"Probably the same thing that makes me think you regret ever having invited me to stay with you in the first place."

Delan stopped. The people behind had to pull up and veer around him. "Why would you think that?"

She looked up at him silently for a moment. Then she made a face as she shrugged, turned, and started walking away slowly.

Delan started after her. Never the luck, he thought. Never the luck. Here finally was a girl he cared for—and he was blowing it. He was uptight, constantly preoccupied, and obviously it had now reached the point where she was no longer willing to tolerate his moodiness. It was his own fault. He had watched it building up in her for several days now. But he had no idea what to do about it. Which in turn only made him even more nervous and unsure. How could he explain to her the huge problems he had on his mind? Hell, he couldn't even talk about it. And even if he could, she was hardly the person to understand. How could he explain he had no intention of hurting her, that he didn't want to make her feel unwanted—not now or ever? Explain that they had both been just plain unlucky, that he simply couldn't handle what it took to nurture a relationship right now?

Clio stopped at a wire-mesh fence and looked at the bodybuilders exercising inside. Delan came up beside her. She seemed to be captivated by an oversized blond girl doing deep-knee bends while holding nearly two hundred pounds of iron above her head. Momentarily she turned and smiled at Delan before looking back. It seemed more like a quick check to see if he had caught up with her than anything else.

He adored her, Delan thought, gazing at her beautiful profile. But sooner or later he would lose her, the way he was going. Lose her because he literally hadn't given her a moment's undivided attention since she had arrived. If he was lucky enough to dodge a bullet in the back, that was. Oh, how he would like to explain it all to her. To confide in her, to nestle in her arms and tell her about his world.

But how? How could he even begin? How could he explain that his mind was gripped by Russian defectors and Machiavellian plots, by Washington mandarins and the terror of being sold out? And if he did, would she understand? Condone?

Not likely.

On the other hand, he had to do something. He didn't want to lose her, and there wouldn't be many more chances before things got totally out of hand. He leaned close to her ear.

"Do you want to talk about this or were you just practicing throwaway lines back there?"

She turned slowly and looked at him. "It's not me who has to do the talking, Nick. But if you're asking me if I'll listen, the answer is yes."

Delan took her hand and guided her through the packed throng toward the beachfront. As they walked across the sand the crowds gradually thinned.

"Okay, let's start at the beginning, shall we?" he said when they were by themselves. "What is it that's upsetting you exactly?"

Clio Bragana stopped and stepped away a foot or two. "Do you really need it spelled out for you, Nick?"

Delan nodded cautiously.

"Okay," she said sullenly. "Let's see now. First you invite a reasonably normal, healthy young lady to stay with you. And then when she arrives all you have time for is a quick dinner before you drop her off to go out for the night. How does that sound for starters?"

Delan turned his head a little and looked at her sideways.

"But before you go out for the night, you just have time to turn down her invitation to make love," she went on. "And that was only the first night, too. The second night you're too tired even for that. All you have the energy for is a quick dinner in the room, a peck on the cheek before falling asleep on the couch.

"As for the third night," she added, "you've got to admit the prospects don't look very good, do they? Not with the mood you're in."

She was angry—and hurt—and with good reason. He felt his heart leap. God, he wanted to tell her. Everything. The whole sorry mess that was his life story. He wanted to tell her and feel the comfort of her solace. To feel her arms around him, to kiss her and make love to her and forget.

"You're right."

"I don't want to be right, dammit. I want to know why."

"There's a reason. A good reason. And I'd like to tell you about it. Just like I'd like to tell you a lot of other things about my life." He paused and they looked at each other, he a mite apologetically, she with gathering suspicion. "But I can't. Not very much, anyway. In a sense, in my own way, I tried to explain the predicament I'm in to you the night before last after La Scala. But I grant you it was incomplete and evasive. The problem is, that is all I can ever be: incomplete and evasive."

The frown that had been gathering on Clio's brow deepened as she stepped forward. "I don't understand, Nick—"

"Let me finish," he interrupted softly. "Please. I'll tell you what I can. But unfortunately that's not very much." He reached out and cupped her right hand in both his. "The fact is, there's a lot more to me and my life than being unusually and unexpectedly busy all of a sudden. For a start, that happens reasonably often. Even worse, that's all I can ever tell you or anyone else about it. That's the way it is. I don't particularly like it. But I have to live with it and can.

"No," he said more loudly, holding out the palm of his hand, "don't even ask it. I'm probably saying more than I should already."

"You haven't heard the question yet."

Delan squinted at her silently.

"If you can live with it, what is it that's bothering you, then? Why are you eating your insides out?"

"Maybe I should have said 'could.'"

"Why?"

"Because you're beginning to mean a lot to me, Clio. And I'm not at all sure how you're going to take it in the end." Delan paused and looked away briefly. "Which makes it a totally new problem in my life. Something I've never had before, not with anyone. That's not to say there haven't been other women in my life. There have. Some I felt very deeply for. But never like this. I've never wanted anyone to understand me as much as I want you to. The problem is, on the one hand, you're a very sensitive lady; and on the other, I'm severely restricted in what I can say or do to put your mind to rest. Restricted even when I want to defend myself, even when I want more than anything in the world, more than you'd ever believe, to tell you everything, to answer any question you might have."

The worry lines on Clio's face deepened as she stared at him uncomprehendingly. In the silence, the serene background noises became a roar: the sea rushing in, planting kisses on the shore; seagulls squawking as they circled high above; the gentle breeze fluttering the leaves and nearby flags.

Nick Delan reached out and brushed back the dark hair billowing around her face and large almond eyes. He brought her closer, embracing her.

"Restricted by what, Nick?" she whispered, nestling her head in the curve of his neck.

He sighed. "This may sound crazy to you but I want you to take my word for it. You don't even want to know that much. Let's just say I'm not authorized to discuss anything to do with my work. Not with anyone."

Her body stiffened abruptly. He raised his arm and caressed her head. "But there's nothing to worry about, Clio. Nothing at all. It sounds much worse than it is. That much I promise you."

She cuddled her head closer as she pressed her body up tighter against his. Slowly the tension inside her seemed to ebb a little, her muscles relaxing. They stood there, hugging each other silently, their bodies forming a perfect fit.

"Nick."

"Yes."

"I want you to make love to me."

15 | SUNDAY, JANUARY 10

The lonely sound of James Cassidy's heavy black wingtips on the diamond slabs of black and white marble reverberated around the labyrinthine corridors. It was close to one o'clock in the morning and the old Executive Office Building, that controversial, overdecorated structure, was deserted. Even, as of a few moments ago, Room 208, the hub of the nation's most secret antiterrorist crisis-management teams. So secret is it, in fact, that it has no name—other than one or two informal terms its members choose to call themselves: "208 Committee" or "Policy Development Group."

This was the room in which Anthony Boyle had chosen to conduct the latest meeting of the four men handling the Sanford affair; three of whom were regular members of the 208 Committee. James Cassidy—like many regional or area specialists called in as needed—was the only stranger present. Indeed, he had never been inside the room before; and, given the inordinate influence this group wielded on so much of the nation's covert antiterrorist operations, the simplicity of the spartan conference room had surprised him.

"Good night," Cassidy nodded, forcing himself to smile politely at the smart young sentries on night duty.

"Good night, sir," snapped the four guards, almost in unison.

At the entrance he stepped past the huge urns on pedestals sprouting winter flowers and down the stairs onto 17th Street NW.

He turned right past the elaborate French mansards and porticos of a building that once had housed the State, War, and Navy departments of the budding Republic. Now it was simply an adjunct of the White House, an office that merely sifted the directives emanating from the mansion next door: an ugly eyesore Dwight D. Eisenhower wanted removed; a treasure John Fitzgerald Kennedy ordered preserved as a national monument.

The dormant Fannie May Candy Store across the street caught the CIA man's eyes as he turned up the collar of his London Fog trenchcoat to ward off the bitterly cold southerly winds whipping up behind him. He had less than half a mile to walk and the stroll in the icy night air would relax him. And God only knew how much he needed that tonight. He was seething with tension.

Just why he felt so worried and nervous, he couldn't understand. After all, it wasn't the first time in his career that he'd been at the center of a national crisis. Maybe it was merely a lifetime of duplicity adding up—as it had been for so long now. This latest round, however, had started as a simple nagging feeling just after the meeting in the limousine with Nick Delan, the AISA man, and he'd been unable to shake it ever since. Poor fucker. What were they really planning for him? In all likelihood nothing, the CIA man concluded uncertainly. Not unless he, Cassidy, had missed something. Or unless his masters were lying to him. Or—as with Delan—only telling him half the story. But then again, there was absolutely no reason for them to do that. Not with him.

Boyle's plan—the Osiris Option, as it had just been formally designated—had a very good chance of working. Cassidy had sensed the enthusiasm, excitement even, it had sparked in the other two men. Cassidy himself had been most impressed. Though extremely elaborate and sensitive and unusually high on resources, it was a cunning and unconventional ploy. A scattershot plan designed to address and neutralize the broadest possible range of Soviet intentions. Yes, it was clever, he thought. And appropriately named, too. According to Boyle, Osiris had been a major deity in ancient Egyptian mythology. One associated with vegetation, fertility, spiritual rebirth, and the concept that the soul was immortal if the body was preserved.

Cassidy's mind faltered. First comes reality, then comes philosophy. Why, then, had Anthony Boyle hidden so much from Delan? Why had he not told the AISA operative about the meeting the two of them had had with Stuart-Menteath just before they flew out to L.A.? Why hadn't Boyle told Delan about Pavlenko's death? And the dire warning the Russian defector had sounded? Why hadn't he mentioned the most frightening of all the many complications they faced: the possible existence of a mole?

Was it, indeed, for the reasons Boyle had cited when he had asked Cassidy "to play along"?

"I'm a little concerned that the complications and heavy-handed killing of the defector might discourage the man," the Deputy National Security Adviser had told Cassidy on the plane out to L.A. "I'm not certain that the existence of moles and deceptions and violent deaths are particularly conducive to an operative's mental balance when he's about to execute a dangerous mission."

The logic had sounded fine back then, thought Cassidy. In fact, it sounded just as good now. But on its own. Divorced from everything that followed. Most particularly, the information Delan had imparted in the car about the sophisticated monitoring sights staking out Sanford's house. That was new; a radical wrinkle in the already complex problem they faced. So why hadn't Boyle opened up to the man then? Why hadn't he placed all the cards they had on the table?

Cassidy had posed those questions to Boyle once the AISA operative had alighted from the car; immediately after he had asked him why they were trying to smooth-talk the operative.

"You saw the way he looked and behaved in the car, Jim," Boyle had replied. "Christ, that's all we need right now. To have him pull out."

True enough, thought Cassidy now. But was it the only reason? He hoped so. But something inside Cassidy niggled, some sixth sense that kept repeating that anyone was expendable at this level.

Suddenly, James Cassidy felt disgusted again. Disgusted with himself and his profession and all the ilk that staffed governments everywhere. But most of all with the concept of pragmatism—in whose name any crime became fair play.

Hell, thought Cassidy, the very response they were going with had in fact been sparked by something Delan had said.

The operative's husky voice sounding a warning resounded in Cassidy's head.

It's immaterial who's actually up there. What we need to know is why

228 · BARRY CHUBIN

they're there. And what it is they're after. Even worse, is it something specific they're looking for? Some sort of reaction they're trying to instigate?

It was that last sentence that had triggered a chain reaction in Anthony Boyle's tactical mind. A reaction that had gone on to incorporate all Colonel John Stuart-Menteath's information before ending up as this Osiris Option they had activated.

It was intricate, though, thought Cassidy, bracing himself against the sudden gust of wind that drove him forward. Intricate and sensitive. Intricate in that it entailed the coordination and use of some of the most sophisticated equipment known to man. Not since 1984/85 and Bill Casey's personal crusade to locate Beirut CIA station chief William Buckley after he'd been kidnapped by the Islamic Jihad terrorists had such a huge and sophisticated technological effort been mounted. Back then they had dispatched two low-altitude KH-12 satellites into geosynchronous orbit over Beirut and thence started to search for one single individual in a city of 950,000 inhabitants.

Sensitive because it all depended on one man. A man who had everything to lose and nothing to gain. A man who, in the end, had to accept all the potential risks and personal sacrifices—and all solely in the name of patriotism.

Nevertheless, it was a good ploy, thought Cassidy. And, like all good schemes, a very simple one on another level. Why the hell was he so worried, then?

He didn't know. Maybe it was simply because the word mole had cropped up—a word that always made everyone in the trade jittery—no matter how often they ran into it during their careers. Maybe it was because Delan was so exposed out there, so vulnerable. Maybe it was Anthony Boyle—and the cold, calculating, ruthless stance he was taking. Maybe it was just a residue of the long, impersonal discussions about what to do with Delan when he had finished his task. Cassidy's boss, CIA director Robert Wilson, had called Delan "a liability under certain circumstances." And what did people do when someone became a liability?

The answer made Cassidy uneasy—even though he had spent a lifetime hearing similar answers. And working on solutions mired in the same ethic.

Suddenly, as he crossed Pennsylvania Avenue opposite Renwick Gallery and continued up 17th toward K Street, he felt too old for his trade. The wear and tear was becoming too much. There was a time when he took these things in his stride. Not anymore. The sort of knocks he had received over the past few days were too exhausting now. Especially debilitating was the news about Pavlenko. He, James Cassidy, had broken the golden rule—he had, as they said, "fallen in love with his agent" and allowed the personal relationship that had developed between them to blind him. Now it was clear that Pavlenko might well have used Cassidy for years. God only knew how much damage his information had caused. Only on his deathbed had the Russian come clean.

All of which, thought Cassidy, meant it was time to quit. When a man started breaking the basic tenets of his trade, when everything he did was riddled with doubts and guilts and regrets, it was time to move on, to retreat to a simpler world.

At the end of Farragut Square Cassidy crossed L Street and stopped at the Connecticut Connection building. There, for a long moment, he stared, as he often did, at the shop window with the wide assortment of toys. As always, his haggard eyes and lips formed a wispy smile that reflected deep and abiding sorrow. As always, his mind faded to a different scene. Of a sobbing Penny, his wife, tearing out of a doctor's office. And rushing to their frail little three-year-old daughter sitting in a playpen in the waiting room outside. Rushing to her and embracing her and looking at her incredulously, not believing—refusing to believe—what she had just heard. Hugging and squeezing and kissing the little child as if willing her love to conquer all.

James Cassidy tore his eyes away from the colorful dolls in the shop window and headed up Connecticut Avenue. He remembered that fateful day four years ago, when for the first time he had heard those two words. *Heard* them, that was, and not dismissed them as other people's problems.

"She has cystic fibrosis."

He could still hear the specialist's voice. Matter-of-fact, unemotionally professional, but filled too with a world of sympathy for the pain he knew he had just introduced into the parents' world.

"Is there anything that can be done to cure her?" Penny's faint, quivering voice had asked when he hadn't been able to speak, paralyzed by shock like never before or since.

"I'm afraid not, Mrs. Cassidy. That's not to say, of course, that there are no treatments to ease Jenny's plight. I think it may also be comforting for you to know that a great deal of research is . . ."

But Penny had heard enough. She had rushed out of the doctor's office in a desperate attempt to get away from his voice. To be with Jenny, to love her and hold her and never leave her—for now the time they had to spend together was limited by God.

Cassidy ached as he contemplated the snowflakes swirling around the streetlight up ahead. Never again had he seen a smile on Penny's face. Not, that was, out of Jenny's presence. With her Penny pretended well. But once alone all she did was pray. First desperately, begging for a miracle. Then, after the funeral, for the little girl's soul.

Cassidy felt the guilt inside mount. For over a week now he hadn't been home. He hadn't been with Penny, to console and comfort her a little, to show her she was not alone. She had sounded so forlorn earlier that evening when he had called to tell her he couldn't make it home for the night. The problem was his absence was not a rare occurrence.

No, he was sick to death with his life. It could not go on. The time had come. He would resign. Take early retirement and leave. Something he should and could have done years ago, having started with the Agency so young.

"Yes," he murmured out loud as he looked blindly down the street. When this affair was over, he was through, he told himself pushing the wooden door of the Mayflower Hotel. Just as a hot gust of air from inside the hotel caressed his frozen face, he heard the cranking sound of a powerful engine kick to life behind him. Instinctively he looked around to see a dark-blue, chauffeur-driven Mercedes-Benz pull out from the curb across the street.

The Frenchman glanced at the tall, slim, middle-aged figure entering the Mayflower Hotel as he glided his car away from the sidewalk. A hundred yards down the road, he removed his driver's hat and placed it on the black-leather seat as he settled down for the short drive ahead.

One hour later the Frenchman parked his rented Mercedes-Benz 300E in the previously allotted spot at National Airport, just across the Potomac. He also checked in on the Eastern shuttle to New York and reserved a seat on the first plane leaving Kennedy Airport for Europe; as it happened, a KLM flight—to Amsterdam.

Fifteen minutes before boarding the shuttle he entered a phone booth, dropped in a dime and dialed: 347-3000.

"Mayflower Hotel, can I help you?" the female operator asked.

"Suite 636, please. This is the White House."

"One moment, please."

The Frenchman calmly extracted the small, pocket calculator-size remote-control device from his blazer pocket and extended a small aerial from it.

"Hello," a gruff, sleepy male voice answered.

The Frenchman pressed a button.

Just under four miles away, three ounces of C-4, cyclotrimethylene-trinitramine, an American-manufactured plastic explosive of devastating power that can be shaped in any form and handled with total safety, shattered the night air and scattered the man's head across the room.

Sublime.

Not since his late teens, and perhaps not even then, had he felt such total contentment at sharing a bed. Pure, clean, simple, tender—all of these feelings were part of the fulfillment. But only a part. For the total harmony was more than the sum of its parts—it was the ultimate human experience: two hearts, two bodies beating as one, murmuring silently, speaking of love.

Nick Delan looked down. Clio Bragana's lithe, shining, exhausted body lay splayed across the king-size bed, her head resting on his outstretched arm. Eyes closed, teeth biting gently into her lower lip, her face held the same expression of complete and utter satisfaction that he felt.

He bent his head and kissed her damp forehead before leaning back to gaze at her again. It was a face and persona he had become very attached to in the past few days—curiosity and compassion gradually fading into something else. Something totally new to him. In the past there had always been the clearest demarcation between love and fascination in his life. But tonight the boundary was blurry and faint. One so very easy to cross. Somehow, too, he had the strange feeling this moment would last. That the powerful emotions he was feeling for this young woman beside him would remain unaltered by time.

It was a little frightening. Delan turned away and tried to concentrate on other things. The softly billowing voile curtains danced with the circulating air. In rhythm almost, it seemed, to Wynton Marsalis' brilliant trumpet emanating from the speakers in the corners of the room.

Strange how smooth the transition had been. He had been imagining all sorts of difficulties, given the Rubicon it must have been for her. Wonder what was going through her head? What thoughts? What hesitations? What fears? Or had Genoa and the frightful memories been forgotten in the relief of transcending what must have been a huge and unnatural mental block? Still, he was happy for her. Happy that it had been so painless.

He smiled inwardly. It was a difficult task, trying to avoid thinking about her when the very air was filled with the addictive whiff of her body. Her body and the most erotic of all perfumes: postcoital scent.

"How about a snack?" she murmured over the music.

"Sounds terrific."

She rose, kissed him lightly on the lips and walked from the bed.

Delan felt the bedside panel and switched off the music, replacing it with a late-night movie. When Clio returned, she placed a thick plexiglass tray bearing fresh doughnuts and two cartons of milk down on the crinkled sheets before sitting in front of him, nude and cross-legged.

Suddenly the engrossing staccato of electronic beats that herald news bulletins sounded, tugging at Delan's attention.

"Good evening," a somber, middle-aged newscaster said. "Once again terrorism has struck the nation. This time within a hairline of its heart." The newscaster paused, shifting with appropriate moral outrage.

"Tonight, in Washington D.C., less than one half-mile from the White House, a bomb was exploded in the prestigious Mayflower Hotel, killing a senior government official. For the details . . ."

Nick Delan felt his stomach muscles tauten. He lifted the bed covers off his body as he sat up to concentrate. Holy Mary, Mother of God, he thought staring at the portrait that flashed on to the screen. No! No!

He scrutinized the picture, absorbed, as the details emerged, recounted by a black reporter with heavy glasses standing in front of the snow-flecked Mayflower Hotel.

Slowly a numbness set in. A helpless sinking sensation that gradually forced his heart up into his throat. In the end only two facts registered. The rest was coloring.

James Cassidy was dead.

Killed by a remote-control bomb placed in his room.

"Nick, what's wrong?" he heard Clio ask.

He did not reply. His mind was consumed by the images on the screen.

"Nick!" she demanded in a louder and more worried tone. "What is it, Nick? You look petrified."

What was there to say? He wanted only to run. To hide. To bury his head.

"For God's sake, Nick, talk to me."

On the screen the image of the black reporter abruptly gave way to that of the earnest anchorman. And in that one instant Delan's mood changed. Fear gave way to dark hate. And determination took hold where impotence had been.

He turned away from the television toward the chirping telephone, the slow arc of his swiveling head absorbed and distant, and yet suspicious in the extreme. Now those glazed, steely eyes swept past Clio unseeingly. They were green, a green as fragile, as brittle as the green of a flawless emerald. But there was not a hint of trepidation in them anymore. None whatsoever. Now they were as cold, as cruel and unforgiving as the lonely Boyacá hills in Colombia from which the delicate stone is mined.

"Hello."

"LAX airport," the instantly recognizable male voice at the other end of the line barked. "Bradley International Terminal. American Airlines Club. Seven o'clock tomorrow night."

"The only plausible explanation available to us, Mr. President," Anthony Boyle said, "is that Cassidy, as Pavlenko's debriefing officer, was killed to further boost the credibility of a—as far as they are concerned—successfully inserted dispatched agent."

The President of the United States regarded his advisers gravely from behind his desk. Dressed in a pair of white pajamas with a blue piping that matched his dark-blue dressing gown, he looked as most men of his age look when aroused from slumber at nearly four in the morning to face a huge crisis—fatigued, dull, yet at the same time wide awake.

"And what that therefore suggests, Mr. President," Boyle continued, "is that they have unwittingly confirmed the credibility of Pavlenko's final statement."

The President puckered his lips, turning slightly until his troubled eyes rested on the flickering fireplace at the far end of the Oval Office. "A statement of some value coming from—whatever else he was—a brave, loyal and committed Soviet operative betrayed and killed by his own side."

"Precisely, Mr. President," Robert Wilson concurred.

"And there's still no evidence to suggest they know that Pavlenko lived long enough to hint at being a plant?"

"None whatsoever, Mr. President."

"So it follows that they're still unaware that we suspect his original revelations were bogus."

"That's correct," the CIA chief replied.

"Illusionary is probably a more accurate word than bogus, Mr. President," Kenny Ellender offered. "In the sense that, rather than being untrue, the defector's original disclosures were calculated and designed—we have to assume—to instigate a specific response from us."

"I agree with you, Kenny. That's the crux."

The President swiveled toward Anthony Boyle, sitting to his right.

"The key question we have to keep asking ourselves, Mr. President," Boyle said, "is why would the Soviets want to blow the Sanford operation in the first place? Why would they want suddenly to give up on a long-term, high-cost, ongoing and enormously successful operation about which no one on our side had the slightest suspicion? It doesn't make sense. Unless, of course, they were giving up long-term priorities for more immediate short-term gains."

"What about the existence of a mole?" the President asked. "Do we have any new information on that? Anything at all?"

"No, Mr. President," Boyle replied. "We don't. And all we can do is what we're doing now. Namely, restrict all knowledge to those present in this room."

16 | MONDAY, JANUARY 11

"I must admit, Nick, I imagined I'd witness at least a small measure of relief on your part."

Nick Delan stared coldly at Anthony Boyle.

"You might have, Tony." He paused. "If I didn't have such a strong impression you're hiding something from me. Or lying to me, maybe. Or both."

Anthony Boyle stared back at Delan for a moment. Then he dropped his tired, bloodshot eyes and loosened his collar and tie. "I guess, in a sense, you're right. There are one or two aspects of this thing you know nothing about. But that's for several good reasons." He raised his head. "Not least of which is the strict need-to-know being enforced in this operation—and there are things you do not need to know, Nick."

Delan stared at him in silence, eyes narrowed, unblinking, and hard.

"You don't. Take my word for it. They have nothing to do with your end."

"Everything has to do with my end, for Christ's sake, Tony. I'm the sucker going in, remember?"

"That," retorted Anthony Boyle firmly, "is precisely why."

Delan hesitated before he spoke again. And in that one fleeting moment a wave of doubt crossed his mind. "What's that supposed to mean?"

"It means we're not exactly playing with the kids in the alley, Nick. It means that if something went wrong and you were caught they'd pump you full of truth serums and have it out of you—everything, that is—in no time." Boyle paused. "And that, Colonel Delan, we cannot afford."

Nick Delan stared at Boyle. That should give you a rough idea about how the desk jockeys have assessed the risks involved, he thought.

Abruptly Delan heard James Cassidy's voice reverberate in his head.

"Speak unto us smooth things, prophesy . . ."

But he still could not place the words. Could not complete the sentence either—even though it was on the tip of his tongue. Where had he heard it? More important still, what had Cassidy meant?

Suddenly Delan felt the distance between himself and Anthony Boyle, his world and that of all the Anthony Boyles—those articulate, smooth but ultimately unprincipled bureaucrats. Men who never left the safety of their warm, comfortable rooms. Who only jabbed and circled, but never actually fought. Men who admitted nothing, denied everything, and had not one abiding belief. Not one real emotion in their bones. In the arena of politics and diplomacy, only the slick, the cool, and the impeccably groomed belonged. The rest were expendable. Particularly the soldiers.

"Trust me, Nick," Anthony Boyle said softly. "Because I'm not authorized to tell you, and I can't. Not now, anyway."

Delan glanced away. There was no point in continuing his silent inquisitorial glare. Anthony Boyle was "not authorized," which meant it had already been decided; and no amount of questioning would loosen his tongue. Besides, need-to-know was standard procedure—and if pressed there was every chance Boyle would lie rather than relent.

All of that he understood; accepted, even. It was not new. He had lived half his life with this kind of restriction. What was upsetting was Boyle's reticence when it came to discussing what the defector had said when confronted with the information about the infrared lights monitoring Sanford's house.

"He couldn't add anything substantive," Boyle had said earlier.

And that was about all he had said regarding the subject, albeit in a number of different ways—and then only when pressed.

It didn't make any sense to Delan. Why didn't Boyle want to discuss the subject? And why was he so sure the defector wasn't lying or holding back? How could a man who had started off knowing every intimate detail about the Sanford story suddenly clam up and claim ignorance about this crucial aspect?

"Tell me, Tony, what if the Osiris Option doesn't work?"

"It will."

"Yes, but what if reality doesn't quite fit in with this myth of yours and complications arise?"

"They won't," Boyle replied confidently. "Take my word for it."

"Fine," said Delan, dropping his tone an octave to underline his growing impatience, "but let's just suppose for a moment, shall we? Let's look at the downside. What happens if Osiris doesn't go along with your plans?"

"There's absolutely no reason to question the viability of the option," Boyle replied matter-of-factly. "For a start, it's not something new we're trying. Hell, the Egyptians executed a variation of it flawlessly with Qaddafi a few years back. With our help, that is. All we're doing is raising the orbit a little, that's all."

Briefly Delan closed his eyes. Maybe Boyle didn't have an answer to give. Maybe there were no choices. That's what it sounded like. But why? It was very strange. Even more suspicious given Boyle's caginess. But what choice did he, Colonel Nick Delan, have? And the plan itself was ingenious. Complex, risky, but brilliant. If it worked—and that was a big if—they would be ahead on all counts. They and not the Soviets would be calling the shots.

But what if it failed?

"The answer to your question is, all hell will break loose," Boyle said uncomfortably. "Well, isn't that what you want to hear?" He paused, staring at Delan. "Look, I can't make you accept it, Nick. No one can. But let me say this before you make your mind up. There's absolutely no way we could replace you if you were to decide to back out now. Not in time: the entire plan depends on timing and location. Once Sanford leaves that house, the plan becomes obsolete."

Nick Delan looked away, briefly casting a circumspect glance around their corner table in the American Airlines Admirals' Club lounge in the Bradley International Terminal at Los Angeles airport. More and more he was learning that some of the most secret meetings conducted in this clandestine world he had been drawn into occurred in hotels and bars, taxicabs and limousines, and airports; not behind the thick walls of "sterile" rooms in various high-security buildings. He had to admit, though, it seemed quite effective. Nothing at all suspicious was apparent. The room was standard Americana, filled with white plastic tables and chairs, bright-red nylon carpets and synthetic flowers and plants. Television screens dangled from the ceiling to announce the terminal's arrivals and departures, while the predominant sound in the lounge consisted of the hushed tones of various business conversations, punctuated by the clinking of ice cubes around two dozen long and short glasses. Occasionally a flight announcement would purr through the loudspeaker system.

It *was* an exquisite plan, Delan thought, looking back to Anthony Boyle. A little bit of the lion and a lot of the fox. Inside, Delan felt the first fleeting sparks of excitement run through his body. Nevertheless, life had conditions; and prudence was one of them. He would do it. Just as Boyle wanted, he would do it. But he would play it safe. He would find a way to insure himself a little. Because if anything was going to go wrong it would—in every likelihood—go wrong after he had undertaken his mission; not before. At that point he, Nick Delan, would be the Achilles' heel of the Osiris Option. And chopping off the limb to save the body was not exactly a concept foreign to the Washington players. Ask the Meo and Montagnard tribesmen of Vietnam, Delan thought, remembering one or two faces of those he had worked with back in Nam. If you could still find one alive, that is.

"Okay, Tony," Delan said slowly, at length. "How soon are you planning to go?"

"I don't know. One or two days, probably more," Boyle said with mounting relief. "I think you should get yourself ready and I'll let you know when everything's in place. It might be short notice, I'm afraid."

Delan hesitated before nodding. "All right."

"And don't worry about it, Nick." Boyle smiled fraternally. "All you are now is bait."

"Live bait, Tony. Let's be precise."

* * *

The shortest route from Terminal 1, the international concourse at LAX airport, to Terminal 7 is across the island of gray parking structures and service buildings that separates the one-way traffic on World Way, the overburdened access road that feeds the massive airport. That way the distance is less than half a mile.

Nick Delan, however, chose to take the longer route: around the wide, bustling, U-shaped road, past the seven other terminals, weaving in and out of the elongated buildings to mingle with the colorfully attired crowds. For although the distance increased by something like a mile, it was twenty minutes to nine, which meant he had some time to kill before the scheduled appointment with Clio. Time which provided a perfect and natural opportunity to see behind himself, to double-check for any would-be tails.

There was little that was noteworthy along his way: a lot of concrete, even more glass, and an inordinate amount of red—as in carpeting and paint and decorations and furnishings—all in various degrees of wear. The one exception was the extraordinary hybrid mix of races and languages of the busy crowds. And it clearly reflected the evolution that had taken place. The shift that had established Los Angeles County as the new Ellis Island of the promised land, opening up a melting pot more diverse, more fragmented and alienated than New York City had ever been.

As he bobbed and weaved through the crowds, Delan checked to see if he was being tailed. Twice he employed established patterns—trap runs designed to draw out, isolate one or more members of a team of professional sidewalk artists by stretching them thin in a given direction. But there was no one; he was clean. So he relaxed and slowed down a little as he passed Terminal 3 and approached the first bend in the horseshoe that curves in front of the commuter terminal housing Sun Aire.

Running alongside him to his left, a line of vehicles snaked along World Way.

Approaching Terminal 7, Delan glanced at his watch. It was five minutes to nine in the evening. He was still a few minutes early. As he walked closer, though, he saw the black Thunderbird parked where they had agreed to meet: in the loading lane outside one of the United Airlines doors.

Delan lengthened his stride, threading more quickly through the packed sidewalk until he reached the car.

"Hi," he smiled, sliding into the black-leather bucket seat on the passenger side. "You got here—"

"Oh, Nick!" she cried, moving to embrace him. "Oh, God, I thought you'd never arrive."

Delan froze. She was pale, shaking.

"What's wrong?"

"Oh, God!" she repeated, burrowing her head in his chest.

He hugged her back. "What's the matter?" he asked softly, patting her back reassuringly. "What's wrong?"

"Someone's been following me. All the way . . ."

Delan's eyes narrowed as a bank of warning lights came alive inside. Who? Why? How long had they been following? Before or after she had dropped him off in front of the Bradley International Terminal earlier in the evening? Before or after he met with Boyle? Had they been seen together?

Delan cuddled her closer, listening to pick out the salient points. The more he heard, the more uncertain he was as to who exactly was being tailed. Her? Or him?

"Come on, now. Slow down," Delan said softly. He released his grip on her arm gradually and then moved his hand up to caress her face before cupping it at the chin.

"Relax," he said soothingly as he lifted her chin, gradually guiding it up until her distraught eyes looked into his. He smiled reassuringly at her before leaning across to kiss her gently on the cheek. The tension in her seemed to ease a little.

"Now, let's back up a minute, shall we?"

Clio rested back on the seat, her hand instinctively reaching up to toy nervously with the simple cloverleaf pendant at the end of the gold chain around her neck.

"How long has he been following you?"

"I don't know."

"When did you first notice him?"

She frowned. "A short time after I dropped you off—I think."

"It's important, Clio. Try to remember exactly."

"The first time I *knew* he was there was when I got to the Bel Air Hotel. It was real quiet and I saw him following me into the driveway. Then when I left the rest of the crew in the bar to come pick you up he was there again, parked near the exit gate at the end of the driveway.''

"And he started following again?"

"Yes."

"You're sure?"

"Yes."

"About seeing him following you before you got to the hotel, too?"

"Yes."

Madonna, thought Delan. "Listen to me a minute, Clio," he said, still not quite certain. "I want you to think about it carefully before you answer. You definitely saw him on the way up? Before you reached the Bel Air?"

"Yes," snapped Clio, turning to face him. Angrily she flicked the pendant she was toying with off to one side of her chest. "Yes— yes—yes—yes. Christ Almighty, Nick, I should be. All I ever do is look around myself. Look around me for . . ."

Even though she did not finish her sentence, Nick Delan knew exactly what she meant. Genoa.

He leaned back on the seat. Someone had for some reason followed them. Him, or her, or both of them. And it was not at all clear how long they had been following. Or how many pursuers there'd been originally. Whether two or more had split up at the airport when Delan had alighted to follow both Clio and him as they went their separate ways. Either way, it was too late now. And it had a bright side. If indeed he was the target of the surveillance, it meant only one thing: that Anthony Boyle was right about many, many things.

He leaned across and kissed her forehead. "I'm sorry. It's all over now. Try to relax a little and we'll see if we can brighten up the rest of the—"

"But he's still here," she blurted, looking into his eyes worriedly. "At least, I think he is."

Delan stiffened.

"Where?"

"He drove by when I stopped here; but he pulled in up there somewhere," Clio said, turning to look out of the windshield at the bend in World Way up ahead.

"One of the assumptions we have to make," Boyle had said to Delan

just before leaving him back there in the Admirals' Club at the airport, *"is that the Soviets will want to continue to build up the pressure on Washington to unsettle us or have us do something rash. Now it follows that, having monitored you crossing the channel and casing Sanford's house, they're on to you. They know you're the point man. And that in all likelihood means that it will be through you that they will try to get to us. It also probably means that they will do everything in their power to unnerve and intimidate you. So for heaven's sake keep your wits about you."*

Delan felt his blood pressure rise. He looked ahead. At the tower that sat at the nape of World Way. Just beyond, the road converged into two-way traffic, a confusion of lights circling around the cloverleaf that fed on and off Sepulveda and Century boulevards. In between lay islands of intermittent darkness: parking lots and structures, small administration buildings, and half-hidden spaces.

The answer was out there somewhere, he thought, feeling the excitement mount inside him. Somewhere in those shadows. And he had to flush it out into the open. One glimpse, one fraction of a look, was all it would take to see if the man was a pro connected to the Sanford affair and not just another normal, everyday horny Californian nut following a pretty chick around town. He had to know. He had to set a trap. But how? Fail-safe?

"There's only one way of doing this," he said at last, his voice tinged with gravel.

"How?"

"Lose him." He looked back, gazing at her across his left shoulder. "Are you game?"

Clio nodded; but slowly, uncertainly, a frown creasing her forehead.

"Okay, start the car."

"Me! You want *me* to drive? Come on, Nick, you do it."

Delan shook his head. "If he's the serious type he might be watching; and we'd be giving away the most potent element we have going for us—surprise."

Her frown deepened.

"Don't worry, just do exactly as I tell you, when I tell you, and it'll be like taking candy from a baby."

She stared at him totally unconvinced.

"Start the car. And then pull into the traffic slowly."

Hesitantly, Clio followed his instructions to the letter and they started inching along World Way. Once off the airport's access road and on Century Boulevard, the traffic steadily picked up speed. They headed past the Sheraton La Reina and the Tishman Center on the left. Minutes later they negotiated the northbound ramp and entered the maelstrom that was the San Diego Freeway.

Delan was surprised how adroitly Clio maneuvered through the forty-mile-an-hour traffic. Especially with her eyes constantly flashing from the side to the rearview mirror.

"What kind of car was it?" Delan asked.

"I don't know."

"Do you remember the color, by any chance?"

"Red," Clio answered uncertainly. "Or burgundy. Or brown. Something like that. Dark, anyway."

"Was it new?"

"Ah . . ." Clio grimaced.

"Never mind. What about the size? Was it big or small?"

"Big, I think. Long."

"Do you remember anything else about it? Anything at all?"

She shook her head.

There was no point in pushing her, Delan thought. She didn't know and prodding would only make everything worse. "Only one man in it, though, right?"

"Yes. Yes, I'm sure of that."

Delan turned toward the window to his right.

"Is he there?" Clio asked.

"I'm not sure." Delan squinted into the passenger-side fender mirror. It was convex. Distances were difficult to gauge. "The traffic's heavy and there's a lot of movement across the lanes."

"I think I saw him!"

Delan glanced at her. "Where?"

"In the second lane. Isn't that a brown car?"

Delan turned slowly and looked out of the rear window, careful to remain behind the bulk of his high-backed seat. Indeed, two cars back and one lane across was the car he himself had suspicions about, nosing in and out of the traffic, trying to catch up. Now two other things about the vehicle were absolutely clear. It was big. And it was brown.

"It's brown. Looks like a Pontiac."

"What about the driver?" Clio asked, her voice trembling. "Is he black?"

Delan squinted into an infinite number of headlights. The shining brown Pontiac cruised thirty yards behind as the bumper-to-bumper traffic gradually picked up a head of steam.

"Can't tell his color. But he seems to be big."

Nick Delan turned back from the rear window and pondered the problem. He looked out at the landscape to get his bearings: Manchester Boulevard passed by; and then Florence. La Tijera and Sepulveda twisting around again would be coming up shortly as the freeway curved left, closer to the Pacific. And then the knotted tangle of cloverleaves where the San Diego and Marina freeways converge.

"What do you want me to do?" Clio asked nervously.

Delan thought for a moment. All he needed was one look, one glance at the appearance of the man to give him some idea of just whom he was up against. In comparison, losing him in the heavy traffic would be relatively easy.

"See the truck up there?" he said. "A couple of hundred yards ahead . . . in the slow lane?"

"Uh-huh."

"Take it easy—but edge up slowly and move up in front of him. You got till Culver to do it. That's quite a way, so stay cool."

Much to the chagrin of the talking on-board computer gauging efficiency, Clio accelerated until they were abreast of the monstrous hulk of the huge semitrailer. Culver Boulevard was still several minutes away when Clio used the indicator to comfortably cut across into the slower lane in front of the juggernaut.

"Now," Delan sighed, reaching up to stroke her hair tenderly. "This is the hard part. I want you to start acting like you're having engine trouble. Jerk your speed around a little. Nothing serious. Five, ten miles an hour or so." He caressed the soft skin of her cheekbone with the backs of his fingers. It was moist with perspiration. "Do you think you can handle it?" he asked tenderly.

She swallowed; and nodded before abruptly jerking her right foot off the accelerator.

Behind them, the huge, cumbersome eighteen-wheeler protested through an earsplitting roar of its air horn.

"Great," Delan soothed. "You're doing fine. Don't worry about him. Just keep it going till you reach Washington. Then speed back up to fifty-five again. Okay?"

She nodded, biting her lower lip.

"Can you see the Pontiac?"

"Yes," Clio answered after checking in her side-view mirror to see directly down the lane they were in.

"What's it doing?" he asked, unable to see it in his own mirror.

Clio glanced nervously at the mirror again. "It's . . . it's pulling out into the second lane."

Delan felt the adrenaline inside building. "Speed up to sixty," he instructed as they crossed the Washington overpass. "What's he doing now?"

"Moving with us."

"Still in the second lane?"

Clio nodded unenthusiastically.

"Okay. See the turnoff up ahead?"

"Yes."

"I want you to come to a stop. A sudden stop on the side of the freeway at the mouth of that exit. Don't use your indicator and don't turn into the ramp. Just swerve off onto the right shoulder of the freeway. Okay?"

Clio said nothing. But Delan saw her tightening her grip on the steering wheel.

"Are you ready?"

"Yes," she said; and swallowed.

Delan could see tiny beads of perspiration now, covering her forehead. But he waited—gauging the speed and distances and traffic; waited—for exactly the right moment.

"Now," he snapped when he was satisfied.

Clio reacted instantly. She twisted the vehicle from the hard, smooth asphalt surface to the soft, bumpy gravel of the shoulder, compensating well for the slide that came from the sudden changes in speed, drag, and holding. But the shattering roar of an air horn sent a wave of thunder through the car as the semitruck behind was forced to brake sharply and swerve to avoid a collision. The angry blare continued as the truck fishtailed momentarily onto the right shoulder, a cloud billowing in its wake. But the dust was blown away almost instantly by the unending procession of cars moving past in the slow lane. The very same train of vehicles, their headlights flashing by like tracer shots, formed a defensive wall across which the brown Pontiac couldn't cross. It was trapped in the second lane and carried away by the relentless tide heading north.

Whoever was driving the brown car was astute enough to improvise, however. Instantly he slowed down, hiding his vehicle behind the bulk of a battered old light-blue surfer van tattooed with psychedelic designs that puttered along in the slow lane.

Nick Delan felt every muscle in his body go hard. He hadn't seen a thing. Whoever it was was a pro. Of that there was little doubt.

17 | WEDNESDAY, JANUARY 13

The strains and tensions of the enormously high-risk/high-reward undertaking were beginning to reflect on the features of the four men. The long hours, the tedious detail, the fastidious secrecy, all being played out against the backdrop of the burdensome daily routines of high offices, seemed nothing in comparison to the rising sense of expectation they felt. For the pace was picking up now; and at stake was nothing less than the control of the Kremlin and the leadership of the Soviet Union. The sweet rewards of victory were becoming increasingly clear. So, too, were the disastrous consequences of defeat.

Only the fifth man in the group, the stooped, disheveled Englishman who was, at that very moment, presiding over the nightly project status meeting, conducted in the extreme security of *D'e'vachka Adee'n*, seemed totally unaffected by the mounting electricity of the drama.

Strewn in front of him, across the green baize of the conference table in the small, smoke-filled room buried deep beneath Stevenson Hall, were documents, pictures, folders, and computer printouts. Mounds of information sheets intricately detailing every facet of an operation that was taking place half a world away—but had as its root objective, now, the removal of the General Secretary of the Communist Party of the Soviet Union as well. The unmaking of Washington, much to the bemusement of the elderly Englishman, was now being even openly called an "added bonus" by his Soviet colleagues.

"How did the assassin respond to the provocations we devised?" asked the oversized Anatoli Andeyev, looking at the next item on the list of questions he'd jotted down during the last two and a half hours.

"Positively," the Englishman replied.

He was the only man still wearing his jacket—a worn, comfortable-looking grayish-brown Soviet attempt at a tweed. All the other men were long since in their shirtsleeves; and even then they appeared uncomfortable in the stifling, claustrophobic atmosphere of the small underground room.

"To both?" Marshal Filatov asked.

"Yes. If anything, I'd have to say even more strongly than we thought he would. Certainly that is true with respect to his violent behavior with regard to the social deviants outside the restaurant. In fact he injured them rather badly. All of which tends to suggest he is extremely predictable. And consequently malleable when the right stimuli are applied."

"And the surveillance?" Filatov enquired.

"Same thing," replied Philby. "Acted as we thought he might, totally reckless in his attempt to flush our man out. However, I must say that that's only a flash report. As you know, we avail ourselves of a twice-daily courier service for the more in-depth written primary source reports. Once we receive that we should be in a better position to know more about the precise details of his behavior."

Philby paused. "Nevertheless, I think this can be said with very little doubt: the psychographic file we've put together on Mr. Nick Delan seems to be reasonably accurate up to now. So far, in every instance, his reactions have borne out what the doctor's report concluded. Which is that he is a highly headstrong, reckless, rather simple and guileless chap at heart. That's not to say, of course, that he's not shrewd, quick, capable, and extremely violent. Rather, I think it tends to suggest what I mentioned earlier. Namely, that he's a predictable sort, a reactive man rather than active. The advantage of these latest field tests is that we can be reasonably certain that the stimuli selected in the laboratory, so to speak, do in fact trigger the requisite reactions we're after in the field. And that, you will agree, Comrades, is a distinct advantage to have over your opponent in any game."

"What is the next step?" Filatov asked.

The elderly Englishman placed his half-moon glasses on his nose and looked down at the sheet of paper he picked up from the table. It exaggerated the slight tremble of old age in his hand.

"To effect the disconnects, I believe. Thereby eliminating the visible layer of the network we have on the scene. The people who could conceivably leave some sort of trace."

18 | THURSDAY, JANUARY 14

In "Boys' Town," officially known as West Hollywood, Cathy Greene turned her yellow Buick onto Santa Monica Boulevard from Fairfax, the bright white beams of its halogen lights sweeping across the ashen faces of the teenage boy prostitutes plying their flesh along the darkened, litter-strewn pavements.

Shit, she thought, looking at the digital clock on the dashboard. Its lime-green figures read 10:33 P.M. She was already three minutes late. And Carl H. Hocher, the local illegals controller, was an exacting individual.

Illegals are deeply entrenched intelligence agents who operate outside the legal status provided by diplomatic posts and international organizations. Thus they perform illegally, operating on false papers and legends—or covers—preferably as citizens of the foreign country in which they operate.

Hocher was a pompous man with a bulbous nose who drank too much, she observed, almost tasting her revulsion. He was coarse and mean and small-minded. He also had a penchant for looking for reasons to dump on others to make himself look blameless. Cathy let up on the accelerator a little. All she needed now was to get stopped for speeding.

Nervously she brushed back her red hair and tried to shake off her anxiety by concentrating on the view ahead, the somewhat bizarre sights along what was commonly known as Gay Main Street—a tiny strip of real estate along Santa Monica Boulevard.

But the relief was momentary, the bad vibes descending as soon as she allowed her mind to drift. It was weird, this hastily called meeting. In fact, she could recall only one previous occasion that anything like this had occurred on such short notice. But even then, it had not been anywhere near as mysterious—and heavy-handed and negligent—as this. A dark, deserted lot just off a major thoroughfare in one of the most police-infested areas of town. What sort of safe, secret rendezvous was that?

She turned the car south on Sweetzer and then immediately right into a small, dark parking lot bordered by trees and dwarfed by low-rise apartment blocks four or five stories high. Earlier in the evening she had cruised by and reconnoitered the meeting place. She drove slowly over the bumpy, litter-strewn surface to the far corner of the deserted plot and parked in the shadows as she had been instructed.

In the rearview mirror the nose of a white Oldsmobile could just be discerned, poking out of the thick bushes in the dark corner behind her.

She alighted and stepped carefully through the vacant lot until she approached the shining white sedan with tinted windows. Surprisingly, when she opened its rear door no light went on. And instantly she noticed the blackness inside the dark-windowed vehicle. Nevertheless, after only the briefest hesitation, she ducked her head beneath the low roof and moved to get in.

Abruptly a huge muscular black arm reached up from the darkened pit and grabbed her by the hair as another massive paw muffled her scream. Like a winch the sinewy arm yanked her, throwing her off balance, sending her diving into the car. Her knees and ankles scraped painfully across the metal rim of the frame as she crashed prostrate on the cushioned seat. The pain, however, was only momentary. For immediately she felt her body spinning again, tumbling downward until her spine snapped agonizingly against something protruding from the floor.

"Don't move, mama," said a cruel, jive tone. "Not an inch."

She looked up. Into the mean, strung-out eyes of a black man she had seen before—where? She could not remember. Nevertheless in that one suspended moment everything else was as clear as day. But the hate that welled in her for Hocher—the man who had set her up—was abruptly cut short. Severed by the most startling sight she had ever seen in her life. Her frightened heart pounded, horror and panic converging into extraordinary strength and energy that gave vent through her thrashing limbs. She kicked out, screaming uselessly.

The movement of the long black arm was relentless. And the long hypodermic syringe it held grew larger and larger as it came toward her face. Now it was a question of inches—so close, so malicious-looking she was scared to punch out any longer—frightened it would throw the thin slithery needle off course—into her eyes.

Frenzy filled her as the long, thin syringe entered her nose, her face unable to move in the vise grip of the huge black giant with a cold, inscrutable face. Then quiet, a hush, a lull she knew would fade to everlasting sleep.

The powerful tubocurarine entered her body high in the undetectable nasal passage, buried among the deep pores and roots of hair. It spread slowly through the bloodstream, down to every muscle in her body, making her drowsy and lethargic for one brief moment—before cold unconsciousness set in.

When she was fully comatose, Aaron "the Baron" Brown moved her body back to her own car with the ease of a butcher handling a leg of ham. There he placed her behind the steering wheel before carefully rolling up the blue sleeve of her cashmere sweater and tying a makeshift tourniquet below her slim biceps. Then he extracted another syringe from his pocket and pumped the inside of her elbow full of the latest designer drug. Products of illicit labs, stronger, more lethal than narcotics from natural sources, these chemical concoctions are custom-made, personalized, for the right price, to individual whims.

The tubocurarine would keep Cathy Greene alive—sedated, relaxed, asleep—until she overdosed on synthetic heroin.

It was the first of the disconnects Kim Philby had instructed.

The second was less than three hours away.

Twenty-two miles north of the White House, just off the bustling Washington–Baltimore Parkway that cuts through the lush rolling greenery of Maryland like the slash of a sword, a massive monolithic compound looms. From a distance, it looks cheerfully benign. Above the verdant woodlands jut three varishaped towers of differing heights, connected by a sprawling, pistachio-green, three-floor A-shaped building. Taken together the cluster exudes the aura of a huge, overgrown bureaucracy—the likes of which are resplendent in the Washington area.

It is, however, a misleading impression; and a carefully cultivated deception at that. For this compound is the headquarters of the most secret agency within the United States Government. An establishment created not by an act of the legislature, but by a seven-page presidential directive issued on November 4, 1952, by President Harry S. Truman—the text of which has never been made public.

This is the National Security Agency, the largest espionage facility in the Western world. And its director, according to the Senate Intelligence Committee, is "the most influential individual" in the U.S. intelligence community in terms of both the sheer size of the operations he oversees and the immensity of his agency's funding. For while in theory the Director of the Central Intelligence Agency is responsible for all intelligence activities, in reality, according to the same Senate Intelligence Committee report, "the DCI controls less than ten percent of the combined national and tactical intelligence efforts. . . . The remainder spent directly by the Department of Defense on intelligence activities . . . [is] outside his fiscal authority."

The NSA headquarters are situated behind Orwellian fences that encircle the one-thousand-acre compound at Fort George G. Meade. Charged by the Department of Defense with the nation's worldwide electronic eavesdropping operations, behind those perimeters lie caves of electronic wizardry; and a city with a little over 5,000 permanent residents. During the day, its population swells to over 40,000 with those commuting in to operate the huge subterranean espionage factory.

Up on the roofs of the compound's buildings, the skyline is awash with a frightening array of exotic antennae: radomes, parabolic microwave dishes, log-periodic, Wullenweber and long-wire antennae, huge satellite dishes, and many others bristle like a hedgehog's carapace. And each is operational on a constant basis: radiating and receiving and disseminating the information gleaned by over 100,000 seconded personnel scattered over 2,000 electronic-listening posts and antenna farms cached across the surface of the globe.

All the variegated efforts of its sister agency, the National Reconnaissance Office, another "black" organization which is responsible for the nation's military satellite program, also converge on this one point—the seven layers of electronic eavesdropping satellites girdling the globe: from the earliest generations of small Sigint beach ball listening posts, the Big Bird satellites, the family of lower-altitude KH models, the Close Looks and Chalet platforms, the high-altitude Rhyolite—on up to the massive new 30,000-pound space-shuttle-delivered Aquacade electronic listening posts. All this capability congeals at one huge, "hardened" Atlantis that lies buried in the bowels of the earth beneath those benign-looking administration buildings at Fort Meade.

This is the National Security Agency's Office of Telecommunications and Computer Services. And it consists of twelve and a half acres of the most sophisticated computers and data-processing and cryptographic machines on earth—a concentration of brain power hitherto unknown to man. Twenty-four hours a day, three hundred and sixty-five days a year, this complex network of artificial intelligence monitors the information pouring in from its electronic eyes and ears across the world. Eyes that have synthetic apertures that can zoom in from outer space to read the text of a newspaper or the make of a watch; and drooping Schmidt sensors that can, with their Teal Ruby capability, home in on and conduct infrared, thermal, and holographic surveillance against the clutter of the earth's background.

Its ears, meanwhile, operate in any number of different ways. They monitor the communications traffic, i.e., every telephone, telex, telegraph, facsimile and computer message being flashed around the world via microwave communication systems. Most of which, under cover of proprietary agencies, belong to them.

All this information is fed into the staggering underground computer network whose primary brain is divided into two hemispheres, as in the human mind, left and right, code-named Carillon and Lodestone. The network's showpieces are the interlinked Cray III machines on display. Each has a capability of 1.2 billion flops (floating points, or arithmetical operations per second). Which means, in lay language, that each can achieve in one second what took several years in, say, 1960.

Along the western wall of this huge underground cavern ten War Rooms are situated—each grotto has the dimensions of a medium-size indoor basketball arena. Seven are used for visual monitoring.

Three are allocated as nerve centers, reserved for crisis-management purposes or oversight of a sensitive operation, providing a constant window on the area of particular interest. These rooms are all identical. At first glance they resemble small, ultramodern aircraft hangars, with copper-covered beams and scaffolding buttressing the plexiglass astrodomes from which soft, opaque, artificial daylight glows. But the impression is held only briefly, as the visitor's attention is snatched away by an incredible vision of the twenty-first century. Hanging at the precise epicenter of the opposite wall as one enters the copper-lined vault doors, extending thirty yards in length and fifteen in height, is an electronic map of the world. It is alive with constantly changing colors and blips of lights, throbbing with dotted bars and permutating numbers and graphs that provide a treasure trove of worldwide intelligence: approaching aircraft, ships, and submarines; Soviet troop deployments, missiles, bases; and, of course, the constant changes taking place. And the movements appear as they occur in multicolored tracer lines that, taken together, indicate the first hint of a trend: buildups; from where; unusual flow patterns; and any and all other ab- or subnormal activity so key to determining the slightest inconsistency in a game designed to forestall the ultimate match.

On the left-hand wall of this futuristic setting crammed with activity are what appear to be two Cinerama-size screens. A closer inspection reveals that they are in fact two sets of twenty separate small screens. They are situated next to one another, two inches apart, five across and four down. These are expressly designed for isolation shots: close-ups and freezes. And of course to view background material from the computer files, or any and all other purposes.

To the right of the room extends an amphitheater where decks of control boards and instrument panels are laid before an army of experts—crypto and traffic analysts, telemetry and signals officers, conversion and communications specialists, and others—with backup engineers on hand to constantly monitor the performance of the equipment in this Aladdin's cave of electronic magic.

Down on the command floor, at the center of the pit of the room, is a series of low-back leather swivel chairs placed around a twelve-man conference table, itself situated in the middle of a giant rotating, slate-black platform.

It was precisely in this spot in War Room 9 that Anthony Boyle, the Deputy National Security Adviser who was the acting executive officer of the mission, sat; together with the Director of the National Security Agency and Robert Wilson, the CIA chief.

"What time is it?" snapped Wilson. Like Anthony Boyle, his eyes were glued, as they had been for nearly fifteen minutes now, to the twenty lit screens in front of him.

The tall, reedy NSA chief, a Navy man who was wearing his uniform, swiveled toward the huge electronic map on his right. He glanced up at the black digital clock, neon red numbers against a black background. "Twenty-three twenty-eight at target site," Vice Admiral Kenny Lee Harmon replied in a refined Texas drawl.

"Near enough," Wilson said, turning to look at him. "Any reason why we can't get started with this a few minutes early? It's only a briefing and orientation session."

"No," Admiral Harmon replied. "Not really. This is more or less what we can offer you throughout the night, irrespective of the hour you choose to carry out the operation."

Anthony Boyle forced himself to look away from the riveting images, pictures that not even he, with his exalted security status and high perch in the White House hierarchy, had known could be produced in "real time" and with such clarity. He turned and studied the NSA director, aware of the new respect he harbored for the man.

He had the gawky, bespectacled look of an eccentric Central European professor with tenure at a small midwestern college. It was, however, a misleading appearance. The Admiral was generally regarded as one of the most brilliant minds in the service of the United States Government. Only the dark-brown near crew cut brushed straight back above the sloping forehead of his long, narrow face gave a clue to the firmly established habits ingrained in him by the traditions of his naval background.

"All right," said Admiral Harmon, leaning forward and extending his long hands to the small panel of levers and dials and switches on the table in front of him. "What you're looking at on these screens is a series of pictures of the West Coast of America in what we call real time, which means *live,* for all intents and purposes."

Boyle and Wilson followed the Admiral's gaze, their heads turning back to the wall in front of them and the bank of smaller screens to the right, all twenty of which were flickering.

"What you are looking at is the target zone. And the pictures are being transmitted directly by the Aquacade satellite we moved into geosynchronous orbit above Los Angeles four days ago," the Admiral continued before going on to explain how, from top to bottom, left to right, each green-tinted infrared picture provided "systematically tighter, or closer, shots" of the same area: "your target zone."

Starting with a cloudy, flat and misshapen wide-angle shot taken from 22,300 miles above, that extended from the black inlets of sea cutting in at the slightly lighter grayish land mass at Prince Rupert in Canada down to Baja California, in the south; and Tucson; Salt Lake City; Butte, Montana; and Calgary, Alberta, on the horizon. Then closer, parts of California, Nevada, Arizona and the northwestern tip of Mexico. Closer yet, Los Angeles: San Diego to the south, Palm Springs and Barstow to the east, San Simeon to the north. Los Angeles proper. Then the area to its south: Orange County. Anaheim. Newport Beach. Until the last picture showed a clear, sharp, computer-enhanced bird's-eye view of a narrow slip of water bordered by two beaches.

"To begin with, I'd like to draw your attention to the last screen. It is the primary target zone up close. In other words, the roof of the building you see beneath this arrow I'm jiggling, in the top center of the picture, which is due west, is Allan Sanford's house. Directly opposite, across the waterway, is the Balboa Bay Club. This," he said, toying with a lever until the small white arrow moved to the bottom of the screen and jiggled around before settling at one precise point, "is where your man stages from; or at least has on his practice runs. It's a point at the northernmost tip of this wharf that runs along here." The white arrow moved parallel with the bottom of the screen, where a long line of black ran alongside numerous yachts and boats of differing sizes. Then the white pointer moved again, closer to the bottom border of the image. "This here is the Balboa Bay Club, as I mentioned.

"Now what I'd like you to do is look at the screen beside it, to the left. This depicts the same area, only it pans out a little to include more of the vicinity. This, for instance," he said, superimposing another white arrow on the new screen, "is Pacific Coast Highway, which runs behind—on the inland side of—the Balboa Bay Club. Again this is the waterway—Lido Channel—we were looking at a moment ago on this side." The arrow moved to the other side of the buildings before heading on to the sandy beach opposite to the west. "And this is Sanford's house.

"But for the purposes of this exercise I'd like you to look at this area." The arrow moved back to the east, across the waterway, past the Balboa Bay Club, over Pacific Coast Highway to the hills that overlooked the coast road from the inland side. "This is where we've detected the infrared surveillance sights," he said, pressing another button.

Immediately five red Xs appeared, shaped in an arc up on the hills. Anthony Boyle leaned forward until his elbows rested on the table in front of him. He was impressed to the point of amazement by the extraordinary technological spectacular he was witnessing. Only the matter-of-fact tone of the Admiral's enlightening commentary made it all too real.

"And it's here that our problems start," the Admiral added ominously.

Boyle looked at him. "Why?"

"Well, because there's a peculiarity here someplace. And it has to do with the triggering mechanism these sights are using."

He looked away from Boyle and toyed with the control panel again. An arrow appeared on Lido Channel, some twenty to thirty yards out in the water, directly in front of the Balboa Bay Club. "Earlier this week when your man went in on his final practice run, as you know we monitored him. And it was exactly at this point"— the arrow on the screen jiggled around—"that he was picked up by those five observation sights up on the hills watching him. No, let me rephrase that. This is the point at which the monitors were activated."

"What the hell is that supposed to mean?" Wilson snapped after a long silence.

"Well, there's a slight problem we have with that," the Admiral drawled, exaggerating his natural Texan accent.

"What is that?"

"Well, Bob, from these points here," the Admiral said, pointing with another arrow to each of the five red crosses that represented the surveillance sights on the hills behind Pacific Coast Highway, "there's no line of sight to the path your man took. Not until he gets to this point."

The second arrow moved sharply west, flitting over the street and store and burger restaurant lights dotted around the broad coast highway. It passed by the club and the terrace and wharf in front of it to a point in the waterway some thirty yards beyond the stationary first arrow indicating where Delan had been picked up by the monitoring sights.

"You see, these buildings here," the Admiral said, pointing to the club, "are relatively high-rise. And they completely block out the view of the monitoring sights behind until somewhere around this point here."

On the screen the second white arrow jiggled where it stood. Which was at a point some thirty yards beyond the stationary first arrow indicating where Delan had, in fact, been picked up.

"As you can see, there's no way they could have—"

"Jesus H. Christ," Anthony Boyle mumbled, slumping back in his chair. "That means they have another observation post somewhere. Up closer. With line-of-sight vision."

"Precisely," the Admiral replied.

The silver-gray Volkswagen pulled up onto the raised apron extending from the impressive Palladian house.

Like the man said it would, the killer thought as he got out of his car, parked at the curb in front of the short, white-balustraded wall of the house. "A little after closing time," he'd said. "Which should make it somewhere around two in the morning." Man was right. Man was always right.

Even before the lights of the Volkswagen had dimmed and the engine turned off, the man closed the door of his own car, but left it slightly ajar to avoid the slightest sound. He moved, too. Quickly, stealthily, like a cat on the prowl, he crossed the seven yards from his vehicle and entered the wrought-iron gate just as it was closing. Sticking to the shadows of the trees and bushes on the left-hand side of the driveway, he crept up toward the idling Volkswagen.

The driver switched off the engine. Simultaneously its lights went black and the door started to open.

The man stopped and waited.

Suddenly the driver knew he was there. She seemed to sense his brooding presence rather than anything else. Half in, half out of the vehicle, she snapped her head up and tried to gasp. It was a muffled attempt, drowned by the chilling reality she saw.

The killer looked at her coldly for one split second. Then he raised his revolver and shot her in the mouth from close range. The silenced bullet made barely a sound as it exploded from the barrel. Entering her skull, it stifled even the smallest groan as she crumbled backward into the darkness of the car.

The assassin cast a calm, furtive look around just to be on the safe side. There was no hint of life in the immediate vicinity. Only the never-ending night-lights of the city spreading away beneath the Hollywood Hills caught his eye. But only briefly, an instant. For almost immediately he looked back and leaned into the vehicle, directly above the blond girl's blood-splattered corpse. He leaned forward and pressed his gun into her left breast and fired again. The burn marks spread away like soot from a miniature chimney on the frilly, peach-colored satin dress that resembled an old-fashioned slip. Satisfied, he released his gloved grip on the revolver—the same revolver he had pressed into Cathy Greene's lifeless palm less than three hours ago—and allowed the gun to tumble to the floor.

A minute later, after using the remote-control device fitted on the Volkswagen to open the electronic gates at the end of the small driveway, he returned to the stolen Chrysler Imperial and pulled out from the curb.

Behind, Aaron "the Baron" Brown left a trail of clear evidence at Cathy Greene's house. Clues that would point an overworked and underpaid policeman to conclude that the young woman found dead there had been murdered by her host. A woman who just happened to have also died that night; and from an overdose of drugs that could possibly have been the consequence of intense remorse. The time discrepancy between their deaths would baffle and tantalize and absorb a lot of man-hours. Then, in every likelihood, it would be forgotten, buried beneath the never-ending flood of other, more recent crimes.

Either way the second of Kim Philby's disconnects had been placed. Miss Jacquie Petit was dead.

19 | FRIDAY, JANUARY 15

From his brown barrel chair, situated directly beneath one of the string of chandeliers hanging from the high ceiling in Lobby Court, the tall, powerfully built black man watched.

Phillip Myers entered the Century Plaza Hotel and passed the clump of *ficus benjamina* trees decorating the right side of the doorway. The man sat, immaculately attired in a beige Italian silk suit, and slowly swiveled his thick neck to follow the diminutive Myers scurrying across the hotel's ostentatious modern entryway toward the elevator bank at the far end.

At the precise moment the brushed aluminum doors closed behind Phillip Myers, Aaron "the Baron" Brown glanced at his watch. It was exactly 2:48 P.M. Casually he raised the pages of *The Los Angeles Times* and continued reading.

A few moments went by before he cast his eyes at his watch again. It now read 2:54. He folded the paper haphazardly and tossed it on the next chair before reaching into his right trouser pocket. From the wad of notes he extracted, he peeled off a ten-dollar bill which he dropped onto the table in front of him, next to the empty beer bottle and froth-stained glass.

He rose slowly to his full, broad-shouldered height and sauntered toward the elevators.

Very calmly, he pressed the call button before raising his hand to his coat. He tapped the small vial in his breast pocket and smiled.

SATURDAY, JANUARY 16

The soft chirp of the Trimline telephone persisted. Reluctantly Nick Delan turned over in the bed and picked it up.

"Hello."

"Mr. Breitenbach?" said the familiar male voice.

Delan's eyes opened wide. "No," he said, quickly propping himself up on his elbow.

"Is this room one-sixteen?"

"No," Delan repeated. He was wide awake now, his brain gripped by the meaning of the words. He rubbed his face with his free hand.

"Oh, I'm so sorry to have disturbed you," Anthony Boyle said slowly. "I asked for room one-sixteen. They must have made a mistake. Have a good day, now."

Delan sat up smartly. He threw off the bedcovers and glanced at the radio clock as he swung his legs to the floor. It read 8:07 A.M. One-sixteen, he thought. First digit: one. January. Last two digits: sixteen. Sixteenth. January sixteenth. Today. He was cleared to go. Tonight at midnight.

He turned and glanced at Clio, lying in the bed. Thankfully the phone and his abrupt movements had not awakened her; her breathing was deep and regular, her face a sea of serenity.

For a long moment Nick Delan sat and looked at the telephone on the bedside table. Tonight. It was all set. There was no turning back.

He stood silently and picked up the terrycloth bathrobe lying on the chair as he trod softly out of the bedroom and down the stairs to the living room of the duplex. He stepped out onto the balcony and sat in a chair, oblivious to the golden Californian morning bursting overhead.

For the next two hours, while Clio continued to sleep, time passed increasingly slowly for Nick Delan. The old familiar mood set in, catalyzed by the sudden speed of events. It was, as always during the final hours of the countdown before an operation, a period of deep introspection. Like the controlled fear athletes experience before the gates of the arena are finally opened and the seats filled.

He thought of many things, but mostly of what lay ahead. The fear he could handle. It was an old friend, easy to placate. All you had to do was respect it. If you didn't, you were crazy. A fool. Besides, fear was in all men. How it was handled separated the coward from the hero. What was more difficult to control, though, was the doubt. The misgivings he had about what he was about to do, the suspicions he had about his own side.

When his thoughts moved to Clio the ambivalence increased. Wasn't it a little foolish to have her here, with him, at this particularly sensitive time? On the one hand she could conceivably be useful when he veered away from Boyle's plan, as he'd decided to do. Valuable as a legitimate alibi, or a cover, or an aid if something went wrong. On the other, was all that just rationalization? Was she there simply because he wanted her there? Needed her there?

He was so absorbed with these thoughts that for some time he was unaware of her presence behind him on the balcony.

The anxiety on his face, the intense concentration didn't escape her notice. And for a long moment Clio Bragana was uncertain how to react.

"A penny for your thoughts," she said finally, stepping out onto the small balcony and bending to kiss his forehead.

Delan snapped his head around, startled out of his reverie. She moved around and sat across from him at the breakfast table.

"Well?"

He shook his head. "I was thinking of you, believe it or not."

"What about me?" she asked, reaching to pour herself a cup of coffee with one hand, while the other held the front of her *robe de chambre*.

Delan stared at her for a moment. And for one split second he wanted to tell her everything. But again it was a fleeting fantasy. He didn't want her hurt. Above all, he did not want her hurt. But he didn't want to lose her, either. Which meant he couldn't even begin to tell her to go away for a little while.

"That bad, huh?" she said mockingly. "Should have known from the look on your face."

Delan leaned forward and lit a cigarette. "I'd like you to be serious for a minute, Clio, and listen to me very carefully. There's something I want to tell you but there are two caveats."

Clio's smile faded.

"The first is I can only be very vague and you'll have to trust me. The second," he said, looking her in the eye, "is that you'll have a whole lot of questions. And I don't want you to ask them."

Clio Bragana frowned. "What do you mean?"

"That's a question."

Clio Bragana hesitated, not knowing what to say. Then slowly she dropped her eyes, the suspicion evaporating slightly. "Okay."

"The next few days are going to be hard ones for me, Clio. I've got a problem that I've got to resolve. And I have no idea what's going to happen. But I want you to do something for me. I want you to stay by that telephone."

"Why? What's going on, Nick?"

"Probably nothing. But then again, I just may need your help."

Because of the time difference, in the Soviet Union it was already January 17.

At *D'e'vachka Adee'n*, in a large, ill-lit office lined with paperback English books and piles of half-read newspapers and magazines, Kim Philby started shuffling the stack of computer printouts scattered over his heavy wooden desk into an orderly pile. In the background strains of Bach's *Prelude in A Major* made a curious contrast with the room's musty atmosphere of stale pipe smoke and calculated clutter.

The old man placed the stack to one side, on top of one of the many piles, some of which were already over a foot high. And still the center of his desk was covered with papers, documents, and charts. He picked up a scuffed black file from his left and placed it on top of everything else, directly in front of him. A thick diagonal red stripe ran across the cover.

Reaching for his pipe, he opened the folder and looked at the picture on the left inside cover. He angled it a little to avoid the glare of the overhead bulb that hung from a faded green shade. Philby placed the unlit pipe between his teeth and for a long moment looked at the face—a face with which he felt a strange kinship, an intimacy he sensed although they'd never even met.

Then slowly he looked at the page opposite and flicked it after absorbing the only five meaningful words it contained: Delan, Nick. Né: Delano, Nicola.

Almost absentmindedly he started skimming the familiar pages he now knew by heart, glancing down the various headings and subtitles. He stopped at: *CLASS BACKGROUND: Proletarian origins prior to embourgeoisement of father following connections with organized crime.*

Of the rest of the twenty-seven-page psychoanalytical report, much of which was highly technical and filled with medical terms, Philby read only those sections he had annotated in his own handwriting, especially the underlined words. *Raised by maternal grandparents . . . strict Catholic upbringing . . . mother murdered by rival gangland family in an underworld territorial dispute with father over drug-trafficking rights . . . poverty . . . alienation . . . estrangement from deviant father continued until latter's own violent death outside a restaurant in lower Manhattan four years ago . . . loner . . . deeply religious . . . excessive high achiever . . . potentially insubordinate, cynical, and mistrusting . . . tendency toward naive idealism and perfectionism . . . prone to oversimplifications . . . extremely physical . . . emotional tendencies, but suppressed . . . simple ethical standards . . .*

At the sound of the telephone Philby dropped his eyes to the very last line of the report even as he picked up the black receiver: *CURRENT MISSION: Assassination of Allan Sanford.*

"Yes."

"General Philby? Zubko here. We've just received confirmation from Elshtayn. The assassin is approaching the area."

Kim Philby pulled a soiled handkerchief from the pocket of his old brown cardigan just in time to trap a sneeze. "Thank you, Arkadi Anatolevich. I shall be right down."

* * *

The gentle waves rolling up Lido Channel toward Turning Basin shimmered beneath the full moon framed in a deep purple sky. From across the waterway came the loud, rhythmic beat of an electric guitar. Somehow it seemed to jive in perfect rhythm with Nick Delan's heart, bursting with rising excitement and tension.

The music was an unexpected bonus. A perfect diversion to draw away the attention of the curious, the insomniacs, and the night owls. In addition it provided another unforeseen and welcome break: cover. The opportunity to blend in with all the spaced-out rich kids celebrating the rowdy pot party aboard the yacht across the way—some of whom were skinny-dipping in this, the midnight hour.

Almost by rote he checked the thirty rounds of 9mm Parabellum bullets in the magazine of the Heckler and Koch MP5SD. The silenced machine pistol was of his own choosing. A firearm designed specifically for antiterrorist operations, only 8.8 inches long—ten in the integrated silenced model he was using—it weighed just 5.4 pounds and was small enough to be concealed beneath clothing. It was generally regarded as the ultimate weapon of its type on the market—reliable and deadly accurate with a cyclic rate of fire of six hundred and fifty rounds a minute.

It was functioning flawlessly. He replaced it in the waterproof knapsack on top of an unusually long, clumsy-looking pistol, large and cumbersome like an archaic flare gun. Before closing the waterproof bag, Nick Delan extracted a pair of binoculars and a small black box. The binoculars he looped over his head. They were the rubber-coated Baird general-purpose night-vision apparatus, night eyes. To prevent them from dangling awkwardly during the swim across he snapped their two Velcro-edged straps to the patches of similar material strategically placed on either side of the buckle of his thick, light brown-webbed belt. He slung the knapsack behind his back, slipping his arms into its shoulder straps. Then he turned his attention back to the small black box.

It was a tiny, synthesized ELF (extremely low frequency) transmitter/receiver that operated on only 2W of power—too low to be audible to hostile trackers. It also contained some of the most sophisticated integrated microchip circuitry on earth, circuitry capable of coding and decoding conversations via instantaneous digital conversion and operating up to a range of seventy miles. Which was five times more than necessary to carry Delan's voice to the U.S. Marine Corps Helicopter Base in Irvine. There the communications room stood ready, patched in to the National Security Agency just outside Washington.

The apparatus also contained a minuscule pinhole microphone that was covered by a waterproof artificial one-way membrane. Delan snapped the receiver into the precision housings on his belt and locked the lightweight, hardened black polymer otoscope connected to it, behind his ear. He adjusted the thin arm that extended from the hearing aid until the microphone stood just to one side of his mouth.

"Claw to Eagle. Claw to Eagle," he whispered into the warm night air. "Can you read me?"

"Eagle to Claw. Eagle to Claw," a flat, cryptic tone replied in Delan's ear. "Roger. We have cross-link."

He was ready. All that was left was a moment's mental preparation. He paused and stared across the channel. After a few moments he slowly, carefully formed a small cross in front of his bare chest. He closed his eyes and bowed his head. At length he looked up and crossed himself again.

"Claw to Eagle," he finally whispered. "Proceeding with infiltration mode."

Looking around cautiously he slipped into the water and waded until the sand disappeared beneath his bare feet.

Deep in the bowels of the earth beneath Fort George G. Meade, the Director of the National Security Agency leaned back in his chair at the table in the center of the command floor in War Room 9. He concentrated on Screen 17 on the opposite wall. Slowly the troubled expression deepened on the man's bony, angular face.

"Does he know we're watching?" Admiral Kenny Lee Harmon asked softly, turning to look at Anthony Boyle.

"No," snapped the CIA chief. "We're in voice contact only as far as he's concerned."

Robert Wilson continued to gaze at the screen, trying hard to ignore the NSA director's tone. Just like the first time he'd seen them, in the "briefing and orientation session" two nights ago, all the pictures on display were clear, bright, well-defined. Nothing at all like the vague intelligence pictures the CIA or Defense Department so grudgingly released when it was somehow propitious. The image content and quality were detailed and accurate to the point of being astonishing. In the lexicon of the trade they were "computer-enhanced." Which meant the pictures and colors he and Boyle were looking at were manipulated, sifted, selected, sequenced, and otherwise processed by computers to offer instantly edited readable images. All that was odd about them was the slight green tinge and the angle of viewing. Certain compensation—in the first instance as to depth and relief—needed to be made before one felt totally comfortable analyzing a picture frame from the air. But it was a knack, learned quickly. One everyone in War Room 9 had long ago acquired, except, of course, for Anthony Boyle and himself.

Wilson shifted forward in his chair, determined not to let his concentration waver under the Admiral's continuing glare. Harmon knew only half the story, anyway. He had absolutely no idea just why Delan must be kept at arm's length. Goddammit, he cursed to himself. If Harmon knew, he would be the first to agree that they were right. Besides, this thing was too big to be governed by normal ethical codes of conduct. Principles, morals, duties, or allegiances, none of those applied to problems of this magnitude. This was above even life or death. It was a matter of national security.

"Roger, Claw," the same passionless voice replied in Delan's ear as he slid into the water. "You are go for infiltration mode."

Dead straight across sat Allan Sanford's house. To the left the college kids and their wild party. Delan studied them as he began swimming—slowly, silently, breaststroking the cold water. The festivities occupied most of the deck of the sixth or seventh yacht away, with the revelers pouring down the gangplank and onto one of the small private wharfs that extended before the patio of a large Georgian-style house. They were not close enough to get in the way. In fact, they were not in any state to notice him, let alone care.

He looked to his right. The small playground a hundred yards down from Sanford's house was dark. As were most of the surrounding houses, except for the flickering of some remaining Christmas decorations and the soft, yellow glow of night-lights. No one else seemed to be awake, other than Allan Sanford—whom he had observed earlier, sitting working at his desk. Delan had not seen any patrol guards yet, either. Which meant he would have to wait until they had come and gone. And then allow them an additional ten minutes to gain enough distance to let him conduct his business and be safely on his way out. Preferably halfway across the water, too—before they could double back to Sanford's house if and when the commotion started.

Abruptly he stopped and treaded water. Five or ten yards ahead he would come into the view of the surveillance sights on the hills behind. The ones he had observed on every one of his practice runs—beaming infrared lighting onto the target zone. What had still not been established was if there were any available light watchers; and if there were, where they were situated. Behind? Ahead? Close? Far?

"Claw to Eagle," he whispered and waited.

"Roger, Claw."

"Approaching Red Line One."

"Looking good."

Paddling gently, Delan undid the Velcro clasps on his belt and raised the goggles. He scoured the island with the more precise clarity of night eyes. The available lighting mode turned darkness into a green-tinged twilight. But still it uncovered nothing untoward. No. It was the return journey that would be the problem. That was where the danger lurked, the point of maximum exposure. And there was at least one good reason to believe that the Soviets were on to him. That much was obvious. Not only had they observed, monitored, even perhaps filmed him going in to reconnoiter the site, they'd also had him tailed. All of which meant that at that very moment they probably had him in their sights. They could squeeze the trigger whenever they wanted. Kill or wound— whichever they fancied.

But they hadn't. Not yet, anyway. Which meant, so far at least, that Tony Boyle's reasoning was sound. Perhaps things would work out as planned. And the chances of that happening increased with every yard he advanced. All Nick had to do was get in and get out— alive. And out was the operative word. For once he'd carried out the task, all the ground rules would change immediately. For a start, he'd have outlived his usefulness from the Soviet perspective. Shit, he could think of several reasons why he'd be more valuable to them dead than alive once it was over. It would mean another body, for one. A corpse that could be linked directly to Washington.

Delan's heartbeat picked up as he stopped and looked back at the mainland again. Getting back to that shore, he thought, would be the problem. And it was there, in those very same shadows he had to reach, that, in all likelihood, the dangers lay. Either that or an undetectable sniper up on the hills. Through the binoculars he scoured from right to left.

Nothing. He stopped the sweep of the binoculars momentarily at his point of departure: the staging point that was the recess beneath the northeast end of the wharf, next to the dark wooden stairs leading up from the beach. Then he started up again, searching the coastline and the small tree-covered embankment that rose to the quiet parking lots behind the bars and eating houses along a short strip of Pacific Coast Highway known as Restaurant Row.

Suddenly, from behind, he heard the angry bark of a dog on Lido Island. He turned. Two security guards, one uniformed, one in civilian garb, led their dogs along the narrow bridle path fronting the island. He studied them for a moment as they walked by, sixty or so yards away, engrossed in conversation.

Wiser to let them gain some distance before reporting in, he thought, turning back to monitor the shore behind yet again. Plenty of time. It would take at least ten minutes before he could continue his approach. Cascades of bougainvilleas and wild flowers led to eucalyptus and weeping willows along the embankment. Recesses and cover behind which a man could hide. He peered more closely, slowing down the sweep of the goggles to a snail's crawl. A gray wooden shed, nearly buried in the exotic vegetation. Small sailing yachts moored on the beach.

A million hiding places, he thought as he turned back toward Lido Island again. He dropped the goggles, letting them sink slowly beneath the water to dangle at his chest.

"Claw to Eagle."

"Roger, Claw."

"We have a hold."

"Roger. What's the Estimated Delay Time on that?"

Delan looked up the path. At the guards now passing the yacht holding the celebrations, a hundred, a hundred and twenty yards away.

"Five minutes or so," he answered. "Depends on how long it takes for the island's security patrol to disappear from view."

*   *   *

"Damn!"

Anthony Boyle's head snapped toward the speaker. Vice Admiral Kenny Lee Harmon's slitted eyes were locked on the bank of screens.

"What is it?" Boyle asked.

The Vice Admiral turned unseeingly toward Boyle for an instant, a world of consternation in that one brief glance. Then he directed his regard back to the screens on the wall as he shifted forward, closer to the panel of controls fitted into the shiny darkwood table in front of him.

"I'm not sure."

Anthony Boyle followed the Admiral's intense gaze to the vaguely green image filling Screen 17 on the left side of the immense wall.

The picture showed two strips of land, separated by a channel of water. Across its gently rolling surface lights danced, buoys bobbed, along with any number of boats of varying sizes. But the most prominent feature about the dark swath of water in the middle of the picture was the whiter shape of a man, whose warmer body and more light-absorbing skin stood out like a sore thumb against the cold, dark, liquid background.

It was Nick Delan. And it was obvious that he was looking back at the shoreline on Newport Beach.

Boyle turned back to Harmon, unable to fathom what had grabbed his attention.

The Admiral had angled his head slightly. He was looking at the picture sideways now. To Anthony Boyle it seemed like an eternity before the Admiral stirred. When he finally did he was slow and uncertain. He leaned forward and hesitated again, his eyes glued to the screen. Boyle felt his anxiety mount. And suddenly the drone of high-technology noises in the background grew ominous: the whir of high-speed printers mixing with the beeps and bops of warning signals synchronized to an untold number of lights and colors dotting the walls and screens. Telephones rang endlessly, momentarily drowning out the hushed whispers of intercommunication jargon and instructions and a constant buzz of other activity.

At last Harmon pressed a button and suddenly his voice boomed, echoing off the huge plexiglass "daylight" dome extending twenty yards above them. "Screen twenty," he ordered. "I need a zoom."

He lifted his finger and turned slowly to Anthony Boyle as he leaned back in his chair. He spoke softly. "I think we got company."

Nothing.

Yet again Delan scoured the recesses of the night. But there was still no sign of life. He looked on, probing the dangerous shadows a moment longer. Knowing, too, that time was crowding in. It had been fully five minutes since the private security patrol had passed by behind him on the island. And ten was the optimum time to strike in terms of the correlation of distances between the roving patrols and Sanford's house. If he missed the first opportunity he would have to wait another twenty minutes before the timing was right again. Wait exposed to three or four dozen spaced-out teenagers roaming the vicinity, the surveillance teams monitoring him from high in the hills; and, of course, any chance encounter.

Abruptly his anxiety mounted. He twisted toward the island. Then he looked back to the mainland, then back and forth slowly, then up to the hills. Or perhaps not just a chance encounter. Maybe it was all meticulously planned. A hit man, waiting in those shadows on the mainland side or up on the hills. And if that was the case, Delan was pincered—rat-holed, in military parlance—in the sea.

Delan downed the dark sinking feeling he suddenly felt. It was too late to worry about that now. Or perhaps too early was a better way of looking at it. He would factor it in. On the way back he would work out something. In the meantime he had nothing to worry about. Not until he had made the hit.

"Claw to Eagle. Seems clear again," he whispered. "Reverting to infiltration mode."

"Roger, Claw."

He began swimming again. A little faster this time, his senses homing in on the shore ahead, scanning, probing, listening. Gradually he drew nearer to the island, until finally he felt the coarse grains of sand coming up at his feet. Remembering the infrared lights monitoring from behind, he carefully raised his torso to a crouch in the shallow water. Bit by bit, with the lowest profile, he crawled as far as he could. Then, abruptly, he stood and rushed to the safety of his preselected hiding place, the hide site, as it was called by his colleagues. It was a narrow corridor running between two houses from the bridle path fronting the island back to via Lido.

Once safely ensconced he immediately reported in: "Claw to Eagle," he said, still catching his breath. "Claw to Eagle. Island One achieved."

"Roger, Claw," the controller replied. "Looking good on timing."

"Yeah," Delan mumbled halfheartedly as he peered around the wooden fence. He raised the binoculars and peered across the water again, at the same all-important landing zone across the channel. A film of water slowly ebbed down the lenses before the image cleared. Delan squinted into the dark mass of shrubbery and trees, the boats and small toolsheds and other shadows on the other side, suspicious and yet at the same time uncertain as to what exactly it was he was looking for.

Nothing happened. Nothing moved. Except for the leaves and flowers fluttering in the breeze. Slowly he raised the Baird goggles further, above the darkened semi high-rise Balboa Bay Club building. Five infrared floodlights beamed back at him from the cliffs behind the club, arcing high above Pacific Coast Highway on Cliff Drive.

He ducked back behind the low wood fence and dropped to one knee as he wrestled the small knapsack off his back. Quickly he tore the waterproof flap open, removed the machine pistol, and placed it on the ground. Then he slipped the other oversize pistol into his thick-webbed belt.

Delan closed the bag and picked up the machine pistol. Carefully, he stood and looked to his right. Nothing had changed: luxurious yachts rocked gently and a hundred yards away dozens of college kids continued to enjoy their Sunday night party. Nothing appeared troubling. He peered around the fence and looked to his left. As far as his eyes could see, to the playground and beyond, the entire area was deserted.

He leaned back against the fence. "Claw to Eagle. I'm going in."

* * *

"For Christ's sake, Tony, don't you at least want to *warn* the man?" Admiral Kenny Lee Harmon asked, his tone an incredulous whisper.

"No," Robert Wilson barked, once again fielding the question. He glanced at Harmon, the natural pout of his crusty old face giving him the air of a stubborn bulldog. "That is something we have absolutely no intention of doing."

"Why the hell not?" the Admiral asked, stunned. He swiveled his head left, away from Robert Wilson toward the younger and less dour visage of Anthony Boyle. The Navy man's eyes pleaded for reason. "That's a sniper out there, Tony. Waiting on the mainland with a Remington 40XB rifle and a night scope to pick your man off."

Anthony Boyle rubbed his forehead gently as he bent his head forward. He looked down and away to the other side.

"I'm sorry, Kenny," he said, turning to stare at the Admiral. "He can't be told. It's absolutely imperative that he is seen to be functioning for real out there."

Harmon's face suffused with blood as his angry eyes glared at Boyle for a long moment. "What you're probably looking at out there, then," he said softly, "is a dead man."

"As long as it's after he's done his job," Robert Wilson said calmly, absorbed with the picture he was watching.

Sweat oozed from Nick Delan's skin. Burning a little as the open pores let the saltwater in. It was a good sign. His body was primed, sensitive, coiled. Even while the brain was calm, organized, in control. He waited a moment longer, pressed against the wooden fence, casting one final look across the terrain.

Abruptly he heard a soft sliding sound carried by the gentle warm breeze drifting from his left. His body went taut as his neck snapped to look across his glistening shoulder. The small sandy beach disappeared into the distance. It was deserted. He scanned the narrow bridle path separating the shore from the houses. Still nothing. He looked closer.

Suddenly he saw a shadow appear through a half-open sliding door. Involuntarily he ducked back behind the corner of the wooden fence. His heart pounded furiously. Very slowly he let his head drift forward again. Inch by inch the view increased—the water, the beach, the bridle path—till finally Allan Sanford's house was in full view. And there on the veranda a silhouette stood.

Delan squinted into the light that spilled from the doorway. It was a man. That much he could make out. But who? Who was it? Who the hell could it be? Allan Sanford had been alone when Delan had observed him earlier. All night, if the last-minute update he had received was to be believed. *Madonna!*

The figure moved. He turned and walked slowly away from Delan, back across to the other end of the small patio that fronted the house. The man stretched his body as he did so, raising his hands to his shoulders and arching his back as if trying to dislodge some pain or tension that had gathered there. At the far end he stopped and looked into the distant darkness for a while before turning and walking back. But in that one brief moment—which was all it took in the soft shower of light spilling out of the house—Nick Delan relaxed. It was Allan Sanford—the celebrated features unmistakable.

Delan breathed a sigh of relief as he studied his target. He was standing still at the near end of the veranda, staring at the extraordinary panorama of beauty stretching away toward Corona Del Mar.

It was a simple shot, Delan observed. Not forty yards. At a stationary target. He contemplated the wisdom of the impromptu option. No, he decided, resisting the temptation. It was an unnecessary departure from the intricate game plan. The stakes were too high. He had to get closer. To be absolutely certain, he had to get within feet of the man.

He glanced at his watch before looking to his right. Then to his left, beyond Sanford. Nothing of concern was discernible. He turned his eyes toward the figure of Allan Sanford, just as the former actor reached out and pulled a white wrought-iron garden chair closer. He sat in it, raising his legs comfortably to the low white cast-iron fence that bordered his veranda.

What the hell was he doing? Why was he outside? This was a scenario Delan had not prepared for. He looked at his watch. It was getting late. He had to move if he was to stick to his schedule. Otherwise he would have to wait for the island's private security patrol to come and go again before going in.

No, he decided, turning his full attention back to Allan Sanford. That was unwise. He had to do it now. Besides, Sanford's presence on the porch did not exactly introduce insurmountable problems. Delan would have to force him indoors again. Nevertheless, what *was* imperative was to reach him undetected.

Delan gauged the elements he had to work with: it was dark; Sanford was absorbed; the distance to cover forty yards. If he moved quickly enough there was a very good chance that Sanford wouldn't notice him until it was too late. Delan cast one final look around the vicinity. Then he turned toward his target, his eyes narrowing as determination took hold.

Now, Delan snapped to himself as he broke out of the narrow alley. Immediately he cut left, sprinting toward the targeted house. He drew closer, the knapsack dangling from his left shoulder, easily accessible; the small machine pistol in his right hand. Allan Sanford had not noticed him yet. His eyes still lingered on the distant scenery. They skimmed Delan's head, absorbed by the view behind. Closer still; ten yards away.

Sanford looked down. The mask of contentment vanished from his face, replaced abruptly by a look of horror. A terror that made him trip and stumble in his desperate haste to rise to his feet.

Delan took the three steps up to the porch in one bound, his eyes never leaving Sanford. He stopped, four yards separating the two men.

The former actor stared back, horrified, frozen at the sight of the black-greased, heavily armed professional killer confronting him. Then abruptly he seemed to take a hold of himself. Composure began to ebb back into his face, and comportment, as if the last scene had to be played out with at least a small measure of dignity. His bearing became stiff and a look of calm but studied resignation settled on his face.

For one split second Delan pitied Sanford, hated himself. This was an innocent man. Ensnared not so much by greed or ambition or any other human failing as by the deadliest trap of any relationship: trust. And now Delan had to make him pay.

"Back," he said, pointing the machine pistol. "Inside."

Sanford didn't move. But abruptly the alarming sound of a police siren erupted. Simultaneously, behind Sanford, off in the distance on the bridge connecting Newport Beach to Balboa Peninsula and Lido Island, a flashing neon blue light caught Delan's eye. Had something gone wrong?

Delan switched the machine pistol to his left hand. Quickly he drew the huge slab of a handgun with a malicious-looking bulbous integrated silencer from his belt. And raised it until it pointed squarely at Sanford's heart.

The former actor stepped backward silently and awkwardly, his right arm extended stiffly behind, feeling for potential obstacles. He nearly tripped over the doorsill as he entered his house. Only the curtains he grabbed saved him from tumbling to the floor.

In the background the siren of a second police car could be heard, perhaps even a third. Delan followed Sanford into the large split-level room, waving him backward toward the far end of the sunken living area. As the sirens drew away, fading gradually into the distance, Delan relaxed a little as he forced Sanford to move closer to the front wall. Near the corner, directly in front of the French window overlooking the veranda and the beach.

Nothing in the luxurious, orderly if impersonal area caught Delan's attention. He took a deep breath as he looked back at Sanford. And fired.

The muffled spit erupted in a fountain of blood squirting out from the center of Sanford's white-cotton Oxford shirt. Even as his contorted body flew backward across a chair, a second shot caught him in midair, not two inches from the first. And a second spray splattered the room, catching in its crimson path the cream-colored wall behind, the beige curtain, and the white Italian leather couches two yards away.

Nick Delan stepped forward quickly. He circled the fallen chair and stood directly above the tangle of arms and legs and pools of red that was now Allan Sanford. He extended his right arm until it was rigid, locked at the elbow—the classic executioner's stance—and fired the third shot at the center of Allan Sanford's forehead. A muffled spit and more blood erupted as the prostrate body bounced violently.

For one split second Delan stared down at the bloody horror he had created. Then he turned swiftly, opened the French window, and stepped back out into the night.

"He's made the hit, for Christ's sake. Why can't you tell him now?"

Anthony Boyle ignored Admiral Harmon's question. Instead his eyes were riveted to Screen 20 in War Room 9; and the black, balaclava-clad figure it isolated, standing behind the chest-high stained wooden wall at the end of the Balboa Bay Club, hidden from Delan's view. Peering across the waterway, the man held a Remington sniper rifle in his right hand. Attached to it was a heavy-duty Redfield scope.

"Tell me, Kenny," Boyle asked, barely audibly and without turning. "What exactly is that man doing?"

"I don't know," the Admiral replied curtly. "But thanks to us he's had all the time and every opportunity in the world to kill your man."

"Precisely," said Boyle, turning toward the Admiral. "But he hasn't. Why?"

Harmon glared at the Deputy National Security Adviser. Then he glanced at Robert Wilson, who remained uncharacteristically silent for once.

"Don't fight me, Kenny. I need your help. All I've got going for me is intuition here. And that's exactly the kind of riddle we've been facing every step of the way."

The Admiral flicked his eyes back again and regarded Boyle's face silently for a moment. "So how's not telling him that there's someone out there stalking him going to change anything, for God's sake?"

Anthony Boyle shook his head softly. "I have no idea. And it is just possible we may not find out until it's too late. For Delan, that is, anyway." He looked away from Harmon, turning toward the relevant screen on the wall. "What I do know is this: we can't interfere. Not under any circumstance. This charade has got to be played out for real. And if that means losing a man, I'm afraid—"

"Screen twenty," the giant jet speakers suddenly boomed around the cavernous operations room, drowning out the clattering electronic machines and printers, and interrupting Boyle. "Unidentified intruder reverting to offensive posture."

Anthony Boyle's eyes narrowed immediately as they focused on the gun the black, balaclava-clad man had raised. It was aimed across the waterway at Lido Island.

"Claw to Eagle. Claw to Eagle. Can you read me?"

"Roger, Claw," replied that same cold, monotonous, aloof voice of the mission coordinator. "That's affirmative."

"The delivery has been made."

"Check. The delivery has been made."

"Roger, Eagle. Request clearance to return to nest."

"Can do, Claw. Come on home."

Delan's eyes stopped their sweep of the immediate vicinity all around him. The night was still. Not a soul had heard or noticed or cared. Only the sounds of the rock party off to his left shattered the serenity of the island paradise. Delan waited a moment longer, though, his heart thumping. Waited behind a rose bush next to Sanford's fence, a sense of foreboding building inside.

It was there, he thought, looking across the waterway to the mainland. There, in those shadows, that the danger lay. He raised the night-vision binoculars. For a moment he studied the terrain to his right. Then, slowly, he started panning to the left. Along the narrow strip of sandy beach fronting the huge houses on Bayshore Drive toward the Balboa Bay Club. Past the small wooded area and the health spa facilities and service buildings to the wharf where luxurious yachts creaked gently at their moorings.

At the end of the wharf, not thirty yards from the stained wooden fence that bordered the northwest perimeter of the club's grounds, he stopped; and started panning back again.

Yes, he decided, that was the path he would take. Before stepping out of his hiding place he cast a look up and down the beach just in front of him and the path along which the security patrol passed on their routes. Both were clear, so he stepped out and walked down the slight slope of sand toward the water.

Abruptly a thunderous crack sounded, a massive splintering of lumber that was cut off only by the tumultuous roar of a huge explosion. Then another, so deafening that they immediately transformed the languid night into a vicious thunderstorm erupting directly overhead.

Instinctively Delan flung himself to the ground. But he was too late. A ferocious tornado blasted him, picking him up like a matchstick and sending him end over end before dumping him in a stunned, tangled heap several yards away.

High above the deep-purple bulge of the stratosphere, the two explosions appeared as minuscule sparks to the Aquacade super-satellite's wide-angle eyes.

Instantly its photochromic phosphor screens filtered the luminance gain, ensuring that the sudden flashes did not, for even the tiniest instant, blind its multitude of eyes. Even as they zeroed in, their Goodyear Aerospace synthetic apertures cutting through the smog overlays like laser beams on a cloudless night, other parts of its brain were processing the information and thence relaying them in digital code to that underground electronic cave beneath Fort Meade.

On the twenty screens in War Room 9, it was an awesome sight. Sequentially the sparkles grew larger on each monitor. From left to right, five rows across, four layers down, each picture became more telling as all erupted in different sizes of brilliant white at the same time. On the fourteenth, fifteenth and sixteenth screens the sight was almost that of flames billowing up toward cameras placed at different heights of a launching pad, practically engulfing them in the flames that were now billowing upward. From the seventeenth screen onward the luminance gain was less bright. For none of these pictures included the point of detonation, and so illumination only flowed across the close-up shots of the waterway, the beach on the mainland, the buildings behind; and a black balaclava-clad man aiming his gun.

He fired it again and abruptly there was a third explosion. And once again sparkling flashes appeared on the screens as the sudden buzz of activity in the room picked up to yet a higher notch. The clatter of printers, the electronic beeps and bops and the whir of computers were all but drowned out now by the sound of raised human voices speaking strangely, almost in another language.

"I need the OST on that," said one voice.

What he received from another man was a series of numbers interspaced by letters here and there.

"Check," the first voice said.

"Communication status?" someone else demanded.

"No change. Up, down, and lateral links in place."

"Hold CRO on standby."

"Roger. CRO on parallel."

"Zero blockout," a female voice interjected.

"Check on blockout. Revert to PI on SDH."

One floor up, in the deathly hush of the glass-fronted observation deck that overlooked the cavernous war room, the mission controller picked up a weak sound on the earphones he wore.

"Eagle to Claw. Eagle to Claw. Please come in."

There. He thought he heard it again. The wheezing seemed a little stronger.

"Eagle to Claw. Eagle to Claw. Acknowledge call signal."

The gasping sound he received in response could easily have been interpreted differently had it not been for the distinct cough that followed. "Eagle to Claw. Eagle to—"

"Claw to Eagle," a whispered croak interjected. "There's been an explosion."

"Yeah, we heard it. Are you hurt?"

"No," the feeble voice replied. "Not too seriously, anyway."

"Good. Can you give us a precise fix on the point of detonation?"

"Hard to tell," the voice replied, still weak but increasingly composed. "All hell's broken loose here. Lot of smoke. Looks like several boats are on fire. Maybe Sanford's. Can't tell."

"Roger, Claw. Suggest you revert to evacuation mode."

The burning diesel fumes shot twenty yards into the sky, billowing orange, red, and black clouds lighting up the night.

As the plumes descended, a shower of burning confetti rained down on the pandemonium below. Already some of the other yachts were on fire. Soon the flames on their decks would spread down to their fuel tanks, then other explosions would follow. The college kids had passed the initial phase of stunned shock. Now chaos ruled as panic and hysteria broke out among the vast majority. Some of the more quick-witted were running away from the rapidly spreading fire. Down the beach, toward Delan, many blood-splattered, others clutching ugly burns.

Across the waterway on the mainland, and on Lido Island itself, lights were coming on. Windows and doors were opening and heads popping out. In the distance the sirens of police and other emergency vehicles could be heard. Vaguely Delan thought he could make out their blurry flashing blue lights as well.

He had to get out of there. Before they arrived. It was a question of only moments.

Delan urged himself to move. To shake off the daze. To down the overwhelming queasiness he felt. For the first time he felt the trickle of blood on his forehead. He forced himself to raise his hand and feel the long, wide-open slit to the right of his crown. He shook his head and squeezed his eyes to force the multi-images into one clear picture as he struggled to rise. First to his hands and knees, then to his feet, staggering as he bent down, collected his equipment, and stumbled toward the water. Behind him the screech of burning rubber could be heard in sync with untold police sirens as their cars careened on to via Lido Nord not half a mile away. Delan urged himself to go faster; to tumble through the dusty, acrid clouds of fumes and smoke blurring the waterline. Suddenly he heard the sounds of footsteps. Then more of them. Running, growing steadily nearer on the asphalt bridle path behind him.

Delan stepped into the water. His arms and legs were responding more rapidly now. He looked back as he waded deeper into the water. Some people were running from the fire, while others approached it, dazed, incredulous, cautious.

The cold water felt refreshing. Against the film of perspiration covering his hot, listless body and the clog of pain dulling his mind. It felt better than an icy mint julep served on a blistering summer night. He ducked under the water and, fighting the gentle current, cleared a path as best he could to his right.

Only when his lungs felt like bursting did he surface. But briefly, only long enough to take a very deep breath before ducking under again. He continued swimming up toward the curve on Bayshore Drive on the opposite side of the waterway.

What the hell had happened back there? It was far too convenient to be a coincidence, an accident, an act of God. No. Abruptly the water seemed to get colder against his bare skin.

Cautiously he came up for air again. But this time he spent one split second longer above the water. A nanosecond that provided his bearings; and one key fact. If the explosions had indeed been planned, then they could have been detonated by only two types of triggering device: a remote-control signal to a pre-positioned bomb, or an explosive projectile; either of which meant line-of-sight vision. And both of which meant someone was watching within the ninety-degree angle that was required for unobstructed viewing.

His heart started pounding furiously. The remote-control bomb was unlikely. The Soviets would never have risked placing a bomb in one of those boats—not after they had observed Delan conducting his sorties at night. They would have automatically assumed the entire area was under intense scrutiny, with teams of monitors deployed around the clock.

That left only one possibility: an explosive projectile fired out of the long, smooth barrel of a sharpshooter's rifle. He came up for air to fight off the grim sensation that suddenly gripped him. Twenty yards ahead and to his left he noticed a round orange buoy. Anchored to the seabed, he thought as he submerged and changed direction to swim with the current toward it.

The slippery hard plastic ball was far bigger than it appeared from a distance. Easily large enough to hide him from the mainland, thirty-five yards away, while he caught his breath and did a little thinking.

Across on Lido Island the fire among the yachts was spreading and the firemen still hadn't arrived. Up and down the beach, small crowds had formed, contributing to a confusion that only seemed to be getting worse. In the distance more sirens wailed as coastguard boats headed out of Turning Basin at the far end of the island toward the spreading flames. Overhead a helicopter loomed low, its two Over-lite metal halide floodlights blanketing the entire neighborhood with daylight. In the night sky beyond, the flashing lights of several other choppers could be seen approaching. Delan zoomed in on Sanford's house. So far it had attracted no special attention. Like all the other houses falling outside the immediate danger zone, it lay still, quiet, ignored.

No. His problems no longer lay on Lido Island. It was the other side he had to worry about now. He turned, careful not to allow any part of his body to extend beyond the luminous buoy, and looked at the mainland. It was here that the dangers lay now.

Delan raised the nightscope. He switched from OFF to AVAILABLE LIGHT, and lowered his head until the binoculars peeped around the buoy, at the precise point of its waterline.

The view he got was not good. Waves rippling across the channel kept submerging the binoculars. It took several seconds each time for the blur to clear. Patiently Delan stopped and started his sweep along the shoreline after each interruption. He panned to his right, down the beach from the South Shores Sailing Club to his far left, down toward the Balboa Bay Club. The first explosion had occurred toward the stern of Sanford's boat, on the starboard side, anchored as it was with its bow inland. If his assumption was correct, that meant that the bullet had been fired from this side of the vessel. But he saw nothing. The narrow beachfront, the embankment leading up to the parking lots, the tiny sailboats moored alongside—all was quiet.

As he slowly swept the area, the green-tinged images of the beach at night slowly gave way to the stained wooden fence that cordoned off the northern boundary of the exclusive Balboa Bay Club grounds and— Abruptly he stopped. And jerked the binoculars back a few yards.

He felt the skin on his back crawl. Somewhere in front of that clump of trees there had been movement. Some sort of life. Had it been a human figure? He probed the area, aware suddenly of a sixth sense that was working overtime.

There. He saw it again. A round black object.

"Claw to Eagle. Claw to Eagle. Come in, please."

"That's a Roger, Claw."

"I think," Delan whispered distantly, every wave of concentration in his body focused on that black half-hidden shadow he was watching, "I got company out here."

"Check, Claw. Need a clarification on that."

"Someone's out here. Someone with a heavy mask and an even heavier rifle."

"Check, Claw. Stand by. We'll get back to you."

The shadow moved again, this time more obviously. Now Delan could clearly discern the balaclavaed head with two large cut-out eyes bobbing behind the fence, eyes cast down almost as if he was toying with something. Then he saw what looked like a long canvas bag appear. It dropped on this side of the fence followed by a tall, athletic figure dressed from head to toe in black. Delan watched. The figure moved with stealth, silently and with catlike grace, always hidden in the darkest shadows, his every move honed by experience.

"Nick." It was the distinctive New England accent of Anthony Boyle coming over the earplug. "Listen to me."

"Shoot."

"This could be the break we've been waiting for. I want you to go after this man you've seen."

Boyle sounded anxious, excited, both. Strangely, though, he had no questions he wanted answered.

"Apprehend him. He could have vital information that could burst this whole thing wide open at the seams."

Delan felt a surge of adrenaline run through his veins. The man was good, he thought, watching him glide effortlessly through the shadows toward the beach at the northern end of the wharf. The rifle looked almost like an extension of his muscular arm, held cocked and locked, down to one side, ready for use at an instant's notice. The man knew his trade, too. He wasn't running away. Exactly like he, Nick Delan, had planned to do, the man was making for the sanctity of the exclusive, private Balboa Bay Club.

"You want this man *alive*?" he asked skeptically.

"That's imperative, Nick. He's useless to us dead."

"He's moved out onto the path now. Heading toward the beach," Admiral Kenny Lee Harmon observed, watching the balaclava-clad man on Screen 19 in War Room 9.

"Isn't that toward the point where Delan staged?" Anthony Boyle asked, noting how deftly the unidentified intruder had hidden his rifle behind the long tennis bag, both in the same hand.

"Yes, it is," Harmon replied. "Right there. Next to those stairs leading to the beach. Underneath the end of the wharf."

"Tony, looks like your man's heading for the other end," Robert Wilson interjected. "Take a look at that, would you?" he said elatedly. "He's cutting the intruder's route off in the tunnel under the wharf."

The two other men turned their attention to the half-lit scene of the waterway on the screen to the left; and the glistening figure of a semisubmerged swimmer, his body greased, heading for the beach at the southern end of the wharf.

"Way to go, Nick," Anthony Boyle encouraged only half out loud. "Come on, come on."

"Shit!"

Boyle snapped his head toward Admiral Harmon.

"The intruder's stopped. What the—"

The intruder had suddenly ducked from the path. He hid now, absolutely still, behind a large clump of bushes to the right of the wooden stairs leading to the beach.

All three of the men sitting behind the conference table leaned forward almost in unison, each feeling the sudden need to move closer to the drama they were watching as the intruder dropped to one knee. They saw him lay down his rifle and then slowly cover its distinctive Monte Carlo stock and inlaid fore end with leaves and weeds. All the while, however, his eyes looked through the bushes in front of him and over the yachts moored along the wharf sweeping down and away to his right. Their focal point: the figure some seventy yards away, swimming just several yards out to sea.

"Looks like he's assessing your man's next move," Harmon ventured. "Yes, yes, he's switching to a handgun of some sort."

Anthony Boyle shifted nervously in his chair.

"Look. He's moving out again. Minus his luggage," Harmon said, more to himself than the others. "Down the stairs. Toward the tunnel. Christ Almighty!"

Anthony Boyle's wide eyes darted from one end of the wharf to the other. From the northern end, under which the intruder had just disappeared—to the southern end, where Nick Delan was coming ashore. Then back, then forth, tiny beads of perspiration suddenly dotting his forehead. He undid the top button of his shirt.

Admiral Kenny Lee Harmon turned toward him, the spare, angular muscles around his jaw bulging with strain. "For heaven's sake, Tony," he hissed. "He's moving in on your man. Setting him up for an ambush under there. You still don't want to warn him?"

"No way," snapped Robert Wilson.

"Why the hell not, for God's sake?" snapped Harmon.

Wilson turned and looked at the Admiral, a pugnacious bulldog expression on his face. "That's classified. Even for you, Admiral Harmon."

In the water, Nick Delan clung to one of the concrete pylons of the wharf. Just ahead, on the creaking wooden planks of the walkway above, he could hear the voices of a small group of people. Some in dressing gowns and bathrobes, others in hastily selected casual attire, the club members had deserted their beds to watch the horrific scenes across Lido Channel.

"Is it *really* true one of those houses is Allan Sanford's?" a middle-aged woman's voice asked.

"Jesus H. Christ. Look at that, look at that, will you?" another man bellowed. "It's spreading to the next boat. HOLY SHIT!"

"Oh, my God," the same woman gasped.

To Nick Delan, though, their words were background noises. Other voices filled his head, voices conducting an inquisition—an audit studded with thorns.

"Where? . . . where? . . . where?" one shrill tone cried. "Why?

. . . why? . . . why?" another demanded. Where was he headed, this balaclava-clad man? And why had he stuck to the shadows? Why, if he was heading for the safety of these grounds? If he intended to escape by melting in with these crowds?

Perhaps . . . perhaps he had been wrong back there, Delan thought. Perhaps he had misjudged the man's intentions. Maybe he was just heading down toward the beach to get closer to Delan. Hugging the shadows to hide.

But that didn't make any sense. If he'd wanted to kill Delan he could have done so at any time. Delan had been floating in the water like a sitting duck. Why had the man held his fire? And where the hell was he now? Delan thought for a moment. What would he have done if he was in that man's place? The answer surprised him with its simplicity. It also sparked off an even bigger fear. Down, the voice answered. And around. Beneath the wharf to circle all these people watching the fire from the grounds; and then circle off to the secluded woodlands to the right to dispose of the equipment, change attire before heading back to the building or the parking lot or a waiting car on Pacific Coast Highway on the other side.

But then again, the passionless voice continued as if with a will of its own, if I had wanted to kill you, I would not have shot you in the water either. I would have waited until you reached this side.

Why?

Because the water might have washed the body out to sea or onto a distant shore. This way you have a body positioned in the most incriminating spot imaginable. With all the right accoutrements: the rifles, the explosive rounds, and the various other pieces of equipment required to create the most perfect fall guy: a dead one who couldn't answer back.

Delan felt the warm beads of sweat trickling down his forehead. He looked to his left, under the concrete arches separating the big, solid concrete pylons of the wharf. A dark tunnel ran under it; and small, frothy purple waves twisted onto the two yards of sandy white shore that ran down its length.

That is what I would have done if I were in his place, the voice repeated. Or better still planned the operation. Shades of Aquino. The assassin killed virtually at the site of the crime. Only this time filmed, too. Clearly identifiable. Nothing could add more to the conspiracy of it all. And God knows, the Soviets had had enough time to plan. On two different occasions Delan had made this very same journey across the water under their eyes, giving them prior notice of his precise step-by-step route. He cursed himself. They could never have dreamed of a more compliant clown.

Planning was one thing though, he thought, his eyes narrowing. Execution another. Somewhere out there in those shadows there was a killer, waiting for him. A hunter who had good reason to believe that his task was essentially nothing more difficult than a Sunday afternoon turkey shoot. And it was true. As things stood now, Delan was holding the losing hand. And in a deadly game of survival that had no rules.

For a moment Delan stayed on in the water, quiet, motionless, sifting through the options available to him. One factor evened the odds a little. He had seen the predator. And that was enough. It gave Delan the most important advantage of all: surprise. An element that totally changed the nature of any contest. Especially the kind of lethal night game they were playing now.

Cautiously he pushed himself away from the pylon and with soft, silent breaststrokes approached the shore. His feet touched sand as he passed beneath the wharf. He stood and pressed himself up against one of the outer pylons supporting the walkway above. Glancing around to get his bearings, he simultaneously swung his knapsack from his back and extracted the Heckler & Koch silenced machine pistol. He was at approximately the midpoint of the underpass, he observed, flicking its safety notch all the way forward to automatic.

Now, he thought, peering slowly around the gray concrete column, looking left toward the northern end of the wharf, how best to draw the man's attention? That was the point. He looked down the dark corridor, punctuated only by the occasional dim shaft of light that slipped between the huge hulls of the yachts parked alongside.

Nothing. Nothing, that was, but the noise of the mounting commotion across the waterway and the comments of the growing crowd overhead. But the hunter was there. Delan could feel it. Somewhere in that darkness ahead.

He bent down and picked up several tiny pebbles lying beside his right foot. Warily, he stood again, raising the night-vision goggles dangling at his chest. Again he scoured the area, looking for one broken line in the simple, uniform architecture, one darker gray shadow on the sand, one blacker blob against the wall.

Nothing. He turned and threw one of the pebbles up against the hull of a boat, as far as he could away from himself toward the north—but careful to use a wrist action only to keep his profile hidden behind the concrete pylon.

It thudded against a mass some fifteen yards away, making a dull, hollow, empty sound before plopping in the seawater below. Quickly Delan raised his goggles and looked back again to the corridor on the inner side of the pylon.

Still nothing. He repeated the action. But again it produced no result.

Where was he? Which nook? Which cranny?

Sweat poured from his skin as he leaned back against the cold concrete. He had to up the ante. Increase the risks to both of them a little. He stopped and calculated the optimum exposure spans needed in the series of moves he had to negotiate in the moments ahead.

Flashes, he decided. He had to move as fast as possible, offering only blurs of movement, too few frames in the moving picture for anything to be distinguishable to the human eye. That way he would be offering the smallest target. If he did it quickly enough, no target at all.

He coiled himself, plastering his body hard against the wall. Cocked ready in his right fist, he held the snub-nosed machine pistol. In his left he carried the knapsack. One . . . two . . . three, he counted silently—before taking off.

He flew through the air and landed, adroitly somersaulting on his right shoulder toward the concrete wall opposite. There in continuation of the flowing, almost soundless, sequence he deftly rose to his feet and immediately slid his body up into the corner of the recess he had chosen, between a buttressing column and the wall.

Nothing. No angry spit of a silenced bullet. No dull thud of pounding lead. Just the gentle sound of small waves breaking softly and the distraught voices from directly above.

Delan breathed out. A deep, heavy exhalation that sought to expunge some of the tension. He waited a moment, using the goggles to scrutinize the critical section of the tunnel. Then he braced himself again, this time leaning his right shoulder against the wall to increase his leverage.

Abruptly he dived again; but this time a searing pain scorched high on his right hip just as he landed, midway through his somersault. A vicious, sharp stab that made him cringe and grab at his back as the jarring throb spread out across his body. His hand was immediately covered with blood. His face contorted with agony as he pressed up against the wall to hide himself behind the sanctuary of thick concrete. For one split second his mind blanked with the excruciating pain. Then his hand, feeling the wound, communicated the good news to his brain: it was a cut. Not a hole. A two-inch jagged vertical line—which meant it could not be a bullet. That would have been a horizontal puncture, from right to left.

He glanced down and cursed the half-broken bottle neck lying in the sand. Then he swept his grimacing regard onward; to the end of the corridor, now again to his left.

Nothing. He turned and looked at the other side of the pylon, just in case the predator had read his plans correctly and was creeping up on him on his blind side. But he wasn't.

He dropped to one knee and felt for the knapsack. Whoever it was down there, coiled ready to strike, would have no way of knowing what Delan was doing. Advancing, retreating, panic-stricken, or calm. All he would have seen was a fleeting shadow, a momentary flash of movement that was gone before giving a clue. But he would be waiting, thought Delan, as he emptied the knapsack, silently placing each piece of equipment on the soft sand at his feet. Waiting, primed, and ready. Waiting for that one small mistake that is all that's ever needed by a pro.

Delan stood and gently let the bag slip down until he held it in his right hand by one of its shoulder straps. Pressed against the concrete column he swung the bag back and forth gently, gauging the arc, the speed, the height, and the optimum combination of the three. Then he let fly. As softly as he could he let go at roughly hip height, releasing it gradually so the drift across the width of the corridor was slower than his own somersaults had been, more stationary.

A spit erupted, a soft deadly hiss that smashed into the bag in midair, sending it flying up and to the right. Instantly another angry spit split the air. And then a third. Each mangled the bag even further as it fell to earth. Somewhere between the second two shots, however, Delan's reflexes came alive. He yelped, a soft but harrowing animal cry of pain. Then he cried out louder, a second and even more agonized howl.

"What the hell was that?" he heard someone on the walkway above demand. It was a male voice.

"What?" asked another man.

"I thought I heard a yell."

"Probably my wife," said his colleague without missing a beat. "It's a habit of hers."

The first man laughed. But Delan didn't hear him. Suddenly his attention was focused on something that resembled the first hint of a shadow. It moved, crawled out inch by inch. Until at last a lithe, reptilian black figure could be made out, slithering from behind a column—slowly, cautiously, full of skill. It hesitated for a long moment before it suddenly and very adroitly moved, rolling across the ground toward the wall opposite and sliding deftly to a standing position, his back against the concrete. In his right hand, which dangled down to his side, he held a firearm.

Delan felt the first pangs of relief. The man had fallen for the ruse. He was moving in to examine what he thought was his fallen prey. Delan gritted his teeth. Come on, mother, he said silently. Come on.

Beneath the beads of sweat covering Delan's greased face, the muscles grew taut. It was a different game now, he thought with satisfaction. The odds had changed.

The tall, powerful shadow drew steadily nearer on the opposite wall. Like a seasoned shark stalking his prey in ever-decreasing circles, the shadow was moving in.

Delan steadied his breathing. The man was less than seven yards away. In his hand, now raised to his belt and flexed a foot forward, he carried a Sterling .357 Magnum. In that one instant all the long tedious hours, every year, of weapon recognition training—all the color charts and graphs and slides and slow-motion films of every type of gun ever made, each with its own peculiar characteristic—suddenly paid off. It was a revolver, and, like most of the revolver breed, it kicked to the right when fired—which made the left a slightly better direction to duck toward in case of necessity. Delan stored the information in the back of his mind as he crouched down a little lower, ready.

Around the rough-concrete column across the corridor, the shiny metallic blue of gunmetal came into view first. The tip of the gun, then the barrel, then the revolving chamber, finally a black kid-gloved fist.

It was enough. *Take any piece you can* was the most elementary rule. The elbow appeared . . .

Now!

He fired—a hail of bullets descending in an almost straight line as he lowered the machine pistol in a short, sharp drop. The hand disappeared. The deadly, silent staccato of spits dispatched the KWT bullets in a short semicircular arc that sliced the arm at the elbow, sending it flying into the concrete wall. Then came the howl of pain. This time the agony was real and loud and never-ending. But miraculously it was lost in the cacophony of rotating blades of the helicopter passing very low and nearly directly overhead. Delan immediately took further advantage of the cover. He stepped out quickly and shot twice more, one in each of the man's ankles. The balaclava-clad man's body bounced, writhing in agony. But the wild shriek died in his mouth instantly, twisting instead now to a soft, defeated whimper. Delan stepped forward and withdrew the balaclava covering his head.

He'd never seen the man before.

Delan knelt beside him. "There's two ways we can do this," he said. "Either you're a dead man here and now. Or you do exactly as I tell you."

For a long moment the man stared at Delan, every feature in his face contorted with agony. Every feature but the eyes. They were cold, calm, realistic. Suddenly gleaming white teeth appeared in the darkness as the man grinned at Delan. Delan glanced down at the man's only hand: the left one, trying to cap the tiny geyser bubbling up a stream of blood from his chest. Sticking out of its epicenter was a longish, triangular-shaped concrete spike—a piece of shrapnel from the bullet-riddled wall. Delan recognized the calm euphoria that comes to a man losing too much blood too quickly. It was called the final high.

The grin broadened. "Don't shit yourself, man. And don't shit me. I ain't goin' nowhere no more," Aaron "the Baron" Brown whispered. His eyes flickered momentarily, lids heavier even though the smile lingered on. "But then again, neither are you, man. Neither are you."

He coughed and suddenly blood appeared around his teeth. Simultaneously his breathing became a rasp as abruptly he wheezed and gasped for air—oxygen his punctured lungs could not absorb. Nevertheless the leering grin never left his face.

"You see, they ain't going to let you live, boy. Ain't no way. Not if they send me in after you in the first place."

His sleepy, smiling eyes flickered, for one moment all white as the pupils disappeared up into his skull. They returned—but not entirely, rising black moons disappearing into thick clouds.

"So run, man. 'Cos dying ain't what it's cracked up to be." He coughed again and the blood running out of his mouth became a small stream. "Take my word for it," he said, fighting to breathe. "Run. Maybe you'll buy yourself a week."

Aaron "the Baron" Brown lay back—dead.

Delan looked at him. For a long moment he stayed on, kneeling beside the dead man, staring at his face. All the while doubts from the past ran through his mind. Delan had to make a judgment call. Had this man been issuing a warning of some kind? Or making some bitter, desperate dying threat? And James Cassidy? What had his last words in that car meant? Another man who also happened to be dead. Delan didn't know. And there was no way he would—not until after he'd committed himself to the course he'd decided to take.

On Lido Island it was absolute chaos now, he observed as he collected his equipment and stuffed it back into the torn bag. Looking at the balaclava he held, he walked toward his staging post. There he slipped on his clothes before reaching and adjusting the microphone again.

"Claw to Eagle. Claw to Eagle. Can you read me?" he whispered softly. "Come in, Eagle."

"That's a Roger, Claw. Repeat, Roger. What's happening there? We must have had a down link for a while. Couldn't pick you up. What were those noises? Sounded like shots."

"Yeah," Delan whispered back, giving his voice an urgent, stressful tone. "I heard them too. Couldn't ascertain direction, though. Get back to you as soon as I run into something."

"Roger, Claw. What is your precise location?"

"I'm under the wharf running in front of the Balboa Bay Club."

"And the direction of your intended probe route?"

"North."

"Roger."

"Out," Delan said, closing down the conversation. He turned the radio off and removed the lightweight headset. He pulled the balaclava on after he'd put the radio in his bag, on top of the rest of his equipment. Then he walked off. His direction was due south.

"The first phase has just been completed, Mr. President," Anthony Boyle reported, looking at his watch as he cradled the phone. It read 3:23 A.M. Pacific Standard Time—three hours behind the Eastern Time Zone in which Camp David in Maryland fell.

"Any hitches?"

"The flow was a little less smooth than we'd have liked. But the overall result doesn't appear to have been affected too much."

"What happened?"

"A couple of explosions occurred during the final phase of the operation. After our man had completed his assignment and was coming out."

"Explosions!"

"They had an operative in place at the target zone, sir. Monitoring our man throughout the operation. He triggered the detonations."

"Why the hell would they do that, Tony?" the President asked slowly and uncertainly. "Why would they suddenly go overt at such a sensitive stage? When everything was apparently going along as they planned quietly?"

"Probably to attract immediate attention to the site, Mr. President, to eliminate any possibility of our shutting the lid on the story or shifting Sanford's body from where they filmed the hit."

There was a long pause before the President spoke again. "Did you apprehend their man?"

"No sir."

"Why not?"

"He's dead."

"Dead?" the President repeated in an astonished tone. "Why the devil was he killed? Why wasn't he—"

"It seems to have been an accident of some sort, Mr. President," Anthony Boyle interjected. "Result of what appears to have been a forced confrontation."

"What do you mean, Boyle? Seems? Appears? What the hell does your man have to say about it?"

"Nothing, Mr. President. I'm afraid . . ."

"Nothing!"

"No, sir. At least not yet."

"Why?"

"Basically because the operative deviated from his instructions, Mr. President. As a result we haven't had the opportunity to debrief him yet."

"What the hell do you mean, deviated?"

"He lied to us. Right at the end of his mission he reported that he was probing northward in search of their man when in actuality he had already killed him. Then he proceeded to evacuate the area via the south."

"Why would he do that?" the President asked.

"That's difficult to say from a distance, sir. Fear. Mistrust. Panic. Anything could have unhinged him."

"In the meantime he's a walking time bomb, though, isn't he, Mr. Boyle?" the President snapped back. "One that may well explode long before we manage to catch up with him."

"Oh, we haven't lost him, sir."

"How's that?"

"I said we haven't lost him, Mr. President. We have, in fact, been locked on to him from the moment he deviated from his instructions. Wilson has had his car fitted with a homing device from the first day of his involvement in this operation."

"Well, pick him up, for God's sake, Tony."

"Ah . . . I'm afraid we can't do that, Mr. President. Not right away, anyhow."

21 | SUNDAY, JANUARY 17

In Beverly Hills it was approaching noon when the chirp of the two-tone door chime snapped Clio Bragana out of her trance.

Relief, that was the instinctive reaction she felt as one word resounded in her head: Nick!

Then all the other sensations, the worries and fears that had plagued her throughout the long and fitful night swept away the momentary joy. She looked away from the television screen—the vague backdrop to most of her fretting ever since she finally gave up all hope of sleep at five that morning—and concentrated on the door of the suite. Her conflict mounted. On the one hand, she'd never been so attracted to a man. On the other, she couldn't allow such emotions to dominate her. Not with him. Not with anyone. Not with her past.

She stood up just as the doorbell sounded again. Oh God, she thought. What the hell have I got myself into?

As she walked across the wall-to-wall white carpet she recalled—as she had so many times throughout the endless night—the mood Nick had been in yesterday: dour, secretive, uptight.

"Don't forget, Clio," he had said as he leaned down to kiss her forehead, "say a little prayer for me before you go to bed tonight."

"Why won't you tell me what's wrong, Nick?"

"Because nothing is," he had replied, forcing a smile.

"Why do you need a prayer, then?"

"Because I've always been a firm believer that He's a good man to have on your side."

"Please, Nick?" she had beseeched. "Stop being flippant; tell me."

"No," he'd answered. "Besides, there's nothing to say. Except: stay by that telephone."

She opened the door of the suite. A casually dressed young man stood waiting.

"Miss Bragana?" he inquired, glancing down at the slip of paper attached to the large gift-wrapped box he held. "Clio Bragana?"

She frowned. "Yes."

"You have a package, ma'am," the boy said, holding out the box.

"Thank you," Clio replied uncertainly. "But it's Sunday today," she blurted suddenly.

"Yes, ma'am," the young man replied matter-of-factly.

"Shops are closed."

The young man shrugged. "I don't know, ma'am. A man gave me twenty dollars to deliver it and that's what I'm doing."

Clio felt her spirits rise. "What man?"

"He didn't mention his name. Just told me to deliver this box to you. Have a nice day, now," the boy said, backing away, obviously nervous and eager to depart.

"Thank you," Clio murmured, looking down curiously at the large box in her hands.

Inside her room Clio cast another eye at the famous name adorning the glitzy yellow-and-white-striped paper: GIORGIO. She smiled. He was safe.

But the relief was momentary. It was a weird and unexpected gesture, this package of his. More so because he had to have planned it, bought it before today. Worriedly she started tearing off the wrapping paper, ripping at it more and more desperately. By the time she reached into the cardboard box she was almost frantic. Inside, exquisitely folded, lay a simple blue hopsack blazer.

Clio stared at it. Then she slowly lifted it out of the box and examined it suspiciously. A plain white envelope was sticking out of a side pocket. She reached for it and walked toward the sunken sitting area as she slit the envelope open.

> *Darling Clio,*
>   *I need your help.*
>   *There is no way I can explain anything to you. Not right now. Not like this. But I will when I see you. Trust me. PLEASE.*
>   *Go to the Beverly Hills Hotel and rent a bungalow. Repeat, it MUST be a bungalow. Tip heavily. Or even turn to one of your show-biz contacts. Do WHATEVER you have to. But get it. And do so under the following name: Jennifer Cristo. They are well acquainted with incognito reservations. I will contact you there—under this name—at 3 P.M. exactly.*
>   *Also, make sure you are NOT being followed. And burn this letter the minute you've finished reading it.*

It was the last line that drove home the poignancy of his appeal.

> *Please, Clio, I need your help desperately. I have no one else to turn to, to count on. All my love, Nick.*

The palpable loneliness of those words, the cry for help, raised goose pimples across the surface of Clio Bragana's skin. This was not a man who launched personal appeals lightly—not unless he had absolutely no choice.

She bit her lip as she sank into the couch, the same violent tug-of-war between nervous self-interest and love that had been waging inside her all night mounted with a vengeance. She looked around the room, her forehead knotted in anxiety. The poor man, she thought. I'm the best he can come up with.

In the silence the words of the local newscaster on the television filtered through.

"Now for an update on the huge three-alarm fire that broke out on Lido Island late last night and swept through some of *the* most luxurious yachts in the world, we go over to our reporter, Gary Morten, on the scene at Lido Island. What do you have for us, Gary?"

"Not a whole lot, really, Brian. The situation here is still very fluid with the authorities taking an unusually cautious approach—

especially with the media. All we know at the present time is that a series of explosions rocked this exclusive area, the island retreat of quite a few stars and many of the Southland's industrial leaders, including probable presidential candidate Allan Sanford, some time between two and two-thirty this morning. And it took the firefighters until nearly five o'clock to get the flames under control. It's believed that a small fire broke out on or near one of these boats you see behind me and spread quickly to the other boats moored beside. The explosions were, it is generally thought, the result of the fire reaching the huge gas tanks of these luxurious yachts. But there has been no official confirmation of that at this point. The fire damaged eight boats in all and the estimated value is placed at over fifteen million dollars. Miraculously there has not been any loss of life, even though a number of very serious second- and third-degree burn injuries have been reported among some college students who evidently were celebrating a birthday party on one of the yachts."

Clio Bragana looked at the television.

"Unfortunately," added the reporter, "the preliminary fire department report tends to suggest that this entire disaster was the result of carelessness. Perhaps an unwitting firebug among the partying kids."

As the commercial break came on, Clio began rereading the letter.

A heavy veil of cigarette smoke hovered above the small circular conference table in the basement bunker beneath Lincoln University's Adlai Stevenson Hall. What the polluted air did not convey, however, was the tension that had been building during the arduously long session now crossing into the new day.

Seated around the green-topped table in the spartan room were the same five senior military and intelligence officials who had restricted their frequent convocations solely to this uniquely safe venue. The table in front of them, however, was now littered with half-eaten plates of food, any number of glass tumblers and empty mineral water bottles, and ashtrays brimming with crushed cigarettes and several half-smoked Havana cigars.

"Comrade Philby," Sergei Filatov, the Soviet Defense Minister, was saying, his tone filled with exaggerated patience, "the hour is late. The deadline for the first phase of the release of the documentation is rapidly approaching; and everything you're saying we've already discussed at length tonight. The fact is we have listened to your concerns. We have considered your recommendations. But unfortunately we—all of us sitting around this table—find them . . . how should I say it . . . unfeasible given the pressures we face in the days ahead."

The frail, stooped, white-haired man shifted uncomfortably as he sighed in frustration, a rare and altogether uncharacteristic show of defiance from this normally most reserved of men.

"Comrade Marshal," he said slowly, his elderly features sagging with fatigue, "with all due respect, these are established facts we are talking about, not recommendations. Unless, of course, you wish to regard the advocacy of caution as a new initiative on my part. Because that is the only thing I'm suggesting here tonight: caution. The deadline you keep referring to is not carved in stone. And while I cannot speak knowledgeably about these domestic pressures that concern you so, I can say this: we need time. We must have one or two days in which to assess the implications of these unexpected wrinkles that have appeared in our plans. We must stop and assess the consequences."

"But these so-called wrinkles of yours, Comrade Philby," the lean, weather-beaten man with the salt-and-pepper hair replied in an equally exacerbated tone, "do not change a thing in the greater order of events. Not substantively. The Americans have committed themselves irrevocably. And the evidence to convict them exists now. We have a *film*. A smoking gun, as they like to call it. How on earth is the other side going to come up with anything resembling plausible denial, let alone a credible defense, when we release a sixty-minute, thirty-five-millimeter film documenting the entire assassination being carried out by one of the most decorated soldiers in America?"

The old man shook his head. "I don't know," he mumbled softly. "But something—"

"We have our 'Abraham Zapruder' in place," Marshal Filatov interjected firmly, his impatience building to anger now. "What is there to gain from delaying his immediate introduction onto the scene as planned?"

"Comrade Philby, tell me," a concerned, intense-looking Geidar Rezayov interjected before the old man could answer, "what is it—

precisely—that is bothering you the most? Is it the fact that the American executive officer was not eliminated as planned?"

"No. The failure of that part of the sequence doesn't upset me in and of itself at all. After all, the death of the American officer, the assassin at the site of the crime, was merely to be the final nail in the coffin, so to speak. An event engineered to facilitate quick linkage between the assassination of Allan Sanford and Washington. But it was not in any way central to the plan. Besides, his demise is only a question of days, if not hours, now. And the same linkage will be achieved when the film is released, anyway."

"What is it, then, that makes you feel so strongly that we should stop and regroup?" Rezayov asked calmly.

Kim Philby contemplated his response as he looked slowly around the table, his tired, watery eyes appealing for understanding. What he saw, however, was not encouraging. Nevertheless, he thought, perseverance was by far the lesser of the two evils. And the man whose interests he seemed to have sparked was by far the shrewdest, not to say pragmatic, of the lot. He looked at Rezayov.

"As I have already said a number of times tonight, it is not any one single element that bothers me. It is the composite. A number of events adding up. The essence of this scheme was an orderly progress that achieved a maximum of surprise. Each step was to lead to the next and we were to be in control at all times, monitoring closely and constantly from the inside. That is why we went to such extraordinary lengths to be plugged in to Washington's every move.

"Well." Philby paused. "That is not what has been occurring. Let me repeat briefly what I am talking about. Firstly, and most importantly, the feedback we've been receiving from Elshtayn has throughout this operation been steadily tapering off—both qualitatively and quantitatively. And every time we do hear anything it conflicts sharply with what we were told before: there is the matter of the timing of the assassination, the delay. There's the matter of an ostensible change in their plans. And now, today, there's the question of the assassin's odd behavior after he executed his task. All in all, it spells confusion. Confusion spells unpredictability, which spells danger. What it also means is that the orderly flow of events we had in mind has been disrupted. And Elshtayn does not appear to have been able to alert us adequately or expeditiously. For what reason, remains to be seen."

The old man looked around the table as if searching for another wavering vote. "Secondly, there is the matter of the circumstances surrounding the death of our contract operative. The Americans moved onto the scene with extraordinary speed. And, despite all our various efforts through different sources, not one single word has ensued since they removed this man's, Aaron Brown's, body. That alone is most unusual for that country. Even if it has been for only less than a day so far. But taken together, these two events, namely the speed of their movements and the unusually tight secrecy shrouding the man's fate—a secrecy that has not provided a voracious media with a single clue to work with despite all our efforts in Washington, Los Angeles, New York, and abroad to spark off the story through rumors—raise important issues that simply have to be addressed.

"Now one can dismiss all this outright. Put it down to the chaos we know exists in Washington, the confusion we ourselves went to great lengths to create. Or one can take a more cautious view. If we choose that approach we then would have to conclude that the flow of events is not going as we planned; that there are things going on that we don't know; that Elshtayn either doesn't know or has not been able to pass on yet. In a sense, I suppose that's understandable. Remember, gentlemen, when you are in deep cover it is not always possible to communicate frequently or accurately. Especially when you are in the center of frantic activity.

"Nevertheless, what all this adds up to is that there are too many questions to which we do not have the answers. Certainly, I don't. What I have is a suspicion that something is wrong. And I believe that I've already presented enough evidence to you tonight to support my contention."

The Englishman paused and glanced again around the table. This time it was a slower and more resigned look. "I therefore believe it is absolutely imperative for us to wait a few days before we go further. We must be certain. If only a part of my suspicions turn out to be correct it would be sheer lunacy to expose ourselves any more than we already have.

"Now," he paused again, "I do not believe a delay of one or two days under these circumstances is an outrageous demand. Two days," he repeated, his voice rising in plea. "That's all I'm saying. Let me pulse our assets, in America and elsewhere, for a line. Probe, to gauge the direction they're taking."

A tense silence suddenly descended on the smoky room. At length, it was Geidar Rezayov who broke the strain. "You think that would suffice?"

"Yes," Philby replied confidently. "At the very least, we would get some intimation as to how things are unfolding. Which would place us in a better position to make a knowledgeable decision about whether to proceed or abort. Besides, if the Americans do have a secondary or parallel counterplan in operation, all the pressure will be on them during this period. They cannot hide Sanford's body forever. In the days ahead there are going to be many questions asked about his whereabouts. We'll make certain of that."

"Two days," Anatoli Andeyev repeated softly. "Forty-eight hours. And how, my dear Philby, do you propose we do that? How do you suggest we keep the General Secretary and his 'enlightened' colleagues at bay for that long?"

"That's the crux of the problem," blurted Marshal Filatov even before Philby could open his mouth. "You refuse adamantly to consider this side of the equation, Comrade Philby. Already questions are being asked. Many more will follow as this story picks up steam. We were, after all, cleared to proceed *only* with a sexual entrapment program, *not* to engineer the assassination of a confounded American icon."

"I grant you that," snapped the Englishman. "But imagine what sort of reaction we can all look—"

"Grant me, too, that you are being cautious in the extreme, Comrade Philby," Filatov interrupted. "None of your concerns, none of your warnings—real or imagined—alter the fact that the Americans have already committed themselves. We've seen it ourselves. On film. There's no going back for them now. They have killed—*murdered*—the next President of the United States of America."

The Englishman dropped his eyes defeatedly. "Perhaps," he said softly.

"Perhaps?" bellowed Filatov. He paused and spoke in a softer tone. "The American intelligence community have an expression, my dear Philby. It's called 'sick-think,' and I believe it's most appropriate here. One of its symptoms is believing distant warnings rather than what you see with your own eyes."

It was useless, thought Philby. These were not men who could be made to understand the intricate weave of delicacy or finesse. Let alone instincts. They were products of the system after all. Symbols of its values and style. And no one had ever accused the Soviet Union of using a surgeon's scalpel where a hatchet would suffice. Strange that a nation whose leaders were as crude, as ponderous and unimaginative as these men, could produce such prodigious champions of a sport as ticklish and perplexing as chess.

Filatov was right about one thing, though. They were going around in circles. They had been through all this over and over for a little more than three hours now and nothing had changed. No. That wasn't strictly true. One thing had—his position. It was weakening with each passing moment. None of these men could claim they were blessed with tolerance. And in the end—even after all these years—Kim Philby still had one major stigma tattooed in invisible block capitals across his forehead: ANGLICHININ.

"I wish I could grant you what you asked of me, Comrade Marshal," Philby said at length. "But I can't. You see, I'm not at all sure how to put this to you. But above and beyond what I've already said there's a phrase in English that you don't have in your language; at least, not used in the same way. It's called: *sixth sense*," Philby said, pronouncing the English words with pride. "And every instinct in my body tells me to be wary, that something is wrong. Just what, I can't say. But I," again he spliced the English word in among his accented Russian, "*sense* it. To the marrow of my bones, I sense it. Something is wrong."

The emotional vehemence of his words, coming from this normally reserved, understated man, startled the four men he addressed.

Then Marshal Filatov leaned forward slowly.

"We Russians have an expression too, Comrade Philby. One I don't believe you have in your country. It says, 'Courage, like the body, is a diminishing asset.'"

Clio Bragana opened the door; and for a brief moment they looked at each other. Then, with a half-stifled sigh of relief, she fell into Delan's arms.

306 • BARRY CHUBIN

"Oh, Nick," she whispered, clasping him in a tight embrace as she pressed her head against his chest.

Gently Delan guided her backward into the small, secluded wooden villa, closing the front door with his heel. Then he held her closer, relishing that familiar whiff of perfume on her body. He raised his right hand and caressed her hair softly, closing his eyes, lost in the warmth of the moment, the calm. Gradually he felt the exhaustion ebb out of his bones.

"How difficult was it to arrange?" he asked at length as he looked around the plainly decorated room behind her.

She leaned back in his arms and grinned at him, her eyes twinkling. "One-hundred-dollars difficult," she said rising up on to her toes.

They kissed, a long passionate embrace filled as much with tenderness as with longing.

In the end it was Clio who broke away. She stepped back and stared up at him. "God, you look terrible. What's happened to you?"

Delan nodded joylessly. "At least I'm not a hypocrite. That's exactly how I feel," he said, walking toward the center of the ill-lit sitting room. "Terrible."

A frown of apprehension swept across Clio's face. "Why? What's going on, Nick? Why all this cloak-and-dagger bit?"

Delan peered out of one of the two windows overlooking the small dark-wood balcony in front of the bungalow.

What to tell her? he thought. How much would it take to satisfy her curiosity? And yet not involve her in any way?

For a long moment he stared silently at the golden afternoon sunlight. He saw no one. No movement at all, in fact—except for the gentle breeze fluttering through the leaves of the tall, old trees all around. It was serene. No wonder this was a favorite Hollywood corner for rest and recuperation from the battles in the studios, boardrooms, and banks. Here, buried deep in the leafy lap of luxurious isolation, a man could lose his cares—even if only for a cozy afternoon tryst with a pretty friend. This place was built for just such subtle games of discretion: protection of confidences and a great deal of laissez-faire. It was an ideal place to hide.

"Nick," he heard Clio say, a hint of harshness in her tone. "You did say you'd explain it all to me."

"I work for the United States Government, Clio," he replied quietly. "And I've been involved with something that may or may not have gone wrong." He paused and released the curtain before turning slowly to face her. "I don't know, and it's going to take a few days before I do. In the meantime, I have to lie low. But to do that I need your help," he said, his soft voice a blend of reluctance and guilt.

Clio Bragana's solemn gaze slid slowly to a look of deep uncertainty. "Is that all you have to say to me?"

Delan shook his head, the right corner of his mouth curling upward in a helpless half-smile. "No. There's a lot more I'd like to tell you. But I can't."

"Why not?"

"Because I don't want you involved too deeply. And if you knew you would be."

"But I'm already involved."

"Involved in what, Clio?"

"Don't split hairs with me, Nick," she shot back. "Not now. What the hell are *you* involved in?"

Delan studied her silently for a moment. No matter what, she had to be protected.

"Look, Clio, I'm telling you the truth. How bad can it be if I work for the Government?"

"Why are you so frightened you have to hide, then?"

It was a good question. "I don't know," he said slowly, letting out a heavy breath of air. He paced toward her. "I really don't, Clio. I'm not at all sure if I'm being cautious or foolish and paranoid."

"Then I suppose you should do it," she said after a long, cold, intense appraisal.

"Will you help me?"

"Yes;" she replied hesitantly.

"Good. Because there's something I'd like you to do for me right away."

"What?"

"The car. It's parked next to the hotel, on Crescent Drive. I want you to drive it away and dump it somewhere. Can you do that?"

She nodded, hesitant and apprehensive.

"But I want you to wear gloves," he continued. "And to leave the keys in the car when you dump it so it'll look like a joyride. On your way back you've got to remember to do two things. One, change cabs so you eliminate the possibility of any cab driver remembering picking you up in the area you dump it." He smiled; and then caressed the side of her face reassuringly. "After all, this is a difficult face to forget.

"And, two, make sure you're not being followed. There, or back. If you are, call me here and ask for . . . ah . . . Tony. Then give me your precise location—and I'll be there."

"Okay," Clio whispered after a long pause. "But you better give me your measurements as well."

"Why?"

"You'll need some clothing."

One nagging question plagued Nick Delan.

All through the remainder of the afternoon, during the long therapeutic shower he took to soothe away some of the aches and pains in his body, it niggled at him. Afterward, while he attended to the two deep cuts on his head and hip, the inquisition continued. Indeed, long after the two hours he'd spent worrying about Clio were over and she'd returned safely, the same troubling question reverberated in Delan's mind: What was he running from?

And each time it provoked a hundred related questions: why was he sitting in a hotel room—petrified? Why couldn't he trust them? run to the safe house down in San Clemente they had picked out? Why couldn't he shake this feeling that he was now expendable? That, given the right set of circumstances, it was he who would be the target? Perhaps of both sides?

Anthony Boyle. That was why. His old friend Boyle. The man whose life he'd saved. What was Boyle trying to hide? Why had he sidestepped Delan's questions about the defector? Why had what he'd said seemed so incomplete?

Delan didn't have an answer. All he knew was that for the first time in his life he felt entirely out of his depth. In a profession noted for treachery, Nick Delan was a novice.

And all the while—through these endless hours of doubt—one phrase jingled constantly in the back of his head, six words he'd not been able to shake from the moment he'd heard them.

"Speak unto us smooth things, prophesy . . ." he heard the late James

Cassidy's voice mumble morosely. Over and over again he heard that phrase, like a scratchy old record stuck in one groove. *"Speak unto us smooth things, prophesy . . ."*

It still meant nothing to him. Only enough to stop him from getting through the night in peace, tossing and turning with each possible new interpretation.

The killer waiting for Delan in the dark. What had he known? Delan cursed his luck. He had not meant to kill the man. Demobilize, yes; cripple, even maim; but not kill. He thought of the concrete shrapnel and cursed his luck.

Who was he? Why was he there? And who had dispatched him? Had he really been there to provide the Soviets with the corpse of Sanford's assassin? There was no doubt he was there to kill. Whose interests would be better served if Allan Sanford's assassin was found dead at the site of the crime?

The Soviets?

Probably.

But there was another scenario that was not altogether impossible. What if the Osiris Option didn't work? What if, for all his confidence, Boyle was wrong and he couldn't pull it off? What then?

A hundred pictures flashed through his mind. Black-and-white photographs that dropped on each other in a growing pile. Images of Lee Harvey Oswald, Rolando Galman, and Bent Singh, the men who killed Kennedy, Aquino, and Indira Gandhi. Mouths open and distorted, faces cringing with agony as the first bullets entered their bodies. And ended their lives before a single question could be asked of them.

"You don't get to be head of the Politburo by being a choirboy," Henry Kissinger had said about the Soviet Secretary General.

Neither, thought Delan, do you get to be the President of the United States that way. Or the Director of the Central Intelligence Agency. Or National Security Adviser. Or, for that matter, his deputy.

Anthony Boyle? His friend? Could he really be so utterly ruthless and underhanded?

Abruptly Nick Delan felt his skin crawl. *The Bible. Isaiah. That was it. That was where the passage was from. He remembered distinctly from all those Catholic schools: "Speak unto us smooth things, prophesy deceits."*

"*. . . prophesy deceits . . . prophesy deceits.*"

Suddenly Delan felt very cold. His instincts had been spot on target. Anthony Boyle *had* been deceiving him. Smooth-talking him, at the very least. And James Cassidy had been uncomfortable about it. But why did Boyle want to deceive him? What about? And where was the smooth, distinguished Mr. Boyle heading with his lies?

22 | MONDAY, JANUARY 18

The morning news stunned the nation.

Allan Sanford was dead.

Or was he?

No one seemed to know for certain. And what made it even more disturbing, every strand of this huge story about the apparent assassination of an international idol was shrouded in mystery. A substantial body of information pointing to his murder had been uncovered. But there were key elements missing.

What had started out as a simple story about a fire just off Newport Beach, California, early yesterday morning had quickly burst into a swirl of international rumor and conflicting reports. And all this speculation about almost inconceivable events had mushroomed very quickly into a domestic storm.

Then another story broke late last night, the focal point of which was a film made available to ABC News under bizarre circumstances: via a courier service, addressed to the network anchorman based in New York but sent by a name that could not be traced from an address that did not exist.

Despite the oddity—and the film's murky quality—the network gauged it as newsworthy and released it immediately on its *Nightline* program. By this morning the dim, foggy pictures had been computer-enhanced. Now they clearly showed a heavily equipped man swimming across a channel under cover of night, then hiding behind a short wall before entering a house—later clearly identified as presidential candidate Allan Sanford's Lido Island retreat. It showed, too, that same figure first menacing the former actor at gunpoint. Then within seconds felling Sanford, apparently by shots; but this was not absolutely clear. The film continued with the mysterious explosion on the boats, the fires, the pandemonium; and the killer's escape.

It was an extraordinary document. Almost as gripping for its Zapruder-like amateurish, grainy black-and-white texture, which gave the pictures an ominous realism, as for the incredible story line: the cold, efficient assassination of a national idol.

The body? The body? Delan kept fretting as he followed the reports intently. That was the one fear he felt about all the unanswered questions that were emerging. Where had the film come from? Who was the assailant? What was the forensic evidence? When would it be made public? None of the key unresolved questions gripping the entire world bothered Delan half as much as the discovery of *the body*.

The related stories did not provide an answer either: the film of the blood-splattered couches, curtains, and walls in Allan Sanford's house, the fire-razed yachts and wharfs, all the comments of various officials crawling all over Sanford's house eventually ended with the same crucial four or five questions. But for Nick Delan there was only one: Where was Sanford?

Aggravating the bizarreness of the puzzle even more, there were suddenly no senior officials from the normally efficient Sanford organization—White House, Inc., as it had been dubbed by the press—available for comment. Why?

In light of the mounting global outcry this became a subject of intense scrutiny.

But it didn't upset Nick Delan. Following the deepening mystery and worldwide shock and outrage, he felt a sense of serenity descending. For, as Boyle had said at the airport, "At worst, without a body, there's no crime." Perhaps he was wrong, perhaps paranoia had distorted his perceptions. So far, events were proceeding exactly as Boyle had projected. Not even the enormous attention being focused on the gunman's face from the infinite number of perspectives which the film provided worried him. The blown-up zoom shots, the circles drawn around his features on still frames, the artists' impressions and identikits being assembled—none of these could strip off the heavy grease on the gunman's face. He was in no danger of being recognized from what was appearing on the world's screens. Not so far, at least. After all, Clio's suspicions weren't aroused. And she was living with him.

It was just before noon when Delan's calm was jolted.

"In what must be regarded as a related development," a television announcer said urgently, "the Los Angeles Coroner's office has just revised its ruling in the three-day-old case of Allan Sanford's campaign manager and right-hand man, Phillip Myers. 'Premeditated murder' is the verdict now, upgraded from the originally announced 'death by natural causes.' He was, the coroner now says, poisoned in his room at the Century Plaza Hotel in Century City with a substance believed to be ricin—a toxin more deadly than snake venom and one that leaves little or no trace. For the details we go over to Los Angeles and ABC correspondent . . ."

Nick Delan closed his eyes, his heart pounding. Something had gone wrong. Something not even Anthony Boyle had factored in.

He opened his eyes suddenly, squinting at the television screen. At least not as far as Nick knew.

At 5:59 P.M. the tiny blinking lights appeared below the dark clouds billowing over the District of Columbia. Floating down gracefully, they grew steadily larger until the purr of the chopper's distant churning blades crescendoed to a roar. Marine One hovered and touched down gently on the South Lawn of the White House.

At precisely that moment, not more than two or three hundred yards away on the western periphery of the presidential estate, a small, inconsequential, gray Chevy Nova with smoked windows turned right off 17th Street into the immaculate grounds behind the old Executive Office Building. The vehicle twisted around the well-lit driveway until it was directly behind the building, stopping out of view on its eastern perimeter: just a few yards away from the West Wing of the White House.

Not one of the 2,000 or so journalists accredited to the White House at any given time was there to witness the discreet arrival of the car. For every one of the nearly two hundred on duty that evening had been enticed to brave the arctic weather on the strength of the latest rumor: that on landing the President would make an important announcement on the Allan Sanford story. The array of microphones erected at the usual location on the floodlit snow-covered lawns added weight to the story.

The President looked extremely grave as he descended the steps of the helicopter. At the bottom he held out a helping hand for the petite First Lady. Ushering her gently ahead, the President strode quickly past the forest of beckoning microphones toward the majestic white building at the end of the lawn. The horde of reporters waiting patiently in the cold night were offered only the briefest of unenthusiastic smiles as they watched the couple stride away, their entourage following.

Nevertheless several of the more astute correspondents did notice one unusual fact. The absence from the receiving committee of John Atkins, the White House Chief of Staff. Only as the President approached the building did he arrive, hurrying out of the doorway to exchange the curtest of greetings before leaning his head closer to the President's ear.

The reporters did not hear him whisper, "Mr. President, the Soviet Ambassador is waiting."

"There is an assassin but no body—that is the gist of the unfolding story this evening as the circumstances surrounding the mysterious disappearance of presidential candidate Allan Sanford continue to baffle the FBI. For the first time, too, there's a whiff of a political scandal in the air as the White House itself suddenly appears on the defensive."

The large portrait of Allan Sanford behind the network anchorman abruptly changed to that of a dour, bald, bespectacled man.

"Tonight, in an unprecedented move," the ABC anchorman continued, "the Soviet Union has formally made just such an accusation. Henrikas Yushkiavitshus, the highly influential chairman of Gosteleradio, the Soviet Union's state-run committee for television and radio, appeared before a hastily called meeting of the foreign press corps in Moscow to announce that the Soviet Union has obtained reliable information that implicates, I quote, 'certain American government agencies in the disappearance of Allan Sanford.'

"Asked about this extraordinary accusation, the White House refused to comment.

"We'll have these stories, plus an updated computer-derived

identikit of the man allegedly involved in the suspected death or disappearance of Allan Sanford, and the stunned worldwide reaction to this story, coming up after these messages.''

In the ensuing commercial interval, a surge of panic welled inside Nick Delan. For the first time in his life he felt a debilitating sense of total impotence. Like a passenger on a runaway train, his life was being shaped by distant forces over which he had no control. People he had reason not to trust. He was trapped in this room like an animal. And inch by inch, minute by minute, the walls were closing in on him.

Too much was happening. Too quickly. Had Osiris fallen apart? Because this was chaos. A shambles filled with curious coincidences. People were dying. Peripheral people—which was exactly what *he* was now.

He glanced down at *The Los Angeles Tribune* on the coffee table in front of his armchair. His eyes immediately focused on the small article he'd read earlier.

WEAPONS DEALER FOUND SHOT IN LOCKED CAR

PARIS—The savage murder of an international businessman on Sunday by what appear to be professional assassins is the subject of an intense police inquiry here in the French capital.

Keyvan Naderi, an Iranian arms dealer suspected of plotting to obtain and sell U.S. weapons in violation of the U.S. embargo on arms sales to Iran . . .

First Phillip Myers. Now Keyvan Naderi? Delan himself was the only direct link he knew between these two individuals, both murdered in the space of forty-eight hours. Could it really be a coincidence? Neither Myers' nor Naderi's deaths had been foreseen by Boyle. Or had they? What had Boyle been holding back?

If the Soviets were planning to control the next President, why not penetrate the inner circles of this one? Cassidy had been killed by the Soviets to provide credibility to Pavlenko's story. Sounded convincing at the time.

Angrily he snapped the newspaper shut and dropped it at his side.

He didn't want Clio to see the article. For reasons totally beyond Delan, she'd truly liked Naderi. The last thing Delan needed right now was to scare her even more. Not least, because she was his sole lifeline to the outside world and he needed to keep her on an even keel. So far she had no reason to suspect any connection between him and the events which were unfolding on television. Their talk had been ordinary and she'd spent much of the day going about her modeling assignment. But with the Naderi story he had to be careful. She had to be protected from herself.

He heard her turn off the shower. No, he admitted, that wasn't the only reason. He cared about her, and—thanks to him—she had more than enough on her plate to deal with for the—

Abruptly his brain went blank with disbelief, his blood freezing. The black-and-white picture of a face on the television screen was now one he recognized well. It was his.

"I don't know," Delan said quietly. "Probably a combination of things."

Gently he broke away from her soft embrace and rolled away toward his side of the king-sized bed. Already reality was beginning to seep back in, forcefully shunting aside the joy of the tender, trembling moment they had just shared.

"Like what?" Clio Bragana asked softly.

Delan felt for the bedside table and lit a cigarette before looking back at her. The shaft of silver moonlight spilling in from the windows caught the film of moisture covering her body. It glistened off the olive skin on one side of her supine legs and the generous curves of her hips, while only hinting at their sensuality in the darkness of the other. She lay on her stomach, her hands folded in innocent prayer, tucked beneath her contented face.

"I joined the Army because I was drafted. I stayed on," Delan paused, digging for an honest answer, "I guess because in the first instance I had nowhere else to go to."

"And in the second?" she asked after a long silence.

"I became addicted."

"Addicted? What to?"

Delan took a deep drag on the cigarette. Clio Bragana thought she detected the slightest shake of his head.

"I don't think I've ever been able to answer that question intelligibly. Not even to myself." He paused.

What had started as a calculated act to distract Clio from the television and his photograph to avoid the stream of awkward questions that would inevitably follow, had now become the most loving moment of their entire relationship. Her reassuring warmth had transported him to another world. Their touch had been passionate and tender, tinged by the heightened bliss that comes to lovers only once they have thoroughly experienced each other's bodies. And now, exhausted, he was delighting in talking to her about himself. Sorry only that he couldn't tell her everything. Couldn't tell her why he'd turned off the television before she had come out of the bathroom. Couldn't tell her his suspicions, his terror at what he had seen. For in this one moment in his life he wanted more than ever before to be close to Clio, to open up to her completely.

"How do you explain the tricks people play on themselves to hide the flaws: the weaknesses and phobias they inherit? What do you do when all your parents leave you is eternal shame on one side? And loneliness and regrets on the other?"

He blew out a heavy lungful of smoke. "You try harder for one. Because, when you're born a loser, you *have* to win. You're very, very hungry. And that's all you crave. You try to hide, too. Melt into a large group of some kind: an organization, a union, a team, a unit in which you're lost among a sea of faces. To me the Army seemed as good as any."

Clio Bragana rolled slightly to one side. She raised her right arm to prop up her head as she gave his ill-lit profile a long silent look. "Were you successful?"

"Successful?" Slowly Delan turned his head to face her. He could see the tenderness his words had aroused in her eyes. It made him feel even more responsive. He held his gaze on her. If things were, by some miracle, to work out, he'd have to tell her all this someday. She had the right to know everything. She had to know. And then to choose. He looked away.

"Depends on how you define the word. Besides, priorities change. In Vietnam I had two goals. In the morning—to get through to sunset. If I did that I considered myself a success. At night it was to make it to daylight. I did that for nearly seven years and twice in every twenty-four hours I congratulated myself. Which is something most of my friends didn't manage to accomplish. So I guess you could call me a success."

"What a hell of a way to exist," she whispered after a long pause.

Delan raised his eyebrows. "It wasn't as bad as it sounds. There were certain things about that life I grew very attracted to. Couldn't live without." He turned and looked at her, and tried to put a world of warmth into his small smile. "Not, at least, back then."

She looked back at him lovingly. "Why? What was it you found so inviting?"

"It's a tough feeling to try to explain."

"Please try. I want to understand you."

Delan looked at her grimly; then he sighed. "In Vietnam I was a member of a unit called the Studies and Observation Group, or SOG. The name is a little innocuous because it was supposed to be an elite unit that specialized in operating clandestinely behind enemy lines. When we went in on most of these missions we did so with helicopters. And we always went in the final minutes of the evening—a period known as 'last light.' That's the worst possible moment in the day for what the military folk like to call ocular orientation; seeing, to those who speak English."

Delan paused, remembering. "It was a weird sensation, Clio, the last ten, fifteen minutes of those rides. Every time. No matter how often you did it. Because you knew that, at best, the odds were even that those last few minutes were probably all you had left of your life.

"The feeling—as you jumped from that chopper floating half on and half off the ground amid a farrago of confusion: bullets and explosions and shrieks and shouts, and ran for your life . . ." He breathed out, obviously unable to find the right words. "Well, it's something more powerful, more potent, more gloriously stimulating than all the fame and money in the world, all the sex and glamour and power anyone, anywhere, could ever have."

Again he paused. "It was a feeling I wanted again in my life."

Clio Bragana stared at his dark, brooding profile for a moment. Then slowly she raised her naked body and leaned across to kiss his brow. "You know something?"

"What?"

"I think I've fallen in love with a romantic."

23 | TUESDAY, JANUARY 19

"The United States of America is the most volatile and violent nation on earth," the General Secretary of the Communist Party of the Soviet Union said softly into the window, the hot vapor from his breath clinging to the cold glass. "It is therefore dangerous to trifle with it. Not because they are strong but because they are unpredictable."

He paused and stood there silently for a moment, his eyes vaguely contemplating the bright lights three floors below. Dotting the snow-covered landscape of Ivanovsky Park, the lampposts stretched across to the dark Arsenal building in front of him and up to Nikolsky Tower to his right. Behind him, the eight men sitting across from his desk, down the stem of the T that was the green-baize conference table, said nothing. The silence in the room was total as they waited, watching his short, robust, peasant body, hands clasped behind the back of his dark-blue suit.

"It is a nation," he continued in the same calm, emotionless tone, "whose first and last reaction to any problem is to shoot it. And this is not some sort of vague and temporary apparition. It is a clearly documented historical tendency. A propensity—as the record indicates—that has only become more pronounced in recent times. Consider the facts. Seventeen of the last thirty-seven years this country has been at war; five times it has invaded Caribbean countries in that period, twice the Middle East."

He shook his head unhappily at the slumbering world outside. "And still some of our comrades wish to continue to play brinkmanship with such a nation," he added sadly.

"How?" he suddenly snapped in a louder tone. "How on earth did these imbeciles from *D'e'vachka Adee'n* apply the first rule that governs any state's international relations—risk evaluation—to this insane scheme of theirs? How can anybody ever hope to predict with any accuracy what the reaction of a nation with so many variables at interplay will ever be? Such numerous power centers and interest groups constantly jockeying for position and shifting their ground. It is insanity. And it threatens to undo everything we've achieved. *Everything*."

The General Secretary paused and breathed deeply before he turned and paced back toward his desk. As he approached it he raised his gaze from the priceless Persian rug beneath his feet and looked at the tall, sallow figure sitting on the opposite side of the table.

"I shudder to think, Comrade," he said with just a hint of a smile easing the severity on his boyish, bespectacled face, "what the consequences would have been if we did not have you to warn us."

The dapper man the General Secretary addressed smiled back contentedly. The General Secretary looked away, to the telephone that had suddenly begun to ring on the side table flanking his desk.

"If only we had had a little more lead time, though," he said, walking toward it. "Prior notice, rather than information after the fact. It would have made a world of difference to our credibility as far as Washington is concerned, don't you think, Comrade?" He paused before he spoke again. "Not to mention that we ourselves might have been able to stop it."

The General Secretary stopped behind his desk and looked again at the confident man sitting erectly.

"But, then again, it is not you, Comrade, who can be blamed for that, is it?"

Again he paused. But this time it was a longer break. An interval in which his facial expression gradually adopted a menacing glare.

"I'm sure the inquiry will exonerate you of any malevolent intentions, Comrade Rezayov. Indeed, I would think only the harshest and most inclement panel of your peers could reach the conclusion that you were perhaps—how should I say it?—waiting to see how things proceeded?"

The smile on Geidar Rezayov's face slid slowly to a look of horror. He seemed to pale as he shied back into his chair, withering under the weight of the General Secretary's implacable glare.

Without looking away even for an instant, the General Secretary picked up the receiver.

"Your call to the President of the United States, Comrade General Secretary."

"Good morning," said the ABC News anchorman, a grave expression on his face. "Amid a cascade of revelations, including an accusation of direct White House involvement in the death of Allan Sanford from a high-ranking Soviet official, an embattled administration, fighting to defuse fierce and mounting criticism, has just released the name and picture of a man it seeks to question."

The newscaster paused dramatically. "In its investigation of what increasingly appears to be the assassination of Allan Sanford, the FBI has just put out an all-state alert . . ."

The picture on the television screen changed. To that of the head and shoulders of a man wearing the uniform of the Green Berets, his right chest awash with medals.

". . . for Lieutenant-Colonel Nicholas Delan, born Nicola Delano, son of the late Salvatore 'Lupara' Delano, a convicted Chicago mobster."

The coffee cup froze in Nick Delan's hand. Simultaneously a black hate welled inside him. This had to be Anthony Boyle's doing.

"White House sources have told ABC News privately that there may be a link between Allan Sanford's disappearance and his campaign promises to clean up organized crime, with the Mafia employing the highly decorated Colonel Delan's special forces skills to eliminate the mob's self-professed Enemy Number One.

"Meanwhile, ABC News has learned from sources in the Pentagon that Colonel Delan is a member of an elite Army unit that was declared officially disbanded in October 1984 for alleged financial misconduct by three Army colonels. The very existence of this highly secret 'black' arm of the government, however, has always been a subject of some controversy. While it was declared officially disbanded by the Reagan administration in 1984, its existence was denied by the same administration a year earlier and it has never been acknowledged by any other administration before or after the Reagan presidency. Within the rapidly unraveling story of the Sanford disappearance, however, there are now new indications that the unit does in fact exist despite renewed denials following the Iran-Contra scandal of the Reagan administration."

The anchorman paused. "What is becoming increasingly clear is that, even if a portion of the rumors and speculations flying around Washington today turns out to be true, this Sanford affair may become the most crushing crisis of the Republic since the Civil War."

Suddenly, Nick Delan knew she was there. Without looking, he sensed her presence in the room, the heat of her accusing eyes burning into his back. He snapped around.

She stared back, eyes agape, mouth open. She stood there, her face still puffy from sleep, her hair unruly, a white towel wrapped around her body.

"It's not true, Clio," he whispered, swallowing in a vain attempt to lubricate his dry throat. "I swear to God it isn't. It's a setup. I'm being framed."

But even to himself his precarious plea sounded feeble.

She looked at him, her face etched with terror. Then back to the pictures passing across the screen. Then back and forth again, searching, praying for one small discrepancy between the two images.

In the end she gave up. She closed her eyes. Tighter and tighter she squeezed them, trying to exorcise even the vaguest memory of what she had only just seen and learned.

"I'm being framed by my own people, Clio," Delan repeated in a desperate whisper. "You *have* to believe me. You're the only hope I have."

24 | WEDNESDAY, JANUARY 20

"What are you going to do?"

"Try to get down to Mexico."

Nestling in his embrace, Clio Bragana was slow to ask her next question. "Then what?"

"I don't know." Delan sighed. "I really don't. Maybe slip across to Guatemala and then try to find a way down to Brazil, Argentina . . . anywhere. I'll have to take it as it comes."

"Oh, Nick," Clio murmured despondently, burying her head in his chest, hugging him tighter. "I don't understand any of this."

"Me neither, Clio," he replied very slowly.

"It's craziness. Why would your own friends want to frame you? What do they gain from arresting you? Except someone who can tell the whole world the full story, including everything they want to hide."

"I'm not sure that arresting me is exactly what they have in mind, Clio."

Delan felt her stiffen. He immediately regretted what he'd said.

He raised his hand to stroke her soft hair and tried to think of something that would lighten the mood. "Do you know what the Brazilians specialize in these days?"

She looked up at him, her fingers toying with the hairs on his chest. "What?"

"Plastic surgery. So don't be surprised if a Cary Grant look-alike knocks on your door one of these days."

Clio Bragana could not stop a sad smile. But it was fleeting, washed away by the next wave of concern. Now she looked at him like an adult looks at a little boy feigning bravado in front of his family and friends.

"You better go now," he said reluctantly. "It's getting late."

She nodded, biting her lip to stop the welling tears. She looked back into his face. "Yes," she whispered with no conviction at all.

"And remember, our meeting at the car has to be casual. And short. There's very little chance of our being seen together. It's reasonably secluded there and it'll be dark. But I don't want to take any chances. I don't want anyone remembering a couple talking and embracing and saying good-bye. Then come straight back up here and call the FBI. Tell them everything exactly as we discussed it this morning. That we met, we had a casual affair, we parted. It seemed like a good idea at the time. That's all there was to it. Tell them you haven't seen me since the L'Ermitage. That you moved here under an incognito listing on Sunday after we had had a row Saturday evening and I didn't show up that night. A fight that you now suspect I may have instigated to walk out on you. Either way, you haven't seen me since."

"Okay," she whispered, lowering her glistening eyes. "What about the package you sent? What do I say about that?"

Delan reached up and caressed the side of her face. "The chances are they won't know about it. If they do, all you have to say is that you have no idea why I sent it. Maybe it was an attempt to make up. Maybe it was for some other reason. Either way, you ignored it and left the hotel before I showed up."

She nodded softly.

"Remember all of that, Clio. The rest of it, too. It's important. Just stick to exactly what we went through. Don't veer off by one word."

She said nothing.

"It's imperative you do what I say, Clio. And, no matter how often they ask the same question in a different way, just keep repeating the same story. Over and over again."

"I will," she whispered almost inaudibly.

Delan felt her chin quivering against his chest. He looked up at the ceiling as he cuddled her even tighter. "I know what you're going to go through. It's going to be hell. What I don't know is how to thank you for it—and everything else you've done for me. Above all, the blind trust you've placed in me." He paused. "I can't say I hope the opportunity arises, but maybe someday I can repay you."

"You already have, Nick," she said softly, reaching for his hand. She brought it to her lips and kissed his palm gently. Over and over she kissed it before she spoke again. "You've given me something I thought I'd never have in my life: love. Real, honest, decent love. I never even dreamed I was capable of it."

They looked at each other for a moment, a piece of each of them dying with what they knew was the long good-bye that lay ahead. Then they kissed, a soft, enduring meeting of the lips that tried in one brief touch to encompass all the things left unsaid, left undone, all the dreams that would never be realized.

"Come on," Nick Delan whispered, his eyes still closed, his brow wrinkled with regret. "It's getting late. You've got to get to the airport, rent a car, and drive back; and there's only a couple of hours left."

Reluctantly she turned away and picked up her handbag. Next to it, in the simple white porcelain vase adorning the coffee table, Nick Delan noticed the bunch of long-stemmed yellow roses the hotel changed daily. He reached down and broke one off.

"Here," he said threading it through the top buttonhole on the collar of her blood-red cotton suit. "For luck."

She smiled sadly, looking at him as if to etch his face in her mind's eye forever.

"Look after yourself, Nick. Please," she said. Then she turned and walked away, glancing one last time in his direction before closing the front door behind her.

For a long moment Nick Delan stared at the hard, impersonal white of a hotel door, a vague hint of moisture glistening in his red eyes.

Then slowly he forced himself to turn away. It was over, he told himself. At least for now. Better to stay alive. To be around just in case their love did last. Alive, he could find her again one day.

But the margin for error was extremely thin. If only half his suspicions turned out to be justified staying alive would not be easy. As he busied himself removing all evidence of his presence from the bungalow, he thought about the various strands that intertwined to form this debilitating knot of fear he felt.

Was it possible? Could Anthony Boyle, the Deputy National Security Adviser of the land, really be a Soviet mole?

Madonna. He didn't know. There was so much he did not know. It frustrated him. Worse, it was his own fault. This vacuum he was now trapped in had been evident almost from the very beginning. And he'd ignored it.

He sat in an armchair and rubbed his tired eyes and tense forehead as if trying to wipe the slate clean. It was a complicated game of chess they were playing and he had to figure exactly what was happening.

The problem was simple: the task was impossible.

He didn't have enough hard information. For the most part all he could do was surmise. Still, there were certain incontestable facts. Not only were they all ominous, there was a certain pattern, a perverse logic that linked them together to suggest a trend.

For a start, contrary to all the vigorous assurances Boyle had given for both the original plan and the Osiris Option, the assassin *had* been identified. And by Washington. Worse, not only had they officially identified him, they had done it in the most incriminating manner conceivable: Nicholas Delan, alias Nicola Delano, son of Salvatore "Lupara" Delano, a convicted Chicago mobster. The only conclusion one could possibly reach was that Anthony Boyle had lied. That he had intended to pin the assassination on Delan all along. And that it was all very carefully planned. What could possibly be more plausible than a trained killer with Mafia links reverting to his Mafia roots to protect Mafia interests? What could be more plausible than the assassination being packaged as a Mafia killing? In direct response to Sanford's pledged war on the Mafia.

Now, in retrospect, it all seemed so smooth. The classic approach to any setup, in fact: factoring in the fall guy, the scapegoat, before you even start.

And you, you dumb bastard, Delan said to himself. You fell for it. You trusted them . . . him. You never stopped to cover yourself. You never pressed Boyle. You didn't look for the gaps.

That's why Boyle had been so ready to graft the Osiris Option on to the original plan. It made sense now. He had a plausible assassin who had to be kept on track. When Delan got cold feet because he'd spotted monitors, Boyle had to come up with something to convince the assassin to stay the course. He never intended to implement the Osiris Option. No doubt Boyle had presented an eloquent argument that convinced everyone else involved—the White House, the CIA, his colleagues at the NSC—that the overriding concern was a plausible assassination. The details could always be shifted around later, if need be.

Delan rubbed the back of his neck for a moment. All that he could understand. It was logical. Perverse but logical. What wasn't was the disclosure about AISA. That didn't fit. What could Washington possibly gain from revealing that connection? It didn't make sense. Within minutes of Nicola Delano, son of Salvatore "Lupara" Delano, convicted Chicago mobster, being identified as the murderer, the information was changed, devalued by an ever more far-reaching revelation. Now the assassin was Colonel Nicholas Delan, Army Intelligence Support Activity. Colonel Nicholas Delan, United States Government agent.

Why? Why would the administration want to shoot itself in the foot? Why was there such a divergence in the two official stories? One linking Delan to the Mafia. The other directly to the U.S. Government. Was someone in the administration trying to subvert Washington? Why else would the Mafia connection be hijacked so quickly by what was obviously an unauthorized and damning disclosure?

Nick Delan slumped back in his chair. The implications were chilling. Either on his own or as part of a group, Anthony Boyle had to be directly involved in some way. It was Boyle who had railroaded Delan into undertaking the operation initially; Boyle who had created the Osiris Option and convinced Delan of its viability when Delan harbored grave doubts; Boyle who was to have masterminded and coordinated all the delicate moves after the hit.

It followed therefore that Anthony Boyle must have had a part in the creation of a neon-lit killer whom he could soon present to the world as a second corpse. A corpse directly linked to the government. Incriminating it beyond any doubt. All of which had to mean Boyle had an even larger goal in mind than simply killing Delan to close the trail. What on earth could the goal of such a huge double-cross scheme possibly be?

Delan felt a sinking sensation. Was it really possible? Anthony Boyle? A deep-level Soviet agent? A sleeper, a mole? The questions repeated themselves over and over. Why had James Cassidy been killed? Had he unwittingly uncovered Boyle's role? His plan? What had he meant by that comment in the car about smooth talk and deceit?

Delan didn't know. All he could think of were the implications: his own death was imperative. Imperative, even if only half his suppositions about Boyle were true. Only Delan could reveal what had been discussed between the two of them at the airport nine days ago. Only Delan knew the details of the Osiris Option and how it was supposed to unfold. Only Delan could finger Boyle and expose all the lies he had told.

But to do that, he told himself, he first had to survive. This time it wouldn't be as easy. It wasn't one killer he was up against now. No. This time it was a ubiquitous organization. Boyle would have mobilized all the vast resources at the disposal of the United States of America by now. The complex network of FBI informers: the petty hoods, the pushers, hookers, pimps, and fences; the choke pointers moonlighting from their official roles as employees of hotels, motels, flophouses, airports, train stations, bus terminals, rent-a-car firms; the underworld connection that comprised all the various tentacles of organized crime, large or small and of every race. All of these and more would be continuously pulsed by their control agents. And on top of all this came the 8,800-man-strong FBI itself. Along with all the other forces of law and order: the local, state, customs, immigration, border, coast, and other guards. By now, copies of his picture had been circulated throughout the land. And if Delan's suppositions were correct, the pictures would be accompanied by a specific instruction: "Armed and dangerous. Shoot to kill."

Nick Delan stepped out onto the small wooden porch of the secluded bungalow at the Beverly Hills Hotel.

Dressed in a khaki safari suit and canary-yellow polo shirt, a long, thin cheroot in his mouth, he blended perfectly with the casual Hollywood crowd. But underneath his new and immaculately pressed clothes, perspiration oozed from his skin. He could feel the tiny beads twisting down the small of his back, making the Smith & Wesson Model 10 pistol he'd lodged there slippery and warm. For a moment he stood still, lighting the cheroot. Then he descended the few steps to the narrow path threading through the exotic greenery. He tried to walk with a carefree gait as his eyes scanned the surroundings.

This was perhaps the most hazardous stretch of his long, long journey. This initial phase took him through the hotel's main lobby, down through the basement galleria to the swimming pool and tennis courts on the other side. It was the only route available to him. Crescent Drive to the west was far too open. He would never get to the car Clio had waiting for him unnoticed—if indeed anyone was staking the hotel. And he couldn't exactly walk around the back of the grounds, either. Not in residential Beverly Hills. No one walks the streets there; not without arousing suspicions.

No. This was the most natural route and therefore the safest path to take. Up ahead he was approaching the hotel's rear entrance. He leaned into the swing door and stepped inside. The small space was buzzing with activity. Delan's eyes swept the lobby as he headed toward the telephone booths and the steps beside them leading down. To his left the famous Polo Lounge was as busy as ever.

"Excuse me." A heavy hand brushed Nick Delan's shoulder.

Delan turned. The man was young, early thirties. Tall. Wiry. Clean-cut. Intense eyes—boring into him. FBI? He forced a reply. "Yes?"

"I'm sorry to bother you," the man said.

Behind the speaker Delan suddenly noticed another man, roughly the same age and type: wholesome, youthful, serious, athletic, looking on from several yards away. How many others were there? Delan wondered as he raised his right hand to his hip casually, closer to the pistol lodged in the middle of his back. He looked back. "How can I help you?"

"Can you change a dollar?" the tall, wiry man asked, smiling coldly.

Delan looked down to his outstretched hand. But it was what he saw just beyond that made his heart pound even more vigorously: the unmistakable bulge in the lines of the man's dark-gray gabardine suit. Just to the left of the open button, slightly in front of his hip.

"I'm afraid I can't," Delan said.

Should he run? Or play it through?

"Any idea where I can get it?" the man asked.

Impatiently, it seemed to Delan. Nervously, even.

"Yeah—"

Suddenly the sound of a beeper erupted.

The man reached down to the bulge inside his coat. "Damn, that's the third time. All my patients are going to be dead before I get through to the hospital."

"There's a cashier right around the corner, there," Delan said, pointing toward the main lobby beyond the telephones.

"Thanks," the doctor said, scurrying away. His friend followed him.

Nick Delan rubbed the back of his moist neck and glanced at his watch. It read 6:25 P.M. He turned and headed down the narrow steps leading to the basement. There he strolled along the corridor, past the snack bar and the small drugstore, past the men's and ladies' boutiques and the barber shop and hairdresser and the travel agency to the doorway at the other end of the building. As he stepped out into the garden, his anxieties ebbed a little. The most difficult and crowded strip of the route was over. He made his way down toward the swimming pool. Delan followed the curving path to enter the narrow corridor that ran in between the high mesh fences draped with dark-green tarpaulins that sheathed the tennis courts on either side. The carefree sounds of popping balls and friendly competition filled the balmy evening.

At the end of the path, he opened the private members' door slowly, and then cautiously peered up Hartford Way to his right. It was an ill-lit, narrow, deserted lane. Only one car was parked at the curb along the stretch he could see. A dark car, deep-blue or black, stopped just before the bend less than a hundred yards away.

Clio. Delan was relieved. Everything was as planned. He stepped out onto the tarmacadam, pulling the iron-framed, wire-mesh door behind him, but cautiously leaving it open an inch or so. To his left the traffic on Sunset Boulevard flowed past him not more than twenty yards away. Closer, less than ten yards away, cars were backed up at the hotel's exit, waiting for the lights at Sunset and Hartford to change. He looked back and extracted a simple, plastic Cricket lighter from his pocket. He snapped it, lighting the flame that was her signal.

Immediately the metallic click of a starter sounded before the purr of a powerful V-8 engine drowned it. Next a brilliant pair of white-hot lights came alive, flooding the tranquil alley.

Nick Delan squinted into the glare. The car pulled out slowly, very slowly—as he had asked Clio to do just as an added precaution—from the curb. It moved to the center of the narrow roadway, gradually building up speed to ten or fifteen miles or so. Again, just as he had dictated.

He relaxed; and reached for the door, softly snapping the lock closed. But when he looked back, the car was less than twenty-five yards away. And it was closing in quickly. Too quickly. Twenty-five, thirty miles an hour at the very least, it was bearing down on him now—and it was still accelerating; roaring down, aiming straight for him.

Holy Mother of God! There was nowhere to go! He was trapped in the narrow lane. Abruptly, in that one split second that was all he had, aided only by the reservoir of unusual strength and agility that desperation brings, he leaped up with all his might toward the dangling branch of a tree that jutted over the fence.

But he was too late. Not too late for the onrushing vehicle itself. That he had gauged perfectly. But too late for the driver's door that opened suddenly, catching his legs and knocking his flying body end over end in a dizzying spin of somersaults before smashing it into the fence.

At first the whispers were hushed, indistinguishable murmurs reverberating down a long, dark hall. But gradually they circled closer and closer, an ever-tighter spiral that soon grated like the roars of a drunken crowd.

Nick Delan forced himself to move. He summoned every last ounce of energy in his body—and tried to flick his eyelids. They were heavy.

"There's no permanent damage. It's all surface injuries: contusions, lacerations, that kind of thing. Nothing a few days of hospitalization won't set right."

Delan reached deep down into himself and tried again, forcing his eyes to open a little. What he saw was a bright fog. A blinding beam of light that made the two shadows standing above him dark blurs.

"How long before he's fully alert, doctor?"

"Oh, I'd say half an hour or so. As you see, he's beginning to stir. Should be reasonably attentive by then, I would think."

"That's too long. Anything you can do to speed up the process?"

"I'd prefer not to. Let him come around naturally."

"I'm afraid we don't have that kind of time, doctor. I need him fully alert in about fifteen, at most twenty, minutes from now."

"O-k-a-y," the doctor's voice drawled reluctantly.

Delan heard the sound of rustling paper. His eyes could discern objects moving above him now. Blurry silhouettes of people. A small dull jab inside his left elbow tickled his senses.

"There," a voice said as the splinter slithered out of the inside of his arm painlessly.

Very gradually, heat started rushing through Delan's veins. A warm front that immediately began to burn off the fog in his mind.

"That contusion on his head could be serious," the hazy, bald, white-frocked man to Delan's left said. "Ideally he should be kept under observation for two or three days. There's just a possibility of complications. Clotting and so on."

"We'll arrange for that," another man answered in a soft voice.

Abruptly Nick Delan pictured the face of the man behind that voice. He jerked his head up with all the strength he could muster, a strength fueled by the panic and hate he felt at the first sight of the picture in his mind. He stared into the real, live face of the man: Anthony Boyle. He stood above Delan's bed in what appeared to be a hospital room. Delan felt a queasiness envelop him. He was weak, the movement too sudden, too fast. But he *was* still alive.

"Take it easy, Nick. Lie back," Anthony Boyle said softly, extending a sympathetic arm to his shoulder.

"Where is she?" That was all Delan could manage to get out before his arms grew weary, the weight of his head and shoulders suddenly too much for them to support.

Anthony Boyle helped him settle back, arranging the pillows behind his head. He then turned to the tall man with the stethoscope around his neck.

"Thank you, doctor," he said. "The rest of you, too. Now I need to talk privately to this man."

As all in the room departed, Delan struggled to raise himself again to glance around his bed. It was a vaguely gray hospital room, plain and simple. Only it didn't have a single window in its thickly padded walls. Dressed in a well-cut dark-brown suit, Anthony Boyle turned toward Delan.

"I want you to listen to me, Nick. There's a lot I need to explain to you."

"Where is she?"

Boyle stared back at Delan just as severely. "I'll get to that in a minute."

"Now," Delan demanded—but the word came out a croak in his parched throat.

Boyle watched as Delan slowly collapsed back on the pillows.

"All right," Boyle said slowly as he held out a glass of water. "Now just relax. She's safe and well. That's all you need to know for the time being."

Delan looked at Boyle suspiciously. Thank God she was all right. But safe? Who was he talking to, anyway? Which side? Who was Boyle? He had to find out. But anger and hostility weren't the right tools.

Be positive, he told himself. Play along. Read the signals. Do anything you have to do—but buy yourself some time to assess your position.

He reached out and accepted the glass of water from Boyle. The ice-cold liquid was soothing as it went down his dry throat. His mind cleared a little.

"But where is she?"

"It would help if you'd wait for—"

"Wait for what?" snapped Delan. His head throbbed.

"Context."

"What does that mean?"

"We have priorities. There are other, more important things you need to know now."

Delan stared at him briefly before he spoke. "What is this, Tony? You just want to talk in riddles? Or do you have something in mind?"

"What I want is for you to listen to me, Nick. Listen and watch and let me explain a few things to you and then judge for yourself." Boyle paused and looked at his watch nervously again. "It would help, too, if you were to agree to do that in the next couple of minutes."

"Why?"

"Because there's something you need to see before we get started on the background."

Bright floodlights lit up the northeast corner of Dulles International Airport in Washington, D.C.

A quarter of a mile away the horde of reporters and photographers watched from the terminal building as the Plane-Mate disengaged from the Boeing 747 that had just landed. The specially designed vehicle used to shuttle passengers between aircraft and the terminal building would soon begin its lumbering journey.

Slowly the rectangular mobile lounge descended from the mouth of the airplane until it rested flush on its fifty-four-foot-long chassis. Once locked in place the Plane-Mate gradually began to move out from under the plane's belly. It twisted past the well-lit circle and headed across the enormous, dark, throbbing airfield toward the main concourse. Less than two minutes later it docked at the terminal. Immediately the pod began to rise, simultaneously telescoping forward ten feet to make a "weathertight" seal with the terminal entrance. Now it was an integral part of the building, a fixed satellite.

When the passengers started to disembark into the huge hall, however, they were shocked by the reception with which they were confronted. Banks of cameras and microphones were pointed at them, while a horde of reporters jostled for position, straining against the heavy red cordons placed around the exit lane. Most of the passengers slowed down, perplexed and inquisitive. Some were thrilled by the excitement of it all, others tired and truculent.

It would not be very long before they learned that their every move was being seen live across the United States and much of the world.

Nick Delan stared at the television screen, confused.

The door of the Plane-Mate opened and almost immediately the tanned and colorfully attired passengers surged into the glaring fluorescent lighting of the gleaming concourse. Why was he being forced to watch this?

He looked at Anthony Boyle. The Deputy National Security Adviser for Political-Military Affairs stood a few yards to the right of his bed now, his left hand toying with his lower lip, his eyes trained thoughtfully at the picture on the television. Delan looked back at the screen.

Abruptly his heart leaped to his throat. He squinted, looking sideways a little, at the familiar silhouette making his way into the airport hall now. The tall figure, dressed in an open-necked light-blue shirt under a navy windbreaker, looked solemn. Delan glanced at Boyle, his heart pounding ever faster. Then back to the images unfolding on the screen. He looked at Boyle again, incredulous. The Deputy National Security Adviser turned and stared back at him. Without a trace of satisfaction, indeed with a degree of nonchalance that bordered on disdain, he glared at Delan.

Nick Delan nodded almost imperceptibly as he closed his eyes. Then slowly he opened them again to see the figure on the screen move toward a bank of microphones.

Allan Sanford waited for a moment, waited for the buzz to die down. The reporters—the hard, cynical, world-weary male and female journalists who had seen and heard it all before—were, for once, astonished. This was not the man they had expected to see. This was not a man who was *alive* even, for God's sake. All they had expected was a statement by one of Sanford's closest advisers, his pollster Steve Raider, who was speeding back from a brief vacation on hearing of Sanford's death.

"Let me begin by saying," the tanned but haggard-looking former actor began in a grave tone, "that I do not intend to make any comments—any comments at all—about what has been going on here over the last few days during my absence. Anything I said would be totally uninformed at this stage. I have been away on vacation in Bimini, and in complete isolation from the world."

Allan Sanford looked down to the piece of paper he held. In the momentary silence the reporters fumbled with their notepads, tape recorders, shotgun microphones, cameras.

"Nevertheless, I would like to make a brief statement. And I think it's imperative that I make it now—at the earliest possible moment. First of all, in the immortal words of Mark Twain, as you can see, the reports of my death have been greatly exaggerated."

Sanford paused and glanced up. But there was no laughter. A deathly silence ruled, a hush punctuated only by the whir of motor-driven lenses clicking away.

Sanford lowered his eyes back down to the sheaf of paper in front of him. "I am not, nor will I ever be," he said in a measured tone, "and this includes accepting the nomination if drafted—a candidate for the presidency of the United States."

Allan Sanford looked up, and for one fleeting moment a hint of pain seemed to cross his face. Then it passed as he reached up and felt under his windbreaker. "That concludes my statement," he said, smiling as he moved away from the podium.

A roar erupted: a hundred voices speaking as one.

"Were you in your house on the night of the incident, Mr. Sanford?"

"Have you seen the so-called Zapruder film, sir?"

"What about Phillip Myers? Do you have any information that might cast some light on his murder?"

"When did you leave on your holiday, sir?"

"Do you have any comments about the explosions that destroyed your boat, Mr. Sanford?"

"What about the blood and the forensic evidence found at your house? How would you explain that?"

"Are you denying *anything* happened?"

"That was the turning point," said Anthony Boyle. "The General Secretary's call to the President."

Delan looked at him skeptically. "Why?"

"Because up to that point we all naturally assumed that this operation was a sanctioned Soviet initiative. He went to extraordinary lengths to convince us we were wrong."

"And you believed him?"

"Yes, Nick," Boyle replied. "He told us everything. Starting with the birth of the 13th Directorate, its history, who was running it, what its purpose was. He told us why and when he'd ordered it disbanded and how he'd been informed that, because of the momentum the Sanford election project had gathered, a sexual entrapment program was the most efficient way to destroy his candidacy. Thereby, of course, terminating the 13th Directorate's raison d'être. The General Secretary apparently went along with this. But what he didn't know or suspect was that he was being lied to. Under the guise of the sexual entrapment program, a disgruntled rogue element in the Kremlin—and that's what the General Secretary called them—had decided to salvage some of the original objectives of the 13th Directorate. That's where Oleg Pavlenko, the defector, came in. The KGB had carefully nurtured his role as a double for years to be absolutely credible if and when they had to send him over to activate the fallback position they had ready. Which was, of course, to leak disinformation that would force us to only one conclusion: to kill Sanford. Once we had done that, this so-called rogue element would then gradually leak the evidence implicating our involvement. Which of course is where the surveillance posts fit in."

Delan shifted his position in the bed. "The General Secretary confirmed all this?"

"Yes."

"So my hunch the first time I went in to reconnoiter the area that it was a setup of some kind turned out to be right."

"Yes."

"So who killed Pavlenko, then?"

"The rogue element."

"Why?"

"They sacrificed the poor bastard to bolster his credibility even further. That's also why they got to Jim Cassidy. To make it appear as if they were desperate in their efforts to plug whatever Pavlenko had leaked to him."

Delan looked dubiously at Boyle. "Are you sure you can trust what you heard? How do you know the General Secretary isn't leading you on? That this isn't just another twist in this tortuous scheme? How do you know he hasn't been *persuaded* to change his mind since, for that matter?"

Sitting in an armchair facing Delan's bed, Anthony Boyle crossed his legs. "Because we knew something he didn't."

"What was that?"

"That the defector didn't die when he was supposed to."

Delan stared coldly at Boyle.

"I know," Boyle said nodding. "But we couldn't tell you. Not under the circumstances."

"What circumstances?" Delan asked.

"I'll get to that in a minute," Boyle replied. "At any rate, it was a combination of what he revealed and what you observed, namely those monitoring units on the hills above Sanford's house, which convinced us we were being set up. So we already knew some of the elements of what the General Secretary was telling us. That was one key factor. The other was that he had no way of knowing that we had a counterruse in the works. One that was going along smoothly, too. I'm talking about the Osiris Option, of course. Sanford, like Osiris of old, had climbed into his own coffin many years ago and of his own accord. And, just like in the myth, we were at that very moment busy making him, quote—cross the threshold of consciousness—unquote. Getting him to realize the truth about what Moscow had been cooking up for him over the years."

Nick Delan felt a strange mixture of wariness, decompression, and fulfillment run through him as he listened vaguely to Boyle's explanations.

He was safe, that was the paramount relief Delan felt. But beyond that he also felt a great deal of satisfaction—professional satisfaction—at a complex task properly accomplished. The finely calibrated plan, a sophisticated variation of an age-old sting operation—faking a murder for those cameras to record—had worked. The red-paint bullets with tiny anaesthetic flechettes inside shot from the refashioned CO_2 pellet gun had worked. When Sanford came round in Bimini he must have thought he was in the middle of his own second coming. After all he hadn't participated in the plan.

Delan sighed deeply. Thank God. In the end everything had gone as planned. All his worries about being betrayed by Boyle had turned out to be unwarranted. All his concerns about something going wrong and Sanford being killed for real after the scam, and his murder pinned on Delan had turned out to be unjustified, paranoid. The by-product of someone out of his league. Or just losing his nerve, perhaps. Boyle's voice filtered back in. "So you see, as far as the General Secretary was concerned the rogue element had succeeded in leading us by the nose. We had assassinated an enormously popular rival presidential candidate. And the evidence was there. On film. Being broadcast by every network in America and across the world. He could have attempted to take maximum advantage of it.

"But he didn't. Instead, when the assassination was announced, he immediately leaned on his own people. That's when Geidar Rezayov, a member of the Politburo, evidently changed sides and informed the General Secretary of the rogue element's real plans. It was at this point that the General Secretary contacted us for the first time. Personally, I believe he choked," Boyle said turning his wrist to show an open palm. "He panicked at how the U.S. would react once we put the pieces together. At best, we'd respond with a massive allied economic and political offensive that would make the cold war look like a Caspian spring. At worst," Boyle shrugged, "World War III? Either way, from his perspective, he had no option but to call the President."

Delan shook his head in amazement.

"And we did one more thing," Boyle quickly added. "We asked for a signed transcript of that original telephone conversation. He agreed immediately and provided it to us, in Washington, within seven hours—delivered by one of their Blackjack bombers to Edwards Air Force Base. The document was duly signed by himself and eight other Politburo members. No, Nick, he wasn't screwing us."

Delan stared at Boyle silently.

"At our request, he did something else, too."

"What?"

"He instructed the Soviet Ambassador to Washington, who made the initial contact with the White House on the General Secretary's behalf, to put himself at our disposal. We flew him down to Sanford in Bimini yesterday and had him explain everything to the man. That's what swung everything around so quickly. Ambassador Gerasimov didn't pull his punches, either. He laid it on the line, convincing Sanford that it was in his own best interests to play along with us completely."

"What about the Mafia and AISA releases?" Delan asked, posing a question that had been troubling him. "Were they really necessary?"

Anthony Boyle looked around the room as if to ponder his reply. He rubbed his chin for a moment longer before looking back at Delan.

"When this happened we thought we detected a huge, if momentary, window of opportunity, Nick, and we decided to play to it. The Soviet Union has been undergoing extraordinary changes recently. Changes that in a very real sense have sparked a great deal of optimism—"

"Tony," interjected Delan, "I want to know. Why did you

drag my father and AISA into this when everything was working out?"

"Because we decided we had to give this so-called rogue element all the help we could to discredit themselves. The purpose of their scam was to use the American media not just to subvert this administration and the whole political process in the U.S.; they also wanted to use the confusion in the U.S. to promote a more aggressive posture back home. In the Soviet Union the temptation to exploit the woes of a weakened U.S. would have been irresistible. The resulting re-establishment of a confrontational climate would have undermined the General Secretary's domestic reform program. We decided to help them. Make them think they had succeeded—and then some. That's where your father and AISA came into it."

A cloud of incomprehension passed across Delan's face. "I don't follow you."

"The people in Moscow who cooked up this harebrained scheme—this rogue element—are only the tip of a huge iceberg. They represent everything that is entrenched, superconservative, and dangerous in the Soviet system. Theirs is the worldview that describes Soviet interests in terms of a permanent defensive posture. This is the culture that has defined the Soviet body politic for the last seventy years. Now, suddenly there is a very real potential for change in the offing. The new Soviet administration is trying to remove the elements within the system responsible for this culture. But it's been like pulling teeth," said Boyle, tugging at his shirt cuffs as if only just warming to his subject. "So we thought we'd help him out a little. By enticing these people more and more into their own scheme we've handed the General Secretary the weapon with which to destroy them. He can now demonstrate that the thinking which this group represents is irresponsible and reckless."

Boyle paused and looked at Delan. "That's where your father and AISA come in," he repeated. "We had to make it look like the mud was really sticking to us. We had to give the rogue element the rope with which the General Secretary could hang them."

"You mean . . ."

Boyle interrupted Delan. "That's right, we turned the tables on the whole scheme. For the first time in over eighty years we have a Soviet administration committed to dialogue, openness, even democracy to a degree, and we want to help them get firmly entrenched. These people are the best bet we've had since the founding of the Soviet Union. They're committed to a peaceful posture, feeding their own people, even a little human rights, all the things that have always concerned us the most. So why not help him?"

Delan eyed Boyle warily for a moment. "Tony, what you're telling me is that the Soviets were set to subvert the American system by manipulating events here, right?"

"Yes."

"And what you're also telling me is that we turned that all around so that we are now manipulating events in the Soviet Union?"

"Well, I wouldn't put it quite that way," Boyle said dismissively. "Besides, the conduct of international relations isn't a morality play. Most of the time it's more like a poker game. Everybody plays the hand they're dealt. And they just happened to slip us a couple of aces."

Delan closed his eyes as he turned away.

He ached. Every bone and muscle in his body hurt in a different way and his still giddy mind strained to keep up with what Boyle was telling him. He was safe. It was over. But beyond the relief, beyond the thrill of victory, beyond the reassurance that it had all been worthwhile, one feeling and one feeling only ruled—joy. He was all right. Clio was all right: both of them were well and safely extricated from this mess. All he felt now was a longing to rest his head on her breasts, to feel the warmth of her body against his, to savor again the subtle fragrance of her soft skin. All he wanted to do was run to her. To end all this. Still, one question nagged; one item that needed clarification.

"What about the assassin?" Delan asked. "The man I killed. Who sent him in after me?"

"The Soviets," Boyle replied authoritatively. "And for two reasons. Firstly, to draw attention to the scene by creating the furor he did. And secondly, to kill you at the site of the hit. Both of which were enacted to severely restrict our options. Not only wouldn't we be able to tamper with the evidence of the assassination, but there'd be an assassin's corpse on display as well."

"That makes sense."

"Yes. Good sense."

Suddenly Delan smiled sheepishly. He brushed back his unruly hair and looked away. "You might find it amusing to know, Tony, that while I was clutching to what I thought were the last few days of my life I began to convince myself that you, my friend, were a Soviet agent. It was the only way I could explain everything that was going wrong, all the things that made no sense to me."

"A little farfetched," Boyle replied dryly.

Something in the way Boyle was staring at him seemed odd to Delan.

"But not entirely off course," Boyle added in a quieter tone.

Delan froze. As the silence stretched, his eyes narrowed gradually.

"There *was* a Soviet agent on the inside," Boyle said, almost casually. "The rogue element in Moscow were in a sense patched in constantly to Washington's responses."

Delan said nothing. He lay motionless, unsettled yet unable to even guess at what Boyle was talking about. "How?"

"An agent named Elshtayn."

"Elshtayn? Who's Elshtayn?"

Boyle uncurled his tall body in the armchair and rose. For a moment he paced around the room, deep in thought. "Someone we have in custody."

"Fine. But who is he? What was his function?"

"To feed them information from the inside, as it happened."

"Yes, but how? Where did he fit in?"

"At an important enough level to be able to pass on critical details of our movements."

"How was he caught?"

"Boarding a flight for Geneva."

"No. I mean, what tripped him up?"

"These are all good questions, Nick," Boyle replied, pacing toward the door. "But I think you'll want to ask them yourself—in your own good time and directly."

He reached down and opened the door.

Nick Delan's heart leaped when he saw the figure of Clio Bragana framed in the doorway.

"Nick, please meet Natalia Elshtayn."

* * *

Not one inch of the route registered in Nick Delan's mind—not a traffic light or a turning or a street sign—as he drove south, toward Los Angeles International Airport. He operated on remote, totally engrossed with the sounds and images from the past that tumbled through his mind in a haphazard mix that did not match.

"She's not what she appears to be," he heard Anthony Boyle repeat in that Groton accent of his. But the picture Nick Delan saw did not fit with Boyle's words. Indeed, it kept changing, too. Like a kaleidoscope of never-ending patterns, it showed a thousand different aspects of the same face. Now it was a picture of a young woman with billowing, dark-brown hair, her almond eyes laughing in the distant fantasy world of a Swiss ski resort.

"You can do what you want with her. We made a deal with her but we sure don't have to stick to it."

"What kind of deal, Tony?"

"We promised to go easy on her if she cooperated."

"Did she?"

"Yes, she did. She was very helpful. Agreed not only to talk freely, but to go along with us in reeling you back in, too. She was the one who told us you were armed. She also suggested you were desperate and would probably put up a great deal of resistance if you had to. That's why we chose the route we did. To save your life. And God only knows how many others you would have taken out with yourself. In any case, I doubt she knows any more than she's already told us. Remember, she's small fry. Just a tiny cog in the huge apparatus."

"When did you know about her?" Delan heard himself asking.

"Know? For sure, toward the end. We suspected almost from the beginning, though. But she was smart. A real pro. We couldn't intercept any of her calls. She kept using different telephones. Always pay phones. And her conversations were never more than one minute long. Sometimes she'd make ten calls in the space of an hour or two. But none of them would be from the same box or last long enough for us to be able to tap in. The closest we got was on the night of the hit. She went to a booth at the Beverly Wilshire Hotel and seemed panicky and nervous as she made the call. She also talked longer than on any other occasion. So long, in fact, that we missed her by less than ten, fifteen seconds. Only when she received your gift, on the morning after you went in, did she slip up and make a call from her hotel room. That's when we were certain." Boyle had paused. "Strange, isn't it? Her making such a simple mistake after so long. Anyway, it was the Soviet consulate in San Francisco that she was calling. Heaven help whoever was her contact. No doubt he's already back in Moscow. Facing a long Siberian holiday, at the very best, I'd imagine."

The voices from the past faded, replaced by images. The picture filling the dark road beyond the smoked windshield of the car was now one of a luxurious dark room. Two naked bodies clinging to each other on a large bed, rolling over and over, perspiration glistening off their skins as they made passionate love. A passion inspired as much by affection as by lust. One that had about it a tenderness he had never known before. A depth, a warmth that still burned in his soul. No. Somewhere in all that delusion, something had been real.

Or had it? Shouldn't he have known? Hadn't the transition gone too smoothly? From someone who looked at men with disdain to someone who opened up so completely, so passionately, with such abandon? It was *too* good to be real.

"Don't blame yourself, Nick." It was Anthony Boyle again. "If it hadn't been you it would have been someone else. They're as meticulous in targeting their prey as they are thorough in training their hunters. Seems, from the series of security disasters we've suffered lately at their hands, the Russians have a comprehensive list of all our top specialists in your line of work. Each of them—we now learn—has been constantly covered in one way or another by various classes of agent; all of whom were sleepers waiting to be activated. The KGB have got this form of entrapment down to a science. Several million dollars and God only knows how many man-hours go into this kind of operation. They go to prodigious lengths to draw up a psychoanalytical profile of their targets, too. And they don't do it like us—long-range and hearsay and with satellites. They go to source, dispatching whoever and whatever it takes to compile an in-depth file of his or her life from day one; an integrated encyclopedic psychographic study analyzing the target's personality traits: childhood, traumas, fixations, sexual behavior, religious upbringing, influences, response to stress, defense mechanisms, friends, everything. They know more about you than you do, Nick. And then they find, sometimes even—if they have enough lead time—they actually train, the perfect foil to manipulate the target's unique characteristics. Unless they've made a horrendous mistake or missed something big about you, practically no one can avoid being programmed to make a fool of himself."

The film flashing across the buzzing freeway before him now was a montage of stills: the carefree smile of a woman skiing. The ravaged look as she recalled memories of rape. A fairy-tale train ride with her through some of Europe's most beautiful countryside. Her excited face as she requested a song to be played for him against his wishes. The terror when she thought she was being followed at the airport. And last but not least, the special way she held her head as she smiled down at him in bed.

"They access the pressure points—and then play to the weaknesses. It's that simple," Boyle had said. "But it's very, very, very carefully orchestrated and monitored constantly. Like a huge game of championship chess. Only their players can call in to their controllers for advice on their next move whenever they slip away from the target for a few minutes. And the controllers have teams of specialists they in turn can call on. Essentially it's not at all unlike a quarterback calling a time-out to discuss a key play with the bank of coaches and their computers and spotters who are scrutinizing the game from different angles on the sidelines."

Her beautiful face appeared again. Screaming now with terror in a deserted Beverly Hills parking lot littered with four injured bodies. The innocent, vulnerable little child slipping off the negligee, the vision of delight as she stood by a hotel door and invited him to make love for the first time. All of it, every instant of their brief affair flashed frame by frame before him. Each tender, trembling moment of their days together.

Still, he thought, as he parked the car outside the Tom Bradley International Terminal. He had to know. He had to know for sure if it was *all* an act. Maybe . . . just maybe . . .

He looked at his watch as he rode the escalator up to the gate. It read 1:15 A.M.

Nick Delan leaned against the glass wall next to the boarding gate, his eyes glued to the elevator at the far end of the packed lounge. It was marked OFFICIAL USE ONLY and, with every opening and closing of its doors, Delan's pulse missed a beat. Then suddenly he saw four burly men and two severe-looking women appear inside the parting doors. FBI. His heart sank as they marched into the hall. Between them walked the tall, shapely figure of Clio Bragana.

As the group drew closer heads turned. Without makeup her face glowed with innocence. Gone was the artificial perfection of cosmetics and highlights, gone the carefully manicured air of sophistication. It was natural now; the tone of her skin just the way he remembered seeing it each morning.

She was dressed in a simple classic Valentino *robe chemise*. Cream-colored silk that danced and stretched in tiny, ever-changing ripples across her curvaceous body with every movement.

Suddenly he knew he had been right. Given more than just a few minutes together, she would hypnotize him again. No. This was the only way he could do it. Immediately. Tonight. A fleeting moment. Only minutes away from her flight.

For a long moment she stood there looking at him. Then slowly she dropped her eyes. "You look terrible, Nick," she said, attempting a smile.

"It's becoming a habit of mine," Delan answered.

He broke his glare briefly, looking up to dismiss the FBI agents with a curt nod. As they walked away, he turned back to Clio. "Must have something to do with these surprises I keep getting." He paused, then added, "Comrade Elshtayn."

"Please, Nick. Please don't . . ."

"You're right. Natalia sounds more friendly."

"Nick . . ." She looked at him beseechingly.

"Why? Isn't it over now? Don't you get a different alias with every new client you take on?"

"I'm sorry, Nick," she said softly. "I really am."

"Why? What the hell, it was only a job."

"No." She shook her head sadly. "We were unlucky, that's all."

"Unlucky? How?"

She hesitated for a long moment before looking up. Delan noticed moisture in her large, soft eyes.

"A lot of reasons."

"Pick out a few of the more relevant ones."

Clio shrugged sadly. "What for, Nick? What on earth could it achieve?"

"A little peace of mind," he retorted. "Maybe."

She smiled forlornly, shaking her head again—but just barely. "Never. You wouldn't believe a word I said. Not now."

"Try me. Run them by me anyway."

"It wasn't supposed to be like this," she said hesitatingly. "I was assigned to monitor your arms dealing activities in the Middle East. It was just . . . just . . . pure chance that you were called back to handle this . . . this . . ."

"Oh," he interjected, a world of sarcasm in his tone. "So it would have been different if you'd sold me out in Paris? Or Beirut, perhaps?"

"I would never have sold you out in Paris or Beirut. Just as I didn't sell you out here, Nick."

"No? What was it you were doing, then? What do you call it back home?"

She fumbled nervously inside her bag and tried to light a cigarette with a lighter that jiggled around in her unsteady hand.

Delan found himself reaching out to help her. He cupped his hand around hers to stop its shaking.

"None of it was true, was it, Clio?"

"None of what?" she asked, avoiding his eyes.

"Genoa?"

She shook her head almost imperceptibly.

"La Scala? The fight? They were fixed, weren't they?"

"Oh, Nick, what difference does it make now?"

Gently he raised her chin until her eyes gazed into his. "It's important to me, Clio."

"Yes," she whispered.

"The man following you at the airport that night . . . and . . . and all the other things?"

"What difference can it make, Nick?" she asked again, even more quietly.

Nick Delan reached out and held her elbows gently to stop her from moving back. "Please."

"Yes. Yes. They planned it all. They wanted you to get closer to me. They know how to get to people and they had you figured out."

Delan stared at her coldly.

"You're vulnerable, Nick," she said, her trembling voice close to tears. "You're vulnerable, for God's sake. They know you're a rootless, homeless romantic, doomed to a lonely life." She paused and spoke more softly. "The only trouble is, they picked the wrong girl."

Now two teardrops meandered slowly down her cheeks, two large diamonds twinkling in the fluorescent lighting of the lounge.

Clio Bragana swallowed. "And as for selling you out," she said, pausing, "why do you think I stayed on these last few days, Nick?"

She brushed the tears away from her cheeks with the back of her hand. "My instructions were to kill you."

Her lips twitched nervously.

"But I couldn't," she whispered, barely audibly. "I'd fallen in love with you instead. So I ran."

Suddenly, Nick Delan felt drained. His mind reeled while his body seemed to give way to all the weariness that had been building up. He was tired. To the marrow of his bones, he was tired. But more than the fatigue, more than the bruises, his whole being was now shattered by what he'd just heard.

My instructions were to kill you. The words thundered in his head. *But I couldn't. I'd fallen in love with you instead.*

"Why, Clio?" That was all he could think of to say.

"Why what, Nick?"

"Why does a person do a thing like this? How can a person live a life of lies?"

"Necessity."

"Necessity?"

"Yes, Nick," Clio replied. "Necessity."

"What do you mean?"

She stared at him for a moment, sadly, silently. Then she raised her hand and toyed nervously with a button on his dark-blue leather windbreaker. "It's a long story, Nick. Are you sure you want to hear it?"

"Yes." Delan nodded slowly. "Yes, I've got to."

She stared at the button.

"It all started really on a street corner in Moscow a couple of years ago. I was there for some debriefing sessions. Anyway, one evening as I was coming out of my apartment complex I brushed past this wizened old lady, a little babushka woman, who was standing there, fixed in the snow. It was a bitterly cold night and I couldn't understand what she was doing there. Then I remembered having seen her in the same spot that afternoon. It struck me as most weird. She hadn't moved. As I passed her she gave me this strange beseeching look, but I dismissed it as I huddled into the car waiting for me. But the same thing happened the next morning. There she was, staring at me intently as I came out of my flat, oblivious to the frightful cold. The next day it happened again. And the day after. Every day she was there—consistently and without fail. I began feeling sorry for her. She looked so pathetic, so gray and shriveled and bent, standing there in the snow. One day I decided to see what she wanted, this little old woman. Perhaps I could help her in some way. But the moment I started approaching her, she scuttled away—half-running, half-limping. By the time I reached the corner she was lost in the crowds. The next day, though, she was there again. And again she was off as if in terror before I could reach her.

"This scene repeated itself—"

Clio's soft voice was drowned out by the announcement pouring through the loudspeakers. "Would all passengers traveling to Frankfurt on Lufthansa flight one ninety-two please proceed to gate thirty-three for immediate boarding."

Her flight, Delan noted anxiously.

"This went on every day for several weeks," Clio continued. "Each time, though, this little old lady stood just that much further away from my front door. And when one day she failed to appear, I really missed her. It was strange. A curious silent bond seemed to have developed between us. The next day when she reappeared, I was not only relieved, I decided I had to know something about her. You see, as an orphan—all I knew about my mother was that she had died in childbirth and I had no other family—I never experienced the warmth of an older woman's love. And here was this total stranger, obviously demented, who seemed to want to stay close to me. She looked so pathetic standing out there, so lonely. She made me feel guilty. No. It was more than that. Part of it was also that I felt needed."

Delan remained silent. He wanted to hear her talk. He needed to know whatever it was she was leading up to.

"Obviously, my contacts in the state security apparatus were good. So I had her checked out. I wanted to know about her. I wanted to know if I could help her in any way, what desperation it was that was driving her to stand out there every day in the biting cold of a Moscow winter.

"They came back and told me she was just a harmless old lady with a long history of mental problems. But from that day on she never showed up again. That worried me. I began feeling responsible for her disappearance. So I decided to dig deeper, but to do so myself. But I wasn't ready for what I found out."

In the distance behind Clio one of the FBI agents was signaling to Delan, pointing at his watch. Delan ignored him.

"I discovered that the old lady had recently been released from a psychiatric ward. Evidently twenty-five years ago she and her husband had applied to emigrate to Israel but had been turned down on the grounds that they were very prominent scientists whose work had brought them into contact with important state secrets. When they objected publicly with other *refuseniks* they were arrested and imprisoned. They went on hunger strikes and were transferred to psychiatric wards. She had been pregnant when she was arrested. And when she gave birth in prison her child was immediately taken away from her. Then her husband died while being force-fed."

A teardrop kissed Clio's lips as her tone became strained. "I pitied the woman enormously when I read her file. As an orphan myself I felt her grief. Loneliness at any age is the same. I wanted to help. But I needed to know more. Eventually I found out everything, including her husband's name. It was Viktor Natanovich Elshtayn."

She looked up into his eyes.

Delan watched as she paused and tried to compose herself. For one fleeting moment he thought he vaguely remembered the story of the name. But then it was gone, lost as she swallowed, closed her eyes and spoke again. "I never saw her again. She'd been exiled to Kazakhstan to keep her away from me, their prized— But it was too late. From the moment I learned I was Jewish something snapped inside me. All the years of indoctrination at *D'e'vachka Adee'n,* all the childhood and teenage brainwashing, the pampering, the material perks, the traveling abroad and all the other luxuries that 'swallows' enjoy meant nothing anymore. The truth dawned. I was a swallow. A star swallow, the belle of the ball—but a swallow just the same. Which meant a state whore. From that moment on, a strange and powerful sense of purpose welled in me. I knew who my people were, what they represented, where I belonged. But I wanted to take my mother with me. To meet her. And get to know her. And to be with her for the last few years of her life. And to do so in that precious promised land that she and my father had been willing to risk everything to see."

Clio looked at Delan again, her tearful eyes glittering with defiance now. "More than anything else, Nick, I was proud. It was almost as if for the first time in my life I knew what it meant to be free. To be a person instead of a thing. To have a name, a past, a rich past, instead of being a state ward."

Abruptly the loudspeakers above boomed again, bursting their cocoon of privacy. It was the final call for Clio's flight and Delan saw two of the FBI agents start walking toward them.

"So I decided to use the only weapon I had going for me to buy my mother back: my body," she said when Delan had turned his attention back to her. "To use it and abuse it and sell it and give it away if necessary and to anybody or anything that could help me get that wizened old babushka to Israel before she died."

She smiled sadly. "It would have worked, too. I'd built up a great deal of influence in all the right quarters."

She paused and swallowed the lump in her throat. "So you see, Nick, I didn't sell you out. I've blown everything. But I didn't sell you out. I'm not sure what love is, Nick. But if this isn't it, it must be close."

Nick Delan's arms did not have the strength to hold on to her, to stop her from turning. His brain, too, was paralyzed: too frozen by what he had just heard to tell her everything would be all right. To beg her to stay. That he would help her. That somehow they would work it out.

All he could do was stare at her as she walked toward the boarding gate. Even when she stopped and glanced back he couldn't move. He watched as she looked into his eyes, tears streaming down her cheeks.

Then suddenly she turned again and stepped into the corridor. But as she walked away the picture slowly lost its focus. Until all Nick Delan could see of her through his tears was a bright blur.

Epilogue

Within a short while a major shakeup began to take form in the Soviet hierarchy, including the Politburo, the Secretariat, the Armed Forces, and the KGB. New, younger figures appeared in the receiving lines where once the familiar remnants of the old guard stood. One of the more surprising figures missing was that of Geidar Reza Alievich Rezayov, the Deputy Prime Minister. Soviet observers in the Western world immediately dubbed the new appointees "technocrats."

When Harold Adrian Russell "Kim" Philby learned he had less than six months to live, he submitted a special invocation to the General Secretary, a rare occurrence for him. His request was to be granted the right to give one last interview to the Western press.

In that interview he maintained that he didn't regret a thing. And that if he had to do it all over again, he would gladly do so. To the very end the man who had not only betrayed his country but the entire free world did not accept that he was a traitor. He said he wanted to be buried in the Soviet Union. The country he considered his own—and had for over fifty years. He died not long after the interview—of "undisclosed causes."

Meanwhile, none of the inquiries initiated by the National Security Adviser's office and disseminated to all the intelligence arms of the United States Government relating to the "fate and whereabouts of one Natalia Elshtayn, aka Clio Bragana" produced a positive response. The standing order was eventually rescinded.